Ancestral Voices

Ancestral Voices

Etienne van Heerden

VIKING

VIKING

Published by the Penguin Group
Viking Penguin, a division of Penguin Books USA Inc.,
375 Hudson Street, New York, New York 10014, U.S.A.
Penguin Books Ltd, 27 Wrights Lane,
London W8 5TZ, England
Penguin Books Australia Ltd, Ringwood,
Victoria, Australia
Penguin Books Canada Ltd, 10 Alcorn Avenue, Suite 300,
Toronto, Ontario, Canada M4V 3B2
Penguin Books (N.Z.) Ltd, 182–190 Wairau Road,
Auckland 10, New Zealand

Penguin Books Ltd, Registered Offices:
Harmondsworth, Middlesex, England

First American Edition
Published in 1992 by Viking Penguin,
a division of Penguin Books USA Inc.

10 9 8 7 6 5 4 3 2 1

PUBLISHER'S NOTE
This is a work of fiction. Names, characters, places, and incidents
either are the product of the author's imagination or are used
fictitiously, and any resemblance to actual persons, living or
dead, events, or locales is entirely coincidental.

Originally published in Afrikaans as *Toorberg* by Tafelberg Publishers,
Cape Town, in 1986. © Etienne van Heerden, 1986.

LIBRARY OF CONGRESS CATALOGING IN PUBLICATION DATA
Van Heerden, Etienne, 1954–
[Toorberg. English]
Ancestral voices / Etienne van Heerden.
p.   cm.
Translation of: Toorberg.
ISBN 0-670-82831-9
I. Title.
PT6592.32.A5235T66   1992   91–41311
839.3′635 — dc20

Printed in the United States of America
Set in Plantin Monotype Lasercomp
Typography by Virginia Norey

For Kaia

'It is of course true that there are many similarities *ex analogia* between the testimony and that to which the testimony refers; but then life itself, and death as well of course, is really a fable endlessly repeated . . .'

Judge Lucius, addressing the Cape Bar Council

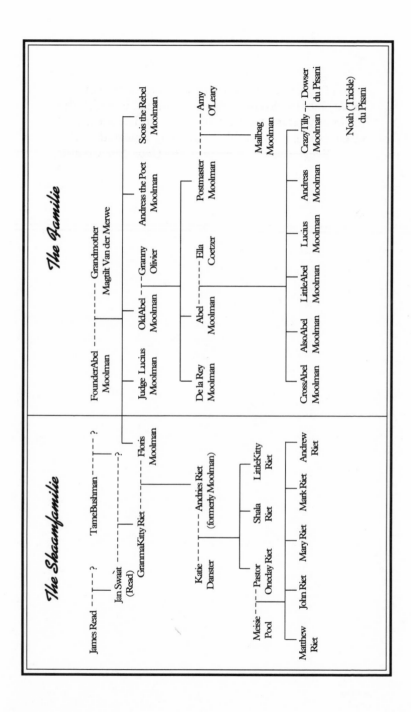

The Skaamfamilie

The Familie

James Read — ? — ?
Jan Swàat (Read) — ?
GrannaKitty Riet — Floris Moolman

FounderAbel Moolman — Grandmother Magrit Van der Merwe

Judge Lucius Moolman
OldAbel Moolman — Granny Olivier
Andreas the Poet Moolman
Soois the Rebel Moolman

De la Rey Moolman
Abel Moolman — Ella Coetzer
Postmaster Moolman — Amy O'Leary

CrossAbel Moolman
AlsoAbel Moolman
LittleAbel Moolman
Lucius Moolman
Andreas Moolman
Mailbag Moolman
CrazyTilly Moolman — Dowser du Pisani

Noah (Trickle) du Pisani

Katie Danster — Andries Riet (formerly Moolman)

Meisie Pool — Pastor Oneday Riet
Shala Riet
LittleKitty Riet

Matthew Riet
John Riet
Mary Riet
Mark Riet
Andrew Riet

Ancestral Voices

Chapter 1

The evidence of great sadness, said Katie Danster, who had been on her way from the Stiefveld to the Halt that morning to collect her pension envelope, was something she saw with her own eyes. She'd set out at first light, just as the mist was curling down past the heels of the Toorberg and the wild geese were starting to cry out to one another. The drought was at its height and every morning started with this mournful crying of the geese for water and wet nesting places.

Before setting out she had hung the iron pot over the embers of the previous evening's fire and gone outside to break twigs into kindling. Coming back inside, she had stepped gingerly over the sleeping children bundled up in their karosses in the front room, and then pushed the kindling into the hot ashes, holding it firmly with her hands and gently blowing the fire into life. Once the kindling had caught, she arranged split sticks and logs over the flame so that the water would boil and the porridge would be ready for the rest of the household when they woke. Getting up stiffly from blowing the fire, she was suddenly aware of her son Shala standing in the doorway behind her. What a fright you gave me, she thought, but said nothing for fear of waking her grandchildren. Shala always moved like a shadow and never wore a shirt. The birthmark across his left ear identified him as a Moolman. So did the boundless rage in his eyes and his habit of never looking directly at the road ahead. Distant, his eyes were, always scanning the horizon or the nipple-shaped hilltops.

'Morning, Shala Riet,' she said, stooping through the front door and glancing at him as she passed. He was still angry. He had been present the night before when, with her grandchildren all round her, she had spoken her heart out about Toorberg and the Moolmans. She felt they had to know, yet later she was astonished that she should have chosen that particular moment to explain to the children the history of their clan.

1

'Morning, Ma Katie,' he said in the voice that always re-minded her of her father-in-law, Floris Moolman – not that she had ever seen Floris Moolman, but when Shala was hardly more than an infant GranmaKitty had said: he's got Floris's tongue. All she'd ever seen of Floris Moolman was the much fingered photograph which they still kept safe, along with her pension papers and the letter in which Abel Moolman had granted them and their descendants the right to live on the Stiefveld for one hundred years.

'There was something trying to get at the goats last night,' said Shala. 'I chased it away.'

'Was it a jackal, Shala Riet?' she asked as they sat down together on the wooden bench beside the front door. Far below in the valley the roof of the big house was visible, shining through the mist – the sheets of English iron which Founder-Abel Moolman had ordered by ship from over the water. That was after the Bushmen had fired the thatch of the first clay house up in the Valley, on the night when FounderAbel and Grand-mother Magtilt had taken refuge under the floorboards.

'I didn't see any tracks, Ma Katie,' he said.

'It must have been the *tokoloshe*, my child.' She looked up at the crown of the Toorberg where the beacon was just visible through the mist. 'There's still plenty of *tokoloshes* in this moun-tain,' she said. 'Just ask the wizard across the valley: that Malay knows. The cliffs are full of caves: go searching through them and you'll find the skeletons of your forefathers.'

'Oneday and I know every one of those cliffs, Ma Katie,' said Shala impatiently. 'There's nothing up there except the Bushman paintings in the cave near the Eye. There's no *toko-loshes*, Ma, and you know it.'

Angered, he stood, and she watched him stride away: her shy son with his upright bearing and his fine shoulders. He threw open the gate of the pen and, using his hips to force his way in between the goats, thrust himself through to the back of the flock, then whistled to drive them out through the gate ahead of him.

He slammed the gate shut behind him and the flock began

to move downhill, whitebeards in front, ewes in milk right at the back.

'Shala,' she called out to him: 'you've had nothing to eat!'

He waved impatiently, following the flock; and soon the red dust, the swirling mist and the blurring in her eyes hid him from her sight.

Of her two sons, Katie Danster thought, Shala Riet was the handsome one: Shala with his proud rage against the Moolmans, his bare chest, his hands that could break or mend; her handsome Shala Riet, with his barren loins and the blemish across his left ear – the tell-tale sign of sterility among the Moolmans. There was nothing wrong with his blood, though; that was the blood of his father, Andries, and of his grandmother, Kitty Riet, and of Kitty's sturdy forebears right back to the missionary James Read from whom they had taken their surname, and further back still, through that holy man's veins, to the misty world across the sea.

Still, she understood that to Shala and to Oneday – her other son, the clever one – these things were not important: they were children of today and tomorrow, not of yesterday. That was why Shala had been so angry the night before. They'd been talking about the drilling machine endlessly sinking holes all over the farm and getting nowhere, when she began to tell them the story of Toorberg. Despite Shala's anger, though, Oneday's children, now bundled in sleep on the floor of the front room after their late night, had listened respectfully.

The story of water, Katie Danster told them, was the story of the Moolmans. High up in the Toorberg, the Eye, source of the now dried-up spring, had been discovered by FounderAbel himself, as he came trekking through on his stallion, with his packhorse and his mounted bondsman Jan Swaat behind, and his tracker, TameBushman, leashed to his stirrup. They say TameBushman had smelt the water four days to the south, eighty miles away, and that he'd led FounderAbel over the pass, through the marshes and up the rocky slopes of the Toorberg straight to where the sweet, clear water spouted from the seven stone fountains of the spring.

They'd virtually had to drag the horses up the steep slopes, but there, among the ferns and duckweed and the reeds, FounderAbel had unsaddled. There, when the horses had drunk their fill and were standing some distance away; while the manservant was having a smoke down-wind and the tame Bushman as alert as a meerkat was scanning the cliffs above, FounderAbel had looked out over the valley below and resolved: he would apply to the nearest landdrost for a deed of title to this land. There, in the groin of the Toorberg, FounderAbel pitched camp and planned his farm.

For three full days he reconnoitred the land in every direction: north, south, east and west. He examined the soil; traced the course of the stream; wandered through the marshes stalking wild geese; saw the startled coots fly up out of the grass at his feet; and observed, on the distant horizon, great herds of antelope and ostrich.

On the third day there he had fired on a small band of Bushmen gathering honey under an overhanging cliff. They had scattered, while TameBushman sat crouched on his haunches, silent beside FounderAbel's horse.

Later, FounderAbel had crawled about under the cliff for a long time, examining the Bushman paintings on the rock face.

By day they had heard troops of baboons barking up in the mountain. At night, jackals and leopards coughed and yelped beyond the fires they had built round the camp.

In those days, Katie Danster told her grandchildren, while Shala listened in morose silence, your great-great-grandfather FounderAbel learnt to love the soil, and because he could not fully understand the strange enchantment of this new world with its Eye, its wet valleys and its dry grasslands, he named the mountain the Toorberg and determined, when he obtained the title-deeds, to call his farm by the same name.

Then he'd returned to fetch his stock and wagons that he'd left camped beside a river three weeks to the south, with Grandmother Magtilt then heavily pregnant with Judge Lucius. He'd led the wagons right to the sweet pasturage of Toorberg, where the stream from the Eye widened into the course of the Toor-

4

berg River, and there he'd set up his camp and decided that this soil was where he and his descendants would forever be established.

FounderAbel had drawn up his wagons in a triangle, enclosed them in a circle of thorn-branches, erected a shelter to cook in and sowed half a bushel of wheat close to the camp. He'd shot a few antelope and set snares in the Vlei. When the strips of biltong hung drying in long rows in the cooking shelter, he'd set off on horseback and in seven terrible days he had galloped to the nearest landdrost and back. On the seventh day, racked with fever, his horse foaming at the bit, FounderAbel had returned to Toorberg with the title-deeds in his saddlebag. He returned a much poorer man, for the landdrost's price had been far higher than he had expected. When he looked into the wagon-tent he'd found Grandmother Magtilt cradling Judge Lucius in her arms.

There were three difficult months ahead for Grandmother Magtilt, daughter of the hardy clan of Van der Merwes from the rugged Koue Bokkeveld. Judge Lucius, like all clever babies, suffered from colic. And, as if that was not enough, Founder-Abel lay in the sickwagon for twelve solid weeks, fighting a raging fever. In those twelve weeks, the old people said, he sweated out all the sins of his forefathers, but in the long nights of tossing about in the wagon seven devils entered into him. For when he eventually emerged from the sickwagon, still shaky at the knees, all hell broke loose.

Within three years, FounderAbel had shot and ploughed and chopped and built till Toorberg Farm was the pride of the frontier. It was the place where wandering preachers, pedlars and fugitive murderers would spend a night, in wonder and amazement as they listened to the sounds of the night: the wild geese calling, the jackals howling, the rasping growl of leopards – and when all else fell silent, the sound of the Eye gurgling away in the darkness.

Once Shala was out of sight, and the flock was out of earshot, Katie got up with a sigh. Thinking about the ancestors always made her sigh. The new generation was young and strong, they could cope, but the ancestors were so utterly spent that she worried about them constantly.

It was still not quite daylight in the front room when she carefully knotted together in her bundle a coin, a quid of chewing tobacco, a knucklebone talisman for luck and hope, and the small cross which GranmaKitty Riet had entrusted to her on her deathbed, saying: 'This belonged to Great-grandfather Missionary himself. Don't ever wear it: it came straight from his sacred breast. His woman stole it off his deathbed. Wrap it in your bundle and take it with you wherever that rubbish Andries drags you.' Those had been GranmaKitty's last words. Then she had breathed her last and Andries had had to go to his cousin Abel Moolman to beg for planks to make her coffin so that they could give Kitty a decent burial.

With the bundle clamped under her arm Katie tied her headscarf tight above her eyes, cast a last glance at her sleeping grandchildren, the offspring of Oneday Riet and Meisie Pool – that slatternly wife of his who kept running away to her people in the Camdeboo – and set off down the valley, out of the meagre Stiefveld, to where the rich, dark soil of the Toorberg valleys began.

Later, she was unable to explain to the magistrate just what had given her second sight that morning. Perhaps it was the tales about FounderAbel the night before, or her thoughts about the *tokoloshe*, or even Shala Riet's sullenness. Perhaps it was all the rumours her clever son Oneday had picked up at Bible school. Or perhaps it was the wild geese crying for nesting places; or the mist and dust rising in the early sunlight that wrapped everything in a haze, so that she could actually feel the evil breathing down her neck, as she made her way down to the Halt on the plain. For suddenly, and with an overwhelming sense of sadness, she noticed little Trickle du Pisani, the lovechild of Crazy-Tilly and Dowser du Pisani, standing on the footpath in front of her, listening to the wind.

Katie later told the magistrate that Trickle had not seen her and that when she had come up close to him she could see that he

6

had already crossed over from life to death. He had been watching the wild geese flying overhead and crying for water. Standing there, he was no more than the ghost of a child. Even afterwards, when they explained to Katie that Trickle had died three days later, she still maintained that she had seen him standing there already as dead on the footpath, listening to the cries of the wild geese.

It was common knowledge that as a baby Trickle du Pisani had never blinked his eyes in the sunlight and that even as a very young child he'd had the habit of peering down boreholes. He had also inherited his mother's fear of the dark and his father Dowser du Pisani's fondness for willow trees. Trickle always loved playing under the willows round the Toorberg farmstead. Katie herself had seen him ducking behind the trunk of a willow or even trying to hide among the low-hanging branches on the ground, whenever Abel Moolman came by. There he would lie, holding his breath until Abel was out of sight. They say that once, when Abel stopped for a while to watch a dung-beetle rolling a ball of dung, the child had held his breath for so long that he'd gone blue in the face and been picked up as good as dead. His father had had to summon the Malay to bring him round.

From the very first time that Trickle had peered down a borehole he could almost always be found near the drilling machine and the new holes that were being sunk. In all the months that the machine was hammering away, day and night, at new boreholes, with the drillers keeping the fires going all night long to be able to see how the rods and gears were functioning, Trickle never slept. He repeatedly ran away from the old farm schoolhouse where Dowser du Pisani and his six children lived, heading straight for where the drilling was going on. There he would lie, flat on his belly on the ground in the dark, watching everything with his wide, calm eyes.

When at last the investigating magistrate visited her at home on the Stiefveld to ask her where she had been on the day that sad thing happened to Trickle, Katie could still see his small pale face before her, as he searched for crabs under the

7

pebbles down in the shallows, or sat, like someone in a dream, beside the windmill listening to the rods at their slow thrusting, into the earth and out again.

Trickle was a child of the sadness, people would say, as they watched the little boy wandering around the farmyard. The Moolmans did not realize that the child was not quite right in the head, though, until one night he crept in through the open window of the big farmhouse and took Toorberg's large old grandfather clock to pieces to see what time it was. Only then did everyone recognize that this child did not take things at face value.

While Katie Danster watched Trickle standing on the footpath that morning, turning his head so his eyes could follow the wild geese, she recalled the night when CrazyTilly, then very near her time, had disappeared up among the ravines in the mountain. The whole family, even the Skaamfamilie from the Stiefveld and Postmaster Moolman's people, had gone up into the mountain with lanterns to search for Tilly. Eventually they found her, crouched beside the dried-up Eye, high up against the Toorberg's steepest cliff, with a wet newborn bundle in her arms. The legend was that for seven months after his birth there was always a tear trickling down the child's left cheek, and whenever any adult wiped it away it would simply reappear.

From then on people said he was truly a child of sorrow.

CrazyTilly's child would never be a Moolman – for that her lover's blood was altogether too dubious and she herself was too confused. The Du Pisanis from the Knersvlakte had always gone hawking their dowsing ability with the willow rods wherever the need arose, but they had never taken root anywhere. They were transients, and Abel would never leave Toorberg to a child with vagabond blood in him – a child that would forever be wondering what was beyond the horizon, even when he stood beside the beacon on the Toorberg and looked out over the plains of Camdeboo to where the earth curved away into the dapple-grey distance. Moolmans were rooted deep in the earth. They did not have the right to leave, even after death. Toorberg was theirs and they belonged to Toorberg.

As these thoughts were passing through Katie's head, Trickle suddenly wandered away into the veld and she never saw him again. She hurried on then, for dawn was far advanced. When she reached the Halt she told Mailbag Moolman: 'I came across little Trickle du Pisani dead on the way.'

Mailbag gave her a quick sideways glance. 'The road is getting too much for you, Aunt Katie Danster,' he said. 'You should send that no-good Shala son of yours instead. Why do your people make life so hard for you?'

At first she made no answer. She just watched his hands sorting the mail on the inkstained table.

'And that Oneday son of yours, Aunt Katie Danster. Everybody knows what sort of churchifying he gets up to in the townships. One of these days he's going to get picked up by the police.'

She looked up, out to where the dark red bus was parked under the pepper trees at the Halt. 'You're only a stepMoolman yourself, Mailbag,' she said. 'You know all about having life made hard for you, you and your mother and your father the postmaster.'

Mailbag's hands were motionless as he looked up. 'Aunt Katie,' he said, and she saw him screw up one eye as he always did when thinking hard, 'the drought that is choking the life out of Toorberg will force even the proud Moolmans to realize what a body feels like when your ribs are no more than bare ridges under your fingers. I'm telling you, Aunt Katie, I feel it in my bones. There is much suffering ahead for the Moolmans. That drilling machine has bored holes wherever there was a green arum – wherever there was even a tuft of grass – wherever Dowser's willow-fork dipped. But all the earth has thrown up are old bones and loose pebbles. You'll see, Aunt Katie, God has drawn off all the water in Toorberg's watertables. Sin cries out for punishment.'

Mailbag looked down again and went on sorting the mail.

Katie was dumbstruck. In all the years she had watched Mailbag growing up and playing round the house with Shala and Oneday, she had never heard him say so much all at once.

9

When he had given the mailbag one last shake to make sure it was empty, he looked up again. 'The pension hasn't come yet, Aunt Katie. Perhaps next week. The Government always takes its time.'

She said goodbye, picked up her little bundle, drank a mouthful of water from the tap under the pepper trees and set off home again along the track that everyone called 'Katie's Path'. On the first of the ridges she put down her bundle, untied the knot and took out a plug of her chewing tobacco. She sat there for a long time looking out over Toorberg. In the distance across the valley she could see a wisp of smoke curling up out of the chimney of her little house.

By early afternoon she had reached the Stiefveld. When she got home Shala told her the news of the frightful thing that had happened to Trickle du Pisani.

Chapter 2

The magistrate did not have much luggage with him on the journey: two bags, the smaller one with the more immediate necessities and the larger one with a few books and court reports on cases which he had thought might prove relevant; also a photograph in a silver frame, a notebook, a flask of whisky, a box of cigars, a small jar of ointment to rub on his stump and a camera for *in loco* inspections. A quiet, thorough man, the magistrate; one who had spent long years working in the courts of the outlying districts.

He sat in the jolting train compartment sipping whisky as he watched the veld moving past the window.

He had been born in a roadcamp, in a tent beside a camp-fire. So his mother had told him. On a night when his father and the labour gang were packing charges of dynamite into the rock crevices of a hill through which the new railway line was to pass. As the dolomite grated and broke and the earth was wrenched asunder, he arrived.

They had never found his father's body. Only the ring which the magistrate wore on the hand now holding the whisky glass had been picked up, days later, without a scratch or even the slightest trace of blood on it, still loosely circling a thin dry fingerbone. The ring had landed near a nest of army ants which had stripped the bone quite clean. They could not very well bury the bone on its own, so till the day of her death his mother had carried his father's fingerbone in her apron pocket, and when-ever she was worried about anything she would lay her hand on it. When she died, the magistrate had had it buried with her, so his father's name could also appear on the tombstone.

Before boarding the train, he had done his preparation thoroughly, acquainting himself with all the facts about the jeal-ous soil of Toorberg. It was a farm with topsoil a hundred feet deep, right down to bedrock – so the drillmen were reputed to have said. Taking samples with the hollowtipped drill, they

11

found nothing but the purest black earth for ninety feet. Only after that did they strike loose gravel, and eventually, at one hundred feet, the hard crust which lay impenetrably covering the mysteries below.

Jealous soil, thought the magistrate. While ploughing in sowing time one year Abel had evidently unearthed the skull of a prehistoric monster. When excavated it was the size of a small Ford and the bone was as white as snow. Abel had the tractor drag the huge skull up to the homestead. There he carefully measured it with a ruler, photographed it from all angles and noted down everything which he thought might prove important or of interest. He realized the value of his find, because he'd read up about it in the *Encyclopaedia Britannica* in his study. Then he ordered the skull to be soaked in old engine oil to stop it rotting and to prevent vermin from gnawing at it, and had it buried under the floorboards of the stable where the rams were housed, believing that the rams' urine would preserve it. Then he swore his attorney to secrecy, had the skull described in his will, and attached a codicil leaving his find to the Royal Museum in London.

The investigating magistrate would have to determine which of these stories were true and which were lies. He knew what his first question was going to be. He had formulated it in the course of the long train journey: 'Show me where the drilling machine was positioned . . .' That is what he would ask first, and when he had the answer to that, the other questions would follow of their own accord. And the answers likewise. Ultimately, he promised himself, he would deliver a judgement in which charge, evidence and sentence would all be clearer than even the purest borehole water.

An extensive family, the Moolmans. At the start of the train journey the magistrate had sketched the family tree on a clean sheet of white paper: on the left the Skaamfamilie, sprung from the loins of Floris Moolman, and on the right the proud Moolmans, from FounderAbel and Magtilt down to the very youngest. Now he was memorizing it. When he closed his eyes he could already trace the bloodlines in his mind. Thoroughness: that is what Justice had taught him.

12

What the magistrate had left out of his reckoning, however, was the Moolman temper – in life as in death – for while he was still on the train, so the story went, OldAbel Moolman, son of FounderAbel and father of Abel, rose from the grave and drove his old jeep down the main street of the town, to await the arrival of the investigating magistrate.

As the train steamed into the station at the town, the magistrate leaned out and looked at the brown-uniformed porter on the platform, noticing at the same time the row of signal lanterns and the dog curled up outside the stationmaster's tiny office. He alighted, beckoned to the porter and asked him to take his luggage to the hotel for him on the station trolley. He decided he would walk the short distance to his lodgings, so as to take the measure of the little town and its inhabitants right from the outset of his investigations. As the magistrate came down the station steps, trying to ignore all the inquisitive eyes staring at him, OldAbel careered into town, spun the jeep round with extravagant speed in front of the co-operative store and stopped in a flurry of gravel as he always had. Flicking a riding-crop against his calfskin gaiters, OldAbel – even in death an impressive figure of a man – slammed the door of the jeep, strode over to the pepper tree and waited.

Slowly the magistrate walked up the main street. When the man emerged from the shade of the pepper tree to confront him, he asked, politely, 'Who are you?'

'OldAbel Moolman of the Moolmans of Toorberg. You go straight back to your bench, Magistrate. Our district has always known what to do about its own sins. We deal with them ourselves.'

The magistrate thought for a moment about the tales he had heard before he arrived. A fevered part of the world, this. In broad daylight people worked hard on their farms, because it was a demanding world which could wring blood from a stone. But when the savage darkness of night sank over the wide plains, or in the intensity of the summer heat when a man's brain simmered in his skull, truth and myth, history and the future, life and death became inextricably entangled.

Impassively the magistrate stroked his stump and asked: 'How do you see the Law, Mr Moolman?' Upon which OldAbel called down damnation on the Bench, compelling the magistrate to ask: 'Do you realize that it is an offence to speak against the Bench in this way?' OldAbel's riding-crop was still impatiently flicking his gaiters. He was not only impatient by nature; by now he was quite obviously in a hurry to get the matter settled so that he could return to his resting place.

'Magistrate!' he shouted. 'You're going to find you haven't got the guts to pronounce sentence on the Sons of Abel. You're altogether too miserable a specimen.' When the magistrate did not answer, he continued: 'Go back to your court instead and lock up all the bloody stockthieves that are the curse of the whole damn district!'

'And you, sir,' replied the magistrate, still apparently unruffled, 'return to your grave, for according to my records you have been dead for years.' He walked round OldAbel – avoiding his shadow, for no one would tread on a dead man's shadow – and proceeded to the hotel where he signed the register, ordered a whisky and sat down on the veranda. Long after he had left, the folk of those parts still related his arrival in this way.

There he sat till late afternoon, speaking to nobody, watching the caterpillar tractors at work in the gravel pit on the slope of the koppie above the town.

He was thinking about that little fingerbone. He didn't know much about his father, only that he had been a cripple. He'd loved books but had never had the opportunity to complete his studies. Evidently from a good family, his mother always said. And crippled, from childhood.

This is my world every bit as much as yours, he thought, the family tree open on his knees. My judgement on the case will be as much yours as mine.

Chapter 3

Ella Moolman walked across the frost in her kitchen garden to pick parsley for the midday meal when Abel and the geologist would be returning from the veld. She hoped they would bring news of relief for Toorberg. She looked up for a moment at the wild geese, crying as they circled overhead above the homestead before flying back into the mist shrouding the crown of the Toorberg. Then, as she bent down, feeling the ice-cold parsley leaves between her fingers, her heart gave a sudden terrified lurch. For right in front of her, one print clearly deeper than the other, were the footprints of Abel's dead brother, De la Rey. In a flash she relived all the events surrounding De la Rey's previous visit, the only one since she had married Abel.

There had always been stories about De la Rey, the Moolman named after the fighting general of the Boer War. People said that following the example of his Uncle Andreas he had gone to the city and lost his soul there among painters, writers, musicians and others like them who made graven images of God's Creation. After a great many years, though, gossip about De la Rey had ceased. Abel had remarked to her: 'They've all sucked their thumbs dry for tales about De la Rey. When they start worrying about drought and stock diseases, they forget to gossip about the Moolmans.'

Until De la Rey, a grey-haired old gentleman all alone in the world, a full-blooded Moolman without an acre of ground to his name, suddenly arrived on the farm. Official records showed that he had died intestate several years previously. No one could tell how he reached the farmstead. There were no wheeltracks, Postmaster Moolman swore he had not alighted at the Halt, and he could not have walked very far, not with one leg shorter than the other.

But suddenly, one morning three years ago, as she was picking cannabis seeds to steep for CrazyTilly's tea, he had come

15

limping through the kitchen garden. Ella did not recognize him, after all the years. When she married Abel and took over the Toorberg homestead, De la Rey had already left for the university in the city to work at his thesis on the Nature of Shame. He was hoping, or so everyone said, that his study would lead to invitations from all the great cities of the world.

As he approached, there was something about the nod of his head which reminded her of OldAbel, and she quickly glanced in the direction of the graveyard. But when he came right up to her asking: 'Where's OldAbel?' she realized that though this was clearly some relation, it was not OldAbel himself risen from the dead.

'Over there,' she said, pointing to the graveyard.

'Oh,' he replied, and from the way he looked at her Ella, always nimblewitted, concluded that this must be De la Rey, the dreamer.

'You're De la Rey,' she said, shielding her eyes from the bright glare of the early morning sun. 'My brother-in-law, the dreamer.'

This morning, as she carefully examined the footprints in the kitchen garden, her thoughts went back to the days following De la Rey's appearance out of the blue. They gave him the room which had been Soois's, still empty after all these years, with Soois's bloodstained uniform still in the wardrobe, and there De la Rey spent all his time reading books taken from the glass-fronted bookcases in the library. Even at night, once she and Abel were in bed, they would hear him shuffling along the passage to fetch or return books. He was restless, said little, didn't eat much; but – to Abel's intense annoyance – he would often beckon Trickle from his hiding-places among the willows and read him tales from the classics. In due course everyone became accustomed to De la Rey's presence, and then suddenly one morning he walked out through the farmyard gate and never returned.

It was not until a full week later, after the search in the mountains had been called off, that Abel realized what must have happened. He was standing in the slaughter kraal at the time, holding OldAbel's Lee Metford rifle and waiting for the farmhands to drag the struggling young ox close enough for him to shoot, when he recalled that the preparations for this season's slaughtering had been going on for a fortnight past: the meat tables had been scrubbed down with bicarbonate of soda; shining new meat-hooks were hanging in the biltong shed; and in the course of that fortnight De la Rey had become increasingly restless and had eaten even less than usual. When Abel looked the young ox in the eye, it suddenly struck him that it was when De la Rey as a child had come across OldAbel in the slaughter kraal, about to shoot seven young oxen in the annual winter slaughter, that he had received his severe setback. After that De la Rey had never been the same again. He had never again been able to stomach cold-blooded killing.

Once these things had occurred to him, Abel felled the ox with a single shot and ordered the carcass to be cut up as quickly as possible. But he then nailed up the doors of the biltong shed and instead had all the biltong hung in the garage of the house in town. Everyone was sure that Abel would eventually get over this sensitivity to his brother's feelings of revulsion about flesh, but the fact was that no ox was ever again slaughtered on Toorberg.

No one knew whether De la Rey had ever found salvation in the course of his travels. Nor could they tell whether in death he had gone wandering once more. But when Ella bent down to pick the cool parsley in her kitchen garden that morning, all these thoughts about De la Rey came flooding through her mind again.

Hastily, she picked a few sprigs of greenery and hurried back to the kitchen. Leaving the parsley on the kitchen table, she went down the long passage to her room and sat down at the dressing-table. She combed her hair and put on some lipstick. Then she pinned on the brooch she had inherited from Granny Olivier and, with her hand to her cheek, looked at herself in the mirror. Toorberg has never yet allowed any Moolman the freedom to leave, she thought, not in life, and not in death either.

Rising, she wandered through the huge old house, past the grandfather clock in the sitting room and the copper pots in the passage, past the portraits of FounderAbel and Grandmother Magtilt above the sideboard in the diningroom. She looked into all the bedrooms, opening the windows of the guestrooms to let in some fresh air, plumping up the pillows and straightening the bedspreads. She blew the dust out of the chamber-pots under the spare beds and rearranged the bathmat in the guest bathroom.

Then she went through the house once more, before sitting down at her stinkwood writing desk in the sun-porch. Opening her calfskin diary, she wrote: 'This morning De la Rey suddenly arrived on another visit. Abel and the geologist are out searching for water in the uplands. My hands are trembling. I can sense that something is about to happen.'

The investigating magistrate later requested Ella – if it would not be an invasion of her privacy – to show him that particular page from her diary. He looked at it for a long time and shook his head, without at first saying anything. Then he took his leave, but turning at the front door, he remarked politely: 'You seem to have great insight.'

After closing her diary and locking it away in its small yellowwood chest again, Ella sat waiting for De la Rey, thinking to herself: He's sure to be wandering about the farmyard somewhere. Or perhaps he's talking to the child down among the willows.

From her writing desk in the sun-porch Ella could look out over the lawn to the rose garden, and farther on across the farmyard to the stock pens and the sheds. Sitting there, she noticed Katie Danster in the distance, coming along the footpath that ran down the hill above the sheds to the lowlands and the Halt. She's showing her age, thought Ella, watching the diminutive figure. She must be nearly eighty, and yet see how briskly she walks. They really are a tough lot. Then Ella remembered that it was the end of the month and that Katie Danster was probably on her way to collect her pension from Mailbag Moolman.

Like Katie Danster's family, De la Rey too was a step-Moolman – those rejected and shoved aside by the pride of Old-

18

Abel and of Abel. Why should he have returned at this particular time, Ella wondered.

When she was just newly married, Granny Olivier had told her that actually De la Rey, and not Abel, had been OldAbel's favourite son. De la Rey was supposed to inherit Toorberg, since he was the eldest, and from his proud walk and the haughtiness of his bearing it was obvious that he was FounderAbel's grandson. He was tough and arrogant, but reserved, and something of a loner, particularly as he grew older and his leg gave him more and more trouble. No one doubted that he would want to further his education, but everyone was sure he would return to farm on Toorberg.

But something happened in his childhood, Granny Olivier said, that changed him. Ella did not enquire any further, but at the time of De la Rey's first visit, when Abel mentioned the ox-shooting, she understood. Coming across his father at the centre of the scene of such slaughter, with three oxen lying dead round him and a further four bellowing and milling around against the wall, had been such a shock to the child's sensibilities that from that day onward he had become even more withdrawn. His horror of meat drove him to spend all subsequent slaughter times at the family's house in town: a quiet, nervous boy, who watched birds through binoculars and was a disappointment to his father. When he finished his schooling he had left for university and never once returned – not even for a by-election or a New Year's Day feast on Toorberg.

Abel had stepped into his elder brother's shoes. According to the documents in the deeds office, OldAbel had secretly transferred to Abel full title and sole ownership of Toorberg on the very day that De la Rey had left for university. This fact was not known even to Abel until years later when OldAbel died and, in the presence of the undertakers, Abel removed the key to the safe in the library from his dead father's neck. That, said Granny Olivier after his death, was OldAbel's way of cutting De la Rey right out of his life at the earliest opportunity.

But to prune away all the deviant off-shoots of the clan completely was beyond OldAbel's power. By the provisions of

19

FounderAbel's will every Moolman woman and every Moolman man who did not himself farm on Toorberg had an inalienable right to a share in the produce of the farm, and on his instruction this provision was to be included in the will of every subsequent inheritor of Toorberg in perpetuity. From the attainment of their majority, for the rest of their lives, all the other Moolmans received two dozen eggs and one head of slaughter stock a week, as well as a can of skimmed milk; a bushel of wheat each quarter; thirty kilograms of biltong every hunting season or slaughtering time; one dressed springbok each winter; a box of quinces from the hedge, when these were ripe; a basket of peaches from the orchard in peach-season; and a daily picking of enough vegetables from the vegetable garden to feed a family with six sons. One final provision led succeeding generations of Moolmans on some dreadful searches up in the Toorberg: once a year one pint of mountain tortoise broth, boiled up from the tender flesh of a Toorberg mountain tortoise – for its medicinal properties.

Every Abel was to provide his kin with these things. They were the things which would remind the Moolmans of their ancestral home and of their final resting-place: the family graveyard where all Moolmans, by the express testamentary order of FounderAbel, were to be buried, with their feet to the East so that at the Second Coming they would rise and face straight into the new dawn. For generations clergymen would remonstrate with the Moolmans about this pagan practice until Abel put an end to the complaints by remarking to a new young minister that they buried their dead in this way for tidiness sake – so that all would lie the same way.

Even after De la Rey's disappearance, he still had his right of usufruct. Shortly after his twenty-first birthday, a telegram arrived from him at the university setting out his wishes regarding the usufruct: he would have nothing at all to do with the biltong; the vegetables, fruit, eggs and milk were to go to the convent in town; the hunting of mountain tortoises he regarded as sinful; the slaughter animals were not to be slaughtered; the springbok was not to be shot; and the bushel of wheat was to be sown in the earth from which it had been reaped.

So, for many years bound by the wills of his father and his grandfather, Abel had to have De la Rey's share of vegetables, fruit, eggs and milk delivered to the convent. During De la Rey's first visit to Toorberg – shortly before he disappeared into the void again – Abel took him into the library one evening, shut the door behind them and, from where she sat crocheting in the sittingroom, Ella heard Abel ranting at De la Rey to sign a document withdrawing this stipulation.

Ever since Postmaster Moolman's secret marriage to the Roman Catholic governess Amy O'Leary and the bitterness which that union had caused OldAbel until his deathbed, Abel would have nothing whatever to do with the Catholic faith. He would not even allow the nuns to call on the Skaamfamilie in the Stiefveld when they visited farms in their battered old Kombi. 'Pagan penguins!' OldAbel had always said. 'Refusing to live under the authority of a husband.'

But De la Rey refused to budge. Abel again threatened to take the wills of FounderAbel and OldAbel to the highest courts in the land to have all the difficult clauses declared null and void, but De la Rey was obdurate. He and Abel had not spoken to each other, even at table, for two whole days.

These thoughts passed through Ella's mind as she watched Katie Danster until the old woman disappeared behind the hill. All morning Ella sat there, as though paralysed by the weight of the footprint on her mind. The previous night had been disturbed. The drilling machine had hammered away all night long. Once, at about three o'clock, there had been a shout. For a moment she thought they had struck water, but the noise quietened down again and when day came she heard that it was a polecat which had run between the fires round the drilling machine. When it ran into the legs of one of the drillers, the polecat had let off such a foul stench that not even washing with paraffin had got rid of the stink.

Hearing the approach of Abel's Land Rover at midday, she went back to her room to smooth her hair into place in front of the mirror. By the smells coming from the kitchen she could tell that the joint was done, so she went out onto the veranda, hoping that this time there would be some good news. Perhaps they had discovered a new underground watercourse in the lee of the cliffs.

Abel stopped the jeep in front of the wagonhouse. He and the geologist sprang out and ran up to the front door. Just for a moment, Ella's heart leapt for joy and she called out: 'De la Rey has also arrived today!' but Abel seemed not to hear. As he ran past her into the house she noticed patches of sweat between the shoulder blades of his khaki shirt.

The geologist stopped in front of her and removed his pith helmet, saying: 'Mrs Moolman, a terrible thing has happened.'

Chapter 4

Grandmother Magtilt sat once again in the sun-porch, in the place that had always been hers, half in the shade of a potted fern – in the wheelchair that after all these years was still lying broken up in the attic – watching compassionately as her grandson's wife prepared the house for the drifter De la Rey. Grandmother Magtilt knew that De la Rey's footprint was no less than a sign of foreboding. After long hours of silently watching her, she understood Ella Moolman's nature very well indeed.

From the early days when the Coetzers of Altydsomer used to drive over to Toorberg for their regular Sunday afternoon picnics with the Moolmans in the shade of Toorberg's tall trees, she and FounderAbel had paused in their silent walks round the farmstead to watch this beautiful child with her jet-black eyes and her pouting little mouth as red as a rosebud. Once, when Ella Coetzer, then in her early teens, had lifted her frock high above her knees and splashed through the clear water of the Toorberg's Eye in her bare feet, FounderAbel had declared: 'That's a wife for a Moolman there.'

Later on, Ella had continued to come – now as an exquisite young woman with huge eyes that looked at the dead as though seeing them – so much so that Grandmother Magtilt and FounderAbel were often startled: had the young Ella's eyes actually rested on them for a moment or had they not? But the next moment she would look away again, at a butterfly or a flower which the youngsters Abel or De la Rey were showing her. From a very early age Abel had paid court to Ella Coetzer. On their picnics, when she sat her rag doll up against the trunk of a poplar tree, Abel would harness his clay oxen and have them completely encircle the doll. 'Look,' whispered FounderAbel to Grandmother Magtilt, 'he's already staking his claim. He's a Moolman all right!'

De la Rey also competed for the favours of the black-eyed Ella, but it was Abel, tough as a cane and as swift as an antelope, who eventually won the contest. It was to him – she in a soft, silky dress of the finest satin and he in corduroy trousers and polished leather gaiters – that Ella one Sunday afternoon, deep in the poplar grove, promised her hand. Even FounderAbel, though by nature disgruntled, had smiled approvingly, while she, Grandmother Magtilt, who still considered herself to be the mother of all the busy inhabitants of Toorberg, felt that this was proper. She was grateful, too; for in those long days on the wagon chest on the foremost of Abel's wagons, she had not been able to see into the future. But when the third generation to spring from her loins brought home a young wife as lovely as Ella Coetzer of Altydsomer, a girl as courteous and as brave as she was beautiful, and when they took their vows and so sincerely pledged each other their troth, Grandmother Magtilt was deeply and thankfully at peace.

Life had never been easy for her. She could not even remember exactly when FounderAbel had asked for her hand – not in those savage days of encircled wagons, sick children and commando expeditions against the black impis. It must have been between one expedition and the next, as her own mother lay dying of malaria in the wagon tent, that the black-bearded and reckless FounderAbel had asked her, just in passing, to marry him.

She could not remember. There had been wagons drawn up in a circle and flames and prancing black bodies. There was the continual crack of gunfire. There were thin assegais hurtling through the air, impis rattling their clubs against their shields, children crying between the wagons, cattle milling round and round and trampling on dogs. Some of the cattle collapsed, one wagon tent caught fire, a man knocked her over, and in their tent her mother was calling for her. She crawled away from the wagon wheel, where she was charging her father's muzzle-loaders for him, and looked into the tent. In the flickering of the flames her mother was sitting bolt upright, staring wildly. She was already in hell, right in the infernal flames, thought Grandmother Magtilt. When she reached her side, she was dead, so she simply drew the blanket up over the yellow face. Not before the

24

next morning while a patrol was out on horseback tracking down and annihilating the impi, and the remaining men were cutting the throats of the wounded cattle, did a woman from one of the neighbouring wagons come to lay out her mother. Only when the woman drew back the blanket did they notice the shaft of the assegai protruding between the third and fourth ribs.

Six months later, with their two wagons, she and Founder-Abel headed into the wilderness. For months she sat through the daylight hours, jolting along on the chest seat of the forward wagon. Round her each morning, as far as the eye could see, were herds of game. In the afternoons, she would occasionally glimpse an impi watching them from the top of a ridge. But some nights, when they had set the wagons at right angles and enclosed them behind a shielding wall of thorn branches, the darkness round them seemed to expand and stretch out, growing ever more silent. Not even the screech of a cricket broke that silence, nothing except the sound of her own breathing and FounderAbel's hand cleaning his gun. Eventually Grandmother Magtilt wanted to scream her fear out loud so that the whole wilderness would hear and come and claim her.

But on they went, thrusting deeper and deeper into the unknown. FounderAbel spent the hours of daylight in wider ranging reconnaissance trips, leaving her under the watchful eye of his halfbreed groom, the deserter Jan Swaat. She never fully trusted Jan Swaat: he had the shifty eyes of a murderer. Once, when FounderAbel had ridden on ahead a little way, she caught him looking at her with his yellow slit-eyes.

'Get away, you Hottentot!' she snarled. 'Don't stare at me. Don't you dare look at a white woman like that again, do you hear?' He turned away, split some wood and lit a fire. But that evening she told FounderAbel, and he went out, found the naked halfbreed asleep in his shelter, and thrashed him with his hippo-hide whip.

'Right,' said FounderAbel when he returned, 'now our deserter has been put properly in his place.'

She was more at ease with the tame Bushman her father had caught at a river-crossing on one of his forays and had given to

FounderAbel as a wedding present. She didn't understand his click-talk, but he had a ready smile. On moonlit nights he would squat on his haunches, rocking back and forth under the moon. Sometimes he would light a fire and dance round and round it like a blue korhaan in a courtship display, but all alone, constantly chewing a piece of sinew, his thoughts far away, perhaps among his own people creeping through the veld somewhere. Where, Grandmother Magtilt sometimes wondered as she watched this little yellow creature trotting tirelessly at Founder-Abel's stirrup: where would the others of his tribe be now?

In later years, from quiet corners of the homestead, she would watch Ella Moolman in the same way – Ella, the woman who so faithfully endured the moods and whims of Abel Moolman. A woman who would suddenly pause in the passage to listen, and then stretch out her hand and touch the curtains beside Grandmother Magtilt's cheek. Then Ella would smile, as though she had discovered a secret, and move on. Often she would simply wander through the house, from room to room, moving a piece of furniture here, straightening a picture there, running her hand across a curtain or plumping up a cushion.

Abel was seldom at home. He was out in the veld all day in his Land Rover, or else out in the yard, when only the grating of his boots on the gravel and the bark of his voice were audible. Sometimes he would come to the graveyard and take a long look at the headstones on the graves where she and Granny Olivier were lying side by side: the women who had preceded his wife. She could not tell what he was thinking, but nobody needed to be told that after the overpowering drive of FounderAbel, every male Moolman would know the weight of bearing the Moolman name. For sheer manliness, none would ever be able to outdo the untameable FounderAbel. She remembered his bold, decisive strides as he paced out the foundations of the Toorberg homestead for her. 'No, stop!' she called out. 'That's enough, that room is quite big enough!' He looked at her, chuckled into his black beard and with a twinkle in his eye took another five paces. 'Just so that you will be able to turn comfortably,' he said. Eventually, when the trader delivered the imported galvanized iron roofing sheets which had filled his entire fleet of wagons, the homestead was the largest in the whole region – the biggest, people said, north of the Hottentots-Holland mountains.

Now the house belonged to Ella. There had been some minor alterations here and there: the odd window had been replaced, the old bathrooms had been done up; on Abel's orders, a new kitchen had been added. Grandmother Magtilt's outside kitchen was now used only when Ella was making soap and at slaughter time. Now it was Ella who kept an eye on the servants, on their knees as they polished the gleaming floors, or rubbed up the brass or brushed the high ceilings with long featherdusters. It was Ella who now strolled through the rose garden snipping off the dead leaves, who picked parsley in the kitchen garden in the very same spot where she and Granny Olivier had stooped to do so. It was Ella, too, who – after giving birth to the sterile CrossAbel and four stillborn babies – had brought the very first Moolman daughter into the world: CrazyTilly, her face just as lovely as her mother's, who could not even find her way inside the house and would then stand crying behind closed doors.

After each of the dead babies had been taken from Ella's bed Grandmother Magtilt had drawn closer, deeply dismayed to see Ella's black eyes growing darker, the pupils even larger, the veins on her lily-white arms increasingly swollen and blue. With each pregnancy Ella allowed her hair to grow longer, till it hung all the way down to her waist. Spread out round her head, it flowed right over the edges of the double bed she shared with Abel. Like that, surrounded by the luxuriance of her hair, Ella would bravely receive Abel again and again until, big-bellied once more, she gave birth eventually to Tilly Moolman. With the cord twisted round her neck and no help at hand, Tilly descended briefly into hell, but then woke again: not only more bewildered than her mother – though even lovelier, some people said – but with all the shortcomings of the Moolmans concentrated in her little body as well.

For Abel, CrazyTilly was the most terrible thing that could ever have sprung from his loins. He believed this was a curse from Heaven. When she started to speak and all that emerged

27

was a strange, incomprehensible jumble, and when she began to crawl round and round in circles like a rabid meerkat, and when she did none of the things that other babies do, Abel summoned the Malay wizard.

Standing in the yard with his pouch of charms in his hand, the Malay watched the black-eyed baby. When she looked up at him with her wild eyes, he declared immediately: 'She will have to be fed quietness for her whole life.' He took five dagga seeds from his pouch and charged Abel fifteen pounds apiece for them. This was no ordinary cannabis: these were seeds from a medicinal plant grown for generations in the garden of a witch-doctor in Mozambique.

The child's mother herself, said the Malay, would have to sow the seeds in her kitchen garden. If all five sprouted, the child would never be able to think straight. If four showed through, there was just a chance that each passing year would grant her a little grace. If three grew, there was a possibility that she would some day actually be normal, provided she was always kept calm. If two, or only one, came up, she would definitely recover her senses. If none at all sprouted but rotted in the earth, then everybody would have been wrong even to think the child was mad, for that would prove that she had been blessed with the Third Eye and the powers of darkness. Then he showed Ella exactly how she was to pick the dagga seeds and brew up a tea with them, three times a day for twenty years. Until the child stops thinking in circles, the Malay said, shaking his head at the baby as she crawled without ceasing in a circle round and round the Toorberg farmyard.

Ella planted the seeds. One morning when she rose and went outside, all five dagga plants had sent their first green shoots up through the soil. Standing among the young maize nearby, Grandmother Magtilt saw something inside Ella break.

Ella hurried back indoors, and Grandmother Magtilt followed her. She heard Ella thinking aloud as she went down the passage: there was a curse on the tenancy of Toorberg by Abel and herself. Toorberg should have gone to a different son, to a dreamer who had also asked for Ella's hand in the poplar grove one afternoon, a hot summer afternoon when Abel had gone hunting guinea-fowl down in the valley, and when Ella with her jet-black eyes as clear as spring water had laughed and said: 'No, De la Rey, I don't love you. Your brother has won my heart. Abel Moolman is the one I want.'

From a few feet away Grandmother Magtilt watched Ella sitting there, constantly putting up her hand to touch her close-cropped hair. Ella had cut off her long tresses the morning the five dagga plants showed through in the kitchen garden. As Ella now sat bowed over her diary, Grandmother Magtilt recalled all the many, many words Ella had written there while her husband was out in the hot sun, labouring, shouting at the farmhands, watching the weather, and patrolling his boundary fences as though he was FounderAbel himself – as though the impis were still skulking in the ravines, as though there was still malaria festering among the bubbles of the Toorberg spring.

All those words, Ella Coetzer, thought Grandmother Magtilt, and still no descendants. All the days in this house, and still no heir. All your nights in bed alone, with Abel's Land Rover brazenly parked in front of the widow's house for all the world to see, and still no son with the strength and force of a Founder-Abel.

Grandmother Magtilt later wandered out into the kitchen garden and all of a sudden she heard the Land Rover and Abel's voice. Then Ella rushed out through the back door with a string of servants behind her, all running with their skirts flapping and their aprons flying, through the low gate leading to the poplar grove.

Chapter 5

The magistrate rose early on the day when his investigation was due to begin officially. Drawing aside the curtains of his hotel window, he looked up towards the gravel pit on the koppie. Although it was still early morning, the trucks loaded with gravel were already crawling up the slope. He pushed up the window and did his breathing exercises in front of it: his healthy arm extended high above his head, the stump stretched up comfortably on the other side (his long-sleeved vest making the effect even more comical) – down to touch his toes with his hand, the stump swinging loosely in the empty vest sleeve flapping in front of him – up again with a deep breath – and again until he was perspiring. Then he sat down on the edge of the bed, feeling the pulse in his stump with his middle finger. Once his heart was beating normally again, he reached into the drawer of the bed-side cabinet for the tin of ointment and started gently massaging his stump. After a bath and a shave, he dressed in light, neat clothes, and closing the door behind him, went downstairs. When he reached the lobby, feeling very much like a tourist, he met the eyes of the receptionist.

As he passed her desk, she greeted him with 'Good morning, Your Worship.' He nodded acknowledgement and went into the dining-room to find himself and a young couple the only occupants. Once he had sopped up the last of the egg yolk on his plate with a scrap of toast, he deftly and one-handedly lit a cigar. The honeymooners stopped whispering their endearments, and stared at him with undisguised curiosity. Before he had finished his coffee, they got up and left, the young man with broad shoulders and narrow hips, the girl, too, beautifully built. As they paused at the door, their arms entwined, he kissed her forehead.

'Anything else, Your Worship?' asked the waiter at his side, startling him momentarily out of the process of mentally formulating questions. At his request the complete Moolman genealogy had been submitted to him, along with other documents – including a report from the security branch on the activities of Oneday Riet, Floris Moolman's grandson. Before his departure and again during the train journey he had carefully memorized it all. He could readily recall all the branches of the family tree, reciting from memory the children of FounderAbel as well as the descendants of his son Floris Moolman.

After spending a long time on the veranda the previous evening, he had gone to his room and opened a commission file. At the back he copied out the genealogy in full and attached an addendum comprising notes on the specific documents he would be able to use as a starting point in his enquiry: the press report that had appeared in the local newspaper immediately after the incident, the police report, the memorandum from the security branch, two photographs of the scene, a report explaining the lack of a ballistic report, an affidavit by the controlling prosecutor for the local court and the resident magistrate's report-in-chambers.

'No, thank you, waiter,' he said, left a tip under his plate and went out into the street. He could feel the eyes following him as he kept to the shade on his way to the court buildings. Unobtrusively, the receptionist crept out of her cramped little cubicle onto the hotel veranda, keenly following the progress of the one-armed magistrate until he disappeared from sight and, disappointedly, she returned to her duties.

He entered the court building through the main door under the national flag. People remarked later that, although there was no wind that morning, the national flag and the flag of the Department of Justice beside it had begun to flap noisily just as he arrived at the court. Passing the clerk of the court's counter, he followed the signs to the prosecutors' offices and having established precisely where these were situated, he looked for the offices of the magistrates. Having located them, he inspected the lavatory, then the children's court, the cells, the small, sparsely stocked library, the parking lot. At last, after spending a while in the blind telephonist's tiny office admiring the man's dexterity at switching and reconnecting lines, he was finally satisfied.

31

He walked back to the hotel and telephoned the court build-ing from his room. The blind operator put him through to the chief magistrate. 'This is the investigating magistrate,' he said. 'I shall be spending some time in your town examining the Moolman report-in-chambers. Would you please have a car put at my disposal?' He knew the fears his voice would evoke in the chief magistrate. He knew them well: the merit reports; the cau-tious, interminable procedures; the seals and stamps and re-ports; the official commissions and hierarchies.

'Thank you.'

He was ready to begin.

Chapter 6

It was not often that a motor car called on the people of the Stiefveld. Katie Danster came out of her cottage as soon as she heard its droning. When she saw the sun glinting on the car's roof, she clambered up excitedly onto the children's rabbit hutch, shielding her eyes with her hand. The car stopped at the gate across the wide, deeply trodden goatpath up to the Stiefveld. A man with only one arm slowly got out to draw aside the concertina gate. He struggled to hook the gate back into its post, but when he had done, he stared out across the Valley as though he was perfectly at home. Putting a cigar between his lips, he lit it with one hand so dexterously that Katie could have sworn he'd used two.

After a while he got back into the car and it proceeded slowly up to Katie's cottage. About a hundred yards out, however, the path became too stony, littered with too many broken bottles, so the car stopped. The iron roof of the rabbit hutch was scorching Katie's feet, since by this time the sun was high in the sky, but she stayed at her post, screwing up her eyes in an attempt to bring in to focus the two men now getting out of the car and heading for the Stiefveld cottage. Shala was up the mountain with his goats and the older grandchildren were at school with Amy O'Leary, Postmaster Moolman's wife. Only she and Meisie Pool and the baby were at home. After Trickle du Pisani's accident, Meisie had returned to the Stiefveld to look after Oneday's children.

When the men were thirty yards away, Katie struggled down off the rabbit hutch and hobbled into the cottage, yelling: 'Meisie! Where are you, you good-for-nothing? Sweep the hearth and empty the chamber-pot under my bed! There are two white men coming. They're sure to be detectives. They'll be turning the mattresses upside down again for Oneday's papers.' She stopped at the cracked mirror behind the screen in her corner of the room to retie her headscarf and tuck in her hair. Then she took a pair of shoes from the trunk under the bed. When the magistrate knocked gently on the outer door, she came out from behind the screen as though she had been there all day, saying: 'Good morning, gentlemen.'

The magistrate and the assistant clerk of the court assigned to him as a driver stooped to enter the cottage.

'I'm looking for Mrs Katie Danster,' he said.

She came closer. 'She is the old woman who's now standing in front of you, sir. Are you sergeants?'

'No.' The magistrate shook his head and smiled. 'No,' he said again.

Katie waited. Behind the screen, the baby began to cry. Dust and ash hovered in the air from Meisie Pool's hasty sweeping of the hearth. The magistrate looked at Katie's bright blue eyes and her wrinkled brown skin, noticing the crooked hands now clasped round her elbows, and the feet in the shoes, too.

'I am the magistrate,' he said then. 'Magistrate Van der Ligt. I have come from the city. I am here to investigate the death of Noah Moolman.'

'After a year?' Katie Danster felt a shudder run down her spine as she heard the wild geese crying up among the cliffs of the Toorberg again, just as they had that day a year ago when she came across poor Trickle on the footpath.

'Fourteen months,' the magistrate replied, and looked round, at the hearth, the iron pot of cold porridge beside the bundles of kindling, the dressed rabbit on a hook beside the fireplace, the tin mugs and plates and the few bits of china arranged on the kitchen shelves lined with newspaper cut into decorative patterns. Against the wall in one corner was a guitar with a worn patch from where the player's palm had brushed across it. A bunch of skins hung from a beam. 'Whose guitar is that?' he asked.

'Mine,' said Katie Danster quickly, startled.

'Do you play?' The magistrate smiled.

'No, sir. I don't know the chords.'

'But it looks as if it has been played.' The magistrate went over to the guitar and picked it up to take a closer look at the strings.

Katie Danster narrowed her eyes. 'It belongs to my younger son,' she said after a while. 'Oneday Riet. He is a minister in the church.'

'Oh.' Carefully the magistrate stood the guitar against the wall again. The clerk shifted about, feeling uncomfortable. 'I wish I could play,' said the magistrate and pointed to his stump.

Katie's eyes were mere slits as she said: 'This is the first magistrate that has ever come to the Stiefveld.'

'There is a reason.' The magistrate's eyes were teasing her. 'If you ask us to sit down, I'll tell you more.'

'Meisie Pool!' Katie called towards the screen. Shyly, Meisie emerged, a smudge of fresh lipstick across her cheek where the baby on her arm had smeared it.

'Afternoon, Your Worship,' she said.

'Good afternoon.'

'Meisie, bring in the benches from outside. Their Worships want to talk. Boil some water. Come on, come on, light the fire!' All at once Katie was scuttling around while the magistrate and the clerk sat down on the benches which Meisie brought in from outside.

As they waited for the coffee, Katie took a seat in front of the magistrate, folded her arms and pulled her scarf low down over her forehead.

'We don't often have white people here, Your Worship,' she said.

The magistrate shrugged his shoulders. 'I hope you don't object, Mrs Danster.'

She shook her head vigorously. 'I am honoured.'

'You see,' said the magistrate, lighting a cigar, 'the Government has sent me to investigate the case of Noah du Pisani.'

He waited for Katie's reaction. At the hearth, the baby on her hip, Meisie was enticing a flame from the coals. Katie looked at Meisie, then at the magistrate.

'But a man from the law came here over a year ago,' she said quietly.

'The Government says . . .' The magistrate gestured towards the clerk. 'We have come to listen to you again.'

35

Katie shrugged her shoulders. 'But everybody knows it all already. It's out in the open. It always has been, right from the start. At the time of the great sadness there was a minister here, a white one, as well as my own son, Oneday Riet. And there were sergeants. There were lots of witnesses. The whole family and all the relatives were there together. It's out in the open. So what does the Government want to come scratching about in our lives again for? After that business Abel just about went off his head, yes, even Abel, and Ella Moolman herself was a sorry mess for a long time.' She shook her head, pulling her scarf down low over her eyes again as though trying to hide the frown on her brow.

'The more witnesses there are, the harder it is to get at the truth,' said the magistrate.

Katie made no answer, her face inscrutable.

'I must take down your evidence, Mrs Danster,' he said, with gentle persistence, stroking his stump. 'Will you tell me what you know?'

'My children and I can tell the court only what we saw with our very own eyes, Your Worship. But more than that, may it please the court, we won't take any part in backveld gossip about this case.'

'My request is merely that you should extend your co-operation. It may then prove unnecessary for me to summon you to give evidence before me officially.' Gently he exhaled the cigar smoke. 'I notice that according to the report you were the last person to have seen Noah du Pisani alive?'

'Yes, Your Worship, I did see him, standing there staring at nothing and listening to the wind as though it had a voice. Yes, I did see him, and he was already dead. I could feel it in my bones. He was dead already by then. Or else he was very near death.'

'What do you mean?' The magistrate leant forward and the bench under him creaked.

'I could see he was dead.'

'But he did not die until three days later.'

Katie looked the magistrate in the eye. 'That's what they say,' she said.

Meisie Pool poured coffee into mugs and offered them

round. The magistrate took a sip of the sweet, strong coffee. 'I hope you like goat's milk, Magistrate,' said Katie. 'It's all we've got here in the Stiefveld. The goats belong to my son Shala. He keeps us all alive with his flock of boer goats.'

The magistrate nodded.

'And were you present when the boy died?'

'No one knows for sure just when Trickle gave up the ghost, You Worship. Some say it was on the evening of the second day, others say it was on the morning of the third day. I just don't know. I won't swear to a death I didn't see.' She screwed up her eyes, sipping from the mug.

They drank their coffee in silence. Eventually she asked: 'Is Your Worship going up to the big house as well, to ask Ella and Abel?'

'I shall visit everyone, Mrs Danster,' said the magistrate. 'Every person who witnessed the episode. It is my duty to find out what happened.' He put his empty mug on the dung floor.

'Yes, it's a pity Toorberg is suffering such lean years,' said Katie. 'It just makes life harder for all of us.'

'Right, Mrs Danster.' The magistrate slapped his knee with his hand. 'Can you tell me now what happened on that last day?'

Katie put her mug down beside his, lightly knocking the tin mugs against each other. 'Which day, Your Worship?'

'But you know which day.'

'The last day?'

The magistrate nodded. 'That last day in the poplar grove.'

'I was looking the other way, at the tree trunks,' said Katie Danster. 'We were all looking in the other direction, here on Toorberg. I didn't see.'

'Did you hear?'

'Yes, I heard, I couldn't do otherwise. I still hear it. I wake up at night thinking it's the crack of Old Abel's stockwhip down in the valley, and then I realize it's that shot still frightening me in my nightmares. No, Your Worship, I heard. I heard.'

'And you saw nothing?'

'Nothing, Your Worship.'

'When the shot rang out, did you not look round?'

'No, Your Worship, I kept on looking away.'

'Were you not curious, Mrs Danster?' The magistrate stood up, walked over to the hearth and turned round to look down at Katie. 'Surely it would have been a natural thing for you to have looked up?'

'I kept looking away, Your Worship, all the time.'

'And after some time had elapsed, after the shot rang out?'

'Then I went over to help the other women hold down CrazyTilly, Your Worship. She'd broken out from where she was locked up, and she was foaming at the mouth again, so we had to hold her down so Ella could get the dagga tea into her to calm her down.'

'Where was that?'

'In the farmyard.'

'And where was Abel Moolman at that moment?'

'I only saw him come past on his way to the wagon house. He was going to let out his boer mastiffs. They had been locked up from the start.'

'And then?'

'Then I came back here to the Stiefveld, Your Worship. That's all I can tell you today. And, with respect, you're lucky I can still remember so much. Because it's more than a year ago, and I can hardly even remember how many kids the goats gave us last year. I'm nearly eighty, you know.'

'I see.' The magistrate moved towards the door. 'Thank you very much for the coffee. Goodbye, Mrs Danster.' He walked out, but turned back to say: 'And I hope to meet your sons, too, some time in the future.'

As the clerk came trotting along behind, a hen and chickens scuttled out of their way. When the car doors slammed shut, Katie Danster turned round in the doorway and looked at Meisie Pool.

'It won't be from the Stiefveld that that poor man gets the story. Let him pick it up where it may found.' With a last glance at the shining roof of the homestead, she went indoors and scratched an ember out of the hearth to light the butt-end of her handrolled cigarette.

Chapter 7

Amy O'Leary Moolman struggled out of bed. She had been up late the previous evening marking her farmschool pupils' work. It was very late when she had gone out onto the veranda, to see if she could sniff any rain. On the lowest slopes of the Toorberg, close to Katie Danster's cottage, a fire blazed, and her last thought before going back indoors was the hope that the Stiefveld was not going to be burnt out again this year as it had been the year that Mailbag was born. Everyone knew what a battle Katie Danster and her sons were having as it was, trying to make ends meet on that barren stretch of earth with only their flock of goats.

Amy was glad that, mercifully, it was the end of the month. As usual, she had given the children the day off school so that they could do their parents' shopping. It was a long walk to the General Dealer's at Voetpad, and many children had to come all the way to the Halt as well, to collect their grandparents' pension money. She told Postmaster Moolman right from the outset, when she started the little school soon after Mailbag's birth: there was no sense in her standing in front of an empty classroom at the end of every month when every child in the district was off on a footpath somewhere, clutching a sixpence or a shilling.

Drawing aside the dining-room curtains, she looked up at the Toorberg and noticed the shroud of mist covering the peak this morning.

'Perhaps there's rain coming,' she said to the Postmaster Moolman when he emerged from the bedroom and sat down to breakfast. She poured his coffee, while he glanced at the day's bus timetable. He looked tired. The hand turning the pages trembled slightly. 'Your blood-pressure is up again today,' she said. 'Haven't you been taking the extract the Malay left for you?'

Postmaster closed the timetable and looked up. 'All that

39

Malay is after is easy money. I'll bet that extract of his is nothing but cowpiss from Abel's milking sheds.'

'Really, Postmaster!' she scolded. 'Have you got a headache?'

'Just a slightly bloody taste in the mouth,' he said. 'Probably from all the biltong I ate last night. I wonder where Abel is getting the biltong from, seeing he still won't allow any slaughtering.'

Amy shrugged her shoulders. 'He probably buys it from his neighbours. Money's no object to Ella and Co. They're flush.' Her mouth assumed the expression it always did when talking about Abel Moolman. She sliced the bread fiercely. Mailbag came in, sat down at the table and blew his nose on his khaki handkerchief. 'If only he met his obligations under the usufruct,' she said. 'Just look when the biltong gets delivered – only now! Five months late. The slaughtering season is in June, not in the height of summer. Next year we've got to see to it that we get it in time, Postmaster. In winter. That is when you want your biltong. To eat in front of the fire. And to fry with your breakfast eggs, early in the morning when it's snowing on the Toorberg. Isn't that right, Mailbag?'

'The devil will catch up with them yet,' said her son, over the rim of his coffee-mug. 'I can feel it in my bones. It's never going to rain here.'

'There's mist on the top of the mountain this morning,' said Amy. 'What do you think, Postmaster? Is it just a dry mist?'

Postmaster Moolman stood up with a sigh, putting the stub of a pencil behind his ear and the folded bus timetable into his shirt pocket.

'Mailbag,' he said, 'you'd better get a move on. It's the end of the month. When I went out to put the brake on the windgenerator a moment ago, Katie Danster was already on her way down. The backvelders'll soon be queueing up for their envelopes, and you haven't finished sorting yesterday afternoon's post yet.'

Amy looked at Postmaster. 'But aren't you going to have another cup of coffee?' she asked, worried.

'No. When my head's all dizzy coffee only makes it worse. And it's not going to rain. Can't you hear the geese? I grew up among them. They're calling for rain. They're complaining.' He went out, and they listened to his footsteps crossing the gravelled yard to the Halt.

'The biltong is six months late,' said Mailbag as his mother sat down opposite him. He took a handful of sliced biltong and as he tipped back his head to cram it into his mouth Amy noticed the ink under his fingernails.

'You need to brush those nails of yours, Mailbag,' she said. 'I tell that to the children at school every day, and here you are in my own house with the skin practically growing over the dirt under your nails!'

He made no reply, just took some more biltong.

After a while he said: 'I heard the drilling machine at it again all night.'

'It's sheer conceit.' Irritated, Amy looked out of the window. 'Abel won't draw water from the government dam, like the rest of the farmers. Oh no, he's too good for bailiff's water. He wants his own water, Toorberg water.'

'And that he's not going to get.'

'Why do you say that?'

'I can feel it in my bones. I just feel it. They've been drilling for months now.'

'It's been years.' Amy got up, wiping her hands on her apron. 'Come on now, Mailbag, hurry up. You know what your father's like when he starts the day squinting up towards Toorberg through his binoculars. You heard him say he'd seen Katie Danster on her way down. Listen, there he is calling you already. Don't try his blood-pressure any further today. We don't want him collapsing again.'

Mailbag got up sluggishly and went out. She shook her head as she watched him through the window, walking over to the Halt with his drooping shoulders and his shirt-tail hanging out. He was a Moolman, all right. You could tell by his eyes. Sometimes when he glanced up quickly, he looked just like Old-Abel. Mind you, some said he took after Granny Olivier's side of the family: they all tended to walk in that sideways-on fashion as though carrying something on one shoulder. And yesterday when young CrossAbel, that idiot of a son of Abel's, had brought his father's Land Rover lurching to a halt in front of her house in a cloud of dust and delivered the sack of biltong – and hadn't even raised his hat to her – she'd caught a momentary glimpse of the resemblance between him, too, and Mailbag. To think that as boys those two used to play together secretly in the Vlei, till one day Abel caught them there. He forbade his son to play with any child of Catholic Amy O'Leary's, and Mailbag came home crying. Later the boy took to wandering up to the Skaamfamilie on the Stiefveld and he, Shala and Oneday became great friends. Amy hadn't stopped him, not even when as an adolescent he used to stay out late up at Katie Danster's place.

'The child can't go on hanging around the Skaamfamilie like this,' Postmaster Moolman had protested.

'Oh, it's company for him,' she'd countered. 'And in any case, Katie Danster's grandchildren are among the brightest children in the school. Ragged they may be, but they come from a good home.'

'What about that tart of a LittleKitty Riet?' asked Postmaster. 'You should just see the way she flirts with Mailbag through the bars on the counter when she comes into the post office.'

Amy was immediately angry. 'Listen, Postmaster, now you are doing exactly what your father did to us. Because I was a Catholic, here we are, forced into penury to live off OldAbel's legacy.'

'Hang on, Amy,' Postmaster protested. 'I only mean that, well, they're cousins, you know. It could cause trouble, and anyway . . .'

Furious, Amy cut him off: 'Look, Postmaster, Mailbag's not going to go interfering with his own cousin! And you know as well as I do that that's not your real reason. As though your own life was not lesson enough for you. Just remember one thing: LittleKitty is descended from a missionary.'

'That doesn't make her a nun,' answered Postmaster and got up.

'You're sarcastic again this morning, aren't you, Postmaster!' She turned her back on him. 'People are people. And Little-Kitty is a lovely child, with those deep blue eyes of hers.'

'Yes, and that deep brown skin of hers, too,' Postmaster called over his shoulder as he slammed the door behind him.

Amy sighed, thinking back on it all. Postmaster's Moolman blood runs deep, she thought as she went to hang up his brother De la Rey's binoculars behind the bedroom door. These were the binoculars through which De la Rey was supposed to have watched birds as a child. Now Postmaster used them to peer up at the homestead whenever the nostalgia for Toorberg came upon him. He would tell her and Mailbag he was just checking the morning's weather on the Toorberg, but with an aching heart she knew that it was his childhood home that he was really looking at, with a yearning so palpable that when he came back indoors again and she stroked his forearm with her fingertips she could actually feel the gooseflesh. So intense was that yearning that he shivered even on the hottest summer morning.

That was why that brat of a youngster who had deposited the sack of biltong on her doorstep with the words: 'Here's your usufruct, Aunt Amy', had made her so angry the day before. When Postmaster came home for lunch and asked who had been churning up the gravel so wildly in front of the house, she was angry all over again, for she saw how his head sank. But all she said was: 'Oh, it's just the biltong.'

He'd spent the whole evening sitting in front of the open window slicing biltong and listening to the drilling machine up on Toorberg. Eventually she had to ask him to close the window to stop the crickets and mosquitoes from coming in to the light.

But the Moolmans would never allow her Mailbag to be one of them. They were far too arrogant ever to share. Even when she had just started teaching at the convent school in town, and Postmaster would come courting her secretly at the boarding house, people had warned her about the Moolman arrogance. When Postmaster eventually asked her to marry him, she took her uncertainty to Mother Superior. In the bare, cramped office high up under the roof of the tumbledown old convent under the pepper trees the old nun looked at her with her penetrating blue eyes and folded her pale hands. For a moment she looked down. 'Amy,' she said, 'the Moolmans are a proud, closely-knit family. They are staunchly Protestant. They are extremely clannish. For them the past is as yesterday, and they speak of yesterday as though it were today. They never bury the dead. And they never forgive.'

She had not understood what the old nun was trying to tell her. 'It may be that this young man is an exception, but whether they will allow him to be an exception is a question which should perhaps be settled before the wedding.'

Mother Superior would not say any more. She promised to pray for Amy, made the sign of the cross with her pale hands and smiled as she stood up to end the interview. Her hand was cool on Amy's when she added: 'You should come and consult Father Diephuis. Have a talk to him, too.'

Years later, when the old nun died, she and Postmaster were already living down on the plain. During the funeral service she'd caught the strong scent of the pepper tree berries again and wished that she had listened more closely and considered more carefully.

Now the same greed has got us, too, in its grip, she thought. See how much bitterness even the delivery of the biltong could cause, and she herself the bitterest of them all, bitter with resentment she would never have dreamt possible when she first heard the tales about FounderAbel all those years ago. Even in his own time, so people said, the pedlars' carts queued up at the gateway to Toorberg, secure in the knowledge that FounderAbel would buy everything that came from foreign parts or bore a Dutch trade mark. He bought three pianos for Grandmother Magtilt's musical fingers; he owned forty guns, one for every kind of animal or native that crawled on the face of the veld. He bought a stock of cough mixture from an Italian pedlar to last a hundred years – Postmaster and his brothers (and Ella's children, too, apparently) were raised on it. He bought a telescope which had to be carried on the back of a pack-mule whenever he felt the urge to climb the summit of the Toorberg and look out over all

44

his wealth. In later years he bought gold shares in the Transvaal mines from a Russian Jew. He bought snuff-boxes, silver stirrups, brass taps and Spanish leather saddles. And he bought a magnifying glass for his old age when he would no longer be able to read the Bible with the naked eye.

Amy had listened wide-eyed to all these tales, for this part of the world was new to her. What's more, they told her, the day came when FounderAbel decided to brand all the stock on the farm with a capital A. Apparently, on the day he bought the branding-iron from an itinerant Jew, all the flocks and herds on the slopes, in the valleys and on the plains had sensed something ominous in the air. They had grown restless and, so the backvelders insisted, a flock of some two hundred of FounderAbel's fattest wethers had raced up the Toorberg and in full view of all had hurtled over the sheer krantzes on the other side, down onto the wild prickly-pears on the plains of Camdeboo far below. There were vultures wheeling round the spot for a full fortnight.

The story ran that branding every head of stock on Toorberg with the capital A sent the smell of scorched flesh forty miles down the wind for days on end. Every hide on Toorberg was branded and at last, on the evening of the fourth day, FounderAbel was satisfied.

Two months later, however, a goldsmith stopped at Toorberg and FounderAbel gave him a permanent appointment. He wanted his initials in gold on every single object on Toorberg – every saddle, every piece of furniture, even under the cups and dinnerplates. FounderAbel had apparently had the gold dust sent down from the Transvaal mines in which he had shares. But one day when a visiting pedlar saw the goldsmith actually working on one of FounderAbel's boots, the whole district realized that FounderAbel's wealth had affected his head. The consensus was that no man could possess so much and remain sane.

The madness in the Moolman blood was an established fact even in those years, but it did not manifest itself unmistakably again until CrazyTilly was born. 'So the sins of the fathers are visited upon the children, to the third and fourth generation,' said Amy, when at the age of two Tilly had her first convulsions.

45

'That is what you get for being arrogant.' First, Abel and Ella had had CrossAbel, born with the mark of infertility across his ear; then the succession of stillborn babies; and finally, when Ella was on the verge of a nervous breakdown, there was Tilly.

Tilly, who from the very beginning had gone wandering restlessly where she had no business to be. Once she very nearly ended up under one of the buses at the Halt. Tilly, who only began to calm down after the Malay had recommended that she be fed dagga tea night and morning. That tea was brewed from boiled dagga seeds grown openly in Ella's kitchen garden, however illegal it was, even in those days. 'It's medicinal,' people said. Tilly, who later wouldn't let Dowser alone and then gave birth to poor little Trickle.

Trickle was as much a stepchild as Katie Danster's children and grandchildren, or her own Mailbag with his sloping shoulders. All these stepchildren, Amy thought bitterly, living here on the edge of Toorberg, unable to break free, but never truly belonging either.

'You are cursed by your blood,' she told Postmaster one day, but as usual he did not answer. Only once had she ever heard him say anything against his family. That was after he, the late Andries Riet and Dowser du Pisani had gone to Abel one day to plead for the recognition of their children in his will, because someone had overheard Ella saying that Abel had decided to have the usufruct clause deleted. At this meeting, Abel had promised that the Skaamfamilie could continue to farm on the Stiefveld for the next hundred years, but he had refused even to acknowledge the presence of Dowser du Pisani, the man who had got his daughter into trouble. To Postmaster Moolman, to his very own brother, he'd said he would be prepared to hire the stretch of servitude land alongside the railway tracks for Mailbag, if the boy thought he'd like to run some cattle on it. They could pay off the cattle in instalments, and once Mailbag was on his feet, he could take over the rental of the servitude from Abel.

Mailbag and Postmaster had accepted the offer and even welded a branding-iron for Mailbag in the shape of a postal

46

franking stamp. But it was not long before the trains had killed all Mailbag's cattle, and for years and years Amy paid for dead cattle out of her teacher's salary. One of the busdrivers said to Postmaster: 'So that's how your Toorberg relations pay you your due.'

That was when Postmaster, looking into the distance, had said: 'They are no family of mine. Abel and Ella have become scum in that house.' The next day he had his first black-out and Mailbag had to start helping him at the Halt.

When Amy came out of her reverie, she was in the bedroom holding the little holy medal that the old nun had given her. Whenever she thought about all the injustice that her husband and son had to endure as stepMoolmans, she always came back to that little medal. Then she would remember the cool blue eyes of the old nun that afternoon when she'd told her that she had finally decided to marry Postmaster Moolman, son of the immensely wealthy OldAbel Moolman of Toorberg. For, lifting the holy medal from her own neck the Mother Superior had hung it round Amy's, with the words: 'This little medal was given to me by an old friend and sister when I left the city to come out here. She said to me then: "Never forget where you come from, but don't let that stop you going where you must." I give it to you with the same words.'

All morning, as she sat on the small veranda in the shade, marking essays, and later, too, as she moved through the house checking that everything was neat and tidy before Postmaster and Mailbag walked over for their dinner, she felt uneasy. She worried about Postmaster's blood-pressure and his black-outs, worried about what would happen to Mailbag when his father was not there any more, worried about the usufruct, worried, too, about the growing avarice which she felt swelling like an unfamiliar, unnamed tumour deep within her.

She was standing at the kitchen window, with her eyes on the Toorberg and the saint's medal in her hand, when someone ran across the gravel outside towards the Halt yelling: 'Postmaster, get the tow-ropes, Abel wants the tow-ropes! Trickle du Pisani has fallen down a borehole!'

47

Chapter 8

'Show me the drilling machine,' the magistrate said when Dowser Du Pisani came out onto the narrow front veranda of the old farm schoolhouse where he lived with his five children. Hooked into Dowser's belt were five forked willow wands of varying sizes: a thin yellow one, supposedly the oldest, for use on limestone soils; then a short thick one, which was best for low-lying areas; next, a very flexible one, worn smooth from much handling, which he used whenever he could feel water in his feet; and lastly, two small ones whose particular effectiveness he had not yet definitely established. Attached all the way round his belt were tiny medicine bottles filled with samples of water from every spring and streamlet on Toorberg. At night he used to soak his willow-forks in water to which some cattle urine and a few drops of water from his little bottles had been added – to toughen the wood. In this way his wands were steeped in an intimate knowledge of the water in the valleys and the mountain.

Standing before the magistrate on his narrow veranda, Dowser, son of the penniless Du Pisanis from the Knersvlakte, touched his hat and stammered, fingering his dowsing rods.

They set off in the direction of the milking shed on Toorberg, watched inquisitively by the bunch of young Du Pisanis from behind the school windows. Beyond the milking shed lay all the dead machinery: pieces of cast iron that had once been lucerne mowers; a crippled thresher, leaning on its draw-shaft; a stump-nosed tractor dating back to OldAbel's time, its front wheels missing and the back tyres completely perished; a harrow with blunt, rusted teeth; and off to one side: another tired pile of gears, levers and wheels slumbering among the nettles.

'Please, Your Worship, this is the drilling machine.' Dowser stamped back the weeds with his velskoens. 'This is the thing that came and brought troubles on us,' he continued, when the magistrate made no move to take a closer look, but instead lit a cigar and pensively looked at the pile of metal. 'Bit by bit,' said

Dowser, 'like a thread in a jersey. There was no way to stop it and everything just come undone at once.' The magistrate noted how Dowser kicked each component of the machine with the point of his velskoen as he walked round the pile of scrap iron.

'Where is the bit?'' asked the magistrate. 'The tip of the drill.'

'No, nobody knows, Your Worship. They say Mr Abel buried it in the deadveld – that's the poisonous piece of land where FounderAbel's wagons stood when he nearly died of fever. Nothing grows there. They say all the devils FounderAbel sweated out then are still living there today. Not even animals go there – Your Worship will never see any tracks there.'

'Where is that, Mr Du Pisani?'

'Down on the plain, Your Worship, on the way to the Halt.'

'And you say Abel Moolman buried the drill bit down there?'

'Yes, Your Worship, they say Mr Abel loaded the bit onto the Land Rover himself, with his soft hands! He's an armchair-farmer: he never touched a shovel or a tractor's steering wheel in his life! And off he went. And when he came back he was the hell in and all covered with dust, and I hear he said: "Ella, I've washed the guilt off my hands in the dust of the deadveld. Let's forget about everything that's happened this year, let's forget about the machine, and let's be pure and clean when the first rains come." That's what he said, Your Worship, 'cos Katie Danster's cousin's daughter was one of the housemaids up there then, and she heard him say it. And as he said those words, Your Worship, the rain came down all over Toorberg so hard that every dam on the farm broke in the cloudburst, and the antbears ran around in the veld with their noses wet, 'cos all their holes were under water, and all the little brats was chasing them.'

'And,' Dowser went on, as the magistrate sat down on a piece of metal and gazed out over the defunct machinery, 'what made the district even more sure that it was the devil himself that had a hand in all this business was this: all those useless, dry boreholes that the machine drilled open on just about every acre of Toorberg – they all started spouting water!'

49

Dowser pushed his hat to the back of his head. 'And another thing, Your Worship. The Moolmans' family graveyard was flooded, and when the water ran off a couple of weeks later, FounderAbel's grave collapsed. And the gravestone was just gone – the wet ground swallowed it, right down into the place of death that makes us frightened to think about.'

The magistrate nodded. 'I see,' he said.

'Please, Your Worship, let's leave the devil alone now. This machine should be covered up and buried. Really it should have a black funeral, and the Malay ought to curse it. 'Cos this thing lying here is the thing what broke the Moolmans.'

The magistrate stubbed out his cigar on a piece of metal, stood up and sighed. They walked back to his car where the assistant clerk was dozing, slouched behind the wheel.

'So what does the Law say about this business, Your Worship?' Dowser asked.

'That is something I have yet to establish, Mr Du Pisani.' The magistrate stuck his hand through the open window of the car to take a fresh packet of his thin cigars from the cubby-hole. The clerk woke with a start and hurriedly straightened his tie. Lighting his cigar, the magistrate felt the immense silence of the plain enclosing him. Mirages were dancing on the horizon in the distance while a single whirlwind funnelled round the foothills of the Toorberg. Everything keeps silence, he thought, except human mouths babbling on and on like bitter water.

'It's dry,' he said to Dowser, pointing with his cigar towards the funnel of dust.

'It's the Stiefveld that is so dry, Your Worship. Trampled to death by Shala Riet's goats. There's not much left on that bit of veld.'

'Really?'

They were standing out in the sun; inside the car the clerk sighed heavily. The bodywork ticked as the metal expanded in the heat.

'Tell me about Abel Moolman's relationship with young Noah du Pisani, your late son,' said the magistrate, looking straight at Dowser. There was an unexpected sharpness in the glance which Dowser shot at the magistrate, before he looked away again, lightly kicking the tyre with the toe of his shoe.

'But you must have heard, Your Worship?'

The magistrate shook his head. 'No, Mr Du Pisani, so far I have heard nothing.'

'Well . . .' Dowser fidgeted with a little bottle at his belt, working it free of the thong it hung from. He unscrewed the cap, quickly brought it to his mouth, gulped down the water at a single swallow, and wiped his lips. The magistrate glanced across in mild surprise to see if the clerk had noticed, but that young man's head was nodding again. 'Well, you see,' Dowser started again, and gave his mouth another hard wipe with the back of his hand.

'Yes, Mr Du Pisani?'

'You see, Your Worship, me and Tilly – what can I say? Me and Tilly weren't married, really. It happened when she got interested in these willow twigs of mine. She used to creep up on me in the veld, you know, Your Worship, when I was dowsing for water. She just flew out from behind a bush and grabbed my twig and ran away into the veld with it. No, she gave me a lot of trouble, Your Worship, she's such a mad thing. You'll see for yourself when Ella shows her to you, Your Worship. If they let her out of that room Abel built after poor little Trickle died. You know, Your Worship, there isn't a single window in that room. And Katie's cousin's daughter told me Tilly's only got a mattress to lie on, and she has to drink one lot of dagga tea after another all day long. But 'strue 's God, Your Worship, you'll see for yourself, she's the prettiest girl in the whole district, with her high stepping legs and her mouth always talking such strange things.' Dowser suddenly stopped and looked at the magistrate. 'But don't you know all this, Your Worship?'

'No, Mr Du Pisani. That is what I have come to find out. Tell me, were you ever married?'

'That's the other thing about Mr Abel, Your Worship. Me and my wife moved into the little school here. It was empty for years, after Amy O'Leary started her little school at the Halt.

51

And that's when the trouble with Tilly started. My wife left me, Your Worship, long before little Trickle fell in. She went to her people in Namaqualand.'

'She left because of your relationship with Tilly Moolman?'

'Just so, Your Worship, just so.' Dowser's fingers groped for another little bottle.

'But tell me, Mr Du Pisani, what precisely did Abel feel about Noah?'

'He wouldn't look at him, Your Worship. He put up with him, like a orphan lamb in the yard, but he never looked at him. No, 'cos he wasn't a Moolman, you see. And Trickle was also a wanderer, and Mr Abel can't stand wanderers. He also says – you can ask him yourself, Your Worship – he says the Du Pisanis are wanderers. "Water-wanderers", that's what he calls us. And Trickle was a proper Du Pisani: always round the boreholes and the willow trees. Come, Your Worship, I want to show you something.'

Dowser rummaged in his bag and took out a small willow fork. 'This one, Your Worship,' he said, and a mistiness came into the eyes under the hat, 'this is the one I cut for Trickle just the day before he fell down the hole. I wanted to teach him to dowse. I could see he had the feeling for it. You know, Your Worship, even when he was standing up, he was listening to the water under the ground. He could hear water, Your Worship, even if it was a hundred feet down. He would have been worth a lot to Abel. When he was bigger he wouldn't even need a rod, he could just dig in his heel and say "Drill!" and we would drill with that dead machine there, and I swear, Your Worship, I swear we would drill open streams of sweet water. Toorberg needed him, Your Worship; it's just the Moolmans, they wouldn't accept him. They only know their own kind of talents, not other talents.'

'What about your own future on Toorberg, Mr Du Pisani?' asked the magistrate sympathetically.

'No, I can't say, Your Worship. Just so long as I respect Mr Abel, he'll let me stay. Over the years I got to know the water courses on Toorberg. I fetched water in the water cart from every kloof for Mr Abel and Miss Ella and their children to bath in. And for Mr Abel to mix with his brandy. Now he wants us to dig wells and pump out the water what collects in them. That's the new plan, Your Worship.'

'You bear no grudge on account of these events?'

'How can I bear a grudge, Your Worship? It was the hole I sank myself!'

'Not even on account of what happened at the end, Mr Du Pisani?'

Dowser took off his hat and ran his hand across his hair. 'We was all there, Your Worship,' he said quietly. 'There wasn't nothing else we could do.'

The magistrate sighed and stroked his stump. 'Are you sure, Mr Du Pisani?'

'Can you ever be sure of these things, Your Worship? I also lie awake at night. That child of mine has melted into Toorberg's water tables now, Your Worship. Every day he is flowing past under my feet. Maybe Your Worship will think I'm mad in the head, but I feel I'm carrying Noah Moolman around with me in these little bottles, Your Worship.' His face shadowed by his hat, Dowser fingered the small bottles.

'I understand what you mean, Mr Du Pisani,' said the magistrate, looking at Dowser's broad sunburned hand resting on the bottles. The funnel of dust playing over the Stiefveld ridges had disappeared and there was a haze over the Toorberg. 'I must go,' he said to Dowser. They shook hands, then the magistrate woke the clerk and the car drove off.

After a while the magistrate became aware of himself, sitting there, in silence, shaking his head.

Chapter 9

That evening, seated in front of the open window of his hotel room, with the hubbub from the bar down below wafting in on a light breeze, the magistrate wrote:

'My dear wife,

'When I bent down and touched the cold metal of the drilling machine on the Moolman farm this afternoon, I had the feeling that possibly the machine itself was the guilty party, that I ought also to take down its evidence – its full story, from the time when it arrived at the Halt by haulier, all wrapped up in grease and cotton, to the present, where it lies covered with creepers, abandoned behind the milking shed where Abel Moolman's prize Jerseys are milked. One can hardly see it for weeds – thorn apples, nettles, devil-thorns – growing in between and around and all over the pieces of the machine. Curiously enough, I did not notice any rust anywhere.

'There were more parts to it than I had expected. Pieces of steel in various shapes and forms – pipes, rods, gears, tangled cables, supports – lay strewn over a large area. I was frankly amazed at this piece of machinery which Abel Moolman, master of the farm, had banished to behind the milking shed.

'Not that the machine had ever broken down or become unusable. They tell me that Abel Moolman personally dismantled the thing section by section and "buried" it above ground. If he had not been so afraid that the machine would perpetuate its demonic work underground, so the hotel barman informed me last night, he would certainly have interred it properly – out of sight and out of mind.

'It is not always clear to me, my love, how I should proceed with the investigation of this case. How often I wish you were here so that we could discuss the matter. I have no one to share my thoughts with. In fact, at night I am left all alone, with only my conjectures for company, and the heat. When I draw aside the curtains, the sultry night air is quite overwhelming and in addition I then have to look out on the dark bite the gravel quarry has taken out of the koppie opposite. By day I have to be content with the dreary company of the assistant clerk of the criminal court – a dull-witted and chronically somnolent young man – who has been assigned to me as a driver on these interminable deserted country roads and who is in the habit of saying not a single word.

'It is true, as you have frequently remarked, that I never discussed court matters with you. The law is a laborious profession, I am afraid, and it is often only in quiet solitude that one is able to see things clearly. But for the first time in my professional life, with the exception of my time as a novice on the bench, I feel that I have a matter to decide which is beyond my capacity.

'This is a strange district. In the heat of the night, one can sense the townsfolk restlessly fidgeting inside their houses. I have no idea what they are doing. Perhaps they are arranging cups of coffee on trays, or knocking out their pipes against veranda walls in the dark, or putting out bowls of water for the dogs – which bark without interruption all night long. Perhaps they are simply walking about, restless on account of the heat. Leaning out of my window, I watch the lights in the houses going out one by one. Eventually the only lamps left burning are in the minister's study and in the house of the old woman across the road who is dying of stomach cancer.

'The farms are far apart and the people are sullen, unwilling to talk. Not that I sense any disrespect for my office – quite the opposite, in fact – but I do feel that their evidence (nothing but informal conversations so far) is not spontaneous. They are inhibited by fears: ancient apprehensions, inherited anxieties, age-old terrors. The folk up in the mountains have superstitions which show in their eyes and spread like a riot of weeds when they begin to talk – and which are clearly perceptible when they look away. They are living under a curse, these people in the outlying districts. I can sense it, but my male intuition is too feeble to be a reliable guide. I need the eye of a woman, a woman like you, to look and judge with the insight of her spirit.

'I am an old magistrate now and I am suddenly weary. The

heat makes my arm throb, which is odd, because it is usually troublesome only in cold weather. Do you remember the winters in De Aar? You used to apply a eucalyptus dressing for me every morning before I went to court. Now it is the heat that makes it ache. It is odd. I wish you were here to rub my back for me. Only in her absence does a man appreciate his wife. Such is the nature of male indifference.

'Finally, I must tell you that there is a feeling in the town (and I do not mention it lightly, nor – let me add – has anyone said as much to me in as many words, but I feel it all the same), there is a feeling in the town, one encountered in an even fiercer form on the farms, that I am here to rake old chestnuts out of the fire, and people do not like the burnt smell, since these are things which they have consigned to oblivion. However, I have my duty to do, and as you know, that has always been my first priority. I should also add, embarrassing though it is, that the co-operation of my colleague, the local magistrate on the bench, is not all that one would have wished.

'He is like a man holding his breath: he knows more than he is prepared to admit. He fears me because he knows I am here on commission.

'My dear wife, I shall write again tomorrow. I hope you enjoyed the serials on the radio today.

'With fond regards,

'Your husband and lifelong companion,

'Abraham van der Ligt.'

After screwing on the cap of his pen, the magistrate folded the letter and went over to the window to stare out over the town. He slowly drew the curtains, took off his shirt, and did his stretching exercises. When his pulse returned to normal, he slowly massaged some ointment into his stump.

I am like an old dog licking its wounds, he thought.

Chapter 10

Shala and Oneday Riet had often sat in the cave on the Toorberg, surrounded by the Bushman paintings on the rock faces, with the name of one of FounderAbel's pedlar friends carved across a herd of antelope. From this vantage point they could look out over the whole of Toorberg and watch the red railway buses crawling along the dusty road before parking themselves side by side at Postmaster Moolman's Halt. They saw the flocks of merino sheep moving across the plains, followed by slow columns of dust. They observed the progress of a tractor and plough breaking the crust of some of Toorberg's sweetest soil, exposing the dark stain of earth beneath. They noticed Katie Danster battling up the valley towards the Stiefveld cottage with a straggling load of firewood on her head. And always in evidence was Abel's Land Rover driving back and forth between the sheds and stock-pens and windmills and dams, all day long.

Up here, high above all noise and social distinction, they could crawl into the warm mouth of the earth and lie flat on the ground among the rock art and pretend: they were Bushmen and all the world was their own possession and the hunting was free and the paintings on the rock walls had come alive and the brown herds of antelope with the tiny hunters after them were rushing out through the mouth of the cave, hurtling over the lip of the precipice, swarming down into the valley below.

'Bang, bang!' went Mailbag and CrossAbel with their imaginary guns down in the marshes. But he and Oneday moved silently, stealthily, an invisible yellow people with sharp poison-tipped darts that whistled like the wind and struck suddenly like the sting of a bee.

This was where Shala was sitting while his flock grazed two hundred yards below. Most of the goats were lying in the shade, their yellow eyes fixed on one another or on nothing, while a few of the kids listlessly tried a gambol or two in the heat. Suddenly, Shala noticed, Abel's Land Rover shot out from behind the poplar grove, charged along the orchard fence at terrific speed, veered rapidly round the sheds, whipped past the stock-pens and came to a stop in a flurry of dust in front of the homestead. Shala narrowed his eyes and saw Abel run into the house. When a procession of folk erupted out of the back door soon afterwards, all heading for the poplar grove, Shala realized that something was wrong. Measuring the angle of the sun with his eyes, he was worried that something might have happened to Ma Katie who had set out for the Halt so early that morning, or to Oneday's children who would be playing down in the marshes since Amy O'Leary had closed the school for the day. Shala whistled to the goats, threw a few bits of ironstone at the stragglers of the flock and started urging them laboriously down the slope. They were reluctant to start the descent while the sun was still so high – they were not used to going back down into the valley before the long-legged shadows of late afternoon.

As he reached level ground, John and Paul Riet, two of Oneday's children, came running up the footpath towards him.

'Wipe the snot off your face,' he said, before they had even stopped in front of him, their chests heaving. 'Blow your noses.' So first, thumb to nostril, they obediently cleared their noses into the low bushes beside the path.

'Uncle Shala, please come and help,' panted John. 'Noah du Pisani has fallen down the borehole in the grove. He looked down it and he fell in. Please come and help, Uncle Shala.'

'Take the goats home. See that you shut the gate properly.' He dashed off to the Stiefveld cottage to fetch the rawhide thong which his father, Andries Riet, had stolen from Abel's storeroom to lower Granma Kitty into the grave with. As he bent down to pull the hessian bag with the rolled up thong in it from under the bed, Ma Katie walked in.

'Why has the fire gone out, Shala?' she asked. 'The ashes are quite cold.'

'Ma Katie, Trickle du Pisani has fallen down the borehole in the wood.'

He hurried out the door, leaving her standing there with her hand still over her mouth. By the time he reached the spot where

Ma Katie had seen Trickle earlier that day, he could hear the shouting among the trees.

He heard the voice of Abel himself and as he ran he remembered the occasion when one of his goats had wandered off and ended up among Abel's merinos on the sweetveld. In Abel Moolman's own farmyard he, Shala, had told Abel to his face: 'I was not raised with snot on my top lip.' This happened after Abel had sent a message to the Skaamfamilie that Katie Danster was to send a representative down to the farmstead for a tongue-lashing.

It was Shala himself who went down. Not hat in hand, like his uncles and aunts and other descendants of FounderAbel's renegade soldier and the tame Bushman whom he was supposed to have made to run all the way from the Great Fish River leashed to his stirrup. No, Shala was a Riet, descended in direct line from the Englishman James Read, the man who had come to bring the holy gospel to this savage land.

'Those ewes have been put in with the ram,' Abel told Shala. 'And now that goat of yours has buggered up the whole business. Now the ewes are refusing to take the ram. That means sixty lambs less this season! Or else I've got to send for the vet and have them artificially inseminated. D'you know what that'll cost?'

'It was an accident,' said Shala. 'The children made a hole in the fence to set a snare for springhares and the goat slipped through.'

They were standing on the Toorberg farmyard, and Abel's boer mastiffs were sniffing tentatively at Shala's heels.

'Right, but just let one more of your goats ever get in among my stud animals and I'll set these dogs on you.' Abel turned on his heel and strode off, angrily slapping his gaiters with his riding crop.

That was when Shala said: 'I was not raised with snot on my top lip.'

The story did the rounds down on the plains. And at the Mission's annual church fete, when Oneday in his smart white clerical collar was preaching the sermon in the lucerne shed at

Voetpad, someone from Altydsomer told Shala people were saying that he had bitten Abel Moolman's head off with the words: 'Don't think because you grew up with snot on your top lip that I have snot on mine!'

Before he could deny the tale, Oneday had started a hymn and the congregation were all singing. It was Pentecost, so a crowd of young girls were there, from Altydsomer, Voetpad and Doornbosch – some he had never seen before. So the story of the wrangle between himself and Abel Moolman went round and round the plains; and each time the circles crossed his path, his triumph and Abel's humiliation were greater than before. He had not set foot on Toorberg's white farmyard since.

As Shala ran through the cool poplar trees, his footfalls smothered by fallen leaves, Abel's voice, high-pitched and furious, was constantly audible. Shala crossed the double-track road specially cleared to allow the drilling machine to be towed to the spot in the grove where, Katie Danster swore, there had been a spring where she had played as a little girl. Abel believed her and ordered a shaft to be sunk there, promising her a slaughter ox for her family if they struck water. But it had yielded nothing, not even at two hundred feet. The drilling team battled on in the dampness among the tall poplars in vain. Day and night the machine stood there guzzling diesel fuel, in vain.

Shala headed in the direction of the shouting and suddenly burst out onto the trampled grass of the clearing.

Everyone had their backs to him. The four anchor-struts that kept the drilling machine upright were still in place. Three empty diesel barrels lay to one side. Deep scars in the soil showed where the machine had stood shuddering and shaking.

Standing closer he heard Trickle du Pisani's voice coming from deep down in the belly of the earth. Trickle was not hysterical, simply crying out to the people above ground. Once in his childhood Shala heard the plaintive wail of a jackal trapped in a burrow that had fallen in: Trickle's cry was like that.

'How deep down is he?' Shala asked someone.

'Forty feet. They've measured.'

'Stand back, you bastards!' thundered Abel's voice. 'Stop

kicking up dust. Stand back there,' he yelled to left and right. 'Go on, go home. Get back to the kitchen!'

'What are you all waiting for?' asked Shala.

'They've sent to Postmaster Moolman for the tow-ropes the buses use.'

'I have a thong here.'

'It's too short.' Shala looked up in surprise, into the face of CrossAbel. It was all of seven years since they had last been as close to each other. 'And anyway,' said CrossAbel, 'it's probably one of ours.'

Shala looked at him in amazement: the strong open face, the blue eyes under the brim of the khaki hat, the crimson birthmark across the ear. His hand went up automatically to his own left ear with the identical mark that had been there since birth – the mark which had led him and CrossAbel, down in the Vlei when they were boys, to swear always to be blood-brothers, since the gods had marked them so.

'Whose thong is this?' asked CrossAbel, and prodded him in the ribs.

Just at that moment the tractor burst through the trees and Abel gestured to the driver to park with the winch facing the borehole. 'Not too close, now,' he warned. 'We don't want the hole caving in.'

'You ask me that now?' said Shala in CrossAbel's face. 'At a time like this, you ask me that?' He flung the thong at Cross-Abel's feet, turned on his heel and strode back through the trees. Trickle's voice was still ringing in his ears as he emerged from the cool grove. With the hot sun on his shoulders he went back up to his goats.

Halfway home, he met Katie Danster coming along at a painful trot, her hand still over her mouth. Seeing him, she asked: 'Has that holy child gone into the earth now, Shala?'

'The child is stuck,' he said curtly.

'Aren't you going to help?'

He turned round. 'They can wipe their own snot off their own lips. I am taking my goats up the mountain.'

He threw open the gate of the enclosure and forced the

61

goats all the way up the mountain. At the top he crawled into the cool mouth of the cave and lay there, in the earth, thinking about the shaft yawning under Trickle's feet deep down to the bedrock far below.

Arguing about a thong, he thought, at a time like this. Talking about a thong, at a time like this. The words milled round and round in his head. He could not get rid of them. He looked at the dancing drawings round him, stretched out his hands to them, but felt only rock under his fingertips. They would not dance out of the dull pigment to him. They were fixed, motionless.

The games of their childhood were past. TameBushman, whose skull he and Oneday had unearthed in the cave one afternoon, was long dead. People said that when FounderAbel saw that TameBushman was near death, he sent him up to the cave to die in the company of the paintings of his fathers. They said the Bushman dug himself a hole deep in the cave, and when they later found his corpse he had half covered himself with earth. Some said he scooped the cool earth over his limbs to draw the fever out of his body.

One afternoon Shala and Oneday were digging about for the truth of these stories and suddenly, terrifyingly, there in Oneday's hand was the tiny skull, whitely preserved from the elements outside the cave.

'God help us,' Oneday shuddered and they raced back down the mountain as though the devil himself was after them. When they could not sleep that night, and both lay trembling under their karosses, shaken with shivering fits, Ma Katie built the fire up high and called them to her.

'You've been up to some great mischief,' she said. 'Out with it.'

When they had confessed all, she picked up a lantern and straightaway they had to go up the mountain with her in the dark, stumbling over loose stones and low bushes, back to the cave. 'TameBushman must rest,' she said. 'He's your ancestor. We must put him away carefully, so that he can rest. He ran great distances at FounderAbel's stirrup. Half-way across the world he ran. He needs his sleep.' So, reassuring and comforting them all the way, she got them right to the mouth of the cave, but further than that they could not go. So, leaving them shivering, crouched on their haunches outside, she went into the cave with the lantern. They heard her busily at work inside. When she came out again, her cheeks were wet with tears in the lantern light.

It was not before his teenage years, when Oneday was away at school in town, that Shala visited the cave at all regularly again. Then, with his goats grazing nearby, he would often lie up here, looking out over the vast expanse of the farm, none of it his.

Quibbling about a thong, at a time like this. In his mind's eye he recalled the boyish face of CrossAbel as in astonishment he touched first his own ear and then Shala's.

'We are blood-brothers,' CrossAbel had said then. 'Blood-brothers.'

When the goats began to stir restlessly, Shala emerged from the mouth of the cave. The afternoon was over, the sun was sinking fast. Only once he had secured the gate of the goat pen across the entrance behind the last of the flock did he hear the thin, high-pitched wailing of Trickle du Pisani's voice again. It seemed to be coming from the very earth beneath his feet.

Chapter 11

Death had not brought Andries Riet the gracefulness which the nuns had promised. When he delivered goat's milk to the convent, they would stand in the cool-room behind the wire gauze and tell him about the Eternal Life awaiting the Lord's elect. Perhaps the hatred in his heart had always been too bitter, he thought now, looking down on the footprints left by Katie as she trotted slowly along the footpath to the borehole among the poplars. Perhaps that was why the release which death had brought him was still unsatisfactory. The long trip years ago to the Union Buildings in Pretoria to buy himself a new name from the General, and the fact that he had taken all his and Katie's goat-money from under the mattress without telling her, had dealt a terrible blow to his system and darkened his heart. For when he returned, Katie held out her empty hands to him and asked: 'What have you brought back, An'ries?'

Though dying, GranmaKitty was still alive, behind the curtained partition, so he spoke softly. He had caught the odour of camphor, the unmistakable smell of death in the Stiefveld, as soon as he reached the wire gate across the goatpath.

'I went to buy us a new name, Katie,' he whispered. 'I'm not Moolman any more. I was christened a Moolman, but now I'm a Riet. I've got a brown name now, my own name.'

She looked at him for a long time. 'And the pound notes under the mattress, An'ries?'

'I had to take them for the journey, Katie. I had to walk all the way to the city with the purple trees.'

Her eyes narrowed. 'You mean you weren't with Ellie Plooi of Middelvlei across the mountains?'

'No, my Katie-love, I was longing too much for you.' He reached out for her, but she kept her distance.

'So what does the General look like, An'ries? Did you really see him?'

'No, Katie,' he said, dropping his head. 'They said he was

too busy, but they took my papers to him and he quickly said it was all right. He understood about the Moolmans. My family's really the Riets, I told them. That's the family I want to belong to.'

'An'ries, people are saying you spent a whole week with Ellie Plooi.'

'That's just stupid gossip, Katie,' he pleaded. 'They are pouring poison into your ears. Don't take any notice of them.' He looked round. 'Are the children well?'

'Yes, but after three months they won't know their father. Shala's standing up against the hearth already and eating like an ostrich chick. Oneday is still very dreamy. GranmaKitty says he's got second sight.'

'And GranmaKitty, how's she?'

'She's very near the time, An'ries. We'd better get some coffin planks.'

'I'll go tomorrow.'

'Yesterday she was complaining that she hadn't heard anyone nailing her coffin together yet. She's worried about her resting-place, An'ries. She wants a coffin.'

'I'll go down to the farmstead tomorrow and ask.'

He'd had to go begging, Andries Riet remembered as he entered the shade of the grove. OldAbel had unlocked the storeroom and watched as he selected seven long boards.

He'd dug GranmaKitty's grave himself, too, while little Shala and Oneday were playing with their knuckle-bone oxen under a thorn tree.

Before GranmaKitty was buried, beside the ruins of FounderAbel's first house, the nuns secretly came out to the farm and sprinkled holy water all over the OuMurasie – including the grave of the old Hottentot soldier Jan Swaat. It was a very long funeral, Andries remembered. It lasted right into the next Sunday, and turned into a celebration of his new name.

'Riet is the name under which I shall die, and my children after me,' he said, 'and neither I nor my children will ever again sit under a window-sill and howl like dogs when one of the Abels dies. Jan Swaat was the last Hottentot: we are free-born. My children will get an education and, as God is my witness: I shall lie in this ground at the OuMurasie for my ancestors and I have earned the right to it.'

People said that he was too bitter, and that his mixed blood had muddled his brains, but Andries knew that the thoughts of his ancestor the missionary were stirring within him, even though he had neither the education nor the words to express them. It would be through his children that he spoke, he decided, and he made sure that they picked up every old newspaper and book cast out of Toorberg's back door. His children would grow up with words, with books and ideas – not with snares and clubs and rawhide thongs as he had.

He had never been ashamed to talk about his father Floris Moolman, thought Andries, quietly moving closer to the clearing among the trees, even though FounderAbel had forbidden all mention of the name on Toorberg, and so had OldAbel, and after him also Abel the Third. Andries had never seen his father, since they had horsewhipped him right off the farm long before anyone realized that Ma Kitty was pregnant. Often, when overcome by the loneliness of the Stiefveld and when the honey-beer that she brewed in the sun had gone straight to her head, Ma Kitty would tell how, as a young girl, they had pinned her down in the outside kitchen on Toorberg, while her father Jan Swaat and the mercenary Malay tried to force a concoction of herbs down her throat to make her miscarry. But the embryonic Andries Riet had clung tenaciously and even though the weals raised by the cane strokes on Kitty's body were clearly visible, so all on the farm could see the bastardy of her pregnancy, he had been born strong and healthy.

'You're a stolen child, Andries Moolman,' Ma Kitty often said, when the honey-beer had taken hold of her again and she wanted to talk about her love for the young Floris Moolman of the white tribe. 'I stole you in that very same Vlei, from a son of Abel's, when everyone thought I was gathering firewood and he was shooting geese. There and then, Andries, your runaway father took me among the reeds. Every marvellous Sunday afternoon, when everyone else on the farm was asleep, he lay down with me among the reeds.' He remembered so well how Granma-Kitty had taken another swallow from the tin mug and leant over to him, saying: 'And then, like a gunshot, FounderAbel's voice. It was too late, Andries, you were already in my belly, growing and growing.'

'But, Ma Kitty,' he had begged as a child, 'is Pa Floris never coming home again?'

'Andries Moolman, you are a stolen child,' she scolded. 'You are cast off like a skin. Marry a backveld girl and forget about your white father. Forget that you're a bastard, but remember to bear yourself with pride. Look – ' she fetched the little hand-mirror from her room and held it up to him, 'look, your eyes are as blue as the sky: that means you must always look up into the blue. Don't ever walk with your eyes on the ground, like a Bushman tracker. Look up, my Andries. That's why God gave you eyes as blue as the sky.'

And again: 'Jan Swaat, your grandpa, was the last of our family with his eyes cast down. From now on, we Stiefvelders must always look up.' But that was only when Ma Kitty was drunk. When she was sober she slaved for him and for blind Jan Swaat, who in his later years could do no more than sit outside in the sun, oblivious to flies crawling all over his half-closed eyes.

'He's running wild again, in his dreams,' Ma Kitty would say. 'Look at him. He's young and free again, him and Founder-Abel together. You can imagine the thoughts churning round in his head. Look at his mouth watering!' Day after day Jan Swaat sat drooling in the sun until eventually, soon after the death of FounderAbel, he refused to eat and then he too died.

That, Andries realized years later, was the Skaamfamilie's greatest humiliation of all: that once the man who'd kept him like a slave was dead, the bondsman Jan Swaat had lost his own will to live.

But till the day she died, Ma Kitty cherished her dreams of young Floris Moolman, the only love of her life. Andries had to wait until she was on her very last legs before he could set out on the long road to buy himself another name. She never knew, though. She died still dreaming that she had left behind a clan of

67

Moolmans who would, together with the white Moolmans, the sons of Abel, enter eternity with the descendants of Floris.

As the thongs lowering Ma Kitty's massive body into the grave creaked and the backveld choir sang 'Praise ye the Lord', Andries looked up at the peak of the Toorberg and buried, with his mother's body, everything that lay behind him: buried the galling childhood bitterness of the Malay's herbs and the taste of his gorge rising whenever Ma Kitty told the story of how they tried to force her to miscarry in the outside kitchen; buried the crumpled face of his father Floris on the photograph which Katie had now inherited from Ma Kitty; buried the name which reminded him every day of what he was not. He looked at the strong, young body of Katie Danster and at the two sturdy little boys clinging to her skirts, and he vowed – since he was always one for taking oaths – that Toorberg would yet know the pride of the sons of Riet. For his ancestor Jan Swaat had tamed this soil just as much as had his ancestor FounderAbel, the sweat of the one was no saltier than of the other, and at evening the bodies of both were equally sore.

Katie could never get Jan Swaat to tell who her mother had been. The old folk said Jan Swaat had once disappeared into the hinterland and stayed away half a year, before returning with the baby Kitty, whom he said was his child. FounderAbel clapped him in irons for a week and thrashed him every day with a horsewhip. When he was tame once more, FounderAbel set him free again. He went to live on the Stiefveld with the baby and reared her on goat's milk.

TameBushman died that same year. One day he felt unwell, and, filled with nausea, wandered aimlessly around the yard, crouched in the shade, and eventually struggled up the mountain into the cave. There he half-buried himself in the cool earth to try and draw the fever from his limbs. But there he died, quite alone, among the paintings his people had made on the rock. All they needed to do was cover up the rest of him with soil.

Many people believed that Kitty's mother had been one of TameBushman's relatives, since someone had spotted Jan Swaat among a band of Bushmen passing like frightened antelope along the Toorberg horizon. Those were the days when the farmers were systematically wiping out the Bushmen, and there was one tiny girl whom Jan Swaat was said to be very fond of. Shortly after that he disappeared into the hinterland.

'TameBushman was an ancestor of mine,' GranmaKitty used to say, 'so you must respect that cave. Let him rest in peace now; he had little enough peace when he was alive. He always had to smell out underground water for FounderAbel, and whenever his nose betrayed him, he was thrashed.'

Andries had now reached the cool shadows where the drilling machine had stood. He'd often come here, to where the huge machine was hammering and thumping as the rods turned and the engine shuddered against its anchor stays.

The drill bit had hiccupped deep down in the earth and the poplar twigs had trembled lightly, often showering down leaves. Now only the anchor-struts remained, beside deep marks in the earth left when the machine was towed away. And in the centre, black and unexpected, the mouth of the borehole.

Down in the hole the child was struggling. As he went up to Katie, Andries noticed her distress, for she had pulled her scarf low down over her eyes. She was getting old. He looked at the age wrinkles in her neck and wanted to reach out and touch her back.

But just as he was about to touch her, he remembered that he was dead, while she was still among the living.

Chapter 12

They unloaded the canvas packages, watched by the large crowd that had gathered. Mailbag himself cranked the telephone handle and rang three shorts – Toorberg's number – as soon as he saw the ungainly red body of the bus lumbering up past the aloes. The bus looked as though it was towing a great ball of dust along behind it: a long, red-headed worm slowly crawling over the plain. Just as the red nose turned in at the Halt, Abel and Ella Moolman arrived in their Land Rover; and Abel had hardly got out, with a curt nod to Postmaster, and whistled his mastiffs off the back of the Land Rover before CrossAbel came over the ridge on his motorcycle, growling through the low scrub and loose stones, and stopped, one foot on the ground to steady himself.

'They said it came from far up-country, Your Worship,' said Mailbag to the magistrate now leaning his elbow on the counter at the Halt. Mailbag's first instinct had been to jump up and invite the magistrate over to the house, but the man with the stumpy arm had indicated that he preferred to stay where he was and talk. 'It was Transport Services's biggest bus, too – we had to book it three months in advance. Well, it stopped and then the mechanic got out, and then – I remember it so well – a whole bunch of roosters in one of those bamboo cages tumbled out after him, and also a tray of seedlings for Aunt Ella Moolman, and the mechanic's tin trunk as well!'

'A technician?' asked the magistrate.

'That's right, Your Worship.' Mailbag gave a loud sniff. 'From the drilling machine company.'

When CrossAbel pulled his motorcycle on to its stand, Amy also came out to see. She'd stayed inside the Halt, because Ella had remained seated in the Land Rover and Amy had no intention of greeting her there. Katie Danster and LittleKitty, resting in the shade of the Halt on their way back to the Stiefveld from the shop at Voetpad, also came closer. Some of the other farmers must also have heard about the delivery somehow, for by the time the last of the bulky canvas packages had been carefully off-loaded, there was a long line of bakkies from surrounding farms parked at the Halt. The canvas packages were of various shapes and sizes, so some of the more curious farmers and their labourers actually dared to touch and feel them, despite Abel's glares.

'The Moolman's tractor – the John Deere with the funny little front wheels so close together, Your Worship – brought a trailer to cart the stuff away. Uncle Abel was like a broody hen, all round the workers while they loaded it; the trailer even had a layer of straw on it to protect all the bits of machinery. Then they all went back to Toorberg, the whole procession. It looked almost like a funeral, with the John Deere leading it.'

'And then?'

'That's all, Your Worship. I wasn't there when they put the thing together. But they say it was quite a business. They only finished late that night, and then CrossAbel went charging round the farmyard on his motorbike shooting off his dad's pistol into the air.'

The magistrate stroked his stump.

'Is it true that the mechanic was Dowser du Pisani's brother?'

Mailbag nodded: 'That's what people say, Your Worship.'

'I see,' said the magistrate. 'Do you smoke, Mr Moolman?' he asked, taking out a packet of cigars.

'Now and again, Your Worship, when I can afford it.'

'Have one.'

Mailbag noticed how deftly the magistrate lit his cigar. As they smoked together, the magistrate let his eyes run over the interior of the Halt. There was a large round clock on the wall, alongside a red fire-extinguisher. Open on the table beside Mailbag lay the bus timetables; also a small black trunk, open, with – the magistrate noticed – some sandwiches and a flask of coffee in it. Against the back wall there was a bicycle with fat tyres. The floor linoleum had been polished, but in places it was worn through to the concrete below. Flypaper spattered with dead black flies hung from all over the ceiling.

71

'Are you happy in your work?' asked the magistrate.

'Oh, yes, Your Worship.' Mailbag flicked off the ash into his lunchbox, over the sandwiches. He sniffed. 'But I'd much rather go farming, you know. I did start farming, along the railway line down here.' He sniffed again. 'You see, there's so many trains running. Every so often there's another one. I lost all my cattle.' He looked up at the magistrate as though expecting a reprimand. 'I didn't have the money to put up a fence between my stretch of veld and the railway tracks. You know, Your Worship, fencing wire costs as much as a car nowadays.'

'I understand it is expensive.'

They heard the drone of an approaching bus. Mailbag looked at the timetable, then at his watch. 'That's the two-thirty,' he said, making a mark in the notebook in front of him before getting up. 'I must just bring in the postbag.' He brushed past the magistrate and went out to wait for the bus in the cool shade of the veranda. As the bus swung in at the driveway, he went out into the sun. The magistrate saw Mailbag's shirt-tail hanging out, smiled and followed him outside. Mailbag jumped onto the front wheel of the bus and hauled himself up to cling like a weaver-bird at the driver's window for a chat, though the magistrate could not overhear the conversation. Mailbag then walked round to the other side of the bus and came back with a canvas postbag over his shoulder. The driver waved and the bus rumbled through the gate again.

Mailbag smiled as he walked back. 'It's only a light postbag today,' he said. 'But Your Worship should see how I have to sweat to get everything sorted at the end of the month when the pension envelopes come!' They went inside.

'I understand your father's health is not too good,' said the magistrate.

'No, Your Worship, he's a bit off-colour today. He's got high blood-pressure. But his real trouble is the inheritance he's never going to get. You should know, Your Worship, with respect, he was cheated out of his inheritance because he married my mother. Just because she's a Catholic.'

The magistrate nodded. 'I believe so,' he said. After

watching Mailbag emptying the envelopes out on to the counter and then sorting them for a while, he added: 'But that will give you the opportunity to take control of the Halt, will it not?'

Mailbag laughed proudly.

'Definitely, Your Worship,' he said. 'That's for sure.'

'Tell me,' said the magistrate, taking out the packet of cigars again, 'this incident surrounding Noah du Pisani. Were you present throughout?'

Mailbag's hands were motionless on the envelopes. 'Not when he fell in, Your Worship, but we took the tow-ropes up from here in my dad's Borgward. We weren't among the first to get there but we stayed to the end.'

'Until the very end?'

'Even till after the funeral, Your Worship. My mother was so heartbroken, we couldn't get her away from the graveside. They laid the gravestone across the borehole, you know, Your Worship, because he was so far down.'

'Were you present at his death?'

'Nobody knows when he died, Your Worship.'

'Who decided that the grave should simply be there?'

'I suppose Abel Moolman, Your Worship? Who else decides anything on Toorberg? And after all, Your Worship, why would he get little Trickle dug out, go to all the trouble and everything, when the child couldn't lie in the Moolmans' graveyard anyway? He's a drifter, you see, a Du Pisani. Your Worship must know Abel Moolman always said the Du Pisanis are people who once lost something and then forgot to stop looking for it. That's what Abel thinks of Du Pisanis.'

'And no *post mortem* examination was ever conducted?'

'With respect, Your Worship, but what doctor would go crawling down the hole?'

The magistrate smiled. 'Another cigar?' he asked.

'Thank you.' Mailbag bent over to the lighter. 'They're nice and bitter on the tongue,' he said. 'My mother won't be pleased if she sees me now. I think Catholics are against smoking.'

'Really?'

For a while they stood smoking. 'But when, in your opinion, did Noah Moolman die? Was he dead before the shot?'

'By that morning there wasn't much breath left in the child any more, Your Worship. I lay with my ear to the borehole and I could only just hear his chest. It sounded a bit like asthma. People say it was the dampness down there in the dark that made his chest so tight, Your Worship. And with all the digging some dust got into the hole, too, even though Abel Moolman did try to stop it.'

'You are of the opinion, therefore, that he was already dead when Abel Moolman stepped up to the borehole?'

Mailbag looked at the magistrate; he wiped his nose with the back of his hand. 'I can't say, Your Worship. How will anyone ever know?'

'And how did Abel Moolman react to the whole incident?'

'You must surely have heard, Your Worship? Not quietly. They say he went round to all the old boreholes and lay down flat on his stomach to see if he could see the water levels. They say he saw the faces of all his dead children down there, the four stillborn babies between CrossAbel and CrazyTilly, floating in the water. Others say he was searching for Trickle du Pisani because he felt guilty. You know, when the gravestone was made, they say he almost decided to show Trickle's surname as Moolman! But that time of grace was very short, Your Worship. He's as hard as ironstone, that man – at Trickle's funeral, he wouldn't let the Skaamfamilie through the church door. But the whole business affected him very badly just the same. It was in that month that he started climbing up windmills, right to the top, so that he could sit there beside the vanes and think. And he didn't only climb up his own windmills, Your Worship – he drove his Land Rover anywhere he liked. He cut his way through fences with his wire-cutters and climbed all the farmers' windmills so he could look down from the heights at the sins of the world.'

'Is that the truth?' asked the magistrate, looking out of the window.

'That's what people say, Your Worship. And I saw him

myself from the bus on the way to town one morning. First I saw a Land Rover in the veld beside the road, down there at Voetpad, past the shop, just this side of the hollow. And then – I swear, Your Worship – I saw Uncle Moolman, sitting up on a windmill like a crow, staring into the distance.'

'Didn't the farmers object to this trespassing on their property?'

Mailbag shook his head. 'No, Your Worship, the Jouberts and the Jordaans and the Van der Merwes and the Kinghorns all just said: let him climb. He needs to climb away from the afflictions of his ancestors. That's what they said. Look, Your Worship, the whole district knew what a mess Abel had created with his offspring. The night CrazyTilly was born he spent with the stock speculator's widow. The cord got knotted round the child's head and for a while, people believed, she couldn't breathe, so that's why she's so wrong in the head. Ella Moolman had no one to help her: she couldn't even get to the 'phone. These are the kinds of stories they tell about Abel Moolman, Your Worship.'

The magistrate nodded: 'You are bitter about Abel Moolman.'

'No, it's just that I know him,' said Mailbag. 'As a child I played at his feet. I saw him from below, from the toes of his boots right up to his hat. I know him all right! I was not good enough for CrossAbel, he said. He chased me out of the Vlei, because I was Amy O'Leary's worthless child. I won't forget that, Your Worship.'

The magistrate nodded again: 'I understand that you find it difficult to forgive,' he said.

They stood there a while longer. 'I must go,' said the magistrate. 'My clerk has been waiting in the car for long enough.'

They shook hands and he went out. When he leant through the car window to nudge the clerk's shoulder, Mailbag was standing in the meagre shade of the Halt. As they drove away, Mailbag recalled the day the John Deere carted the bulky canvas packages up to Toorberg. Late that night they heard the growl of CrossAbel's motorbike and the pistol shots. Sitting in front of

75

an open window in their cottage, he and his father and mother had lifted their heads. Postmaster hurriedly got up and went outside, with Mailbag following. Outside in the cool night air, they listened to the motorbike engine and the echo of the pistol shots reflecting off the cliff-faces of the Toorberg at them.

Before breakfast the next morning Postmaster called to him from the wind-charger. Mailbag rushed out past his mother, who was slicing bread. His father handed him the binoculars. As he peered through the lenses and focused, suddenly the fuzzy red patch was a clearly-etched definition: a blood-red machine, gleaming in the first rays of the morning sun.

Chapter 13

Everyone is guilty, thought the magistrate in his hotel room.

That is why it was so difficult to apportion the blame. Besides, it was summer and in the sluggish heat confidences were not as readily forthcoming. The town, like all other small towns of its kind, had a great deal of reserve. In his time as a public prosecutor, in all the many transfers that accompany appointments in the Department of Justice, he had got to know such towns well. The very situation of the place deprived its inhabitants: it lay crouched up against a low stony ridge, topped with flat outcrops of rock as rough as tortoiseshell in all the emptiness of the wide plain – just too far from the fertile Sneeuberge of which Toorberg was the highest peak, and beside a watercourse which was normally no more than a trickle, but which could flash flood violently in the rainy season: a wall of water carrying everything before it, only to subside and dry up again just as suddenly, as though there had never been a cloudburst at all.

The magistrate's years on the bench had taught him that this was a country that made people feel guilty, a country which made one feel there had to be a reason why it so seldom knew the blessing of rain.

He had studied the District Commandant of Police's report on the Toorberg incident very carefully indeed, in the course of the long train journey. According to the station commander's accompanying letter, the last good rains had also burst through the roof of the police station and caught everyone by surprise. The report had suffered some water damage and evidently no one had thought to re-type it neatly before it was submitted to Justice for perusal by the investigating magistrate. The magistrate preferred it that way, actually: it was authentic. So too were the few yellowing newspaper cuttings which the editor of the town's newspaper had submitted, at the magistrate's request.

Then there were the sworn affidavits, couched in a country

77

lawyer's pompous phrases; and the report of the local magistrate, written after careful consideration of the police report.

And there were the unbroken plains endlessly passing by the train window as he sat and pondered.

Once, as clear as the taste of a·first sip of whisky on the tongue, a woman on a white horse had appeared beside the railway track. This was near the station where he was due to get off, and he had leant out, his eyes screwed up against the soot from the engine, to watch her glide away and become just a speck on the plain. Soon she was swallowed up by the illusion of water on the horizon.

He lit one of his cigars.

These were his last truly private moments, for when he stepped onto the platform, inquisitive eyes were already there to watch him. Not because of his arm, though. He knew the way people looked when they were looking at his stump. No, the look with which they assessed him on arrival was different.

Now he regularly drew the curtains of his hotel room aside every morning before starting his exercises. From the street the townsfolk could see him comically bobbing up and down in front of the open window. He deliberately avoided reading the morning paper, in order to keep his brain clear and uncontaminated for the day's investigations. He ate breakfast down in the dining-room, smoking one cigar after the braised kidneys and eggs. He was exceptionally polite to the waiters and the receptionist, but never said more than 'Good morning' or 'Good evening' or 'Is there any mail for me today?' A man of few words, who took his first two whiskies in the shade of the stoep each evening, and his third and fourth up in his room. Always with soda and two ice-cubes. Sometimes he sent a little silver whisky flask down to the bar, asking the steward to see that it was filled and left on his breakfast table. He would take it with him on his inspections – usually, the barman noted, on days when the weather was threatening and his arm was probably troubling him.

On some evenings – though this was very rare – he would go into the bar and sit down alone in a corner, without attempting to engage anyone in conversation. No one ever came over and sat with him, either – simply because it didn't look as though he would welcome such intrusion. On those evenings there was a subdued atmosphere in the bar. The dart players bit their lips and played more grimly, wanting to impress the clever man in the corner, the man who had come to rake open the sins of the richest family in the district. The barman paraded his best jokes along with his shiniest glasses. The old soaks preferred to sink into sleep out on the veranda. Late in the evening he would get up, nod to the barman and slowly climb the stairs to his room, leaving the table littered with cigar-butts.

He never set foot in the church – something which the town noticed immediately. But on Sundays he regularly went for a stroll in the park beside the graveyard, and then usually passed along the graves reading the inscriptions. He would raise his hat amiably to the few folk visiting the graves. It was obvious to everyone that he was a lonely man. But they were also in no doubt that he was an astute observer of all around him.

Only once did the drunken blockman from the butchery announce loudly in the bar that the Department of Justice had forgotten all about the magistrate it had sent – he was probably going to be left to wander around there for ever. The magistrate made no reply, finished his whisky, got up and walked out.

He generally spent Monday mornings in the public library, reading. He never entered into conversation with the librarian, but sat for hours in the reading room going through the previous week's newspapers and magazines. Occasionally he would move quietly between the shelves, take a book out here and there, leaf through and then replace it.

Everything about him was so ordinary that the townsfolk simply could not stop speculating about just what it was that was unfathomable in him. How had he lost his arm? What part of the country was he from? Where was he educated? What was the purpose of his investigation of Toorberg? Who, in his opinion, had committed the crime? And what was the crime?

Chapter 14

Sitting astride his motorcycle, CrossAbel buckled the crash-helmet under his chin and covered his eyes with the dust-goggles which his father Abel used with the thresher. One kick from his right foot and the engine under him began to sputter. He had stripped the machine of its silencer, mudguards and headlamp since he only ever used it at midday to go racing round the track he had made in the veld. Years back, even before his military service, he'd had the course laid out between two rows of limewashed stones on the level stretch behind the dam in the vlei. Nobody could see him there – except that he sometimes caught sight of Katie Danster's grandchildren lying flat on the ground, peeping at him through the bulrushes on the dam wall. At other times Trickle du Pisani had left off playing in the mud at the dam's sluice and taken to his heels like a startled rabbit as soon as CrossAbel kicked the machine's starter.

But generally it was just himself and the machine, the hot sun, the sweat in his armpits and eyes as he rode time and again into his own dust, obliterating his own tracks, faster and faster every time, more and more skilfully and ever more nimbly. He knew of only one feeling to beat this racing, and that was what he felt standing bolt upright on a Casspir charging through the black township with the wind in his hair and the plastic visor in front of his eyes grotesquely distorting the black faces in the open doors of shanty-houses, almost like goldfish in a bowl.

In places his racecourse was rockhard by now, worn smooth as polished slate. But only a quarter of a second farther there would be a good pile of powdery sand, and round the next curve, unexpected by anyone unfamiliar with the course, a patch of sticky clay in the upper reaches of the streams feeding the dam, where the route swung through the rushes across the clay crust.

Every day, implacably, recklessly, CrossAbel raced through half a tank of fuel. He countered Ella's objections: 'It's my hobby, Ma. It costs nothing, nobody hears me, it's just me – and it's a lot safer than cleaning up the townships with the other guys. Nobody throws petrol bombs out here.'

'But that's the whole point, CrossAbel,' she would say. 'It's so solitary. Why don't you do something with the other young men in town? Play rugby on Saturday afternoons. Or join the tennis club.'

But he had refused. It was his track and his bike. From early morning his thighs would yearn to grip the tank of his machine, and his hands would itch to clutch the handlebars, so that he could charge into the dust again and with each circuit pit his body and that of the machine against the soil of Toorberg.

'It's treacherous soil, that,' he liked to say. 'One moment you're still up, because the track's as hard as rock – the next the bike's sliding out from under you because you're a couple of inches into the dirt or you're run into loose gravel, and you fall your arse off. When you find the machine again, it's lying on its side, grinding its wheels into a bank of earth all by itself.'

He remembered hearing as a child that every day at noon his great-grandfather had taken a horse and charged up to one of the boundaries of Toorberg. In the old days those boundaries would have been a watercourse, or the ridge of a hill, or a row of thorn trees. Later they were stone cairns erected at hundred-metre intervals. Eventually, in Toorberg's Golden Age, Founder-Abel put up proper fences of wire which he imported from Australia.

It was said that FounderAbel rode his horse like a maniac. After an hour he would return, exhausted, and with a layer of saltpetre white on the horse's flanks.

CrossAbel often stood in front of his great-grandfather's portrait in the homestead, and as he looked into the black eyes, he felt as though he was seeing himself, and only the motorbike could dissipate the restlessness and frustration he saw there.

He needed his racing: his whole system yearned for the machine. Afterwards, he could relax, lie down in his room and smoke a cigarette. On the many, many quiet Sunday afternoons of his childhood he had gone wandering around Toorberg,

81

interminably: the motorbike had cured all that.

He'd be able to farm very successfully here, he often thought, if it weren't for that brand mark of sterility across his left ear. All his life he'd be able to remain here, if it weren't for his useless ping-pong balls. He often thought about these things when racing round his track, and they made him curse: under his breath at first, but gradually louder and louder – a string of obscenities, screaming and blaspheming, cursing Abel and Ella, cursing OldAbel and Granny Olivier, cursing FounderAbel and Grandmother Magtilt, cursing the stubborn soil, the obstinate earth, the sullen sun, the turmoil in his chest, the burning sweat in his eyes – a string of invective streaming out of him louder and louder as he raced round and round, lap after lap. If he could remain, if he could become master of Toorberg's eight thousand morgen, he'd lay out a whole lot of new circuits, each with a challenge of its own: one track in the black soil of the Bovlei, zigzagging between dense tussocks of grass, with deep skidpans in the mud where the bike would sink in to its footrests and roar in protest; and a track high up on the slopes of the Toorberg with klipspringers scattering in terror as he swung through the boulders and the roar of the engine echoed from the cliffs. He'd lay out another track between the white trunks of the poplars in the grove and that would be the most dangerous of all: slippery fallen leaves rotten under the wheels and the hairbreadths by which the treetrunks would have to be avoided would make that the most treacherous racetrack of all.

He'd have a further course all along the railway line, a straight one disappearing into the distance beside the rail-tracks, so that he could race the black locomotives; and another track all round the Skaamfamilie's cottage, with loops round Shala's goat-pen and the corrugated iron hutch where Oneday's children kept their white rabbits: that would be a track he would race round unexpectedly early in the morning, just to see them rushing out of doors with stunned and sleepy faces. And then the best one of all: a track right round the homestead, which he'd race round at night when all the veranda lights were on. He'd go so fast that Abel and Ella wouldn't be able to stop him. The roaring of the bike would fill every room in the house and his father's boer mastiffs, locked up for the night on the sun-porch, would break out into a frenzy of barking. That would be a track to ride while Abel shook his fist in fury at him, and Ella in her dressing-gown stood with folded arms on the front veranda, listening to the night and imagining that De la Rey or Soois or Judge Lucius was back on a visit.

Stiffly, his ride over, CrossAbel dismounted. He pulled the motorbike up on its stand and sat down to rest in its shade, his hands cradling the crash-helmet. The weariness in his arm muscles made him think again about his idea of selecting a young heifer from the calf-pen and walking twice round the milking shed every day carrying it on his shoulders. As the calf gained weight, he'd grow stronger and stronger. Perhaps he'd be the first Moolman ever to be able to carry a fully-grown ox or cow twice round the milking shed. He was much stronger already, because the dumb-bell which he welded together out of two old lucerne-mower wheels and an iron bar had developed his thighs and shoulders very well indeed. The weekend commando training sessions in the military camp outside the town had helped to make him fit, too. He was sure no one on Toorberg would be a match for him now, not even that savage Shala Riet who spent all his days up among the cliffs and was as sinewy as a goat.

At table one day Abel mentioned that, as a child, Judge Lucius once worked out that if he tamed a heifer calf and carried it round on his shoulders every day, he would still be able to carry it round when the animal was fully grown. This was not simply some theoretical arithmetic either: Judge Lucius was well on the way to proving his point when the calf suddenly disappeared. When it casually reappeared three days later, it was too heavy for CrossAbel's great-uncle to lift. After that, apparently, Judge Lucius had never lifted his hand to do anything physical again. He took to the world of ideas and became a judge who was alleged to have completely altered the law concerning Crimes of the Right Hand.

CrossAbel was sure that such a clever man's idea could yet work. Still holding the crash-helmet in his hands, he decided to catch a young calf in the pen the next day, lash front and back legs with a thong to prevent it from slipping off his shoulders, and then jog twice round the milking shed. He was still considering this idea when he heard a shout, the rumble of the Land Rover's engine, gears grating. Someone was ringing the farmyard bell. With the echoes of the cast-iron slave bell ringing in his ears, CrossAbel kicked his bike into life and raced back to the farmyard. Something had happened. The last time the slave bell had been rung in broad daylight was when General Smuts had lost his safe seat in parliament. The time before that was when OldAbel had suddenly put his pocket-knife and his strip of biltong down beside him, asked what the time was, sighed deeply and died. It happened at eleven o'clock in the morning, the very same day, time and date as his father, FounderAbel, had died. When the country was proclaimed a Republic, Abel wanted to ring the bell again, but at the first tug the thong, old and perished after years of disuse, snapped off short and fell in a heap at Abel's feet. Everyone regarded this as a very bad omen.

As CrossAbel charged through the farmyard gate, Ella ran out of the back door, followed by three kitchen servants with flapping aprons. Without stopping to talk to him, they gestured towards the grove of poplars. He raced on ahead, into the trees – the first time he had ever ridden in there. Abel had always forbidden him to ride in the grove because he was particularly fond of trees and besides, FounderAbel's own hands had planted this grove. So now CrossAbel opened the throttle wide, nearly knocking down three farm labourers running in the same direction as himself, on three separate bends in the footpath. All of a sudden he burst into the clearing where the drilling machine had stood. Making a quick sharp turn, he skilfully came to a stop between the three fuel drums and the borehole, where LittleKitty Riet was kneeling, calling down the hole: 'Noah? Noah du Pisani!'

'What are you shouting?' asked CrossAbel. When she looked up at him, and he saw the tears trickling down her dusty cheeks, he realized, and just stood there, opening and closing his hands. Then Abel rushed into the clearing and crouched down beside the hole.

'Fetch Postmaster Moolman's tow-ropes!' yelled Abel. 'We've got to get the child out before he falls any further.'

Looking round with her eyes wild, Ella then approached the hole. CrossAbel felt himself withdrawing to deep within himself, as he always did in times of crisis. Slowly he walked up to the hole, looked down into the darkness, saw nothing and didn't really care anyway. Only once, when Trickle's first scream came up out of the hole, did CrossAbel feel the cry move over his cheek like a warm hand. He was tempted to escape into another bout of roaring round his racetrack – but then the fear passed as he heard his father barking out one command after another. Within minutes Postmaster's cables would be on the way, likewise two tractors with winches, a powerful torch used for hunting springhares, rawhide thongs and pulleys, a can of water to sprinkle round the hole to prevent any dust from sifting down onto the child; also a doctor and the minister from town. Abel himself dropped the end of a measuring tape which he always carried about with him down the hole and established that Trickle was stuck at a depth of forty feet. By the light of the hunting-lamp they could see his little crown of hair and his squashed shoulders.

Abel sent Ella off to give CrazyTilly a double dose of dagga tea and lock her in the library. If she started snatching books out of the glass-fronted cabinets again, Abel ordered, they were to lock her in the feed shed. And a farm-worker was to sent on horseback to fetch Dowser du Pisani from down on the flats where he was exploring possible underground watercourses with his willow wand.

CrossAbel heard the tractor approaching through the trees and then saw Shala Riet with a long rolled-up thong in his hand. Going up to Shala, he again felt the shudder of the motorcycle between his thighs. He was on the Casspir once more and through the field-glasses he could see Oneday Riet walking through the crowd, hear them cheering as he entered the community hall in the township. Gradually he opened the throttle, felt himself overcoming the resistance of the earth, racing,

racing recklessly, overtaking everything in his path, wheels grinding into the earth. When Shala Riet threw down the coil of rawhide thong at his feet and strode away, CrossAbel picked it up and went over to his father with it.

'There's a good thong here, Dad.'

'Tie it to the anchor strut,' Abel ordered. As CrossAbel knotted the supple thong round one of the struts, he felt that it had recently been oiled and worked. They certainly know how to look after the goods they've stolen, he thought. The fact that he had seen the tracks of Shala's goats running under the boundary fence between the Stiefveld and the Vlei was not without significance. The Skaamfamilie thought he didn't know that Shala was driving the goats underneath the fence at night to graze in the Vlei.

The Vlei was the special pasturage which his father had set aside as a recuperation paddock for his stud rams after they had covered the ewes. There they grazed the sweet grasses and twice a day were fed their ram-pellets and chopped prickly-pear leaves mixed with molasses and yellow maize kernels. But he knew that when the rams were not in the Vlei, Shala would let his goats in through the wire to steal grazing. He would catch them at it yet, thought CrossAbel, and he'd put a bullet through the head of the whitebeard, right between its stupid little eyes.

A tractor was standing ready at the mouth of the hole; the dust in the vicinity had been damped down with a watering can; everyone was waiting for Postmaster Moolman to arrive with the tow-ropes. Abel, his legs wide apart, hair in disarray round his high forehead, eyes restless with frustration, was standing beside the hole. Ella, her hands held up to her cheeks, was seated on one of the fuel drums. Katie Danster, her eyes closed, was murmuring quietly as she squatted among the fallen leaves at the edge of the clearing. With an unlit pipe in his mouth, the tractor driver was leaning against one mudguard. CrossAbel squatted down on his haunches beside his motorbike. It was quiet in the grove. Occasionally they heard bits of gravel becoming dislodged, sliding down the hole, falling past little Trickle and making tiny splashing noises in the water far below. It was a dry hole: what had collected at the bottom was only seepage and a little rainwater.

As they were waiting, everyone suddenly became aware of the regular thump of the drilling machine in the distance beyond the grove. It was working behind the homestead, near the family graveyard, where the geologist reckoned there was a fracture in the solid rock shell of the earth. Ella looked up at Abel. Katie Danster's lips stopped moving. She opened her eyes and stared at the deep grooves the machine had cut into the soil as it drilled.

Abel turned to the tractor driver. 'Go and tell the drillers to stop that machine,' he said, then rubbed his hands across his eyes and went on staring fixedly at the hole.

Chapter 15

'From your Cousin Andreas' was the way he always ended his telegrams from Cape Town. They didn't appreciate the Anglophile 'Cousin' at all: not while Soois's blood was still wet on the garden wall, and FounderAbel was still riding his stallion up the mountain every day trying to sweat the grief out of his system.

He said other things, too, both before he left Toorberg and in the course of odd visits later – like the Sunday morning, many years before. The horses were harnessed, everyone was seated on the wagon ready to set off on the drive over to a neighbouring farm for the church service, when Andreas announced, with deliberate loudness: 'Going to church is an underestimation of God.' That was the beginning of the end. In those days Founder-Abel was quick to thrash, so the whole family had to sit waiting on the wagon, reins and hymnbooks in hand, while Founder-Abel chased Andreas through the maizefields to thrash him for blasphemy.

There were always things they didn't understand, those narrow-minded relations of his who could sit in the big house at night by candlelight, simply staring straight ahead of them. But for him there had been the wonderful discovery of soft red clay at the spot where the Eye's waters bubbled up out of the earth with such perfect clarity. He'd been able to prise the clay free from the sticky earth around it and see it suddenly come to life in his hands. Shapes: FounderAbel's face – the nose, the beard, the hair combed back; a galloping horse; the narrow hips of a man; the lazy udder of a cow. Who had understood? His brother Lucius, perhaps? Lucius had once started painting quite seriously: now he would only stop to offer some sneering Latin tag about graven images.

Here, among the playful shadows of the poplar leaves, these thoughts all came fluttering through Andreas's mind. It had been utterly repulsive, quite disgusting, to see Dowser rush into the clearing a little earlier, sweat dripping off him, his face wet with tears, his mouth drooling. Dowser had fallen sobbing over the hole, till Abel strode over and jerked him away. Meanwhile, from deep down in the earth, again and again, came the voice of the child: pretty little Noah du Pisani.

The clan were all there, sitting or standing, for once jerked out of their sanctimonious pride. The folk from the Stiefveld were there, too, the descendants of his unmentionable brother Floris. People with Floris's flashing blue eyes – even young LittleKitty Riet. United for once, he thought, at the spot where the child was undoubtedly going to die.

Actually, his leaving Toorberg had been inevitable. First it was school in the city – and in the holidays the lengthy political arguments with his brother Soois who always wanted his own way – exactly like CrossAbel now. Later, when the young Scots subaltern from the British garrison came on the first of his weekend visits, FounderAbel had warned: 'I see he's arty, too.' And on the veranda that evening, once the young officer had retired to bed: 'They're not like us, the Scots.' When the young officer came a second time, Mother Magtilt made him a bed in the spare room opposite Soois's, and Soois spent every night that weekend with his door open, like a guard on sentry duty.

No, he couldn't have stayed. The Jew with the wagonload of paintings, who had fruitlessly tried to hawk his wares on the farm, had made him an offer he couldn't refuse. The art pedlar had reckoned that Andreas would soon be able to sell art to the farmers with great success from the very same wagon. He was a Moolman, after all, a scion of one of the pioneer families.

But the hectic life of the salons had swallowed him – the perfumed nights, the evenings in the officers' mess at the Castle, the beautiful bewildered young men from the British regiments, lost and far from home, and eager to learn more about local culture from a native like Andreas. There had been the sedate clubs with their oak panelling and deep pile carpets, their discreet stewards. Newspapers from England, America, the Orient. Smoking-concerts and whole new worlds opening up before him. Baths amid the languid bodies of others like himself, all seeking an alternative lifestyle.

Only occasionally, out in the street in the middle of the night, did he catch the sharp scent of dew and early morning, and then suddenly the ravines of the Toorberg would crack open deep within him and in an instant everything was exposed: the smells, the sensations, the dark blue mountain lifting its proud head above the plain, the Eye spouting clear. Then he would wire that he was coming home. Sometimes, particularly in the early years, he'd actually gone, sometimes he hadn't. Eventually he'd stopped going altogether. 'From your Cousin Andreas . . .'

During the war an English-language daily had appointed him to write heroic ballads to keep up the morale of the troops, particularly when the Boer Commandos invaded the Cape Colony from the North and it looked as though the war was going to spread southwards. His facility for turning out verses was as great in English as it was in Dutch; the ballads were acclaimed at the Officers' Ball, and also at the Governor's Reception, and were said to have been read eventually by Queen Victoria herself. She was particularly taken with the one which described her as the Empress of Sovereigns. And it was that ballad that some enterprising pedlar put in his knapsack and took to Toorberg. The poem reached FounderAbel one week after Soois was shot, before Andreas had even heard of Soois's death.

After that, Toorberg turned its back on Andreas Moolman. FounderAbel sent a single telegram: 'Never again set your turn-coat feet on the native soil of your fathers.'

Years later, wearing a false beard borrowed from a theatrical friend, he called at the farm with a load of paintings. The visit was a comic one, but sad, too. He'd remained seated on the cart, with the reins in his hand, while sending his young friend up to the front door to knock and enquire whether the people of the house would care to buy some fine Cape paintings – paintings so true to life that one could simply ignore that new-fangled invention, the camera.

No one had opened the door. Later one of the farm-workers appeared and explained, apologetically, that the people of the house were spending a week in the town house. The auctioneers were in town and they had gone to buy and sell.

As they left, Andreas and his companion passed the Ou-Murasie. When they reached the Halt, the mailcoach had stopped under the pepper trees for the coachman to water his horses. They swung off to the left, and trundled their way down the pass to the plains of Camdeboo. From there Andreas looked back. Majestically, the mountain lifted its blue head above the lower slopes – some dark green, some hazy purple – and above the rugged, morose and grim cliffs. High above, two eagles swooped down from the mountain, wheeled, plunged and then lazily swept away. The grandeur of such wide open spaces was too much for Andreas, agorophobic after years spent indoors and on city streets. At the first railway station after the pass he made the consignment of paintings over to his young colleague and caught a train back to the city.

And now, he thought sadly beside the borehole, your Cousin Andreas is here, and you don't even know him. For now your Cousin Andreas is free to wander at will, invisible and unrestrained, leaving no trace behind him, for at last the farm is his, too. No door is closed to him, no footpath is unfamiliar any more.

Detached, Andreas the poet turned away from the scene round the borehole. I'll wait for little Noah du Pisani, he thought, I'll take him by the hand and, without interference, I'll lead him to all my favourite places, all over this beloved farm, everywhere on Toorberg, and no one will stop us.

Chapter 16

'All right,' said the police captain to the magistrate sitting opposite him. A long cylinder of ash threatened to drop off the end of the magistrate's cigar. 'You can see him, but I'm only allowing this because you're an officer of the court.'

'Thank you,' said the magistrate, a light movement of his hand letting the ash fall to the wooden floor of the captain's office. 'I must see him now,' he continued, getting up.

The captain rose, too, with a quick glance at the caterpillar of ash on the polished floor. 'He's down in the cells,' he said. 'The third door on the right in the corridor leads down. I'll give the warder a ring.' Placing his hand on the telephone, he waited for the magistrate to leave.

As he went down the corridor, the magistrate avoided looking at his own reflection in the glass panels of the swingdoors. The pain in his arm was excruciating. He had taken a painkiller and two quick whiskies before leaving the hotel, and for a while he'd experienced a pleasant drowsiness, but that had passed and now he regretted hesitating with the empty whisky flask in his hand before setting out for the police station.

He went down the steps to the basement under the police station and stopped in front of a barred gate. He pressed the button above *Ring for service/Lui vir diens*. The blank face of a warder appeared. They regarded each other in silence for a moment or two. In his days as a public prosecutor the magistrate had avoided visiting the cells: the smell of sweat and urine in the stone rooms always reminded him of Biblical passages about Hell. Weeping and wailing and gnashing of teeth, he thought, looking over the shoulder of the warder with the fat, boyish face towards the open space between the cells where two warders were setting up the net across a green ping-pong table.

'I am the investigating magistrate,' he announced. 'I am here to see the prisoner Riet.'

The warder looked at him suspiciously, deliberately allowing his gaze to linger on the arm and the empty sleeve.

'The captain upstairs,' the magistrate said with a tired gesture, 'said he would telephone to inform you.' The oppressive heat between the steep staircase behind him and the bars with the warder in front of him made him dizzy.

'Nobody phoned me,' said the warder.

'Then perhaps you should telephone the captain?' suggested the magistrate. As the warder walked away, grumbling, the magistrate leant against the wall. He would have preferred to sit down, but noticed splodges of something on the concrete stairs: probably spittle or urine, he thought. Or possibly blood.

He lit a cigar and inhaled deeply. That made him feel better. Odd, he mused, that the nicotine eased the pain in his stump. It probably contracted the blood vessels. Or dilated them.

Then the warder was there again, busying himself about the heavy iron lock. The door squeaked open. 'You may come in, magistrate,' he said, adding apologetically: 'We have to be a bit careful with security prisoners, you see.'

'I realize that.' The magistrate waved the cigar and entered the central area onto which all the cells opened. The two warders at the table had begun to play: two oafs in uniform, batons at their sides, smashing a little ball back and forth with ping-pong bats.

He remarked to the warder: 'It's stuffy in here.'

'Yes,' said Boyface, 'but they're not here for fresh air.' The magistrate attempted a smile before asking: 'Where is Riet?' He sensed a reawakening of his own interest: he was looking forward to this opportunity of forming an opinion on Katie Danster's pastor son.

They went over to the gate of one of the cells. Watched by the warder, the magistrate approached the bars. His eyes needed time to adjust to the gloom. There were five men leaning against the walls of the small cell. Without a word, they looked up at him. The magistrate tried to fathom their faces. 'Oneday Riet,' he said.

No one moved. The warder strode forward. 'Riet!' he bellowed. Behind the magistrate the smashing of the bats stopped.

One of the men came forward. Sluggish, thought the magistrate, but when the man stopped in front of him, he caught the impudent look in the eyes which he had fleetingly noticed in Katie Danster.

'Are you another of the magistrates supposedly sent to check whether they pull out our toenails?' A sharp question, but not insubordinate. One of the men behind Oneday shifted his position slightly. Another sniggered softly. The little ball was bouncing off the bats again.

'Are you Pastor Oneday Riet?' asked the magistrate politely. Oneday nodded. 'I am.'

'To answer your question: I am a magistrate. But I am here on an investigation quite different from what you may be thinking.' The magistrate took a long draw at his cigar. 'I am here on commission. I have been sent to investigate the death of Noah du Pisani.'

Oneday looked at him sharply. What exactly is the expression in his eyes? the magistrate wondered. Then he turned to the warder: 'May I see Pastor Riet in private, please?'

The man nodded. He unlocked the cell door, beckoning with his head to Oneday.

'Out,' he said, adding 'You can use that one,' pointing to an empty cell opposite. They walked across to it and the warder locked the door behind them.

The magistrate offered Oneday a cigar. 'So,' he said, 'one of Toorberg's folk on a security charge.'

Oneday took the cigar, bent over to the flame and inhaled deeply. When he made no reply, the magistrate continued: 'I didn't know pastors were allowed to smoke.'

At that Oneday looked him straight in the eye. 'A pastor of God in detention,' he said. 'Is that also something you find strange?'

The players at the ping-pong table had changed. The boy-faced warder had now taken up the bat against the winner of the previous game. Strange to see two big men crouching round the table. Out of sheer boredom, the prisoners watched, following the little white ball with their eyes. Once when the ball bounced sideways and landed in one of the cells, it remained the possession of the three inmates for a while. After some rueful laughter it was thrown back through the bars and the game continued.

'I must tell you,' the magistrate resumed the conversation, 'that the details of your detention here fall beyond the bounds of my jurisdiction.' Since Oneday made no answer, looking past the magistrate at the wall instead, he asked: 'Have you scratched your name on the walls here yet?'

Oneday looked at the graffiti with a faint smile. 'No.' He exhaled the smoke slowly, tensely. Then, unexpectedly, he looked at the magistrate in a more friendly way, saying: 'I am pleased to see you. I don't get any visitors here, except the interrogators.'

The magistrate was relieved: conversation would be possible after all. He bent down to read one of the names on the wall. 'There have been quite a number of artists here before you.' Then he stubbed out his cigar against the wall, carefully putting the butt back into the cigar box. 'I have come,' he said, 'to talk to you about the death of Noah du Pisani. This is not an official interrogation. At present I am still finding my way. Actually,' he said, swinging his stump forward slightly, 'I should like, first, to establish by means of informal conversations whether an official enquiry with evidence given under oath will be necessary.'

Oneday nodded. 'Perhaps the Department of the Law should rather concern itself with the living who are dying now, today, in the townships.' Once again, that momentary flash of impudence in his eyes. 'Rather than with a little boy who has been dead for ages.'

'The mills of justice grind slowly.' The magistrate shrugged his shoulders. 'As I told you, Pastor, my jurisdiction is limited to the case I am investigating. I should warn you that I am not permitted to become involved in conversations with you on any other topic.'

'Very well.' Oneday threw the cigar butt, still burning, into a corner of the cell, where it lay glowing in the gloom.

'I understand that you were present at the borehole. I trust that as a Christian and a pastor you will be willing to tell the truth.'

95

'Insofar as the truth, in its true Christian sense, is still recognizable.'

'Now you are talking theology,' said the magistrate. 'I am a lawyer. I shall weigh your evidence against that of others.'

Oneday nodded. 'Very well. What are your questions?'

'I have one further problem,' explained the magistrate cautiously.

'Putting it bluntly, I feel there is a conspiracy of silence surrounding the death of Noah du Pisani. There would appear to have been a whole crowd of people present at the borehole, but no one is prepared to state categorically what happened.' He came right up to Oneday. 'Your own mother,' he said, 'is not prepared to say what actually happened.'

'Ma Katie is very old,' Oneday countered. 'And in any case her nerves have been so on edge since I was arrested that she'd be unlikely to talk about anything at all if she knew you were investigating like a magistrate.' He turned away. 'She doesn't have an easy time of it.' He was silent for a moment. 'She never did. Shoved aside onto that barren stretch of veld on the bare slope of the mountain.'

The magistrate did not react to Oneday's statement. 'And yet,' he said after a while, 'I think she knows.'

'You must draw your own conclusions.'

'And you are not prepared to assist me?'

'I'll help where I can,' said Oneday coolly. 'But I know you're simply going to use everything I say to coerce my mother and my brother and sister.'

'You can hardly object to my testing the validity of statements?'

'Certainly not,' said Oneday. He turned back to the magistrate. 'Would it be rude to ask for another cigar?'

'Oh, no, not at all – do help yourself.' Each took one. Boyface came up to them.

'All still under control, Magistrate?' he asked.

The magistrate nodded.

'Round the borehole,' he then said to Oneday, 'were: yourself, your mother, your brother and sister, Abel and Ella Mool-

96

man, Dowser and Co – in short the whole family. Is that correct?'

'That is correct.'

'I put it to you that Abel Moolman left the hole to fetch his hunting rifle from the library, and that he then returned and cold-bloodedly – but with the best of intentions – gave Noah Moolman the *coup de grâce*, from above, into the crown of the child's head.' He waited for some reaction, but Oneday's face remained inscrutable. 'What is more, I will put it to you that the whole crowd of you Toorbergers then conspired to never mention a word about the matter again.'

Oneday gave a crooked smile. 'With respect, your legal system is bedevilled by conspiracy theories. Look,' he said, pointing to the other cells, 'look at us sitting here. We're working for social justice – and it's called conspiracy! Or an even more sinister word: subversion. A rose by any other name . . .'

'But how do you react to my assertion?'

'What did Ma Katie tell you?'

'That there was a shot.'

Oneday nodded. 'That's true,' he said. 'But then the Moolmans were always fond of shooting. And you know: shooting is nothing unusual in this country of ours. Ask Abel's son, Cross-Abel. He's really the one for guns.'

'You are playing games with me.' With audible impatience, the magistrate exhaled. 'And you cannot afford to do so.'

'Why not? What have I got to lose, Magistrate? Look at me: in sackcloth and ashes.'

'You will compel me to turn again to your mother for information.'

Oneday looked at the magistrate with suspicion. 'Ma Katie is old. She doesn't remember things very clearly any more.'

The magistrate noticed that Oneday was watching him closely. He went back to the graffiti.

'Strange slogans,' he said, drawing his finger across the rough wall.

There was a cheer from the ping-pong table. Boyface had won. Smiling broadly he walked along beside the cells with the bat in his hand, hitting the fingers of any prisoners holding onto the bars. 'D'you convicts see that?' he asked the expressionless faces in the gloom. 'That's the way to play tennis! I wonder how any of you'd get on? All you lot can do is burn and steal.'

'Listen to that,' said Oneday. 'One sometimes has one's doubts about the poor in spirit.'

The magistrate smiled. 'Your mother tells me she still hears that rifle-shot in her dreams at night,' he continued. Oneday stiffened. 'It would appear to be troubling her.'

'She was very fond of little Noah. He used to come and play with my own children from time to time.'

'I see.' The magistrate again stubbed out his cigar against the wall. 'By the way, why did you go into the Church?'

Oneday shrugged his shoulders. 'You people don't believe that we "social gospellers", as you call us, have a vocation. You think it's all political.'

He waited for a reply, but the magistrate said nothing. Earlier in the interview he had forgotten his stump. Now it was throbbing painfully.

Oneday continued: 'It was really what my father wanted. He wanted his children to rise above the poverty of the Stiefveld. I did quite well at school, won a bursary, grew increasingly conscious of the plight of my people, became a pastor.' The magistrate nodded. Then the sharp comment: 'A man of God.' Again that provocative expression in the eyes. 'And that is what I shall remain, no matter how long these warders keep me here.'

'Your mother must be very concerned about you.' Instantly, Oneday was on his guard again and the magistrate knew then that he had found a chink in Oneday's defences.

'She often comes here. One of the warders intimated as much. She sits out there under the trees; she asks permission to see me. They refuse her every time, so she sits out there till late in the afternoon and takes the bus back to the Halt.'

'I shall tell her that you are in good health.'

'Thank you. She doesn't really understand.' Oneday stubbed out his cigar, too, before throwing it into the corner next to the other butt which was still glowing. 'She is still one of the old generation. She is still proud of the Moolman blood. You know, Jan Swaat, my great-grandfather, lived like a dog under Founder-Abel, and died like one when FounderAbel died. My Granma-Kitty was thrashed for having a child by Floris Moolman. My father was a half-breed outcast, in every sense. I was the first to get an education. I was the first to have the opportunity to ask why.'

'It hasn't helped you much,' said the magistrate drily, rubbing his stump. 'See where you have landed.'

'It's the principle.'

The magistrate nodded. Turning to the bars, he called the warder.

As the gate of the cell closed behind him with a clatter, he said a hurried goodbye, and waited for the warder to unlock the gates to the stairs for him as well. At the ping-pong table the click of the bats had started up again. The magistrate climbed the stairs carefully, trying to avoid the splodges. It must be spittle, he thought. Spittle from people who had been down in the nether regions and now needed to spit to purify themselves. He went down the corridor, through the glass doors. He stopped for a moment in front of the police station, enjoying the sunshine, then walked back to his hotel room, where a few stiff whiskies and an afternoon nap beckoned.

Commission work, he thought as he crossed the sidewalk, was not without its advantages.

Chapter 17

'My dear wife,' wrote the magistrate that evening, sitting at the table in front of the window of his hotel room, with the twilight darkening over the town. 'I am at present engaged in the exhausting task of assessing the opinions of every witness in this case. At this stage the interrogation is still informal. Only when I have been able to reconstruct the details of the presumed incident clearly will I be able to enter upon the second phase of my investigation: the taking of sworn affidavits where necessary.'

He looked up across the roofs of the town and took a sip of whisky, hearing the tinkle of ice in the glass. Then he wrote: 'At this stage it seems unlikely that I shall have to subpoena anyone to appear formally. Sworn affidavits should afford sufficient material for a decision.

'I am becoming better acquainted with the various branches of the Moolman family. What was only a family tree to me on the train journey is now becoming flesh and blood. People. They certainly are an eccentric bunch, and some of the personalities (a considerable number of whom are already dead) are fascinating. As happens even in a clinical game like the Law, I have a greater affinity for some of them than for others.

'But then, my love, telling you about such characters is probably an exercise in futility. This is a case which I shall have to battle through largely on my own: where exactly is the fine line between deliberate intent and negligence – what is the extent of the culpability of accomplices – when an entire generation of one family is involved in a chain of events leading to a crime? Who is accountable? Everyone, surely? Add to that a situation where the victim is a child not wholly in possession of his faculties . . . This is something which the Law would perhaps characterize as extremely delicate – and there are a great many other disturbing questions besides.

'I know, my wife, that your common sense will simply ask: Who stabbed, or who stoned, or who pulled the trigger? But this is not a simple criminal case requiring mere clinical investigation – however my heart yearns to be home with you, I am afraid this is a case which demands the most meticulous consideration. I have to probe the chain of causality, the *causa debilis*, right back to the incident which initiated the chain. This may well lead me to the very beginning of the clan itself, to incidents years ago, where history and legend merge in the nightmare of the past.

'I am certain of one thing, though – and I say this without pretension – the same thoroughness which has characterized the course of my entire career to date will help me to get to the roots of this case. I only hope that here, in the isolation of my hotel room, I shall not lose perspective.'

The magistrate took a last sip of whisky from the glass and sucked the ice-cube till it melted in his mouth. Then he bent over the letter again. 'You know how I always strive for clear and balanced judgements. That is precisely what has brought me to such a position of trust that the Department of Justice can send me on investigative missions to test, discreetly, the findings of my colleagues. It is in the light of this position of exceptional trust that you should regard my prolonged absence.'

He got up, rang the bell beside his bed, and then waited in front of the window, the empty glass in his hand. There were still a few lights burning behind the drawn curtains of the houses. When the steward arrived, he handed him the glass.

'Wait!' he called after the steward. Fetching the whisky flask from the wardrobe, he said: 'Please fill this, too, and bring me a jug of iced water.'

He closed the door and returned to the letter, re-reading the last two paragraphs. 'But do be assured,' he wrote, feeling slightly dizzy as a result of having stood for a while, 'that it is only in the flesh, not in spirit, that I am separated from you.'

When he heard the steward's footsteps in the corridor, he concluded:

'Your loving husband,
Abraham van der Ligt.'

101

Chapter 18

When the drilling machine had fallen silent and each person could hear only the sound of his own breathing in the oppressive silence of the poplar grove, FounderAbel Moolman and Grandmother Magtilt came through the trees. Ella, sitting beside the empty fuel drums, looked up for a moment. CrossAbel felt a gentle breeze brush his cheek. For a second Katie Danster imagined she saw a shadow moving across the grove.

FounderAbel went up to the hole where the child was wriggling in the half-light, up to the open earth of Toorberg, where water seeped down into the borehole and the capillary roots of the poplars hung down inside like Spanish moss. For a man of action like himself, whose temper was formidable even in death, these were not easy moments: he was bursting to frighten the hell out of the lifeless bunch gathered round the hole.

He would long since have lowered the wiry yellow body of his tame Bushman down the hole to take hold of the child by the head, and he would have reeled them in together. If necessary he would yoke up eight pairs of oxen and make them strain against the yokes until the earth released that child.

All he could do instead was merely to watch his descendants: his grandson Abel, his great-grandson CrossAbel, Abel's wife Ella, one of the jealous Coetzers of Altydsomer whose ancestor had lost his way and died of malaria while searching for the Kruger millions in Mozambique. Katie Danster represented his son Floris's Skaamfamilie – though she, too, looked as though she was in need of her long rest.

Beside him, with a tenderness for him which she retained even in the grave, was Magtilt. It was for her, FounderAbel realized, that he had tamed his land, so that she would be able to lie in a proper bed when the birth-pangs were upon her; so that she could step out into a properly laid out and carefully watered kitchen garden; so that she should have a proper oven for her baking and a window to sit beside to look out over her husband's fields.

She was the one he had protected on the night when the little yellow people had come and set fire to their first homestead. It was for her that he had ordered lace from the pedlars, and good English baking powder, and the finest cinnamon and pepper all the way from Cape Town, and pure caustic soda for when she wanted to make soap. And when all their sons except OldAbel had left the farm, her devotion had repaid him for all that he had given her over the years.

When he needed to charge up and down the boundary fences, she'd let him be; when he fired his gun into the sky at night to tell the world that he was awake and that the farm belonged to him, she'd understood. When he was out on forays in pursuit of the blacks, she longed quietly for him to return. She never asked why he kept on buying additional land.

She was a wife to him, a mother to his sons; the matriarch of Toorberg.

The boys had not always been easy. Lucius, the clever one, had picked up too much knowledge for his own good in the city; Soois had rebelled against the British; Andreas had taken to writing poems; and OldAbel had inherited a great deal of his father's stubbornness.

Lucius, the one who had spoken Latin before High Dutch, had gone to the city, and when he had returned on visits as an eloquent barrister with a gown, a gold watch and a pince-nez – not to mention strange ideas – they had spent long hours in argument. When Grandmother Magtilt, listening in silence, saw that the discussion was becoming too heated, she would bring them melktert or koeksisters. They talked about guilt and blame, about capital punishment, about Christians, pagans and the Law, about the Ten Commandments and the Twelve Tables, Parliament and the Government, the British and the Dutch, the Bible and the nature of sin. His head teeming with concepts and ideas, Lucius had been lost to Toorberg and later became a judge.

Andreas, who even as a baby had persistently kept crawling into Toorberg's library and, sitting there on the floor, had stared at the spines of the books as though expecting something to hap-

103

pen, turned out limp-wristed and effeminate, and lost his soul to the arts.

During New Year's Day picnics on Toorberg, Andreas visiting from the city and smelling like a city woman, would entertain the old ladies with long rhymes and ballads about the British Empire. As gentle as a calf, he was, a poet and a dreamer. He would never appreciate the recoil of a rifle-butt against the shoulder muscle, never cut out the heart of an antelope and grill and eat it with bloody hands. No, Andreas was a puff-ball.

Soois the Rebel was as hot-headed and cussed as Andreas was gentle. When some Cape Boers rose in revolt against the British, in sympathy with their kinsmen to the north, Soois called up a band of his peers – all farm boys like himself, without property or wives of their own yet, all itching to display their manhood – and they rode out together and encamped up among the ravines of Toorberg. They made a sortie one night to steal FounderAbel's telescope from his library so they could spy on the British columns. Whenever they spotted a British patrol, they would ride down into the Camdeboo and, with bravado and ineptitude, engage the British in a skirmish. Shots would be fired, a horse might be wounded; then they would wave their hats and tear off again as though they had conquered the entire British Empire.

Afterwards they would hide up in the Toorberg again, knowing that the Tommies' superstitious black trackers were convinced that the *tokoloshe* dwelt in the Toorberg. This fact, and sheer good luck, enabled Soois and his companions to stay alive.

At Grandmother Magtilt's insistence FounderAbel went up the mountain regularly to plead with Soois to lay down his arms, but the young men were having fun camping up there at the mouth of the cave above the Eye. 'They're actually getting constipated from all the prickly-pears and fat venison they're eating up there,' FounderAbel reported to Grandmother Magtilt, after one of his visits to plead with the rebels.

Soois grew as portly as a lord and cultivated a beard like a combat general's. But one night, on the occasion of a family gathering in the Toorberg homestead, a patrol of Tommies and Boer renegades ambushed him.

After Soois's death, FounderAbel ordered more poplar cuttings from Swellendam and enlarged the grove in memory of the son whose temper had flared up like the wild shoots of the poplars. When the young saplings were waist-high, he and Grandmother Magtilt started going for walks in the grove each afternoon. As the shade cast by the growing trees increased, so they began to learn acceptance, until one day when the first poplar stood taller than his own head, FounderAbel said to Grandmother Magtilt: 'Now, at last, I have forgiven that renegade.'

So, FounderAbel learnt in his old age, there is serenity in all things. Now that the poplars had met above the heads of his descendants, he had peace within. Shooting and farming, he'd worked it all out of his system. His last battle had been against tick fever, and that was what had finally sent him to his rest.

FounderAbel knew, that day when he walked through the gate of the kraal and felt an itch on the inside of his thigh – and there and then undid his trousers to pick off the little red tick attached to his flesh – he knew then, deep within, that he was destined to die of the bite of one of the smallest pests on earth.

That was Providence's way of forcing him, on his deathbed, into humility, so that he would be able to understand – he could see that now – that things of the greatest import may be contained within the tiniest part of Creation. The fever devastated him, wrung the sweat out of him, almost caused his head to burst for the pain in it, throbbed in his temples and along his spine. He recovered for a couple of days, believed he'd not been beaten after all and got up. But he'd hardly walked from his bed to the sitting-room before they had to help him back to bed. There he lay fighting, long after the little scab on his leg had completely disappeared.

Eventually, realizing that his fight was over, he'd surrendered and in the end it was an easy death. Magtilt and OldAbel were at his bedside. As he took farewell of his wife and son, his groom, the bondsman Jan Swaat, who had trekked north with him all the way from the South and side by side with him had helped tame the wilderness, sat outside under the bedroom window and howled like a dog. When FounderAbel heard the footsteps of Judge Lucius hurrying down the passage – his coach had only just arrived from the city – he embraced death.

Jan Swaat dug the grave himself, and for twenty-one days after the funeral he refused all food. On the twenty-second day he too died.

As FounderAbel was wandering through the events of his life, Trickle began to whimper again. Abel stepped forward to talk to him but stopped when wild geese flew over the wood. For a moment Trickle was silent. Everybody knew he was listening to the geese. But when Postmaster Moolman, Mailbag and Amy O'Leary came panting into the clearing and Mailbag dropped the tow-ropes from his shoulder onto the ground, the whimpering started again. Amy stopped when she saw Abel, but then hurried forward and lay face-down beside the borehole, calling: 'Noah! Noah!'

Grandmother Magtilt placed her hand on FounderAbel's arm. Postmaster Moolman came forward and offered Abel his hand, then went over and shook hands with Ella and with Cross-Abel. He nodded to Katie Danster and then looked at his wife, prone beside the hole.

'I have stopped all the buses,' he said. 'The Halt is closed for the afternoon.'

Abel nodded and picked up one of the tow-ropes, testing its strength. Satisfied, he bound one end tightly round the tractor's winch.

FounderAbel was pleased by the skill in his grandson's hands: the knot was as good as a sailor's. From the tractor's toolbox, Abel then took a hammer and wrenched off its head by standing on it and jerking the handle. Everyone watched his hands. Sweat trickled into his eyes. The shadows cast by the anchor stays were longer than the stays themselves. Abel knotted the other end of the tow-rope round the shaft of the hammer and walked back twenty paces. Taking a firm grip on the hammer shaft, he dug in his heels. The driver started the tractor, put the winch into gear and Abel's feet began to slither as the cable towed him in. When he was satisfied as to its strength, he bent over the borehole.

'Noah!' he shouted. For an instant everyone froze at the realization that for the first time Abel Moolman had called his grandson by name. 'Noah!' Abel called down the hole. 'There's a rope and a stick coming down to you. I'll let it down slowly. See if you can take hold of the stick, Noah – we're going to pull you up. Hold your head to one side as the rope comes down – it's got to go past your head so you can take hold of it in your hands. Hold it tight, see, and don't let go. D'you hear me, Noah?'

Trickle du Pisani did not answer. Squatting on his haunches, Abel wiped the sweat out of his eyes once more. He nodded to the driver and as the winch slowly turned in reverse, Abel carefully fed the cable down the hole, hand over hand. Eventually he indicated that it had gone far enough.

'Noah!' Abel called again. 'Can you feel the stick above you?' There was no sound from the hole. 'Bring me the torch,' he ordered. By the light of the torch he peered down the hole, but then shook his head. 'His arms are stuck at his sides,' he said. 'He can't take hold of the rope.'

Ella's face dropped into her hands. Abel looked round towards her. 'Go home, Ella,' he ordered. She shook her head.

Again he called to Noah. When there was no reply, he turned to Ella in annoyance.

'I'm staying,' she said with determination.

'Reel it in!' Abel waved to the driver. The cable wound up slowly till the haft of the hammer appeared. 'We'll have to hook him,' said Abel. He looked at Ella, then at Katie Danster. 'CrossAbel, get on your motorbike and fetch one of the meat-hooks from the cold store.'

'There must be another way,' said Postmaster, intervening.

Abel dusted his hands against his thighs. 'There isn't,' he said brusquely. 'There's dust down there. The child is going to choke. We've got to get him out before he smothers.'

CrossAbel kicked the motorcycle into life and disappeared down the footpath, leaving a cloud of blue exhaust fumes among the trees. FounderAbel watched Abel wiping his eyes, and noticed Amy worriedly placing her hand on Mailbag's arm. Katie Danster had not moved, but now with the lengthening shadows falling over her she looked older than ever.

So FounderAbel and Grandmother Magtilt wandered on. They knew what the living did not: that the earth of Toorberg would never yield up what it had once taken unto itself.

Chapter 19

The magistrate's car stopped in front of the Toorberg homestead. For a moment he did not move from his seat beside the
clerk, who had switched off the engine and was watching him
expectantly.

'Wait here,' he said, using the remark he had used umpteen
times to the clerk already. Taking the tin of ointment from the
glove compartment, he massaged his stump, using the index and
third fingers of his right hand to apply the salve.

'Does it hurt, Your Worship?' asked the clerk. The magistrate looked at him, noticing a large red pimple at the corner of
his mouth. The hands folded loosely round the steering wheel
were covered with scratches. An engine-fanatic, the magistrate
had long since decided, observing again the old oil under the
finger nails.

'No,' he said. 'It's just uncomfortable. That's all. It's the
heat.' Then he got out and walked slowly up to the front door. On
the gable above, as he stepped into the cool shade of the veranda,
was the motto: *Celebrate Life*. He took in the beauty of the garden
with its lawns and rose trees, noticing in a quick glance over his
shoulder that the clerk in the driver's seat of the car was shifting
his clumsy frame into a comfortable position for a nap.

As the magistrate knocked at the door, he recalled Dowser
du Pisani kicking his shoe against the pieces of the drilling machine in the deadveld and saying: 'Please, Your Worship, we
must go now,' and Mailbag lightly hopping up onto the large
front wheel of the bus and chatting to the driver through the
window.

The door opened, and Ella stood there, cool and fresh in the
doorway.

'Mr Van der Ligt,' she said.

'Good morning, ma'am,' he said with a slight bow. She
inclined her head and stood aside to allow him to enter. He
immediately noticed the furnishings: the thick pile carpet under

his feet, the wooden curlicues of the hall table, the mirror set deep in a heavy gilt frame, in which his reflection looked sweaty and embarrassed.

As she led the way into the sitting-room, he noticed her fine legs. Only once they were seated did she speak: 'May I ask the reason for your visit?'

'I must request you,' he began, and leant to one side to get his cigars from his jacket pocket. He took one out, but before putting it to his lips, asked: 'Do you mind?' She shook her head, so he lit it, looking at her through the smoke: 'kindly to introduce me to your daughter Magtilt.'

He noticed the shutters coming down over her face. 'Tilly?' she asked, unnecessarily, after a moment or two.

'Tilly, as you call her.'

She looked at him wryly, with a crooked smile. 'No, sir,' she said, 'you are mistaken. Tilly is something we never call her. What we call her, in all love,' – she smiled again – 'is CrazyTilly . . .' She looked him straight in the eye. He watched her unwaveringly.

'As you wish, Mrs Moolman,' he said, waving the cigar. 'As you prefer.'

'And since she is *Crazy*Tilly,' Ella continued, emphasizing the first syllables of the name, 'there would not be very much point in your interviewing her. She is, well, . . . confused, you know . . .'

'I understand, ma'am,' he said. 'But I have to see her. For the record. And for my own satisfaction.'

As she regarded him in silence, he realized that she was weighing him up, and shrank back: his drooping shoulders, his stump with its pink tip glowing in the heat, the pouches under his eyes. He thought of her husband: proud, erect Abel with his strong arms resting on his hips.

'I must see her,' he repeated emphatically and with some impatience – more at himself than at her. 'Otherwise I shall have to subpoena her to appear before me in court, which is something you certainly would prefer to avoid.'

Ella sighed and got up. 'I'll go and see whether she is

asleep,' she said as she went out. 'But please don't exhaust her. If you do, we shall have to battle for days to calm her down again.'

'I shall be careful,' he promised the empty doorway as Ella's angry footsteps disappeared down the passage. He smoked in silence. From the depths of the house he heard household noises: the rattle of crockery and kitchenware, servants' voices, a canary singing in a cage somewhere and pecking at a tiny bell. A dog barked out in the yard and farther away there was the drone of a tractor. At the heart of Toorberg, he thought.

Why, he wondered, should the Afrikaner have such an inordinate regard for the family home – it was only a house, after all, like many others. It may have been larger, than most, perhaps, with more beds, more seats round the table, more servants, a family Bible with a genealogy on the flyleaf, testifying to an awareness of kinship ties – but why the shrine-like ambience of such a home? The dour ancestral portraits on the walls; the walking sticks in the umbrella-stand in the hall, some with a patina produced by hands long since crumbled into dust; the attic like a collective memory accumulating the flotsam of generations.

The magistrate recalled his own parental home: the small-town cottage with the red brick fireplace and his mother's sewing machine humming away in the corner day after day; the radio that was never silent; and out in the yard his pigeons waddling out of the loft, spreading their fantails and whirring over the roof of the house before disappearing high into the blue sky.

Suddenly Ella Moolman reappeared in the doorway: 'You may come now.' He followed her down the long corridor and turned into a side-passage, past a number of open doors – he noticed made-up beds, vases of flowers – past some closed doors on either side, until Ella stopped in front of the door where the passage came to a dead end. It was gloomy, far from the noises of the rest of the house. 'Shh,' whispered Ella as she gently pushed the door open.

The room had no windows. There was a sweetish smell which he recalled from his days as a public prosecutor: state evidence in green plastic packets – and then he remembered

Tilly's cannabis tea. Ella stood aside so he could see. In the corner, in a simple, seamless frock, her thick black hair combed back from her pale face, stood Tilly. The magistrate fingered his stump. She is beautiful, he thought. Impossibly beautiful. Clearly the daughter of Abel and Ella: Ella's jet-black eyes and thick black hair; Abel's lithe frame, his high forehead, his pride in the arch of Tilly's neck.

'Tilly,' said Ella, gently, 'there's someone here to see you. He's a nice gentleman from town. He's a magistrate. He won't hurt you.'

The magistrate doubted whether Tilly could see him. 'Tilly,' he said, and stepped forward.

'Wait a moment,' said Ella. 'She needs to get used to you. She doesn't often see strangers.'

He fingered his stump: the ointment had already dried out. He thought of the little tin in the glove compartment of the car. The clerk had probably dozed off by now.

Ella touched his shoulder. 'You can say something, if you like,' she whispered.

The magistrate took another step forward. Tilly's face remained expressionless. He coughed. 'I should like to talk to you, Tilly,' he said. 'There is nothing to be afraid of.'

She made no reply, but slowly started to move. Keeping her eyes on him, she moved warily sideways, her bare feet making no sound on the thick mat covering the floor. In the corner were only a mattress, two pillows and a large, brightly coloured ball.

'Tilly,' he said again, as she circled round him.

'She will soon accept you,' whispered Ella. 'She is just being careful.'

He turned along with Tilly, in the centre of the white room. When he looked around Ella had gone. She had closed the door without a sound.

'Tilly,' he said, putting out his hand to her: 'My name is Abraham van der Ligt.'

She came closer, extending a soft, warm hand. What a beautiful woman, he thought. 'Do not be afraid,' he said. 'I shall not hurt you.'

112

She was watching him closely. 'You look scared,' she said. 'You've only got one arm.'

He smiled. 'That's right, Tilly, I was born like this, with only one arm.'

She smiled at him. Her red lips parted to reveal white teeth. 'You can't ride a bike,' she said. 'You've only got one arm.'

'Oh, I can,' he said. 'To ride a bicycle one needs two legs. See, I have two legs.' She looked at his legs. 'But do you know what, Tilly?' He spoke more softly, so that she narrowed her eyes and leant her head forward to catch his voice. 'You are not to tell anyone, but I have another arm which I keep at home. I only take it out when there is no one about. When no one is looking, I put it on.'

She laughed. He was relieved; he'd won her confidence.

'It's going to rain,' she said. She stretched out her hands on either side of her. 'The flying ants are flying this morning.' She spun round on her feet, looking like a ballet dancer. 'It will rain, it will rain,' she crooned.

'Tilly, may I talk to you about little Trickle?'

'It will rain, it will rain . . .'

'About Noah, your little boy.'

She suddenly stopped, looking at him expressionlessly. 'He's gone,' she said.

'How do you know?'

'I never hear him any more.'

'Where do you not hear him any more?'

'There.' She pointed to the corner of the room.

'What do you mean, Tilly?'

She smiled, went over to the corner and knocked with her knuckles on the wall. She waited a moment before replying in the same code.

'Did Noah come knocking here?'

She nodded and smiled. 'Noah talks to Tilly,' she said, 'his mother.'

'Every day?'

'Every day.' She looked at him suspiciously. 'Daddy doesn't know,' she warned. 'Noah is scared.'

113

'So am I, Tilly, I am also scared.'

She stretched out her hand. 'You needn't be scared.'

'Tilly,' he asked, 'when last did you see Noah?'

'At Christmas,' she said. 'Everybody was in the forest round the drilling machine.'

'And Noah?'

She went over to pick up the ball, threw it against the wall and caught it again. 'Antjie Somers came and caught him,' she whispered, without looking round at him.

'Antjie Somers?'

She was dancing lightly with the ball. 'The one that runs on padded feet and catches little monkeys.'

He came closer. 'Was Trickle one of the little monkeys?'

'Yes,' she whispered, almost inaudibly. She clasped the ball to her chest and looked at him. 'But don't tell anyone?' He shook his head. 'He had fine little fluffy hairs all the way down his spine.' She was panting; she had told a secret. But she looked at him triumphantly. 'Do you see?'

He nodded. 'And a tail?'

She grinned, bouncing the ball against the wall again. Then suddenly she was suspicious. 'But he wasn't a little coloured boy,' she warned.

'Oh?'

'All of a sudden it was raining!' she shouted. 'All of a sudden!'

'And then?'

'I'm not telling.' And at once she was a little girl, sitting cross-legged on the floor.

'But I really want to know.'

'The drilling machine wants rain.' Her eyes were glazed. She hugged the ball on her lap, rocking back and forth.

'Can you still hear it calling?'

'I feel him, in the floor. I feel him calling. It's going to rain.'

'Why is it calling for rain?' He squatted down beside her.

'He's an Abel!'

'Why do you say that, Tilly?'

114

She rocked the ball on her lap. 'Shiny machine. Feet stamp. Drill it open. Dowser will point. Drill it open! Drill it open!'

Tired, he looked at her. 'What about Trickle?' he tried again.

'Antjie Somers caught him. When everybody was having a Christmas party in the forest.'

'What about you?'

'They put me away, they hid my present. They gave me sleepy-tea. It tastes horrible. I don't want to drink it. It's not Christmas. It's New Year, it's New Year!'

'Who says Trickle has gone with Antjie Somers, Tilly?'

'It's raining.' Her voice was flat, ordinary.

'Tilly,' he tried, taking her by the arm, but he could not get through.

When he stood up, turning away from her to light a cigar, she got to her feet as well.

'Drill it open, drill it open,' she whispered, rocking, her hands clasping her shoulders.

'Tilly!'

'You'll wake the rain.' There was a reprimand in her eyes. She tucked her hair back behind her ears. Slowly she came up to him, much too close. In the silent room he could hear the breath passing her lips. She reached out and touched his stump with her hand, stroking the taut, shiny skin.

'Who are you?' she asked. 'Are you Antjie Somers?'

The magistrate felt a dizziness come over him. He swung round towards the door. The cigar was burning his fingers as he opened the door and went slowly down the passage in the half-light. Through one of the open doors he caught sight of Ella sitting on a made-up bed. It was clearly a guest room, with a neat bed, wash-basin and jug, two paintings on the wall, a Bible on the bedside table.

She looked out through the open window. 'Well, have you had enough?' she asked. There were only the two of them in the vast, silent house.

115

Chapter 20

'It would seem,' the magistrate wrote to his wife that night, 'that the Moolmans are attempting to escape into a legendary world where normal rules do not apply. But however they try to disguise their sins with tales of the fabulous adventures of their ancestors, I find – instinctively, without even being able to lay my finger on it yet – the evidence of their transgressions.

'In the end all the myths will have to submit to the truth as it is revealed by the inexorable probing of the independent bench and the Department which has been so good to me over the years, Justice.'

He listened to the laughter in the bar down below. The neon light of the hotel's name yellowed the tarred road.

'Perhaps, my dear, I should regard this one incident in isolation and reconstruct only the relevant facts. But the longer I stay here, the more it seems to me that this is a case where one form of causality flows into another, with one incident leading on to another and then another. But I must admit that the scope of it is much wider than my field, since it concerns the influence of blood and pride, as well as the sources of guilt and blame.

'This may well be the crime of an entire clan, rather than that of an as yet unidentified individual man or woman.

'I cannot phrase it more appropriately tonight.

'Perhaps, when you receive this, you should let me know whether you think I am setting the limits of this investigation too wide? Am I permitting myself to be carried away by this country where the limits of truth and fantasy have long since ceased to be hard-edged?

'Your husband and lover,
Abraham van der Ligt.'

Chapter 21

There was a golden moon above the Toorberg when Oneday Riet, Katie Danster's clever son, veered off to the left from the Halt onto Katie's path up to the Stiefveld. As usual, he sang as he walked: hymns and psalms and spirituals, but also protest songs about the struggle ahead, and the day that was coming. It was his bitter father who had christened him Oneday: Andries Riet, who had declared before the whole congregation, after the christening in the lucerne shed at Doornbosch: 'I called him Oneday, because one day the day will come. God is my witness.'

Even as a toddler, he had been an exceptional child. Following the white ribbon of the footpath in the moonlight, he recalled Katie Danster sitting on her haunches beside him at the hearth watching him playing with the dolosse on the floor and saying: 'He's my tender one. He's gentle. Look now he handles the dolosse. He's going to be a man of God.'

Shala was the one for the outdoors, the one who visited his snares in the boundary fences every day and came home in the evening with a scrub hare or two dangling from his belt. He, Oneday, was the Skaamfamilie's great hope for education and social betterment, and he was never allowed to forget the oath his father had sworn before the whole congregation. As he crested the ridge, leaving the dim lights of the Halt behind him, he considered how similar the congregation which had sat on the floor of the shed that day was to the one which now sat there. Little had changed. Shala, if he were able to father children, would also be able to stand up and swear: 'Oneday the day will come.'

Near the OuMurasie he swung off the footpath. Behind the mounds of baked clay and stone – the remains of FounderAbel's first, burnt-out homestead – half hidden under a tangle of wild vines and creepers lay the grave of his great-grandfather, Jan Swaat the army deserter.

Oneday stood beside the grave for a while, feeling uncomfortable, as he always did when visiting the resting-places of the dead, since he knew they were elsewhere: either in bliss or in hell. But he honoured their memory, and was respectful towards their earthly remains as well, since these had borne their souls through the grinding struggle of a whole lifetime. And in Jan Swaat's case Oneday had the sure and certain knowledge that his ancestor had earned his rest.

According to family tradition – and this was a story that had been regularly told round the fire place for as long as he could remember – Jan Swaat had earned two rixdollars a month as a corps member of the Cape Pandours. As a young man, the son of James Read and his Hottentot wife, he had started out as a vagrant, a man who lived by his wits and his veldcraft. But when the British fleet dropped anchor in Table Bay and the government was in need of every hand that could handle a musket, he acted on the spur of the moment and became a Pandour.

Granma Kitty Riet used to tell how Jan Swaat had fought bravely but that the killing of other human beings had become too much for him. One night he took off his uniform, shoved it under a bush, paid a pedlar a rixdollar for a couple of skins and disguised himself as a savage. He'd crawled through the lines, scraping virtually all the skin off his belly in the process, and fled northwards for eight days, trotting all along water-courses, keeping hidden by day and moving only when the coast was clear.

On the fourth day, dropping over the edge of a steeply eroded gully into a patch of shade, Jan Swaat had suddenly encountered a man whose leg was so badly festered that he had given up all hope of survival. Like Jan Swaat, he too was wearing skins, but in his hands and pointed straight at Jan was a gun.

Jan Swaat stopped in his tracks. There was no returning: the sides of the gully were too steep and its next bend was too far. The man was only fifteen paces away.

'Are you a good shot?' Jan Swaat asked the stranger.

'I am Windvogel Valentyn,' the man answered cautiously. 'I shoot to kill. But you can come closer, I'm also a deserter.'

Jan Swaat thought of the six rixdollars in the pouch between his shoulder blades. 'First put your gun away, friend,' he said. 'I'm not taking one step closer to the mouth of a musket.'

Windvogel lowered his gun and Jan Swaat joined him. They had a smoke together and swapped experiences; and then Jan Swaat examined Windvogel's leg. The swelling was the size of a child's head. The ball must still be lodged in there somewhere, thought Jan Swaat to himself.

He made a fire next to Windvogel and heated the blade of his knife. Then he said to Windvogel: 'What on earth is that over there?' The moment Windvogel looked away, Jan knocked him out cold, with a stone behind the ear. He cut open the wound with the red-hot knife and removed the ball. When all the pus had bled away, he packed what herbs he had into the wound and bound it up tightly with a leather thong. When Windvogel came round, Jan Swaat was away spying out the lie of the land ahead.

'How long was I asleep?' Windvogel asked when Jan Swaat came back down the gully.

'Half a day,' replied Jan Swaat. They never mentioned the episode again; fleeing together they became firm friends. On the eighth day of their flight, however, a patrol caught them sleeping beside a stream and arrested them. Along with two other deserters they were tied to two pack-mules and forced to walk all the way back to Cape Town.

In the dungeons of the Castle a German missionary prayed for them from breakfast till dinner and both were converted. With hallelujahs on their lips they were marched out on to the Parade to face a twelve-man firing squad. But at the very last moment Jan Swaat pulled out a knife, no one ever knew from where, and stabbed his friend Windvogel in the chest.

Grandma Kitty Riet always maintained: 'It definitely wasn't murder. Windvogel Valentyn was a child of God when he died. All Grandpa Jan Swaat did was to help him into paradise a little sooner.'

When Windvogel fell, there was chaos. A member of the firing squad evidently stopped Jan Swaat at the gate of the Castle and fired a shot into his chest at point-blank range. But because only every second musket issued to members of the fir-

119

ing squad had live ammunition in it, and all this man had in his gun was a charge of powder, all that happened was that Jan Swaat gained a black scorch mark on the chest. Jan headed into the Cape bush, on a horse which happened to be hobbled outside the Castle.

He rode very hard and very long, for he knew there would be no mercy for him now. He nearly died from thirst and hunger, but he was still resolved never to beg, scavenge or tell hard-luck stories. Jan Swaat knew he had only one life left, and he was a Christian now, so the issue of Windvógel Valentyn's blood on his hands was a matter which still needed to be sorted out with the Lord as he rode.

One day, exhausted after weeks of flight, as he sat on his half-starved horse, his mouth watering at the sight of a fat springbok ram grazing on a tussock of sourgrass at a distance of only fifty yards, a shot suddenly rang out. Jan Swaat dropped off the horse – he had crossed the Great Fish River into the wilderness by now and was no longer expecting firearms – but just before he slid from the saddle, he did notice that the springbok had also dropped. The horse neighed wildly and broke into a gallop, with Jan Swaat's foot caught in the stirrup and his head bouncing from the stones and anthills.

A horseman appeared out of a patch of trees, stopped beside the springbok, swung the dead antelope onto the stallion with a single movement, dug his heels into his horse's flanks and rode over to where Jan Swaat's horse was dragging him round and round in a circle. The man grabbed the runaway horse by the reins and looked down at Jan Swaat, flat on his back, covered in dust and grass, but mercifully still alive. From the ground the man looked savagely fierce: huge hooked nose, fiery eyes, dense black beard, hair swept back off the forehead and eyebrows.

The man looked down at Jan Swaat and said: 'I'm leaving on an expedition to the north tomorrow morning with a tracker. I need a helper.'

Jan Swaat followed FounderAbel Moolman back to his camp beside a river, and the next morning they left, accompanied by TameBushman who led them from one small stream to

120

another until they eventually reached the clear Eye of the Toorberg.

As a child Oneday had heard this story over and over again – especially on Sunday afternoons when the Skaamfamilie visited Jan Swaat's grave. 'Sleep peacefully, Jan Swaat,' Katie would say. 'You left your missionary father; you searched and found Toorberg; and gave yourself to it completely. You're sleeping in your own land.'

Oneday sighed and walked back across the loose stones and broken earth. As he hurried on again the moon was much higher. Deep in the dark valleys of the Toorberg foothills he heard the howl of a jackal and it gave him goose-pimples; he was relieved as he came closer to the bright lights of the Toorberg homestead. He caught the glint of a number of parked cars and noticed people standing around on the veranda. A soft breeze cooled his face as he passed through the marsh and began to lengthen his strides into the smell of woodsmoke coming down the wind.

He was longing for the hearth in his mother's house. When he pushed open the door and selfconsciously put his hand up to his clerical collar under his chin, the warm little bodies of his children hurled themselves against his legs. He hugged them all. Their hair smelt of the hearth, their necks of the grasslands of Toorberg and their breath against his face told of maize porridge and crackling.

'Ma Katie!' he called over the screen. 'I came by bus as far as the shop at Voetpad. Why are the buses not running to the Halt tonight?'

'Granny Katie's in the forest,' said one of the children.

'In the forest?' he asked, startled.

'She's praying for Noah Moolman.'

'Why, is he sick?'

'He's down the borehole.'

'You stay here.' Oneday ran out of the cottage and by the time his eyes were accustomed to the dark, he was a good thirty yards past the rabbit hutch. Once in the wood he followed the glow of the flames till he came to the clearing where a sheet of canvas had been hung between two tractors and lanterns were swinging from the anchor stays of the drilling machine. There was a large fire blazing off to one side.

He saw his mother sitting up against the trunk of a poplar, looking older and more tired than he had seen her in a long time.

'Oh, Oneday,' she said as he approached, 'the child is down that hole.'

He looked at the black mouth of the borehole, at the thongs and cables lying around, at the figures under the canvas.

'Since when, Ma Katie?'

'Since the sun was high, Oneday. He's cried himself hoarse.'

'Where's Shala?'

'He had an argument with CrossAbel. I think he's gone up the mountain.'

Oneday looked at the figures under the canvas again. 'Who is there?' he whispered.

'Abel. Ella. There's a doctor here, too.'

Uncomfortable, he adjusted his collar, stood up and went towards the canvas, turned round and came back. He bent down over the hole and looked down. Listening carefully, he could hear the rasping of little Trickle Moolman's breath.

He went back to Katie, asking 'What are they doing now?'

'They're trying to think of a new way to get him out. This afternoon they tore a piece of flesh out of his shoulder with a meat-hook. He's stuck. The doctor says if they don't get him out before tomorrow he's going to die. His ribs are crushing his lungs.'

'I must pray for him, Ma.' Oneday looked at his mother in the dark. It was difficult to fathom the expression on her face.

'A white minister has been here already, my child.'

'Where is he now?'

'He's gone again. He said a prayer at the borehole.'

'But I can also pray, Ma. I am here now, after all.'

Katie Danster reached out her hand. He felt the old, dry skin as her fingers closed round his wrist.

'Better pray in silence, Oneday. Perhaps God will hear you better then.'

Oneday looked at her for a long time, but she did not relax her hold. 'The Lord belongs to everybody, Ma Katie.'

She released his arm and sniffed. 'But not everyone belongs to the Lord, Oneday. Didn't you learn that in the far place you went to?' He heard her joints creaking as she got up. 'If you didn't, Oneday, then all your learning was a waste of time. You could have learnt it better on the Stiefveld, or here among the old men on the farm.'

She left him, walking away into the dark. He could not catch the sound of her footfalls, but as she passed through the fallen leaves of the grove and out onto the worn footpath, he could sense the movement of her feet: cracked feet, small feet with shrunken toes, feet tired from all the walking, feet twisted by arthritis and many, many miles, feet burnt by the sun and washed by the rain, feet frosted like leaves and yellow with age, feet that had once carried him, too – better than his own legs could do so now.

Chapter 22

'It was without any doubt the most terrible day of my life,' Amy O'Leary Moolman told the magistrate as they sat in the Moolmans' house at the Halt having a cup of tea. 'It was just too terrible for words.' She played absent-mindedly with the little medal at her throat.

'That medallion round your neck?' said the magistrate. His cup tinkled lightly against the saucer as he put it down.

'Oh, oh this.' Amy looked embarrassed. 'It's the face of my patron saint. You see, Mr Van der Ligt, strange as it may sound, I am a Catholic, even though I married a Moolman.' She shrugged her shoulders and smiled: 'My Irish ancestors must be turning in their graves at the thought of an O'Leary married to a Protestant!'

'Has it caused you many problems?' He lit a cigar and blew the smoke away from him, saying: 'I hope you don't mind my smoking?'

'No, not at all. The curtains always smell of Postmaster's pipe. Please carry on. This isn't Ella Moolman's parlour.' He smiled.

'Has the difference in religious affiliation caused many problems?' he asked again. He could not help but observe that the woman facing him was highly attractive: luxuriant black hair swept back into a thick bun, bright blue eyes, a youthful complexion.

'Indeed!' she cried. 'But like the Afrikaners,' she added with a gesture, 'we Irish are used to problems.'

Smiling, the magistrate nodded. 'You were telling me about that terrible day at the borehole . . .' he prompted her.

'No,' she checked him. 'No, you misunderstood me. The really terrible day was the day of the funeral. That was the day.'

'How come?'

'Well, you know, there was that whole fuss about the Skaamfamilie not being allowed into the church. You must surely have heard?'

He smiled around his cigar. 'I hear surprisingly little.'

'Oh.' She smoothed her skirt, looking slightly nonplussed. 'Well, anyway – Katie Danster's people wanted to attend the funeral, naturally enough. The service was to be held in the church in town and afterwards everyone was going to drive out to Toorberg for the filling in of the hole. Trickle was one of their relations, after all. Actually he and Katie Danster's grandchildren were cousins.'

'Yes?'

'And of course Katie's son Oneday, the pastor – who I hear has been picked up in the black township for his political activities – he wanted to say a prayer at the funeral. He felt it was a family occasion, after all, and he's the only minister in the family, do you see?' He nodded. 'And Katie, particularly, was deeply concerned, because she was the one who had shown Abel the spot in the grove where they should drill, because there had been a spring there in her childhood, she said. She felt that in one sense it had all started with her.' She paused for breath. 'Would you like some more tea?'

'No, thank you.' His stump was tender; he was thinking about the tin of cool ointment in the glove compartment of the car, the feel of the soft ointment between his fingers: massaging, massaging.

'Am I boring you?' she asked, but he shook his head, banishing all other thoughts.

'No, no. Not at all. Please continue.'

'Well, then the church council refused to allow the Skaamfamilie to attend the service. Simply refused; point-blank. Just like that.' Amy got up and took the cup from the magistrate's little table. 'I'll pour you some more.' The steam spiralled from the spout of the teapot.

'Thank you,' said the magistrate.

'Of course Abel Moolman is an elder in the church, and that son of his, that CrossAbel, who is the devil incarnate, is a deacon! I'm told that it was Abel himself who said the Skaamfamilie would be permitted to come to the hole but they were not to be allowed in the church. So Katie Danster's people simply had to wait outside in the shade. After that, only Katie would go to the grave. Shala and Oneday stayed away, which is perfectly understandable – to me at any rate. We took Katie in the car with us from the church back to Toorberg. If we hadn't, she'd still have been on the cart behind those mangy donkeys.'

'You pity them?' He tapped the ash off his cigar into the ashtray.

'What do you mean, Mr Van der Ligt!' She drew herself erect. 'Of course I pity them. Go and see for yourself how they live! StepMoolmans, just like us. Living on Toorberg's castoffs. The small mercy of the usufruct from FounderAbel's will keeps us all going. Thank God Abel has not been able to get the will altered. I believe he took a motion to the Supreme Court about it, but they refused to alter it.'

'Would Abel be capable of murder?' the magistrate asked suddenly, stubbing out his cigar.

Amy put a hand up to her hair. 'I couldn't say,' she said slowly, looking distractedly through the window. And then: 'I don't know. But there are other means of murder apart from shooting.'

The magistrate nodded. 'The Law sees matters in a different light.'

'The Law is clinical. It cannot measure suffering.'

'You are right.' He looked at his hand, at the nicotine-stained fingers. 'Were you present at the borehole on the final day?'

She nodded. 'We were all there.'

'And at whom, do you think, should the clinical finger of the Law be pointing?'

'You are wanting me to say Abel Moolman.'

'Not at all. I would not presume to put words into your mouth.'

Amy looked at the magistrate: a tired, ageing man with hunched shoulders and a stump of an arm. His hand, she noticed, was pale yellow. The fine wrinkles round his eyes could crease into a smile one moment and the next circle those eyes with lines of fatigue.

'What did they send you out here for?' she asked.

He shrugged, smiling. 'Every day,' he replied, 'I see more reasons why Justice should have sent me. An incident occurred which required the attention of the Law. There was a death; possibly a murder. Perhaps it was mere negligence: someone neglected to cover an old borehole into which children could fall. But it is my duty to establish whether there was *dolus*, or *culpa*. Guilt and negligence – that is my job.'

'And what is your own opinion?'

He smiled. 'I do not have one, yet.' Embarrassed, her hands smoothed over the skirt of her dress. 'I do not mind your asking,' he said. 'I am putting a great many questions to you, too.' He sighed, and then continued: 'My investigation is taking longer than I anticipated.'

'What do you think of Toorberg, then?'

'It is a beautiful farm. One of the most beautiful of all.'

'Is that all?'

'For the moment, that is all.'

He smiled at the Irishwoman. Here was someone who would be capable of understanding the significance of all his years as a public prosecutor and a magistrate: the interminable procession of criminal faces; lying faces; stupid, closed faces; scarred and tattooed faces; open, friendly faces which had committed naive murders; so many faces that after all his years in court he was quite unable to call to mind even one.

'Some more tea?'

'No, thank you.'

They heard the noise of a bus leaving. When the roar of the labouring engine had faded, he said: 'You have a very peaceful home.'

'Oh?' she said, surprised. 'Thank you. It sometimes bothers me. Homemaking is really the woman's responsibility, you know. But this business with Abel intrudes even here. Postmaster's health has deteriorated quite badly. Every morning he stands out there beside the wind-charger, looking at the Toorberg farmyard through De La Rey's binoculars. He watches Abel walking through the pens full of sheep – sheep which

127

should have been Postmaster's too. By rights.' She emphasized the final phrase, and then passed a tired hand over her eyes and laughed apologetically.

'You are living a good life, Mrs Moolman,' he said gently. 'You have a good husband and a good home, and you are doing good work at your school.'

'It could all have been so different.'

'But it isn't. That is all I can tell you.'

'You are right.' She smiled. 'You are quite right. Here you are trying to find a murderer and here I am boring you with all my own complaints! It's not really as bad as it sounds.'

They sat for a while not speaking, but without feeling uncomfortable.

'I understand your son Mailbag is rather friendly with a daughter of Katie Danster's?'

Amy did not bat an eyelid. 'Where did you hear that, then?'

He shrugged his shoulders. Suddenly, she noticed, he looked tired again. 'It is a small district,' he said, 'even though the distances are great.' She made no anser. 'Were you aware of it?'

'Yes,' she replied. The clock behind her chimed the hour. 'You should know, Mr Van der Ligt,' she continued softly: 'that I don't mind.'

'And your husband?'

'My husband will never know. I trust that you will not tell him.'

He smiled at her. 'I doubt whether my investigation would ever necessitate that, Mrs Moolman.'

'But?' She raised her eyebrows.

'That is all,' he said, with a shrug of the shoulders.

'But you raised the matter anyway?'

Looking at the mat in front of him, he stroked his stump. 'You should know, Mrs Moolman, that in this investigation I am having to feel my way in the dark. I need to form an image of . . . well, of an entire, extensive family and the relationships between its members.'

'And that is why you want to know more about Mailbag and Kitty Riet.'

'That is correct. And that is why I want to know more about everyone in the family. That, after all, is the whole purpose of my visit.' He needed to moderate the sharpness in his voice: it was not directed at her. It was more the result of impatience with the pain in his arm, and the sleeping clerk in the car outside, and the whispering intrigues about Toorberg which kept coming to his ears in the hotel.

'I wish I could tell you more about Mailbag and Kitty, but to the best of my knowledge it is an innocent friendship.' She smiled. 'I am a mother. I know things without my son having to tell me. I could see, at Trickle's funeral, when we stopped the car beside Katie's donkey cart to give her a lift back to the farm, how Mailbag looked at Kitty. There was something between them even then. She often comes past here, on her way from the Stiefveld to the shop at Voetpad, and always calls in, supposedly to fetch Granny Katie's mail. She's a very pretty child, believe me. I've noticed, when she's here at the Halt, that the buses have to hoot for attention – so she and Mailbag were probably having a cuddle on the quiet.' Amy's eyes had a mischievous twinkle. She winked and the magistrate felt himself blushing.

'You have a very open mind,' he said, trying to conceal his embarrassment.

She shrugged. 'I'm Irish. I'm not one of your Afrikaners. For me, a man is a man and a woman is a woman. Love is always the same. So what if he's half-Irish and she's half-English and descended from a missionary? It makes no difference.'

He did not reply, but noticed the reproof in her words: she made no mention of Kitty's Hottentot ancestry. A clever woman, he thought – not to be underestimated.

When the silence became too protracted, he lit another cigar. 'Are you sure you don't mind?' he asked, with the lighter-flame quivering at the tip of the cigar. 'What would disturb me,' he said, changing the course of the conversation, 'is the fact that these youngsters are blood relatives: after all, they are second cousins.'

She shrugged her shoulders. 'Inbreeding is a fact of life here. It has been going on for generations on these farms. It's such a small community. Tilly is a classic result of it. So was little Noah.'

He nodded, and then said: 'Mrs Moolman, I should like to pose the question once more: when, in your opinion, did Noah du Pisani die?'

She sighed and touched her hair. 'If I had known, I would have told you immediately.'

'I would have hoped so,' he teased, through the cloud of blue smoke. 'You see, he could already have been dead, when everyone thought he was still alive.'

He watched her face cloud over as her thoughts went back. She shook her head: 'I really couldn't say.'

'You see, when the shot rang out . . .' But before he could complete the sentence, she got up.

'I'll pour some more tea.'

'No, thank you. Truly, no more for me.' When she sat down again, he continued: 'You do not wish to be reminded of the incident?'

'Noah was one of my pupils. I knew the child well.'

'Was it really possible for anyone to know him?'

'He was slightly backward . . . retarded, if you like. But a dear child.'

'How seriously retarded?'

'Not really seriously. He could read a little, and write a bit. Perhaps he was just a late developer. But he spent very little time at school, actually. He was forever out following his father around the veld dowsing for water.'

'Do you think it likely that he could have fallen down a borehole by accident, or might he possibly, as a result of his handicap, have . . .?'

'I really don't know. I cannot see how he would deliberately have fallen down a hole. It must have been an accident.'

The magistrate sighed. His sinuses were itching from the cigar smoke. Amy sat watching him quietly.

'Tell me, Mr Van der Ligt,' she said guardedly, 'What would the law say if someone dug a hole into which no normal person was likely to fall, but then a child like Trickle came along

130

and tumbled in – what would your laws have to say about such a case?'

He smiled. 'You should have studied criminal law,' he said. 'For a layperson, you ask very intelligent questions.'

'My father was a barrister.'

'Oh, really?'

'Yes. In Ireland.'

'I see.'

They sat in silence for a while, until she asked: 'Well, what do your laws say about this case?'

He smiled again. 'It is a complex matter.'

'I am quite sure,' she said, once more patting her hair, 'that your laws will have nothing at all to say about mercy.'

'How do you mean?'

'You will see yet. Once your investigation has been completed, you will understand.' When she got up with the tea tray, he knew she wanted him to leave.

He stopped at the door, to remark lightly: 'Actually, I should have made you my assistant in this investigation.'

'Oh,' she said, laughing. 'I wouldn't have been terribly objective!'

'Who is?' he said, stepping out into the bright sunlight and across the gravel to the car, where the clerk was asleep with his head on the steering wheel.

Chapter 23

'When one examines the theory of criminal law,' wrote the magistrate to his wife that night, as the noise in the bar below set off a persistent barking among some dogs farther down the street, 'I, like many others involved in the administration of justice, incline towards the theory of the *conditio sine qua non*, according to which, my love, every act which constitutes an indispensable requirement for a particular condition is regarded as a cause of that condition. You will immediately appreciate that in criminal law causation is not the only condition for criminal liability. The issue of causation answers only the question regarding the causal relationship between the act of, say, Abel Moolman and the condition of, say, Noah du Pisani.

'Pursue the matter further, through an examination of the likelihood of intention or negligence, and one enters the field of my investigation. However, I have to confess to you tonight that in this inquiry I have already exceeded the bounds of my commission.

'The matter could become still more complicated, even if only to justify my commission by a display of theoretical punctiliousness: if Abel Moolman pushed Noah du Pisani into the borehole and Noah's father, Dowser du Pisani, (strange names, are they not?) arrive some time later and gave Noah the *coup de grâce*, there would appear to me to be a causal connection between Abel's act and the death of Noah.

'But only by virtue of the fact that it was a *coup de grâce*. In German law, if my memory serves me correctly, there is mention of an *alternativen Konkurrenz*, and both parties are held to be guilty of murder.

'That, my love, is the position. Does the Law ever ask moral questions? Here in this little country town all the clever theories seem to me no more than pompous procrastination. I fear that, for the first time in my professional career, I am straying from the precise parameters of my brief.

'You should understand that this is not something which I do lightly, particularly since it requires me to transgress a self-imposed rule. However, my affinity for the mystery of Toorberg is such that it has tempted me, my dear, to look further than mere intention or negligence, towards something which I am as yet unable to define, but which has gripped my imagination as no previous case has ever done.

'That, my love, is the excuse I have to offer for my long absence. I hope, as I know you do, that in due course I shall arrive at a decision. So far, though, I do not see my way clear either to overturn or to uphold my colleague's finding that there was no reason to suspect foul play. The consciousness of my responsibility in this regard weighs heavily upon me as I bid you good-night.

'Your husband and friend,
Abraham van der Ligt.'

He sat poring over the letter for a long time. It covered six pages, in the even, elegant script he was so proud of.

Then he folded the letter, but as he tapped his cigar on the ashtray, a scrap of hot ash landed on the paper and burnt a tiny hole in one page. The magistrate did not unfold the letter to see which word had been scorched: he slipped it into the envelope just as it was and put it on top of the little pile of unposted letters in the drawer.

Chapter 24

The question of how the child could have fallen down the borehole transported the thoughts of the aged Judge Lucius back to
his notorious lecture to the bar in which, starting with the Roman Twelve Tables, via Voet and Grotius, down to contem-
porary commentators both on the Bench and in the legal acade-
mies, he had been able to show that the entire corpus of the Law
could be centripetally focused on a single point: Crimes of the
Right Hand.

Now, however, he watched as Dowser du Pisani threw
more wood on the fire before going over to lie on his belly and
listen at the mouth of the hole, his head held on one side.

'We've got to dig,' Dowser said, pushing himself upright.
the light of the flames drew long lines round his mouth. 'Oh,
God help us, Mister Abel,' he said as Abel stooped to emerge
from under the canvas. Judge Lucius noted the heaving of the
dowser's shoulders. 'The child's dying down there, Mister
Abel,' he cried. 'And we're just standing around doing nothing.'

'Pull yourself together, Du Pisani!' Abel knelt at the hole,
sighed, and stood up again. 'Right,' he said. 'We'll try. Fetch
picks and shovels.' He paced out six metres from the mouth of
the hole, threw down his hat on the spot where he had dug his
heel into the ground and ordered the empty fuel drums that had
been standing around since the drilling operations to be rolled
closer. Some of the farm workers up-ended the drums between
the mouth of the hole and the site where the digging was about to
commence, to keep the worst of the dust away from the hole,
while Abel had the earth sprinkled with water and ordered that
the watering-cans be filled continually and kept ready.

Four men with shovels stood to one side waiting for two
others with picks to break the crust. Two wheelbarrows stood
ready to cart away the soil. Abel ordered brandy to be brought
from the library in the Toorberg homestead – the diggers would
be working through the night: they would need encouragement.

134

As the first pick bit into the earth, Trickle let out a high-pitched scream in the borehole. On the farmyard Abel's mastiffs began to bark, jumping up against the inside of the wagon house doors. They have scented death, thought Judge Lucius, and they won't stop hurling themselves at those doors until the child is finally silent.

Dowser du Pisani tilted one of the watering-cans to his mouth, drinking in long gulps. Between the pick-strokes, Judge Lucius heard him swallowing, water slopping down over his lip into his shirt. The men wielding the picks broke through the top few inches of earth and stood aside to allow the diggers to load the loose soil into the wheelbarrows for removal.

At first the picks sank easily through the loose leaves and humus, before their points bit into the crust of the black clay, leaving shining stroke-marks as they broke the earth. Abel leant against the tree, looking at his watch every few minutes. Inch by inch, the picks sank deeper; by the time Judge Lucius wandered off again, the hole was shin-deep.

He passed through the grove, then through the half-open gate into the farmyard. For a moment the dogs were silent. There was a yellowish moon just over the roof of the great house as he approached Ella's kitchen garden, so he kept to the shadow of the trees in the darkness, watching people moving about inside the house. Ella was standing and talking to a police sergeant in the sitting-room, her face pale as wax. Judge Lucius noticed the way she kept looking back over her shoulder as if expecting someone. The kitchen windows were steaming up on the inside as the servants worked with large pots. Passing down-wind from them, Judge Lucius caught the smell of soup.

A strange sensation overcame him in the hall: he was a child again, creeping into the house on a sultry Sunday afternoon while his parents were sleeping. He, OldAbel and Andreas had been outside, playing, in defiance of Grandmother Magtilt's orders.

He noted with satisfaction that virtually nothing had changed. Some of the paintings in the hall were by painters whom he did not recognize; there were unfamiliar magazines on the hall table; but FounderAbel's gilded cane with the capital A was still in the umbrella-stand in the passage; and his telescope, which had been moved from the library to the hall, still bore the dents which the brass casing had suffered during Soois's rebel sojourn among the ravines of the Toorberg. It was not people he missed, though Judge Lucius to himself, but things: New Year's Days, when the house was filled with people – not for the sake of the people, but because then the house was so full of life; Founder-Abel's cane in FounderAbel's own hand – not his father, but the cane itself, vigorously pointing here and thrusting there; Grandmother Magtilt standing in front of the mirror – not herself so much as the actual mirror, dimly, sadly, holding the image of a face.

In the bedroom which had been his as a child, he was surprised by a small vase of flowers on the bedside table. There was water in the tall porcelain jug beside the wash-basin, too, and the window was slightly open. A corner of the bedclothes had been folded back, ready for someone to slip in between the sheets.

Ella certainly keeps an eye on things, he thought. There were few signs of his occupation: a small watercolour which he had painted, somewhat ineptly, before it became clear that Andreas was the one with artistic gifts; a framed Latin poem by Cicero. He recognized the smell, though: it was the Toorberg smell, coming up from the floor, out of the water in the porcelain jug, off the plaster on the walls.

Farther down the passage he went into the library. On a rolltop desk stood the bust of FounderAbel which Andreas had made during his first visit from the city, with the sole but unsuccessful aim of winning his father's favour on behalf of the arts. That desk was the one FounderAbel had imported from England before his death. The larger desk, in the centre of the room, was one which OldAbel had had made, as were the glass-fronted bookcases. The new gun-rack with its twenty gleaming guns of various calibres ranged one above the other was probably one of Abel's relatively recent additions.

Here, in the heart of Toorberg, Judge Lucius suddenly felt like a trespasser. Half-ashamed, he turned back before he had even allowed himself enough time to savour the smell of old books, gun oil and cigar smoke properly. Outside in the night he knew that he had left no footprints on Toorberg. His years at the bar and on the bench had brought him recognition and renown, but the right to leave his footprints on the farm of his birth was denied him.

In the wagon house the barking boer mastiffs were still leaping up against the locked doors. He wandered on among all the places where he had played as a child. The irrigation furrow to the peach orchard, which he as a small boy had bravely helped to dig, was lined with concrete now, and had neat cement sluices.

The silver leaves of the trees were trembling in the moonlight. Stopping in front of the ram shed, he was again struck by the pungent stench of the urine of generations of rams, and went inside. At first the animals stirred nervously as he passed between them.

How the great stud rams used to butt him, always gently, sniffing at his open palms! How rough the outer surface of their fleeces always felt when he ran his hand along their backs, but how wonderfully soft the wool was when he burrowed his fingers deep into it, before withdrawing them again, sticky with lanolin. He would push his way through the rams to the back door of the shed, slide it open and look back at the indistinct humps staring silently at him.

When one of the rams now started urinating loudly, Judge Lucius went out through the back door.

Voices were wafting towards him from the direction of the poplar grove. Odd, thought Judge Lucius, how on every visit he made to Toorberg his route always remained the same: the poplar grove, the kitchen garden, the great house – always ending with the library – then the orchard, the ram shed and eventually, after the implement sheds and the outbuildings, the open veld behind the stock pens where one could walk and walk and walk, over low bushes and tussocks of grass, over stones that had been undisturbed for ages, over the dew of night and the faint tracks left by nocturnal animals. There one could rest as one walked without ever needing to pause for breath.

Judge Lucius remembered the visits he had made to Toor-

berg while he had been in practice in the city. He and Founder-
Abel would sit on the riempie-bench on the front stoep, and
after their second glass of brandy FounderAbel, cautiously but
with barely repressed aggression, would start his interrogation.

'How many souls do you send to the gallows each month?'
FounderAbel would ask. Or: 'What does the Law say about the
taxman's demands for my wool income?' And, without fail:
'Can't the Law get rid of the British for us?' Patiently Judge
Lucius would then try to respond, but he learnt eventually that
the only way to silence his father was by quoting a string of legal
terms and precepts from Roman Law at him in Latin. Founder-
Abel would listen in amazement at the words bubbling out of
Judge Lucius's mouth, then suck audibly at his pipe and impatiently snatch at a mosquito. 'Yes, we'd be a lot better off without the Law,' he would say, and end the conversation.

At the feed store Judge Lucius heard a noise. It sounded
like a woman talking softly. At first he thought he might have
come upon CrossAbel and a girlfriend, and was about to turn
away – but when he noticed that the door had been locked from
the outside, his curiosity got the better of him.

Peering through the window of the feed store, he saw Crazy-
Tilly sitting on a pile of sacks, hugging her shoulders as she
rocked back and forth in the moonlight. When she threw back
her head, and he saw her shining eyes, the beautiful bloom on
her cheeks and the clean, straight lines of her mouth and chin, he
understood why she was regarded as the most beautiful woman
in the district. She was mouthing a constant stream of words,
but he could not make out what she was saying. Then she got up,
took a hessian sack in her arms and facing the window, slowly
began to rock on her feet. Then the rocking became a dance and
her crooning increased in volume until it became a high-pitched,
incomprehensible keening.

All of a sudden she stopped and looked directly at Judge
Lucius. Coming over to the window, she fixed him with a de-
mented stare, the sharp, focused blackness of her pupils stark
against the whiteness of her eyeballs. Soon, unnerved and upset,
he had to turn away.

He did not stop moving until he reached the open veld, out of earshot of the bodies of the rams chafing against one another, of the singing Tilly, of the thudding of picks, and of the banging of doors in the great house. Here, far from the graveyard with the stone bearing his carved name and *Carpe Diem*, his life's motto, he was able to regain control and persuade himself that he had a real body and a firm step again. Here he could fill his lungs with the freshest winds blowing off the slopes of the Toorberg and start moving, weightless, wingfooted, free as an eagle, nimble as a meerkat. Round and round, over and over he spun in the moonlight: a silver tumbleweed bouncing in the wind.

Chapter 25

The magistrate took the week's pile of letters, with his wife's name and address on each envelope, to the bathroom. There he slowly tore them up and watched the scraps of paper fluttering down into the toilet bowl. It was a long process since he had to flush repeatedly to prevent the pipes from blocking up. Eventually, though, the task was done. He took a clean shirt from his suitcase, put it on and sat down in his shirt and underpants at the small table in front of the window.

'My dear wife,' he wrote. 'It is years since last I wrote to you so regularly. It is a new means of conversation, one to which I have yet to become accustomed. I trust my letters do not sound like court pronouncements? It is usually only my judgements which I write on paper, and to express an opinion on the behaviour of others in the formulations of the Law. In fact, I am not capable of doing anything else in writing. Or in life as a whole either: perhaps you would understand this even better than I do?

'Thus far, I have been unable to establish the limits of human sin. All my years on the Bench have brought me no nearer to a solution. But if I . . .'

The magistrate sat looking at his pen for a long while. The unfinished sentence had many possibilities, but he knew that only one would be the truth. For that reason, and because it was already dinner time, he closed the writing pad and stood up from the table.

He had his dinner under the lazy fans in the dining-room and then went out into the dusk for a leisurely stroll under the row of pine trees in front of the hotel. It was Sunday evening and the town was quiet.

'But if I . . .' he said to himself. The unfinished sentence was haunting him. As he passed the church, he heard the droning of the organ.

At last, when the congregation's cars had all long since left, he realized that he thought of his wife as he did of himself, that there was no distinction between them any more, that he could not love her any more, since their lives had become one to such an extent that he could no longer move out of himself towards her.

Chapter 26

The news reached him as he sat in the small office assigned to him in the court building, looking out at the courtyard where the convicts were engaged in their daily task of raking the gravel. Abel Moolman had disappeared without trace. That this should happen now, he thought in the moments of initial alarm, when he was gradually but inexorably gathering sufficient information for the interview which would probably be the most important of all: the one with Abel.

It was his colleague, the magistrate Botes, still in his court gown, who came in panting with the news. 'The search for him has already fanned out as far as the Camdeboo, apparently. He has been missing for thirty-six hours.'

'Well I never,' said the magistrate in surprise when his colleague left. 'Well I never.' He drew the file on Abel Moolman nearer, letting his eyes run swiftly over the notes he had made so far. Then he noted: 'Urgent report: Abel Moolman has disappeared. Leaving immediately for Toorberg to investigate.'

He had the clerk stop in front of the pharmacy first, though. With the empty ointment tin in his hand, he asked for a refill. 'The pharmacist promised to order some of this for me.'

The assistant returned with a new tin. 'Here it is, Your Worship,' she said. 'We have more in stock should you require any.'

He thanked her and paid for it.

'Abel Moolman has disappeared without a trace,' he told his driver. The clerk reacted politely but without interest. The magistrate massaged the cool, pink ointment into his stump. Having been asked to hurry, the clerk was driving faster than usual. The magistrate opened Abel's file and carefully studied the notes he had made after each interview.

As they drove up through the avenue to the homestead, Ella appeared on the front veranda, peering as though she had been expecting them.

142

He got out, but Ella remained motionless, regarding him with a strange, fixed stare as he approached.

'Good morning,' he said, as he mounted the lowest step.

'For a moment I thought you were De la Rey, Abel's brother,' she said. 'When the sun caught the car's windscreen as you came up the avenue . . .'

'Yes, indeed,' he replied. 'We left in haste and in a different car from the one we have used previously.' He smiled. 'It must be your concern for Mr Moolman.' She nodded. He mounted the stairs and stopped in front of her. She was about an inch taller than he was. 'Have you informed the police?'

She shook her head. 'We'll search on our own first.'

He touched his arm. The clerk in the car had watched them for a while, but now sank back into his seat. This time he had brought along something to read. The magistrate noticed a lurid dust-cover on the book. Abel's surly mastiffs were circling the car, cocking their legs against the wheels.

'The dogs no longer even bark when you drive into the yard,' said Ella. He did not know whether to regard this as an insult or a compliment.

'I have noticed that,' he said, 'but they were never excessively aggressive towards me.'

'It's odd, actually. They usually bark at every stranger.'

He shrugged.

She then asked: 'Have you come on business?'

He sighed. 'Partly out of concern, Mrs Moolman. When I heard that your husband had disappeared, I came immediately.'

She raised her eyebrows: 'And partly?'

He waved his arm: 'Partly, you will understand, on business.'

'You think he has run away because you are here on commission?'

'That would be putting it too crudely.'

'But that is what it boils down to.'

'No, Mrs Moolman, it is merely my task to ascertain what happens here. It all falls within my jurisdiction. That is all. If this visit is inconvenient, please forgive me.'

She smiled indulgently: 'I am being unfair on you. Come in and have a cup of tea.' He followed her indoors. As they went down the passage, she said: 'He will come back. This is not the first time a Moolman male has disappeared without leaving any message. The Moolmans are like that. When they get restless, they simply take off. They don't think they owe anybody an explanation.'

They were in the sitting room. 'Not even their wives?' he asked.

'FounderAbel would regularly take his horse and his bondsman and head off into the blue when things on the farm began to get on his nerves,' she said. 'And OldAbel once disappeared for three months on end, before returning with a wagonload of ivory. He'd been across the Limpopo, as far as the great falls. Granny Olivier simply had to sit and wait. So did Grandmother Magtilt. How could I expect any greater consideration than they got?'

The magistrate lit a cigar. 'But did they also send out search-parties, Mrs Moolman?'

She looked at him for a long time. Finally she asked: 'Would you prefer tea or coffee?'

'Tea, please.' As she went out, he heard a bakkie stop outside and, looking through the window, saw CrossAbel striding up, binoculars round his neck and a water-bottle in his hand. The front door banged. There were footsteps in the passage and CrossAbel appeared in the doorway. He looked at the magistrate, then fixed his eyes on the stump.

'You are the magistrate,' he said.

'That is correct. How do you do?' Over the handshake, he looked into CrossAbel's ill-tempered eyes.

'It's the wrong time to come visiting.' CrossAbel stood with his legs apart on the lionskin rug. The chill, green glass eyes of the stuffed lion's head stared up from between his wide-set feet.

'Abel . . .' It was Ella, but before she had said anything, the maid came in with the tea tray, so she turned away. When the servant withdrew, she said: 'Let's have tea.'

'I am sorry if my visit is inconvenient,' the magistrate began. He looked at CrossAbel. 'Do you have any news?'

CrossAbel shook his head. 'Nothing.'

'He will come back,' said Ella.

Uneasily, CrossAbel strode over to the window and looked out. 'I've come for more drinking water,' he said. 'It's bloody hot up in the mountain. And dry. The windmills in those back fields are sucking up nothing but wind. I've been telling Dad for a long time that we should get the drilling machine going again . . .' Ella silenced him with a sharp gesture of the head. He swung round and went out; the lionskin remained crumpled on the floor.

'It's a beautiful skin,' said the magistrate as Ella handed him his tea. 'Is there a big-game hunter in the family?'

'This was the last lion shot in this area,' she replied. 'OldAbel shot it high up in the mountain. They say it moved up from the plains of Camdeboo when the British were laying the first railway line. A great deal of wild game fled at the approach of the first steam locomotives.' She patted her hair. 'Sad, really. They say that when FounderAbel set up his original camp here, lions were plentiful.'

'That is what civilization does.' They sipped their tea in silence.

'When Abel and I were married,' said Ella, 'my father-in-law made us a present of the skin. It was a rather fine gift, don't you think?'

'Certainly.'

'De la Rey would never have accepted it, even as a gift,' said Ella. 'He doesn't believe in shooting.'

'Oh, really?'

'No. He is quite different from the other Moolmans. It's no wonder he fled to the city. This is not the sort of country he could live in.'

'But he used to return frequently on visits, did he not?' The magistrate set down his cup. Ella stood up to close the curtains slightly, to keep the sun off her face.

'Yes, he did,'' she said. 'In his own way.'

'How do you mean?'

'Oh, De la Rey was always different. And he'll go on being different till the day he dies.'

The magistrate cleared his throat, and then said gently: 'But I was under the impression that he was already dead?'

Ella looked at him, her eyes clear and bright. Then she rose, went over to the wall, took down a portrait and brought it to him. 'Look,' she said, 'this is De la Rey. Years ago, of course, as a young man.'

'Oh. Oh, I see.' He looked at the man staring up at him out of the photograph. 'So this is what De la Rey looked like.'

She returned the portrait to its place. 'Would you like some more tea?'

He gestured, replying: 'No, no. Thank you very much.'

She poured herself another cup.

'Your son is very concerned about your husband's disappearance.'

'Oh, Abel,' she said, resuming her seat. 'He takes after his great-uncle Soois. As bloody-minded as can be, if you'll excuse the expression. He's forever in the army. He goes into town on patrol in the locations every weekend, you know. I've given up worrying about it. It's in his blood.'

'Is Soois the one who was shot here on the farmyard?'

'Yes. You know your history well! Yes, he disliked Queen Victoria, so he formed a commando with a number of young men and they hid up in the Toorberg. One day when his father wanted to see him, the Tommies ambushed him. Their patrol was cunningly concealed. When Soois took a peep over the wall, he was shot in the throat by the younger brother of the Roman Catholic governess at Doornbosch. They say he was an ancestor of Amy O'Leary's, but nobody has ever proved it. Anyway, it was one of the reasons why OldAbel would have nothing to do with Amy. The O'Learys all came to Africa because of their asthma. When they heard how Cecil Rhodes's asthma had improved, and how he'd made money too, and become famous into the bargain, a whole swarm of Irishmen and Englishmen and Scotsmen with lung complaints embarked for the Cape. That's how the O'Learys got here. They say Mailbag, too, suffers from a tight chest occasionally, when the buses kick up too much dust down at the Halt.' She looked at him. 'You know Mailbag, don't you?'

146

'I have had some conversation with him.'

'Well, do you know,' Ella continued, 'when the anniversary of Soois's murder comes round each year, that wall still shows a red tinge of his blood. Every year we try to paint it out, but it's queer – if you touch the wall with your finger, it feels warm and sticky.' She was leaning over towards him intently.

'Really?' said the magistrate.

'But we keep away from there,' she continued. 'You'll never see a Moolman walking down beside the garden wall. Even CrossAbel is as scared of that part of the farmyard as he is of the devil himself. Apparently, the gardener won't do any hoeing down there before he has paid a visit to the Malay. Or so the maids in the kitchen tell me.'

'May I smoke?'

'Please do.' As she went on talking, he gained the impression that she appreciated having a willing ear to listen to her. 'The British took and buried Soois in quicklime in an unmarked grave, somewhere in the servitude land beside the black location outside the town. But Soois's rebellion was no disgrace to the Moolmans: he had the spirit to rise up against the British colonialists. He and his commando were almost the only young men in the district who did not become tame little Englishmen during the Boer War. All the others went up north to help the British fight Generals De Wet and De la Rey.'

'I see.' He exhaled slowly. 'Toorberg has a rich history. You must be proud of it.'

'It's not always easy to be the wife of a Moolman.'

'I could imagine that there would be many demands made on you.'

'The Moolmans are never content with only a little.'

'Your entire history, your beautiful farm, are testimony to that.'

'Do you really think,' she asked, 'that ours is a beautiful history?'

He thought for a moment, letting his eyes run over the portraits. 'The history of the taming of a country,' he said after a while, 'can seldom be completely beautiful. Inevitably,' he

147

pointed to the lionskin, 'there will be cases such as these. Perhaps there have to be Sooises too. But there must also be the De la Reys who turn their backs on such things. That is the course of history.'

'But you believe there is something rotten about it, don't you?'

'How do you mean?'

'I mean the reason for your being here on commission.'

He was silent for a while before replying: 'Noah du Pisani's death might have been an accident.'

'You don't really believe that. It is well known that you are sounding everyone about the story.'

'Surely you are sensible enough to realize that that is my duty?' he asked, stroking his stump. He could not be angry with her – this intense, troubled woman. 'I have been sent here by the Department of Justice with the express purpose of determining whether or not justice has been done. I must take every single possibility into account.'

'And you think it possible that my husband could have murdered Noah and that he has now run away on account of all your questions?'

'You are placing me in the dock.'

Ella laughed. 'You are my guest. I should never wish to treat you discourteously. You serenity reminds me of De la Rey.' She looked at the portrait again, took a deep breath and then looked straight at him. 'I must tell you,' she said, 'the Moolmans are people who do things their own way. You should not try to relate everything which happens here to the death of Noah du Pisani.'

'I am doing my best to conduct a rational investigation.'

She smiled again and looked at her watch. 'It's nearly two o'clock. It seems CrossAbel has gone off again. Would you like to stay for lunch? You and your driver?'

'Oh,' said the magistrate, surprised. 'I should be delighted.'

Chapter 27

Wet with sweat, the men with the picks were up to their waists in
the hole when Postmaster Moolman got up and went over to
where Mailbag was sitting up against one of the tractor's wheels.

'Mailbag,' he said, 'take the car and make sure everything at
the Halt is locked up. And don't forget to take the brake off the
wind-charger.'

'And feed the fowls,' Amy called after him as Mailbag disappeared between the dark trunks of the poplars.

It was a beautiful moonlit night. The picks had passed to a
second team of labourers while the first gang were on the back
stoep at the homestead, drinking tots of brandy dispensed by
Abel into shiny tin mugs. Ella hurried out of the back door,
followed by two maids carrying large pots of soup.

Mailbag had trouble getting Postmaster's car to start.
Eventually, with some jerking, he drove off, the headlights
sweeping shakily over the wagon house, the sheds, the flower
garden and the avenue.

The barking of the mastiffs made him wind up his window,
mumbling 'Bloody mongrels.' The next moment, from behind,
a hand moved over his eyes.

'Omigosh!' He braked so hard that the old Borgward
skidded on the gravel road. In the rearview mirror he saw the
laughing face of LittleKitty Riet. The car jerked to a halt and the
headlamps faded to a dull glimmer. 'LittleKitty! What a fright
you gave me!' He turned round, pretending to be angry. 'And
now the car has gone and died on me too!' She giggled mis-
chievously. 'What are you doing in my dad's car?'

'I was at the borehole when I heard your dad sending you
home, Mailbag, so I took the short cut past the graveyard and
ran and hid in the car.'

'I didn't know you were at the borehole.'

'I was sitting near the back, with Ma Katie.' She leant over
to him. 'Aren't you glad?'

149

'Oh! Oh! Am I glad!' He learnt back and pulled her forward till she tumbled over the seat beside him. She smelt of wood-smoke and dung-floors and everlastings and Sunlight soap: the smell of all the Skaamfamilie. '*Meidjie,*' he teased, tickling her in the ribs.

'Mailbag!' she scolded. 'You're not to call me that.' She pushed him away. 'Oneday says we don't take that sort of language any more.'

'Yes, and see where it's landed Oneday,' he teased. 'A clever pastor in the location.'

'Not location either,' she said, with mock acidity. 'Oneday calls them townships.'

'And you? What do you say?' he tickled her. 'You're my cousin, I can call you whatever I like.' He drew her closer. 'And do whatever I like too!'

He bumped the hooter with his elbow by mistake, which set Abel's dogs barking and jumping up against the doors all over again.

'Poor little Noah,' said LittleKitty, suddenly quiet.

Mailbag sighed. 'Yes,' he said. They looked out ahead of them. Then he turned round and looked back. 'We must go. Soon someone will come and want to know what is happening.' He turned on the ignition.

She leant over to him as he drove. 'Old Floris Moolman,' she teased him. 'Always scared that Abel is going to catch you.' She dug him in the ribs. 'FounderAbel's going to kick you out if he catches you with the *meidjie.*'

'And you,' he retorted. 'Jan Swaat's old Kitty! Daughter of the tame Pandour, the runaway son of James Read: I'd keep my mouth shut if I were you!'

She played along: 'Why, Floris Moolman?'

'Because, GranmaKitty, you don't even know who your mother is, and what's more, 'cos Jan Swaat crawled out of a donga in the desert.'

She sat up quickly. 'No, Mailbag,' she protested. 'No, we'd better stop talking about the old people like this. They've earned their rest.'

At the junction he did not turn right towards the Halt, but swung the Borgward left.

'Where are you going now?'

'Away!' he said. 'Down to the Camdeboo, down to the Cape, away from the whole lot of them!'

'What about your mother's fowls?'

He put his foot down. 'Let them eat grit, like my dad!'

'No, Mailbag!'

'They're StepMoolmans!'

'And the brake on the wind-charger?'

'It can brake itself to bits!'

They rolled down the windows and raced along the road that stretched white in the moonlight to the edge of the farthest hills.

'And the red buses!' she shouted above the rush of the wind and the clatter of gravel under the car.

'I hope they all crash into the ditch!' he shouted joyfully, as they slithered round a bend. 'I couldn't give a damn!'

'And what about your mailbags, Mailbag!' she taunted him.

'They've lost their stamps,' he laughed. 'They're not worth anything. They can't go any farther than the ditch!'

'And CrossAbel, Mailbag?'

'Oh, he can crash his motorbike into the cowshed, the cramp-arse!'

'Cramp-arse!' she laughed. 'CrossAbel the cramp-arse!'

'From sitting astride that motorbike. Brrm, brrm, here I come, the boss's son CrossAbel. Get-outa-my-way-I'm-the-hell-in!'

The road climbed and twisted up to the top of a rise. Below, the plains of Camdeboo stretched away into the black distance beneath them. The pass wound its way down the mountain, the bends marked by white-painted railings. Mailbag turned off the road.

'There it is: the Camdeboo.'

Kitty leant against him. 'It's quiet here,' she said. And a while later: 'Think how dark it must be round poor little Trickle.'

'My mother thinks he keeps losing consciousness,' said

Mailbag. 'She says she doesn't think he knows any more what is happening round him.'

'Perhaps it's better that way.' The fresh scents of the veld wafted in through the open windows.

'Look,' he said. 'Do you see that light? That's old Ben Spiekeries's farm. And over there, if you screw up your eyes a bit, you can just make out the lights of Eerste Station. Look carefully.' They sat there for a long time.

At last she said: 'We're on top of the world here.'

'There are ghosts here,' he cautioned. 'In the war, Great Uncle Soois's commando hid up here watching the British troops. The British couldn't move anywhere on the plain without their knowing it.'

'And the ghosts?'

'Dead British soldiers were killed here in the pass pursuing Soois's men.'

'Ugh!' she said. 'Peace is much better than war.' She squeezed her shoulder into his armpit. 'I like peace.' He kissed her. Her tongue played across his lips. 'And I like Mailbag Moolman too.'

'There's a car coming,' said Mailbag. Kitty sat up, and they watched the car winding slowly up the pass.

'We'd better turn back, Mailbag.'

'Not necessary. We'll just sit still.'

'But what if they recognize you?' she asked, frightened.

'Stay where you are, Kitty. They won't stop. People are too scared to stop here on the road at night.'

The car was so near they could hear its engine.

'Mailbag? Shouldn't I get out and wait behind those thorn bushes till they've passed?'

'Damn it, Kitty, will you sit still? Just listen to me. Stay where you are.'

When the car crested the rise and the headlights played full on them, Kitty ducked down, lying with her head against his knees. He could feel her heart thumping against his thigh. The lights dazzled him as the car whirred past in a haze of dust and fine gravel.

'Gone,' said Mailbag. 'See, nothing to be afraid of.' But then the car stopped and slowly reversed.

Kitty ducked down again. A stranger rolled down his window. 'Everything OK, mate?' he asked. Mailbag smiled at him. There was a jacket hanging from the hook behind his head. A sales rep, thought Mailbag.

'Fine, thanks,' he nodded to the stranger. 'I'm waiting for another chap. We're going to hunt springhares.'

'Oh, I see,' said the man. 'I just thought I better stop. It's such a deserted part of the world, this. How far to the nearest bar?'

'Fifty kilometres to town,' said Mailbag.

'Where are you going hunting?'

Kitty bit the back of Mailbag's hand. 'Down in the Cambedoo.'

'I see. Well, "Happy hunting", as they say!' The man waved and drove off.

When Kitty sat up again, Mailbag noticed tears shining on her cheeks.

'The man's gone Kitty. Were you frightened?' She shook her head. 'But Kitty! Why are you crying? The man didn't see you. You were beautifully hidden!'

'That's the whole point,' she sobbed. She sniffed, wiping away the tears with the back of her hand. Mailbag sighed. 'I'm just a *meidjie*,' she said. 'I have to hide like a thief.'

'But Kitty!'

'No, Mailbag, I keep getting headaches from all this lying. And Ma Katie knows, too. She sits watching me in the evenings, with those clever little eyes of hers. She never says anything, never asks anything either. She just sits there, and when I complain of the pain in my head, she gives me that brew of the Malay's. And whenever she gives it to me, she says: "Kitty, you've got the most beautiful blue eyes." That's all she says, Mailbag. Never anything more. Like: Is there trouble between you and Mailbag? Or: Are you having your red time regularly? Or: Are you still meeting him in the Vlei? Or: Have people found out about you? No, all she ever talks about are my blue eyes.'

153

'But they are beautiful eyes,' he comforted her. When she made no reply, he continued: 'Aunty Katie is trying to tell you that you've got white blood, Kitty,' he said gently. 'She doesn't want you to feel like . . .'

'Like what, Mailbag?'

'Oh, I don't know. It's just, she's just trying to comfort you, that's all.'

Kitty sat up straight. 'You think she doesn't want to make me feel like just anybody? She wants to tell me I'm a Moolman?'

'Well, yes. You know how proud she is of the connection.'

'But can't she see that neither Shala nor Oneday nor I want to be Moolmans? Our father specially went and bought us a different name!'

'Your mother is different.'

She sighed. 'We must go, Mailbag. There poor Noah is, stuck in the hole, and here we are in the car high above the Camdeboo.'

As they drove off, she asked: 'Do you think they'll be able to dig him out?'

'I think he's already dying,' said Mailbag. 'I went over and listened just before I got into the car. It was dead quiet in the hole.'

She put her hand up to her mouth. 'Poor little white boy,' she said, as they turned in to the Halt and Mailbag parked the car behind the house.

'Are you coming?' he asked.

She shook her head. 'The dog will attack me.'

'Oh, nonsense. Come.' He held the gate open for her. Just to one side of the dark house he loosened the crank-handle on the wind-charger. It squeaked noisily, and then they heard the wind catching the vanes. 'We must oil the thing,' he said, fumbling with the front door keys.

There was a kettle smoking on the stove. 'Oh, my mother must have forgotten about the kettle when we went haring out of here to the grove. It has boiled dry. May as well thow it away, I suppose.' When she made no reply, he looked round and saw her leaning against the far wall. 'Kitty?'

'This is the first time I have seen where you live,' she said softly.

He nodded, put the kettle back on the stove and dropped the potholder on the table.

'We must go, Mailbag,' she said when he got close to her.

'I want to show you my room first.' She would have protested, but he took her hand and steered her ahead of him down the passage. In the dark room, he had to fumble for a candlestick, but eventually managed to light a candle. 'Look!' he pointed excitedly. 'This is where I lie at night, thinking about all that we have talked about.' He saw her looking at the dart-board with its red darts. 'I take it over to the Halt,' he told her. 'None of the bus drivers can beat me.' He opened his wardrobe. 'And here is the Post Office Certificate that I told you about. I want to have it framed one day. Look.'

'It's nice, Mailbag,' she said. 'Sixty percent is high.'

He smiled. 'Sit on the bed, Kitty. Feel how comfortable it is.' He crouched at her feet. 'Better than the reeds in the Vlei, eh, Kitty?' His eyes were shining.

'Stop it, Mailbag.' She got up. 'We must get back. People will come looking for us. Noah is dying down in that hole.'

'The Moolmans can tidy up their own mess,' he grumbled.

'Could the Noah-child have helped being born?'

He shook his head. 'I suppose not.'

'Ma Katie always says he's a child of heaven. You can tell from the way he listens.'

He nodded. They went outside and he locked the house behind him. She watched him feeding the fowls. Back in the car, she said: 'It's a nice house, and I like your room.' She cuddled up to him again.

Just before they reached the gate to the Toorberg homestead, he stopped to let her out. Her fingers were still warm on his arm as he drove up alone to the brightly lit house.

155

Chapter 28

Floris Moolman watched with interest as a twelve-man search party fanned out over the foothills of Toorberg. He was standing beside one of the few remaining pillars of the aqueduct, watching CrossAbel shouting orders to his men, binoculars in one hand, water-bottle in the other. OldAbel's grandson all right, thought Floris.

Ruefully, he thought of the story about himself which he'd picked up in a pub years before. The last traces of Founder-Abel Moolman's errant son, so the boozy breath of the drunk had told him, were the marks left in the dust of the farmyard by FounderAbel's hippo-hide whip. Between the whiplashes, said the drunk, you could see the marks left by Floris Moolman's elbows and knees as he scrabbled in the dust to escape his father's fury.

'And all that fuss, mind you,' the drunk giggled in his face, 'because old Floris was carrying on with the daughter of FounderAbel's tame Pandour – a murderer that escaped the firing squad at the Castle years before. And the girl had no mother either.' The grinning drunk nearly knocked over Floris's rum. 'Nobody knows where on earth Jan Swaat got hold of her.'

That drunk was the last man Floris ever hit with his fists, and with his butting head, too – something he'd learnt from Jan Swaat – and with the same knees and elbows that the drunk had so contemptuously dismissed.

He'd never really been a fighter – not willingly anyway. He'd sacrificed a lot of honour in life; some would probably go so far as to say all his honour. But there comes a time for every man when breaking point is reached, and that point had now come for Floris. He gave the man the hiding of his life, but then of course he had to flee again. Even now, when he ought to have shed his fear of the living, he could not rid himself of the flinching inherent in his nature. That thrashing on the farmyard, his father's wordless mouth and flashing eyes, his silent brothers, his broken-hearted mother: these were things he would never be able to shake off.

He was watching now as LittleKitty appeared in front of the cottage, shook out a blanket and then stood staring up at the mountain and the band of searchers. She was the spitting image of her grandmother: the same fine, high cheek-bones and narrow nostrils, the same almond-shaped eyes. But the colour of her eyes, like his own, were Moolman-blue. He found it hard to believe, across the chasm of the years, that this was his grandchild.

When travelling from one district to another in charge of the mailcoach, he'd heard that his child was a boy, and that they'd called him Andries because the Moolmans had refused permission for him to be given a family name. Born to Kitty Riet, (daughter of Jan Swaat, who maintained that the English missionary James Read was also one of her ancestors), and begotten of Floris Moolman, son of FounderAbel, the pioneer of the Agter-Sneeuberge. That was what pedlar told him one night at an outspan in the Camdeboo.

Wherever he went under his false name, Floris Moolman acted the gossip-monger, cautiously probing everyone he met for information about himself. Everybody knew the story, and everyone had something further to add: how FounderAbel had caught Floris and Kitty among the reeds down in the Vlei; how he had caught her in broad daylight under Floris's bed; how Jan Swaat had himself dragged the two of them before Founder-Abel; how Floris had resisted to the last, demanding his birthright; how to a man the other brothers had ducked when Floris suddenly pulled out a pistol and began shooting wildly; how the child had been born with a caul and his fist in his mouth – a half-caste bastard with a curse on his descendants . . .

It was strange, Floris Moolman often thought in those years after he had been driven from Toorberg, how low a man would sink in search of himself. Time and again he denied his identity, just to be able to hear something about Floris Moolman from someone, anyone – just to feel that he was somebody, something more than a flinching dodger driving a rickety government coach from outspan to outspan.

157

Like this, in the half-truths of dozens of distorted tales told in the bars of the Camdeboo and the Great Karoo, he had ensured that his name would survive.

Until that night at the Eerste Station outspan. After a long haul he had brought the mailcoach to a halt beside a spring where two other drivers had already unharnessed their wagons. One was a pedlar, the other with an escort of five horsemen was transporting guns for the government. With the five guards posted round the ammunition coach, Floris, the pedlar and the coach driver got to drinking round the fire.

'Down Cape Town way,' said Floris after a while, steering the conversation in a new direction, 'the blokes are all going for nigger girls, one after another. It's a disgrace the way the Church says nothing about it.'

'That's true, you know,' said the pedlar. 'Ten days ago I stopped on a Huguenot's farm up in the Northwest. When he called his wife to come and look at my stuff, would you believe it, when she came up to me, there was no mistaking it – she was a raw Hottentot straight off the Bitterlands. Clumping about like an ostrich in the shoes her husband made her wear. And such wild eyes – you could see she couldn't wait to get back to the bitterveld.'

The pedlar sucked dramatically at his pipe, knocked it out and continued as he refilled it: 'There and then, I decided, even though business could not be worse, this is where I take my cart and I go. Before the Frenchman could buy his nigger girl a bead or a rag, I was on my way. He just stood there with his pound note in his hand. As I drove off I shouted to him: "Du Toit," I snarled, "those brats of yours, do you call them Huguenots or what do you call them?"'

They shook their heads as Floris threw another log on the fire and the sparks flickered red against the darkness. 'Yes,' said the coach driver.

'There was a similar case quite close to here not so long ago,' said Floris. 'You must have heard of the Moolmans? They're the owners of Toorberg, stinking rich, huge herds of cattle, pots of money. One of the sons got off with the daughter of a Pandour, but that Abel Moolman thrashed the living day-lights out of his son – chased him clean off the farm and out of the district.'

'Yes,' nodded the driver of the ammunition coach, 'I heard about that. Floris Moolman was his name.'

'Strewth, eh, even here in this area?' The pedlar shook his head.

'Oh, yes,' said Floris in confirmation, before asking the coach driver: 'What else have you heard tell about the rich Moolmans, friend?'

'Not much. Just that they're stinking rich, as you said.'

'It just shows,' said the pedlar, ending the discussion, 'money isn't everything.'

They turned in for the night, and when Floris woke the next morning the pedlar's wagon had already left. Floris harnessed his team and was just about to offer the driver of the ammunition wagon his hand when the coach driver looked at him through narrowed eyes, spat a thin stream of tobacco juice through his teeth and then took Floris's hand. 'Have a good trip, friend,' said Floris.

'Goodbye, Floris Moolman,' said the coach driver and waited without moving a muscle till Floris had mounted the wagon chest in alarm, whipped his horses and driven wildly away.

Driving across the open plains through a herd of lazy springbok that day, Floris discovered that a man is never too grown up to cry like a child.

That was the end of his enquiries about himself and his kinfolk. It was also the last time he did the mailcoach run in the Camdeboo. He visited other districts; he went prospecting for gold in the streams of the far north; he joined a circus and looked after the horses. Sometimes, when one of the performers was ill, he would appear in the ring with a painted face beside the flanks of the gaudy, shining horses.

But sooner or later he would resume his wandering, driven by his yearning for farmland and cattle and the hot veld sun on his back.

Rumours of Soois's death reached him; so did the news of Andreas's defection to the British. He heard reports about Judge Lucius's speech on Crimes of the Right Hand. He heard, too, how for sixteen months OldAbel and a gang of forty convicts dug away and banked up earth till they had constructed an irrigation furrow to bring water all the way from the Eye to the fertile uplands of Toorberg.

First OldAbel built a sluice up in the Toorberg to divert the water, and then he constructed an aqueduct. In the low-lying areas it was raised as much as three feet above the ground, but to maintain the levels in other places they had to drop the concrete channel as much as ten feet. Vast fields were sown and planted, Floris heard, until Toorberg had the largest stretch of planted grazing north of Swellendam. OldAbel was a progressive farmer, a worthy successor to FounderAbel. He was the only one of FounderAbel's sons not to lose his head over a woman, or art, or the Law, or the war. He deserved Toorberg.

And now, thought Floris, I can wander at will here, as though at last it was mine too. I have to tread warily, of course, because I have not earned a grave in the family plot. But I have returned, like all the Moolmans, because my descendants, too, are here – even if all they have inherited is the Stiefveld, and even if they are bitter and rejected. They are still here; they can still wake up in the morning and look up at the crown of Toorberg and think: We belong here.

Chapter 29

From the Toorberg homestead that night one could see the torches flickering like fireflies against the slopes of the mountain. From where Ella and the magistrate were sitting on the back stoep, it was a beautiful sight. 'They're like summer glow-worms,' whispered Ella. They caught the continual sound of voices from the paraffin store behind the cowshed as fresh search parties came in to replace their torches.

In the outside kitchen a team of women were making torches out of baling twine, old rags and molten candle wax. Ella had seen to it that a large pot of soup was simmering on the stove.

'I am so glad you agreed to spend the night here,' said Ella to the magistrate as they sat there in the dark. He was quite unable to make out her expression, though whenever he drew on his cigar, she was able to see his face for just a moment: glowing, pensive, younger. Bored and sullen, the clerk had already retired to the room which Ella had allocated to him – Soois's old room, with the bloodstained uniform still in the wardrobe.

The magistrate had a fleeting glimpse of the uniform when Ella opened the wardrobe doors to check whether everything was in order for the visitor. Now, out on the veranda, he enquired about it. 'Yes,' she said, 'they actually did order uniforms from the Boer Republics up north. How they got them here through the British lines, goodness knows. But the day they rode out of the farmyard Soois was wearing the uniform of a Boer veld-kornet and all his men had hats with the upturned brim of the Transvaal Republic. As far as they were concerned this was war in earnest. But I don't think any of them realized that death is part of war – not even Soois. My own CrossAbel does not think so either, in spite of all his tours of duty on the Border.'

The magistrate thought back to their lunch together. A servant, in white cap and apron, had held a tray containing a tin plate and

161

spoon so Ella could serve CrazyTilly's food. While the servant held the tray, Ella said grace, holding her hand over Crazy-Tilly's lunch. In Abel's absence Ella sat in his place, explaining to the magistrate that this was their custom. She filled the chair with authority and even though there was only herself and the magistrate in the room, the meal proceeded with dignity, as though the fourteen empty chairs round the table were all occupied by important guests. The clerk had indicated that he was not hungry. From the dining-room the magistrate could see him dejectedly kicking his heels against a low wall in the garden.

'A dull young man,' said Ella, also looking out through the lace curtains.

'Please do not think that he is refusing your hospitality,' said the magistrate politely. 'I may say that often the civil service offers a young man a great many disappointments. One needs a considerable degree of patience in order to reach a position of responsibility.'

'You think he is disappointed?' She ladled some more gravy over the slices of roast mutton on his plate.

'I think he is frustrated. So was I, frequently. But I persevered and eventually I became a public prosecutor and later a magistrate. It requires a great deal of patience and prudence, and of course there are also all the examinations to be taken, but ultimately there is a reward. I do not think he has realized that yet.'

'Perhaps you should tell him so.'

'I should, indeed I should,' he replied, wiping his mouth with the napkin. He appreciated Ella's hospitality – and also the discreet way in which she had cut up his meat before passing the plate to him.

'When was it that FounderAbel first pitched his camp here?' he asked.

'Oh, a very long time ago,' she replied. 'Abel would be able to give you the precise date. It's in the family Bible, too, of course. But it was a long, long time ago, before the Afrikaner actually realized that he was anything other than a pioneer on a wagon. You know,' she continued enthusiastically – he could see

162

she enjoyed these historical tales – 'they say FounderAbel loved telling the story of the young Hendrik Bibault from Stellenbosch who was the first to shout: *"Ik ben een Africaander!"* FounderAbel used to say that when the fact of Afrikaner identity was proclaimed like this for the very first time, Bibault and his four companions were on a binge and as tight as ticks.' She laughed. 'Bibault may have been quite disreputably drunk when he made that statement, yet his words have become a highly respectable part of our history.'

'True,' he assented, 'and yet it is difficult to believe.'

'There were few men who were better Afrikaners than FounderAbel,' she said. 'He drove out the Xhosa and the Bushmen, and with his tame Pandour at his side, he cleared this part of the country for succeeding generations. I don't think everyone realizes what sacrifices our forefathers had to make: no doctors or shops at hand – only the occasional Jewish pedlar or Malay passing by. None of today's Afrikaners are better than he was.'

She poured custard over the preserved peaches. 'A little more custard?'

'No, thank you. That will be fine.'

'Do light your cigar now, if you'd like to. You needn't wait for the coffee. I remember so well how my father used to enjoy his cigar with his dessert.'

'Thank you, but I am in no hurry,' he said. A while later he asked: 'This son of Katie Danster's, this Oneday fellow. Do you know anything about him?'

'Oh, I did hear that the police had arrested him, but then I suppose everyone knows that. Don't you?' He nodded. 'Apparently he was involved in inciting blacks in the location and promoting the bus boycott. Postmaster would be able to tell you more about the buses – even here there was hardly a bus that passed that hadn't had its windows smashed. Until Oneday and a couple of others were rounded up. They don't take their theological studies seriously, that lot, their collars are political not clerical. Out here in the country we'd rather not have the problems which you're having in the cities these days. So I'm glad

163

he's been detained. He was always cheeky, even as a child. It was always Katie's dream that he should have a decent education, but see how badly he's turned out.'

'When did he start getting involved in these matters?' prodded the magistrate cautiously.

'I don't know. Abel banned him from the farm a long time ago, but we know that he very often still comes up the footpath at night to visit the Stiefveld people. And Katie doesn't set him right either. Instead she welcomes him in her house, even though he is a political agitator. Abel will have to have her on the mat about it yet.'

'And your other labourers?'

'No, they're still of the old sort. As you know, they have been out searching day and night for Abel. They know their place.'

'And Katie's other son?'

'Oh, Shala. Now he really is a troublemaker. But he's not an agitator. He herds his mother's goats up on the slopes of the mountain. Abel let them have a piece of veld -- one couldn't very well dump the whole family on the highway. They cultivate prickly-pears, too, and in times of drought they chop up the thick leaves and mix them with molasses to sell to the farmers as stock feed. Often you'll see Katie's grandchildren hawking red prickly-pears beside the road. You're sure to have seen them there – they've put up a small stall made of reeds.'

'I believe I have noticed something of the kind.'

'But Shala causes us plenty of headaches. CrossAbel reckons he lifts the boundary fence at night and drives his goats into the Vlei. But by morning they're all back again.'

'Surely they would leave tell-tale tracks?'

'He only does it when it's raining, so the tracks get washed away. He's much too cunning, I'm afraid.'

'I see.' the magistrate looked up at the portrait of Founder-Abel on the wall and FounderAbel stared furiously back at him. 'I have interviewed him.'

'Who?' Ella looked up, the coffee-cup in her hand.

'Oneday Riet.'

'Oh?'

'Yes.' In a calm and leisurely way he lit a cigar and exhaled a cloud of smoke between himself and FounderAbel. 'I found him an extremely decent young man, although somewhat embittered.' He rested his cigar in the ashtray and picked up his coffee-cup. 'Highly intelligent, though.'

Ella's cup rattled sharply as she replaced it in the saucer. 'Of course you found him decent!' was her comment. 'He knows when to show his best colours.'

'Is it your opinion that he is seriously engaged in . . . subversive activities?'

'Why else would they have arrested him?' Ella poured more coffee. The hand holding the coffee-pot bore two heavy rings. Diamonds and rubies, thought the magistrate.

'I would assume that someone denounced him.'

'In this district nobody denounces anybody else without good reason. As a pastor he held services in all the farmers' sheds, and from what I hear there was very little talk of religion in them.'

'I see.'

'Of course, they hear over the radio what is happening in the big cities, and then they do the same things here. But these are the signs of the times, I'm afraid, and that is what my son has to spend months and months every year fighting, up on the Border and in the location.'

'Yes,' replied the magistrate, 'they probably are the signs of the times.'

They each had a third cup of coffee.

Eventually he said quietly: 'You conceal your distress extremely well.' The servants came in and cleared the table round them. Ella waited until everything had been cleared before replying: 'Abel will come back. If he wants to.'

The magistrate nodded.

'In any case,' she continued, 'there's an old family saying, The Moolmans always return to Toorberg, even if only in death. They cannot escape.'

'You must not think in terms of death,' he protested.

'Oh, don't worry: it's just a saying.' She looked out of the window.

She invited him to follow her out onto the back stoep, where they sat in the shade. They heard CrossAbel's bakkie stop beside the sheds, then drive off again, its wheels scattering gravel.

'I have not yet asked you,' said the magistrate as they sat in the drowsy shade of the afternoon: 'When last did you see your husband?'

'He went to town,' Ella replied, 'on business. He was supposed to spend the night there. But he never arrrived at our house in town. The Land Rover tracks show that he turned off into the veld just before he reached the Halt, but the wheelmarks die away in the grasslands. There's no sign of the Land Rover either.'

'Is there anything missing from the house? Did he take anything unusual with him?

'His clothes,' she said. 'His briefcase. That's about it.'

'Is that all?'

'Yes.' Her face showed no emotion. Somewhere on the farmyard some labourers were shouting to one another.

'Nothing more?' he asked, with gentle persistence.

'His gun,' she answered softly.

The magistrate stroked his stump.

'He sometimes does take his gun,' said Ella. 'Sometimes not. Farmers like driving around with guns. It's not unusual.'

'No,' he said, 'it is not significant.'

'Not in the slightest,' she emphasized.

The shadow of the roof was edging across the farmyard. 'When do the search parties return?' he asked.

She shrugged her shoulders. 'They will come back as soon as there is anything to report.'

'Are you sure you do not wish to call in the assistance of the police?'

Ella shook her head. 'Abel would have a fit. He'd never forgive me. In any case, who knows Toorberg better than its own people?'

Now, sitting here in the dark in the same chairs as during their conversation after lunch, the magistrate's thoughts kept wandering back over the afternoon at Toorberg: to tea, served at four o'clock, among the potted green ferns under the kudu-horns on the wall; to the clerk clearing his throat uncomfortably and slopping coffee in his saucer; to Ella becoming gradually quieter and quieter until, when they were preparing to leave, she pressed them to spend the night. 'Please?' she asked. The clerk had nodded sullenly; but when Ella looked enquiringly at the magistrate, he had accepted her invitation with alacrity.

She led them to the guest rooms, where the bedding had already been turned down as if in expectation of visitors. There were fresh roses in the vases and a small New Testament on each bedside cabinet. 'You may have Soois's room,' Ella said to the clerk. 'It has become a tradition that young men visiting Toorberg sleep in this room.'

Ella then took the magistrate down the passage to the next door. 'I have put you in the room that was De la Rey's,' she said. She plumped up the pillows and straightened a rose in the vase. 'You reminded me so strongly of him this morning in the car.'

He smiled. 'You are very kind.'

'If there is anything you need,' she explained, 'just press the bell above your bed. The servants will be in the kitchen until eleven o'clock tonight. And please don't be alarmed if the dogs should start barking. For several nights now, there has been a polecat making a nuisance of itself round the house. The dogs will eventually smell it out. I only hope they do so before it gets in among my laying hens.'

Then he was alone in the room. By that time it was late afternoon. The linen smelt fresh and clean. Above the bed there was a portrait of De la Rey. Leaning over the bed, the magistrate stared intently at De la Rey. Then he turned round and looked at himself in the mirror. He brought his face right up to the glass, smoothing away the pouches under his eyes. Then he went to the clerk's room. The young man was stretched out on the bed with his shoes on, but jumped up when the magistrate entered.

'Relax,' the magistrate gestured. 'If you want to read,' he

added with gentle mockery, 'may I suggest you page though the New Testament?' He walked smiling down the passage to the sun-porch, where he found Ella making an entry in her diary.

'Some days,' she told him, 'there is more to write about than on others.'

Chapter 30

Soon after LittleKitty Riet had run past him on her way to the farmstead, Soois Moolman heard Postmaster's Borgward start up, stall, and then drive off. He understood haste: in all his life he'd never had time for messing about. As a child he had taken no notice at all of Grandmother Magtilt's admonitions to keep calm – how could he, when from the day of his birth his eyes had watched the restless boots of FounderAbel?

Grandmother Magtilt always said FounderAbel's boots had such a restlessness in them that they would carry on striding on their own, even after FounderAbel himself collapsed and died. Soois, born when his father was quite elderly, was troubled in a very high degree by the same restlessness. Hence, people said, his hatred of the British, even though he'd grown up under a roof made of English iron.

Soois's rebelliousness meant that FounderAbel's latter years were filled with anxiety. At an advanced age he continually had to ride up into the Toorberg in one attempt after another to restrain Soois and his commando of rebels hiding up beside the Eye and plotting mischief against the queen of England.

It was the drilling operations near the Toorberg homestead that suddenly caused the dead to walk again: there wasn't a moment's peace and quiet left to them underground. Soois, from his vantage point beside the beacon on the crown of the Toorberg, brooded on the matter for a long time. For days on end he'd watched the farmyard, when suddenly he saw the crowd of women rush out of the back door as though possessed.

At first he thought the drilling machine had struck water, but then he noticed that the women were not running in the direction of the red machine but heading for the poplar grove. The tribe of Abel are up to something again today, he thought.

He went down the mountain to watch the commotion round the borehole, only to wander off again, intensely irritated by all

169

the bungling. Now, more from boredom than any real interest, he was back to see how the operation was proceeding.

Once the drone of the Borgward had finally died away, Ella and two servants came past Soois from behind with heavy pots of delicious-smelling soup, hurrying along the track where the moonlight filtered through the leaves.

He would never forget that night: the moon had also been full, with the dark bulk of the Toorberg behind him. In the great house there was a single light burning – the lamp in Founder-Abel's library. Soois had deployed his men up on the mountain and then quietly rode down into the valley. He knew every bush and stone; the terrain was like the palm of his own hand. He couldn't put a foot wrong.

Odd, he thought now as he came out into the clearing round the borehole, that he hadn't noticed the deathly silence on the farmyard that night. The cattle weren't even chewing their cud as they did on other nights when he had crept past. Also, the doors of the labourers' cottages were tightly closed. Only a light whiff of smoke was left in the air, since the last fires in front of the cottages had been stamped out just a short while before. As he kept to the trees, slipping from trunk to trunk, there wasn't a breath of wind stirring in the avenue. Once he kicked against a stone and immediately crouched down to listen. He sat like that for a long time, his ears pricked up and wary, but nothing broke the silence.

Until he reached the whitewashed farmyard wall and again squatted down to listen: across the bare yard he heard the family clock strike once – one brazen echo and then, before he risked the last open stretch of the farmyard, he took a quick look over the wall. Where on earth were the dogs?

The shot caught him in the throat. Words gurgled out of his lungs as the force of the bullet knocked him staggering backward. The earth exploded against the back of his head. The words in his mouth were sticky mucus, but there was no sound in his throat. Only the clatter of approaching feet, dogs howling at the ends of their chains, and the question: why didn't the dogs have free run of the yard as on other nights?

With a lantern swinging against his knees, the huge figure of FounderAbel thrust the Tommies aside, crying: 'Stand back, you vermin!' When his father bent down beside him, Soois looked at the flickering flame of the lantern. He smelt the paraffin and pipe-tobacco on the rough hand of his father as the old man stroked his face for a moment.

'He's gone,' said FounderAbel.

Now Soois sat watching Ella ladling out mugs of vegetable broth while the servant, straining under the weight of it, held the pot for her. Then Abel too strode back into the clearing, followed by a gang of labourers. There was, for a moment, a smell of brandy on the air.

The previous evening Soois's frustration had expressed itself as an urge to sabotage the drilling machine. The prospect of another raid was one he found exciting, but this time he would be able to see better in the dark than he had the time the bullet shot his throat away. Sadly, he thought back to his commando days when they had crept stealthily, just as he was doing now, from farm to farm, the bored boys of the rural districts, to avenge themselves on the queen and her lords.

If he was closer, he was sure to be able to hear the drillmen talking. Using his finest commando technique, he would leopard-crawl right up to them, silent as a snake. The moon would not yet have reached the full, but as he inched his way stealthily, panting and covered with dust, right up to the very feet of the drillers, the moonlight would shine brightly on the blood-red drilling rod and the gleaming plungers that made the earth beneath his belly shudder with their pumping and thrusting. While the gears grated and the drill-bit hammered away deep in the bowels of the earth, it sounded like the distant thumping of the Long Tom.

As he felt the drumming, he thought: Toorberg is fighting off that machine, that red thing with the moonlight playing on it, that wakes the dead out of their graves and sets the ancestors wandering as though they weren't the blessed Christian dead at all, but pagans buried by a Malay wizard.

It was not right, Soois reckoned: it had to be stopped. He

would crawl past the drillers' gumboots and take from his back pocket the wire-cutters he had used to snip the telegraph lines in the district during the war. With a single skilled snap he would sever the cable from which the drill bit was suspended.

What a crack there would be! Metal grating on metal! One of the drillers would come running up with a flashlight. The engine would stop. Cursing, they would try to recover the drill-bit, and then silence would descend on the farmyard. He smiled. He knew it wouldn't take long to repair the machine, but for a few hours there would be silence – as was fitting.

These thoughts reminded him of his brother OldAbel's words to him long ago: 'You're just as much of an itchy-arse as your brothers. Who is going to farm Toorberg if all the brothers are such a bunch of itchy-arses?'

'You, Abel,' he'd replied, 'you are the Moolman who's going to farm here. You and Hetta Olivier. I saw you down in the Vlei on Sunday afternoon. Aren't you ashamed of yourself, putting your hand up under her skirt like that?' When Abel aimed a blow at him, he leapt over the garden wall and hared off into the hills. Abel hurled a handful of furious clods after him, but six months later he married Hetta Olivier, a girl who seldom smiled but who insisted on having the largest outside kitchen in the entire district built for her.

By that time Judge Lucius had already become a barrister in the city. When he came home for holidays he would sit on the front stoep with their father, FounderAbel, arguing about the ways of the just and the unjust. When OldAbel reproached him with exchanging his patrimony for fame and fortune in the city, Judge Lucius would push back the little gold-rimmed glasses on his nose, look at OldAbel and FounderAbel with his bright, clear eyes, and calmly explain that he would always be able to walk in the land of his birth. *Nulli enim res sua servit*, he said, and when FounderAbel coughed impatiently, he translated: No one needs a servitude over his own property. My birthright, Judge Lucius then explained, gives me a right to this soil, Abel, even if the title-deed states that it belongs to you. I should have that right even if the farm belonged to the devil himself. By virtue of my birth, I have a right of way here and here, *ex defectu sanguinis*, in the absence of issue, I shall wander on my own, even after my death. Mark what I have said.

At the end of this act of defiance by Lucius, FounderAbel stood up with a snort and strode off to his library. Shortly afterwards they heard him at his evening devotions. In his thundrous voice, as he knelt beside the huge fourposter which he shared with Grandmother Magtilt, he prayed in High Dutch for the farm; for Lucius's reluctance to get married decently and to abandon the ways of the city; for Jan Swaat's folk; for the government and the water-bailiffs; for rain; and for God to ward off the Ten Plagues and to keep the devil at bay until, by strict appointment, he, FounderAbel, should again kneel beside the bed at five o'clock the next morning.

The few visits made by the poet Andreas also added colour to the evenings on the Toorberg veranda. His mouth was full of ballads and his heart overflowing with hope for the arts in the wilderness of his mother country.

Soois had a violently fierce argument with Andreas the day he heard that Andreas had written a commemorative ballad in honour of the Queen. 'You rotten renegade!' he'd snarled at Andreas. 'You Tommie's pet, you Pandour, you . . . you Englishman!' He was just as furious when the news came that Andreas had won a ten-guinea prize in an eisteddfod where he had recited his own poem before the officers of a British regiment and their wives.

FounderAbel had simply shaken his head at this news, and Abel had begun to talk about putting fields under cultivation. Lucius absolved Andreas from all blame since he had acted without *dolus*, finding him guilty merely of mild negligence. 'It was an improper act,' he announced in his court voice, 'for a Moolman to celebrate a queen, for we, after all, are republicans.' Those were the days when Lucius the young barrister was still fond of showing off his Latin witticisms. In later years he became more reserved, more pensive, and seldom said anything at all in that foreign tongue which he had been able to speak with such miraculous fluency even as a child. Lucius had seen too many crimes, people said; they had made him despair of the prospects for the human race.

When his sons took to quarrelling like this, FounderAbel would go out into the yard with his favourite hunting gun and shoot three shots into the air. That was the signal for Jan Swaat, his groom, to come down to the farmstead. 'Saddle two horses, my boy,' FounderAbel would say to Jan Swaat, and soon afterwards the old infantryman would be back with FounderAbel's shining black stallion and a second horse. Their hoofbeats would die away rapidly. Hours later, when everyone else had gone to bed and only Grandmother Magtilt was still up, waiting patiently beside a single candle in the parlour, the returning horses would be heard snorting.

Where the two of them rode to and what they talked about no one ever knew. Perhaps, when they were far from the farmyard and the rest of the family, they talked about Floris, all mention of whose name was forbidden on Toorberg.

Who it was that caught Floris and Kitty no one would ever know. Judge Lucius once expressed the opinion that it was FounderAbel himself. Certainly FounderAbel was waiting for Floris to return that day, Floris with his tousled cowlick and the don't-care swagger of his thighs.

That day FounderAbel brought his whip to the dinner table with him. When he said grace, it was with Grandmother Magtilt's hand under his right hand and his left hand on the whip. The servants waiting at table kept an anxious eye on the whip all through the meal. When FounderAbel had taken his last sip of coffee and pushed his plate away, he looked at Floris.

'Floris Moolman,' he said. Floris, knowing like all the rest of the family that there was trouble coming, looked up, his mouth full of roast potato.

'Yes, Father?' His voice was muffled as he awkwardly tried to swallow the mouthful of food.

'Have you no respect for your own kind, Floris Moolman?' FounderAbel's hand played over the whip. Afterwards, Soois often thought that, for a man who was about to drive one of his sons off his farm and right out of his life, FounderAbel was remarkably calm.

'How do you mean, Father?' Floris had gone as white as the starched table cloth.

'You know, Floris.'

The dining room was ominously silent. In the kitchen the servants had stopped moving pots about on the iron stove.

'No, Father.' Floris looked at the table in front of him.

'What? Are you a coward, too?'

'No, Father.'

FounderAbel rose from his seat and walked round to Floris. Grandmother Magtilt was going to put out a hand to stop him, but it was too late. Floris half-stumbled out of his chair, but FounderAbel's hand closed round his upper arm. He half-dragged, half-carried Floris down the passage and out of the front door. On the farmyard, in front of everyone, without Floris or himself uttering a single word, he laid into his son with the hippo-hide whip.

The blows rained down left and right on Floris's back and legs, so that later there were lash marks visible even on the hard earth. When he had finished, FounderAbel looked at Jan Swaat. 'Bring me my horse,' he said. He rode off into the veld and did not return before nightfall. By then Floris was gone. Weeping, Grandmother Magtilt had salved his entire body with suet, and then given him a small leather purse with a hundred pounds in it, money she had collected and kept hidden in her underclothes for just such a desperate day as this.

At first no one had any idea what the thrashing was for, but when they saw Kitty Riet passing the farmyard with a load of firewood on her head the next day, and they noticed the weals that Jan Swaat's cane had raised on her body, then everyone knew.

Floris never returned. In Toorberg's outside kitchen the Malay forced a concoction of herbs down Kitty's throat while Jan Swaat held her down, but the baby would not come away. So on New Year's Day Andries Riet was born, with the eyes of his English forefather and the high forehead of the Moolmans.

175

They say Jan Swaat gave Kitty another hiding after the birth of the baby just because the child was so strong and healthy, but apparently that was only so that FounderAbel could see the marks. In the privacy of the stone-and-reed hut which Jan Swaat had built on the Stiefveld, he took his grandson in his arms, so they said, and cried like a woman. The story went that after that he took and hugged Kitty, too, where she was soothing her strokes with fat, and cried again.

Jan Swaat was a man with two lives: one was his own, but the other belonged to FounderAbel Moolman, the man who saved him from the reach of the Cape garrisons.

As the sweating men wielding the picks rhythmically dug away beside the borehole, Soois decided: Ultimately, the only son who could have filled FounderAbel's shoes was OldAbel. The others were wanderers, all itchy-arses, himself included. He, Soois, was too angry with the Queen; Andreas's trouble was that he wasn't angry with anyone; Floris was altogether too obsessed with girls to have the time to be angry; and Lucius was angry with Unrighteousness.

Only OldAbel was angry enough with the hard ground to want to tame it and farm it. He had a foul temper, just like FounderAbel, and he was always on the look-out for something to break or to set right again.

A man with a firm grasp, thought Soois as the picks passed to the next gang, the quintessential Toorberger.

Chapter 31

Meisie Pool noticed LittleKitty slipping away through the poplars after Mailbag. As if Ma Katie, Shala, Oneday and she, Meisie, knew nothing about it, she thought. It was no secret from
Postmaster's folk either. Nor from people farther afield, for that
matter: was there anyone who had not seen Mailbag and Little-
Kitty completely engrossed in their conversations across the
counter at the Halt? There was even a rumour that they sometimes shared the sandwiches which his mother so carefully
packed for him.

Everybody could see how recklessly Kitty flirted with any
man in trousers – it was from being stuck up on the Stiefveld
with Ma Katie that LittleKitty had become so shameless. But
when Oneday suggested that it was high time LittleKitty found
herself a proper job in town, Ma Katie flatly refused. LittleKitty
was to stay on the farm of her birth, in the house of the grandmother for whom she was named; she had to rub Ma Katie's
chest with Vicks and eucalyptus oil at night; and she had to see to
the cooking whenever Meisie ran off to her people and simply
left Oneday's Bible-children to fend for themselves. Ma Katie
believed that a woman should put up with even the worst of her
husband's whims. It was her simple duty to follow him to the
end of his days, no matter how poor and bare those might be.
'Even when there wasn't a crust left,' she would say, 'with my
hungry stomach, on my hungry feet, I followed Andries Riet. It
was lucky that in the very worst times I had either Shala or
Oneday in my belly, so I didn't feel so hollow inside. I stood by
him, rotter though he was, Andries Riet, the bitterest man in the
Agter-Sneeuberge.'

But Meisie was not always prepared to put up with Oneday's whims. First all the sermons in the farmers' sheds, then
the long weeks that he was away getting his training at the Bible
College, then the long nights when he was preaching the Word
in the town location, and after that yet another month away

while he graduated and got his collar. The day he came walking up Katie's Path to the Stiefveld and they saw the bright white collar straight across his throat, Ma Katie shouted 'Hallelujah!' and ran, with her wobbly old breasts and her crooked headscarf, down the dusty road, over sharp stones and devil-thorns, to fall on the neck of her clever, clever son. Meisie had hoped that that would be the start of better times for her and Oneday. A more peaceful life. Not like the past few years when Oneday would suddenly appear, make long speeches, sit around looking sour when nobody understood him, and then leave another baby inside her before making off back to the towns or cities.

'Who are your sheep, Oneday, the ones whose shepherd you're supposed to be?' she asked him one day. 'Where's your congregation?'

'I am an itinerant preacher,' he replied. 'My people are everywhere, wherever there is poverty and oppression.'

'And your church, Oneday?' she asked. What she wanted was to be the Minister's Wife, with a smart, wide hat, and sit in the front pew in church on Sunday, with her children all in a row beside her wearing white knee-high socks. O Lord, please give Oneday a congregation, she prayed, often, and an organ that rumbles deep down out of its belly, and flower arrangements beside the pulpit.

But Oneday was one of a new generation of pastors. From shed to farmer's shed he travelled, sometimes by train, some-times on his old balloon-tyred bicycle, and occasionally in the company of a strange man who fetched him from the concertina gate in a black car late at night when the folk in the great house were asleep. Sometimes he came for Oneday on Sunday after-noons, too, when the Moolmans were resting behind drawn curtains.

The man never came in. He would drive his car only as far as the gate and then hoot. He was a black man, that they could see, with a black hat on his head. 'No, Oneday,' Ma Katie had protested. 'These aren't our people. That man comes from the city. Look at his number-plates.' And the man really had come

178

from far – one could tell by the mud on the sides of the car and the dust on the bonnet.

But they could never understand Oneday. Meisie remembered how he'd taken her up into the mountain one day soon after they started courting. They climbed up past the hut where the Malay lived and stopped for a while to watch the old sorcerer crouched over the little fire in front of his hut. When the wind turned they caught the strange smell of the concoction he was brewing.

Oneday shuddered. 'Come away,' he said, 'that is Ma Katie's *tokolosheman* cooking up wickedness again. He was up on the cliffs gathering herbs all of yesterday. Shala says he spent the whole day among the ravines, shouting as he went.' They climbed higher, up the dry course of the upper reaches of the Eye spring, right to the Eye itself, where they sank down, panting, on the smooth slabs of rock.

'Here,' Oneday told her, 'Grandpa Jan Swaat and Tame-Bushman lay and rested. They were the ones, the two of them, who brought FounderAbel here. They caught malaria with him, too, and they drove out the Xhosa alongside him. Jan Swaat because he couldn't go back to the Cape and TameBushman because he was leashed to FounderAbel's stirrup. But when FounderAbel went to the Governor, he was the one who got the title-deeds. Because he was white, Meisie. Because the other two were a poor half-breed and a step-Bushman. But they were earth of this earth, the two of them: TameBushman's people knew this Eye when FounderAbel's grandfather still lived in Holland, across the sea. And when FounderAbel's father came over the sea and landed in Table Bay, scurvy and all, the Bushmen were already living here. By that time Jan Swaat's mother's folk were already moving through here. But who's got the title-deeds today? And who is stuck out on the Stiefveld with a plot of prickly-pears and a goat pen and a few rabbits? The Riets here, the Moolmans there!'

She'd leant over to him comfortingly and asked: 'Please show me the cave in the mountain now.'

Oneday showed her where the water used to gush forth

from the Eye. There were seven stone mouths washed smooth by the water that you could put your hand into, Oneday explained. When he and Shala were children they could still touch the moisture with the tips of their fingers if they lay stretched out on their stomachs and shoved in their arms right up to the shoulders.

There was nothing but dust down there now. 'And scorpions, perhaps. Or a cobra.' He showed her a snake's trail across the path. 'See: Satan himself.'

One night when he was quite small Oneday had dreamt that the Eye was bubbling up full of clear water again and that he was a pastor, standing knee-deep in the shining water, baptizing a great crowd of people by total immersion. That, he explained, was the dream which made him decide to make the Church his life.

Stooping at the entrance to TameBushman's cave, he led Meisie inside and showed her the paintings: tiny hunters clustered round an eland; semi-circles of dancers; a herd of ostriches, but look more closely and you saw they had human legs – that, Oneday told her, was the way they stalked the game – beautiful kudu with proud horns; delicate gazelles darting across the roof of the cave; and right at the back of the cave, the small heap of earth covering TameBushman's bones.

Oneday made no reply when Meisie asked: 'Was he a heathen?' He simply stroked the rock faces with the tips of his fingers as though he wished he could bring the little pictures to life under his hands.

Later, sitting at the mouth of the cave, he told her how the last Bushmen lived in the great Kalahari desert now; a tiny remnant, driven thousands of miles to the north. And now, Oneday told her bitterly, the army had herded them all into a camp and issued them with guns and uniforms – these little people who for centuries had been so content with life that they had invented nothing new at all. They had simply gone on living in the way they always had.

As always, she had simply taken Oneday's hand in hers. There, as they looked out over the farm to where the farthest

180

fences disappeared into the blue haze, the cleverest of all the Skaamfamilie asked her to be his wife.

Perhaps, thought Meisie at the borehole, drawing her skirt tighter about her knees to keep off the evening chill, perhaps she should not have accepted him. Perhaps she should have realized from his conversation that afternoon that he would never be a stay-at-home. But how could she have known he'd be a man to leave babies in his wife's belly and then clear off to the poor of the locations? Afterwards it was too late – with Mark or John on her hip. 'They're Bible-children,' Ma Katie said proudly, and gave them all names out of the New Testament.

'Stepchildren, more likely,' Meisie, complained later. 'Children without a father.' Once, in a rage, she even shouted: 'Kids with a dad who hangs around the location women!'

To which Katie firmly replied: 'You shall follow your husband in the sweat of your brow.' It was after one such argument that Meisie first packed her things and left – away from the pouting Ma Katie who always knew better – away from the surly-faced Shala who stank of goats and sweat as he sat staring into the fire at night – away from her whining children with their everlastingly snotty noses. Back home to her own folk she went.

But eventually she always returned, on the back of her father's donkey-cart with its buckled wheel. It took them a whole day to trundle up the Camdeboo pass from Eerste Station, and while they were struggling up the pass and her father was laying into the calloused backs of the donkeys with his whip, Meisie had time to think things over carefully.

It was better to have a husband than no husband at all. It was better to have a roof over her head than no roof at all. It was better to plant prickly-pear cuttings, when you saw rainclouds gathering above Toorberg's blue crown, than to have nothing at all for your hands to do. It was better to have a husband with a dog-collar than a man who had to slave his guts out over a white man's shovel or walk his feet off after a white man's sheep for one pound a month, plus a bag of maize meal and a handful of bokkoms.

181

It was better to have a Ma Katie whose chest closed up at night from living with a smoking hearth all these years than to have a drunken old mother who brewed her own beer each weekend and then lay with her swollen stomach in the air sleeping off her imprudence. 'It's better, it's better,' she told herself with every sluggish yard that the old cart wobbled up the mountain. 'It's better,' she murmured when they reached the wire gate. She had the dropper-pole in her hands again and was shifting the hook which she knew so well, when she looked up and saw Ma Katie standing on top of the rabbit hutch, ragged and tattered, with her hands over her eyes.

'It's better,' she said as she walked up the slope, leading her father's donkeys over the small hoofprints of Shala's flock, and caught the smell of goat-droppings and rabbit straw. When she felt the warm bodies of her children pressing up against her, she cried.

Ma Katie looked down at her from the roof of the rabbit hutch and said: 'There's coffee on the hearth, Meisie. It's been brewing day and night since you left. Pour some for yourself and your father.'

Later she promised Ma Katie she would stay, even if Oneday never returned. This was her home, this was where her body had made itself a hollow in the mattress, this was where she would die and they would bury her in the OuMurasie. Not before late that night, when she was rubbing Ma Katie's wheezing chest and the Vicks was making her eyes water, did she move the candlestick away so as to leave her face in shadow and ask: 'But, my mother, where then is Oneday?'

Katie shook her head. 'Meeting,' she said. 'He's having a meeting.'

The next day Oneday returned, tired out. He hadn't even known she'd been away. He'd heard the story from somebody or other – at the Halt or in the location – and had come home immediately. Was there illness among her folks down at Eerste Station? Was she herself in good health?

She could see his mind was elsewhere. Late that night he opened his trunk and showed Shala some papers. Shala, sitting whittling at a walking stick, shook his head. Ma Katie refused to look at them. She sat to one side of the hearth, chewing her plug. From time to time she would send a stream of brown tobacco juice hissing into the coals.

When Oneday produced photographs, however, she looked up and recognized the town location, the beer hall, and the new stone church that was built after the other one burnt down.

'Evil tidings,' she said, shaking her head.

'Look,' Oneday pointed. In front of the beer hall stood a bunch of soldiers with rifles. Behind them one could see a Casspir on its high wheels. 'Who is that?' asked Oneday, pointing to one of the men in uniform. His finger trembled. 'Do you recognize him?'

As she sat here at the borehole watching CrossAbel helping one of the labourers fit a new handle to his pick, Meisie wondered why her mind kept going back all the time. It must be the child so slowly dying that is making me so absent-minded, she thought, and having to wait so long for them to rescue him, and everyone sitting or standing silently round the hole unable to do anything, their faces deep in shadow and abstracted, as though they were all lost in thought somewhere very far away.

Chapter 32

Writing to his wife that night in De la Rey's room, the magistrate asked: 'Who gives me the right to delve into this family's past? Tonight, after the hospitable reception which I have been accorded here, I feel like a conceited and pedantic old man who insists on picking at the same scab.

'I want to assure you, my love, that I have not lost my sense of perspective and that I still feel myself to be perfectly capable of passing judgement on the vices of the Moolmans. Too many years on the Bench have certainly taught me objectivity, but it is only human for one to be tempted occasionally by one's personal preferences.

'I feel that I am tonight in the very heart of a family: these stiffly starched sheets do not smell at all unfamiliar, and the pillow against which I am now leaning folds comfortably round my back. I have a sense of having lived for a long time in this room with its elegant furniture – indeed, as I look at the portraits of earlier generations of Moolmans, they seem much more familiar than strangers generally do.

'Can you understand that? To me, in a strange way, it seems logical: this farm is like so many other farms in Afrikaner hands, the family reminds me of so many other Afrikaner families, its individual members are like so many other people who have appeared in court before me times out of mind. In a way I have a sense of kinship with the Moolmans, and particularly here in De la Rey's room there is a strong sense of *déjà vu.*'

The magistrate leant back and looked at his own shadow against the wall. The window was slightly open, so the shouts of the search party from the paraffin store were audible. He heard the clerk leave his room and go to the bathroom. Then, meticulously, he folded the letter.

When the clerk returned, the magistrate rose, put on an old dressing-gown of De la Rey's which Ella had hung over the end of his bed, and cautiously walked down the passage with the

184

letter clutched in his hand inside the pocket of the gown. The musty smell of the old garment rose to his nostrils as he moved through the half-light. Then his fingers touched something in the pocket: a nail-clipper. He went into the bathroom and closed the door behind him. Only then did he switch on the light. He looked at himself in the mirror for a long time: he looked broader and taller in the paisley dressing gown. The cut of the robe gave the impression that there were arms in both sleeves. Sitting on the rim of the bath, he examined the nail-clipper. It had 'De la Rey' engraved on it. He ran his fingers lightly over the letters, wishing: If only I could clip my own nails with this.

After a while he took the letter from the pocket of the robe. With his teeth and one hand he carefully tore it into tiny pieces and watched the scraps of white paper flutter down into the toilet bowl. He had to flush twice to make them all disappear. Before going out into the passage again, he took another look at himself in the mirror.

Coming down the unlit passage, Ella was startled to see him. Her hand flew up to her mouth, but the magistrate pretended not to notice.

'I found this in the pocket of the dressing gown,' he said. 'It may have been there for years. Perhaps no one ever noticed it.'

'What is it?'

He opened the door of his room so that the light shone into the passage.

'It was De la Rey's,' she said. 'Look, here's his name.' He nodded, watching as she turned it over in her hands. 'It feels so warm,' Ella said, holding it to her cheek, 'as though it had lain in someone's hand for a long time.'

He nodded. 'I was holding it.'

'I think you should keep it,' she said suddenly taking him by the elbow. 'Have it as a memento.'

He shook his head. 'I have no use for it.' He smiled wryly at her uncomprehending look. 'Only one hand,' he said, lifting his hand to wave away her embarrassment. They were standing in the passage in front of a wall mirror in a gilded frame. Earlier she had told him that this had been a gift from Granny Olivier's

185

father to Toorberg. Looking at the mirror, he saw their two shadowy images in it, with only the strip of light from the half-open door of his room clearly reflected.

'I'll help you,' said Ella. 'Come.' She led him into his room and made him sit on the bed. As she bent over his hand he studied the few pale liver spots on her long neck. She had beautiful shoulders. Her satin nightdress was showing above her dressing gown. Delicately, while nothing else in the house around them was stirring, she started clipping the magistrate's nails with De la Rey's nail-clipper.

Strange, he thought, but there is nothing improper about this intimacy of ours. It is as though I were her brother and she my loving sister.

Chapter 33

After breakfast the magistrate went into the kitchen. 'Where is OldAbel's grave?' he asked the servants. They explained: beyond the kitchen-garden, just before you get to the poplars. He paused for a moment beside the neat plots in the kitchen-garden, surrounded by the freshness of the morning. There was a slight mistiness round the highest cliffs of the Toorberg; somewhere a tractor came stuttering to life; milk-pails clattered above the animal noises and the shouts of people.

His footprints left a meandering track through the frost behind him. He bent down to touch the moist leaves of Ella's parsley; dewdrops clung to his fingertips. What a beautiful part of the world, he thought later, standing in the graveyard beside the graves of FounderAbel and Grandmother Magtilt, OldAbel and Granny Olivier and the others. Carefully he pulled up a few weeds from between the marble headstones, and when all was clean, he turned round and walked back up to the great house.

In the library, he hesitated for a considerable time before turning the key in the glass-panelled door of one of the bookcases. He took out a heavy volume and sat down in front of the desk. He would never have presumed to take the seat behind the desk – that was reserved for the men in the portraits on the wall:

There was an old sepia of FounderAbel in extreme old age, one foot contemptuously resting on the shoulder of a dead lion, his rough, knobbly fists clenched round the barrel of the gun. Only the eyes bespoke his robust, cunning intelligence; intelligence that was more than mere cleverness, thought the magistrate, standing before the portrait, but a gift blessed with raw energy as well. Otherwise, he thought, all that intelligence would have been quite worthless in this part of the world.

There was OldAbel, with his foot on the mudguard of the district's first motor car. Indistinctly in the background behind him, under a white parasol and with a high lace collar: Granny Olivier.

187

There were various portraits of Abel himself. In the most recent he was standing, legs set wide apart, beside the scarlet drilling machine. It was a colour photograph, beside a framed article from an agricultural magazine describing the drilling machine and the search for water on the largest farm in the district.

In the silence of the library, conscious all the while of the search parties now also fanning out across the plains of Camdeboo, hundreds of feet below the Toorberg plateau, the magistrate could order his thoughts properly. He sensed here the peacefulness of the wide acres round him and realized again that any man who found himself at the centre of thousands and thousands of morgen of land, and sole owner of them all must have a remarkably strong, clear mind.

Eventually the magistrate found himself facing a photograph of CrossAbel in army uniform on the back of a Casspir with a bunch of other soldiers, triumphantly brandishing a machine gun. Behind them crouched the hovels of the town location, a crowd of people, some spindly pepper trees, and far in the distance the Toorberg, clearly silhouetted against the smoky air.

The magistrate stopped, fascinated, in front of the photograph. He thought back to Oneday in the police cells; to Katie Danster, hedging about the owner of the guitar propped up in the corner of her Stiefveld cottage; to Mailbag and LittleKitty Riet.

Later, he went out to the cowshed and asked one of the labourers to direct him to the Malay's hut.

He had to pass the dam in the Vlei, but stopped in amazement at CrossAbel's mud-track: in some places the track was compressed into a smooth sheen; on the bends there were deep scars where the biker had had to put out his foot to keep his balance; the track swept on, cutting through the bulrushes; up at the pump an S-bend ended triumphantly in a right-angled turn, before the track suddenly dropped into shallow mud where a trail of oil smears disfigured the surface. Finally there was another straight stretch covered with the tracks of hours and months of racing.

The Malay's hut was perched on the left-hand slope of the

great Toorberg ravine, opposite the Stiefveld. Slowly and sweatily the magistrate climbed the footpath, stopping frequently to catch his breath. It was amazing how steep the rise was; how suddenly small the homestead and the farmyard became, how close to one another the red buses at Postmaster's Halt were parked, how few goats Shala seemed to have grazing on the slope opposite.

As though expecting him, the Malay was sitting outside in front of his hut.

'Your Worship comes for an interpretation,' he said, with his sly eyes on the magistrate's deformity.

'That is not correct,' replied the magistrate. 'I shall provide my own interpretation. I have come to question you.'

'You are the magistrate,' said the diviner. As he got to his feet, the small bones and pieces of metal hanging all over him tinkled. There was a jackal skin on his head and the animal's sharp ears stuck straight up behind his own, creating an effect at once faintly comic, yet also somehow frightening. In a shelter slightly apart, a small fire was flickering under a three-legged gridiron and a small simmering cooking pot.

The magistrate went over to sniff at the mixture, and then turned round to ask: 'Do you live alone here?'

The Malay nodded. 'Like my fathers before me.'

'Your father was also . . .'

'Yes, he too was a wizard. And so was his father,'

The magistrate sat down outside on the bench beside the wall of the hut. He could see the whole farm from there: the mountainside, the cliffs, the road to the Halt. Wisdom gained from long hours of observation, he thought. Pointing down he said: 'From here you can see everything that happens.'

'I see inside.' The hand with the rings and the strips of animal skin round the wrist tapped against his breastbone. 'Inside.'

The magistrate nodded. 'I see,' he said.

The wizard's cunning eyes caught and held his gaze. 'Your Worship seeks medicine?'

'No, information.'

189

At that, the Malay's face became a mask. No information would be volunteered. After a while he replied: 'What the wizard sees is costly.'

'You do not have the right to charge me any money at all. I am a magistrate. You can be forced to divulge everything you know to me without payment.'

The wizard picked up a twig at his feet and went over to stir the mixture on the tripod. 'What the wizard sees with the eyes which see outward – that the Honourable Magistrate can have without money. That the court can have too. The wizard has been in court: they said he killed a small boy for the medicine in his little balls. The wizard knows about courts and honourables. The wizard knows about swearing too: so help me God.' Stopping in front of the magistrate, he taunted: 'But what the wizard sees with his inward eyes, that the Magistrate cannot have for nothing. That is not the court's business. That is the wizard's business.'

The magistrate lit a cigar. He thought fleetingly of Ella's gentle hands holding his hand, of the nail-clipper at the tips of his fingers. In his memory, she was standing perfectly still in the passage, in front of him. He thought of the shredded letters fluttering down into the toilet bowl. 'Your husband, Abraham van der Ligt,' the words flashed momentarily before his eyes.

He inhaled deeply. The climb had raised his blood-pressure; his heartbeat was throbbing in his ears. He nodded to the Malay. 'I shall pay,' he said, tiredly, and held out a green banknote. The Malay took it from him, rolled it up and stowed it in the leather pouch at his hip.

'Your law doesn't help you?' asked the Malay. Was there mockery in the eyes narrowed against the glare, or was it provocation?

The magistrate exhaled a cloud of smoke. Irritated, he thought: I, too, hide behind my cigar rituals. Then he asked: 'Will you tell me what you know?' He made the request politely, but tiredly. He had to remain precise, he thought, despite the heat. He had to reach a verdict, within the next few days. Abel's disappearance would raise new questions. Justice would take an

190

extremely serious view of the matter: where had the principal suspect disappeared to? And why? Perhaps the local magistrate had been right after all: no foul play, a simple accident in the midst of a respected family, a tragedy that was more the province of the family and the Church than of the Law?

'Tell what you know,' he repeated.

'Trickle saw a ghost,' began the wizard matter-of-factly. He lit a dagga cigarette with a coal which he then kept rolling round in the palm of his hand.

'What do you mean?'

'I saw when he saw the ghost.' The coal was rolling round and round in his palm. The Malay blew on it till it glowed red. 'The farm is full of ghosts. At night I see them walking. White, they are, walking, like boer goats, across the fences, everywhere.'

'Whose ghosts?'

'The fathers of Abel. The old men with the beards. The women with their hooped skirts.'

'And you see them with your own eyes?' He exhaled sceptically. Hear him out, he thought. Somewhere behind the cunning there is information hidden.

'I see them with my inward eyes. My outward eyes will not see them. The Law, too, has only outward eyes. The Law will not see them. But the wizard looks and sees.'

'And?'

'Trickle went into the grove that day. Trickle also had the inward eyes. He was the child of Tilly. And Tilly also has the inward eye. And her husband that walks with the willow-forks. They've all got the inward eye.'

'Why do you say that?'

'They see the water. They see the ancestors. They look and they see. Not like the other people here: they only see what lies before them on the ground.'

'And what happened when Trickle saw the ghost?'

The Malay got up to stir the pot again. Is it possible, thought the magistrate, that someone could have pushed Trickle into the hole?

191

From the fire behind him, the Malay spoke: 'It was in the grove. Trickle was playing there. He stood listening to the geese. Then the ghost of his ancestor appeared to him and Trickle was afraid. When his ancestor stretched out his hand to him, Trickle stepped back. When the ancestor came closer, Trickle fell over backwards down the borehole.'

Inside the murky hut the magistrate noticed a human skull, a pair of goat's horns, a bunch of ostrich feathers hanging from the roof. Stroking his stump, he looked out over the farm. 'Who was the ancestor?' he asked.

The Malay squatted down in front of him. The magistrate caught the sweet, stupefying smell of cannabis. The Malay removed the *zol* from between his teeth. 'The one they call De la Rey,' he said. At such close quarters, his eyes were yellow.

Chapter 34

Every now and again Dowser du Pisani grabbed a pick and hurled himself at the earth with a terrible fury, and each time Abel let him dig for a minute or two before taking him firmly by the arm and leading him away to the trees to rest. Sitting there, Dowser felt weeks must have passed since he saw a man on horseback picking his way through the boulders and thorn trees on the slopes of the Toorberg.

He recognized him as one of Abel Moolman's farm labourers, so after he had filled the last of his little bottles with the murky water of the streamlet beside which he was crouching, he got to his feet and shaded his eyes with his hand as he waited for the messenger to arrive. The streamlet was the last one still running on Toorberg, and the little seepage water left in it was muddy. His intention had been to leave it overnight, and then to pour off the clear water above the sediment and to soak one of his willow-forks in it. Perhaps, he hoped, the fork would then go rigid when he crossed the source of the streamlet.

He knew, with absolute certainty, that there was water beneath his feet. When he lay resting high up in the mountain at midday, he could hear the murmuring of the veins of water underneath Toorberg. He knew the sound of water – his ancestors, who had divined just about every borehole in the entire drought-striken north-west, had bred him to dowsing. He might never be able to smell water as well as a Bushman, but he could feel in his trousers the drawing of the nether waters when he passed over them.

He could tell where the veins of water ran, he could feel the willow forks stubbornly twisting in his hands, resist them as he might. Water had power, that he had learnt, and the drier the region, the more powerfully and stubbornly the willow wand would curve in his hands – so much so that it took the skin off his fingers as it bent, trying to get down into the earth, down to the cool wet chambers of the innermost earth.

193

He hooked the little bottle into his belt, wiped the sweat out of his eyes and waited for the horseman to reach him. The horse was lathered white: every now and again Dowser caught the smell of the animal as it approached. The rider took off his hat and waved it at him, so Dowser knew: he was bringing important news, either good or bad. Good news would be that somewhere Abel Moolman and the clever geologist from the city had found an aquafer that he, Dowser, had overlooked. But for him, that would also be bad news: that it should be the man who knew stones that found water, and not he, who was a man of water.

When Abel first spoke about having a geological survey done, Dowser had asked: 'What's the point in getting a man here what understands reefs and rocks, if he doesn't understand about water? Maybe he can only say where the best slate is, or sandstone, or something else. Or maybe he can be lucky and find a gold reef. Or oil: the government never stops looking for oil. But he can't smell out water, not through all the layers of rock on Toorberg, can he now?'

But Abel Moolman persisted with the idea and soon the geologist arrived on the farm. Every day Dowser watched him and Abel driving from one field to another and from ravine to ravine. Everywhere the man in the pith helmet picked up bits of stone. He even chipped bits of rock off the cliffs of the Toorberg with a little pick and stowed them in his rucksack. For weeks they drove around all over the farm collecting soil samples – even on the Stiefveld. Wouldn't it be a joke, thought Dowser, if they found water right in front of Katie Danster's house! Then the Riets would have a thing or two to say!

'If the horseman is bringing bad news,' Dowser thought, 'it must be about CrazyTilly. For quite a while now she's been building up for something. The dagga-tea that Ella Moolman gives her every day doesn't always calm her down any more.' Often while he was in the veld Dowser suddenly heard the bell ringing in the gable of the little schoolhouse where he lived. It would be CrazyTilly who had broken out again and was tugging at the bell just as she had that day, years ago, when she proudly showed her big belly to all of Toorberg.

194

It was her way of calling him, to show the whole world she was calling the father of her son. Would he ever forget that day at the bell? When he discovered that CrazyTilly was expecting his child, he didn't tell a soul. Martha was still living with him then, in the schoolhouse, with the five children. That was before she went back to her people in the Sandveld. He'd often come across CrazyTilly in the veld. She would stalk him and then jump out at him, pulling off her clothes for his hands to touch that beautiful, crazy body of hers. How could he control himself when that lovely girl was sitting astride him? When CrazyTilly realized that her swollen belly was not the result of eating too many prickly-pears, she ran down the footpath to the little schoolhouse at noon one day, past poor dumbstruck Martha, grabbed hold of the bell-rope and jerked and jerked it till the clanging of the bell could be heard all over Toorberg.

Martha simply could not get her to release the rope. It was only when CrazyTilly saw her father approaching that she let go, and then, with the bell still swinging in the gable, she pulled up her dress to show her father her big white belly.

Abel spun round on his heels and ignored Tilly's existence from that day on. But Martha went berserk: she threw pots and pans and clothes around all over the house; she ripped down the curtain partitioning off their sleeping quarters on the teacher's dais; she stamped on all his little bottles and smashed them; and she broke all his best willow-forks across her knee. Then she packed the trunk and, without even saying goodbye to the children, walked to the Halt with the trunk on her head, and caught the first bus down to the Camdeboo. At Eerste Station, he later heard, she bought a ticket to the Sandveld and disappeared out of his life for good.

He also heard that Abel had applied to the high court in the city for an abortion for Tilly's baby, on the grounds of Tilly's mental deficiency, but the application was so delayed that Noah was born before the court decided. When the court decision eventually reached them, Trickle was blissfully sleeping in CrazyTilly's arms as she sat all day long rocking him under the willows.

195

Tilly never changed a nappy. When the child was taken off the breast she was not capable of giving him a bottle. Ella saw to all that, without ever personally touching Trickle, however. Two nursemaids were always at hand, and when Tilly left the child in the yard and absent-mindedly wandered off, they stepped in and took over.

The horseman, one of Abel's farm labourers, had reached the first of the cliffs by now. Dowser indicated to him to wait, and started clambering down, the bottles at his waist tinkling against the rocks. When he reached the man, he could see that the news was bad.

'What is it?'

'Noah's down the borehole. He fell in. In the one among the poplars.'

Without a second thought, Dowser pulled the messenger off the horse and leapt into the saddle himself. The horse was wet with sweat and its legs were unsteady as it started off down the slope again but Dowser punished the animal. I don't care if you're the last horse in Abel Moolman's stables, he thought, today I'm going to drive you till you're white with salt.

Noah, Noah, poor little Noah. Noah, the waterchild, named after the great water man in the Bible – the first man who ever saw the rainbow. The first man who understood the power of water. 'That's all I ask,' he said to CrazyTilly. 'Just call him Noah.' He told her over and over again, till he knew that she wouldn't forget, and at the christening Noah it had been. Abel had not offered much resistance; they could call the little bastard anything, provided he did not bear a Moolman family name.

The horse's hoofs struck sparks from the rock as Dowser charged down the mountain; they left long shining streaks in the clay of the marsh in their haste; they simply cleared the boundary fences, rather than waste time searching for gates. He had lost his wife for the sake of Noah. Noah was his Toorberg child, his child of this beautiful farm with its dry Eye and its miserly aquafers. This farm where, if you closed your eyes and stood out in the wind at night, you could always hear water running somewhere. Sometimes you could even smell the water on the wind, and you could tell that the animals were smelling it, too, and pricking up their ears. Somewhere there were streams of bubbling water, but they were keeping hidden, as though the earth was shy. This farm with its dry Eye, the Eye which Tilly in her crazed state had sought out that night and where she had given birth to Trickle, on the rock slab washed smooth by the spring water of centuries, while the whole farm was out with lanterns and flaming torches searching for her. Only he, Dowser, standing at the foot of the mountain, had smelt the birth, but by that time the search had so exhausted him that he'd had to send a team of labourers to fetch Tilly. When they reached her she was biting through the cord with her own teeth.

She lay convalescing in the great house for a fortnight, but not once was he invited in. Nor did he request it. He waited. By day he waited in the dry water courses, and at night he waited in the little schoolhouse, as he listened to the breathing of his five sleeping children. He waited to see his Noah child, and when Tilly came down the front steps one day with the baby in her arms, and then walked round to the poplar grove, he knew she was waiting for him, too. She showed him the child, while murmuring unintelligible nonsense. The eyes looking up at him had more in them than the eyes of any of his other children. 'Noah,' he said, and then: 'Tilly. Magtilt.' As she sat there with her back to a tree trunk, he thought: Even if she never says two sensible words in a row, I love her. Just look at her face, the line of her throat, her breasts full and rounded with milk. Look at her pretty feet, stretched out in front of her on the grass: close enough for him to touch. Look at how the leaves cast their shadows over her face.

She knows more than people suspect, he thought. She knows things like tenderness, gentleness, dreaminess. That is why she can give love with her body like no other woman can. Afterwards she is always quiet and sleepy.

'Tilly of the Veld' he called her, because she would sometimes follow him for days without his being aware of it. It was only in the evening, when he was on his way home again, that he would see her footprints superimposed on his wherever the wil-

197

low-wands had led him that day. Where he had spent a long time working in one spot, somewhere behind a bush or a stone nearby there would be a slight hollow in the dust where she had sat: the pretty half-moons of her buttocks in the dust, the soft pattern of her feet, the peeled twigs and curls of barks that she had played with as she watched him. Sometimes there were drawings in the sand: stick figures, houses, windmills and often incomprehensible lines as well. One day, shortly before she fell pregnant, there was an obscene drawing of a man and a woman, neatly outlined on a patch of smoothed earth.

All these things were whirling through Dowser's head as he drove the horse with his knees in its sides, the flat of his hand on its rump, his heels in its flanks. 'Please let Noah live,' he prayed. He knew the boreholes, and the gestures of the messenger drove him to the one borehole where he had always been sure they would find relief – the one in the middle of the grove. Sometimes, even at the height of the worst drought, mushrooms would appear there: a clump of delicate death-cap toadstools with lacy white gills and impudent stems. Or sometimes there was moss, bright green under the dead poplar leaves. There was moisture, clearly; somewhere there was water; yet the machine thrust and thumped till it blunted and eventually broke its bit on the bedrock.

Try as they might, they could not break through the shell. 'We must get a better drill,' he told Abel, 'a drill what can go right through that slab, because under it, God knows, Mr Abel, there's the sweetest, clearest water just rushing past.' Man and beast alike could smell it if they bent over Toorberg's empty boreholes: the smell rising up out of the darkness was sweet and wet and heavy. The rich breath of the earth caught in your throat. There's water there, he would think as he lay awake at night, tossing and turning in a cold sweat, while his forks lay soaking in the water of the juvenile streamlets. We've got to strike water, he thought as he paced up and down in the dark schoolhouse, listening to his children breathing like five little pairs of bellows. His dreams flowed happily with the gallons and gallons of water that they would release, surging up out of the earth, an abundance that would stream down your arms when you plunged your hands into it, of an Eye spouting three feet into the air!

In the morning, when he opened the door, the funnels of dust were again dancing across the plain. The forks lay sleepily in his hands. His tracks criss-crossed the farm, up hill and down dale, north and south, east and west, as if he had completely lost his way.

Even so, Abel Moolman had not fired him. Abel had the drilling machine moved to a different spot each week, following the advice of the willow-forks. Up in the ravine, down near the Skaamfamilie, in the grove, behind the sheds, alongside the Ou-Murasie – at every spot where anybody could remember ever having smelt water, or where some child might have stumbled across a colony of arum lilies.

Once, CrazyTilly returned to the homestead with an arum in her hand and Abel pestered her for the rest of the day to find out where she'd pulled up the bloom. The lily stalk was firm with sap and its white funnel was smooth and moist, but all CrazyTilly would talk about was the stiff yellow pollen stem inside the funnel. It was late in the afternoon before she took Abel to the place where she had supposedly picked the flower – the woodyard, where there was a pile of willow stumps. Abel had had the trees chopped down and dug out when the new ram-shed was built. There was no sign of any arum plant or moisture there.

For weeks Abel had Tilly watched, but she never went any-where she had not been before and the riddle of the beautiful bloom remained unsolved. Even the geologist, soon after his arrival on the farm, tried to talk to Tilly about that arum lily, but she was unshakeable. She simply led him to the bleached white willow stumps. 'Here,' she said, scratching under a stump with her fingers, but anyone who stuck his hand in there found nothing but dust. It was as dry as a bone – certainly no place where an arum would grow.

The Malay couldn't help them either: he threw the bones; he rubbed Dowser's willow-forks with aloe sap, but the drought was beyond him too. One day he told of a dream he'd had: he'd seen a great dam break and water had flooded the entire farm. The only things left standing were the chunks of stone and mortar of the OuMurasie, nothing else at all. He had this dream, he maintained, every time the moon was full and all the bones were full of marrow.

As Dowser was galloping towards the grove, he decided that the wizard's dream must have been a reference to Noah, so by the time he rode into the wood, tears were streaming down his cheeks as he wept for this dreamy child of his who could sense water better than any Du Pisani before him.

Chapter 35

His interrogators asked him whether the disappearance of one of
the most respected farmers in the district was part of his pro-
gramme of subversion. Stupefied, Oneday shook his head,
rolled over onto his back on the floor of the cell and stared at the
graffiti on the walls: diminutive ostrich-men hunting a herd of
yellow antelope, tiny arrows speckling the rock-faces, three
hunters with quivers full of arrows dancing round a smudge of
fire. He crawled over to the mouth of the cave to look down over
the valley, but bumped his face against the bars. Turning, he
forced himself back in the direction of TameBushman's grave,
but became entangled in the blanket on the floor. He called out
to Shala and Ma Katie, and both appeared befcre him, Ma Katie
saying: 'You're a Moolman, my child. You should be proud of
it.'

But then his interrogators returned to ask why he, a pastor,
had a complete list of the times of main-line trains in his pocket.
Why were the arrival and departure times of all the trains that
came to Eerste Station in his inside pocket? And what about the
buses that stopped at the Halt? Were such things necessary for
the work of the Church? Was that the way to serve God? And
what did Shala mean by following those goats up the mountain
every day? Couldn't they graze by themselves? Weren't there
boundary fences to keep them in? What was Shala up to in that
Bushman cave on the mountain? They would go and dig it all up
anyway, they'd search the cave inside out. And find? What
would they find there? Wouldn't he prefer to tell them now and
get it over with?

Three interrogators went up the Toorberg and Oneday
clutched at the bars. They returned with TameBushman's tiny
skull in their hands and asked: Is this a child you murdered?
They threw TameBushman into the cell with him and he told
Oneday the story of how their small band of Bushmen, the last to
resist the white farmers of the Agter-Sneeuberge, had retreated

201

into a cave of their ancestors in the Tandjiesberg. The men had taken up position in a half-moon at the front. Behind them, famished and dying of thirst, were the women and children. They had imprisoned all the old people and the twins born that year in an enclosure of thorn branches down on the plateau and left them there for death to take. From up among the cliffs, before withdrawing into the cave, they had seen the commando approaching the enclosure far below.

The old man began to tell his story to Oneday against the backdrop of the drawings on the rock-face. The commando had sent in a tame Hottentot, stark naked, wearing not a stitch of clothing, to parley with them. But they, the Bushmen, had knocked him down and cut him open, so that he had crawled out of the cave with his guts in his hands, back to the commando. Then the shooting started. The women and children buried themselves up to their noses in the floor of the cave. The farmers wove shields of branches, held them up in front of them and crept closer. The poison-darts stuck quivering like porcupine quills in the shields. Three of the whites were already thrashing about in the poisoned throes of death, before their leaders were able to light a bonfire at the mouth of the cave.

They were smoked out, TameBushman said; most of the women and children suffocated in the smoke, and those that survived were shot just where they were, half buried in the ground. The whites simply searched for yellow noses among the clods, and shot every one they found. The men fell at the mouth of the cave. Bewildered by the smoke, they had rushed out, straight into the muzzles of the guns. But in the confusion he, TameBushman, then a boy of nine, had managed to slither away on his belly and hide himself under the body of a dead farmer. While the massacre of women and children was going on inside the cave, he'd been able to crawl under some vines.

But down where the commando's horses were tethered was one man who had refused to take part in the massacre. Confused by the smoke, TameBushman had walked right into him. The man had caught him, tied his ankles and wrists together, laid him across the back of his horse and taken him back to his wagons. Later, when the man's daughter was married, TameBushman was given to the man's son-in-law as a wedding present.

Tied to a stirrup, he traversed the whole country together with FounderAbel Moolman. They arrived on Toorberg together. At the Eye they lay down on their bellies and drank the clear sweet water, together.

Oneday took the skull from the interrogators and crawled to the mouth of the cave. Again the iron bars, and then a man throwing a bucket of water in his face. The soles of his feet were throbbing. Where would Abel Moolman be wandering? Was he wandering like his daughter did that day when she came walking over to Oneday, high up near the dry Eye? He'd shaken his head at CrazyTilly Moolman when she came towards him, beaming, as though she had known him for years. She must have escaped from the great house. Her legs were covered with scratches, and her elbows and hands were dusty. She was singing: 'Red-red thing, water-thing!' She didn't see him at first, even though she was right beside him. She was imitating the sounds made by the drilling machine when she suddenly turned to him, laughing: 'Antjie Somers, Harelip Man, Antjie Somers, Harelip Man!' She ran giggling down the mountainside, so fast that he was afraid she was going to fall and hurt herself, but she bounded off as surefooted as a goat towards where the drilling machine was working on the Stiefveld beyond the concertina gate.

She was in the cave before him. She was hanging there limp between the interrogators. 'She doesn't know,' said the one at her left arm. 'Or is it that she just doesn't want to talk?' answered the one at her right arm. 'Try again,' ordered the magistrate with only one arm. He came into the cave with TameBushman's skull in his hand. One leg, sticking out of the end of his trousers, was the shining drill-bit. 'What can you tell us?' one of the men asked CrazyTilly. 'We know what you know,' said the other man, 'but we want you to tell it to us.' She lifted her head and looked at Oneday. 'That,' she said, 'is Antjie Somers. Didn't you know?' Oneday jumped up and ran away, but the Malay had set a snare in the footpath ahead of him: a circle in the dust with a spike-thorn in the middle. Leap over the snare! Don't tread in it! O God, help me jump.

But the wizard was standing beside the path. Oneday couldn't jump. He had to land with his foot in the centre of the snare. The thorn bored into his flesh and the snare whipped up out of the dust and wrapped itself round his neck – a round white collar. 'You're a pastor now!' shouted Ma Katie from the corner of the cave where she was sitting with the *tokoloshe* on her lap. The *tokoloshe* spat at him: a jet of tobacco juice that splashed against his left cheek.

The interrogators came to him again. They set down a table and a chair in the cave, with a book and a pen beside it. 'Tell us about your boycott,' they said. 'Why are people no longer allowed to buy from the shop at Voetpad? Who are you carrying the train times around in your pocket for? Who is the man in the black car who comes to fetch you?' And the magistrate with the missing arm came up to him to ask: 'Did you see the gun go off?'

Later he was able to sit upright against the wall. The Bushman drawings stopped moving. Slowly, like the light bulb above the interrogators' table, his thoughts swung back and forth in his head, slowly back and forth in the gentle breeze of the fan.

Eventually he couldn't see CrazyTilly any longer – nor Shala, nor Ma Katie, nor the one-armed magistrate. Perhaps TameBushman was under the heap of blankets? For a moment Meisie was there with the children, but she'd only come to ask: 'Why have you not called to us?'

Perhaps he was back in the township house where he had been caught? The children were screaming outside in the streets and swarming past the front of the house in droves. There was a cluster of Casspirs at the bottom of the street, crowded together like giant corn-crickets. Then they advanced, growling, their wheels bouncing over the burning car tyres and fuel drums. As Oneday peered cautiously through the door of the house, a young lad lit the fuse of a petrol bomb right in front of him and hurled it at the leading Casspir. There was a dull thud, the sound of glass shattering, flame splashing up against the nose of the vehicle and dripping down onto the ground. Then the shooting began, and there were people falling round about him. A bunch of them burst into the house, thrust him aside and rushed screaming out of the back door. The girls' skirts swirled up high above their smooth, young legs as they leapt over the wall. Tear gas burnt his nose and eyes as he bent over one of the children who had fallen on the gravel path in front of the house and was now lying half across a bed of crushed flowers. Coughing from the tear gas, he lifted the child in his arms and when he looked up he had to wipe the tears from his eyes.

The soldier raised his visor and looked at him. 'Oneday Riet,' said CrossAbel Moolman. They faced each other in the burning street. Later CrossAbel pulled him by the arm to the corner of the street where an incinerated man was lying in a puddle of melted rubber. Only the fingers of one hand remained, comically upright in the ash-grey residue.

'One of your own people, Oneday Riet,' said CrossAbel. Later, on the Casspir, Oneday had to duck just like the soldiers to avoid the wires strung across the street at neck-height for troops on the Casspirs.

Above the smoky haze of the township, far beyond the plain, the blue-grey crown of the Toorberg was visible. Cross-Abel turned to him and said: 'Toorberg.' Through the township hovels they rushed before he handed Oneday over to the interrogators, whose first task was to help him remove his collar.

Chapter 36

Quietly, Granny Olivier watched Ella and the man in De la Rey's dressing-gown sitting in the deserted sitting-room sipping liqueurs. By this time the night was far spent, and she would not have approved of such behaviour were it not for the fact that there was a constant coming and going of search parties on the farmyard outside. Ella was talking to the magistrate with unselfconscious honesty, exactly as she had with De la Rey long ago. There was no sign of the evasiveness and timidity that characterized her conversations with Abel. In De la Rey, in that disabled man with his love of books, people always said, Ella would find a soul mate, a friend and a confidant. All she had from Abel was fear and despair; he was a man whose duties left no room for love of a wife. In the silence Granny Olivier thought yet again: the life of the Moolman women was cheerless, her own perhaps the most miserable of them all. For first her father, Japie Olivier, went off with the forefather of the Coetzers to search for the Kruger millions in Mozambique, and was lost. Then Soois and his commando launched their campaign of defiance up in the Toorberg just when she and OldAbel were on the point of being married. Then, soon after her wedding to Old-Abel, there were all those strange telegrams from his brother Andreas the Poet, as well as the rumours about Judge Lucius's indiscretions on the Bench. Lucius disturbed the entire system of precedents with his eccentric judgements, particularly his decisions in connection with Crimes of the Right Hand. He was alleged to have asked, rhetorically, from the Bench: 'Is there any difference between life and death? Surely one is no different from the other? The death sentence, therefore, is no punishment.'

For OldAbel who had no taste for Soois's rebellion, nor Andreas's ballads, nor Lucius's judgements, those were difficult days, for he'd had to step into his father's boots and when FounderAbel had tamed that wild stretch of country, he had done it with fierce determination.

One Abel is like the next, people would say. You can't tell the difference between them. They're all equally stubborn, equally arrogant, equally afflicted with avarice and land-hunger. But Granny Olivier had known three Abels, and was now watching the fourth and youngest. Perhaps they were all similar in their fear of being unable to rule their possessions adequately, but there were definite differences between them. These were things which she had not realized until after her stroke, until she had to spend day after day on the sun-porch, sitting motionless under the crocheted rug, watching the activities on the farm-yard. Sometimes they had wheeled her outside and there, under the willows beside the homestead, she would watch the hairy grey caterpillars crawling up and down the tree-trunks, and a praying mantis rubbing its forefeet together, and an ant search-ing and scrabbling across the gravel of the yard. At shearing time and on dipping days they sometimes took her out to the kraals. There she would sit under the corrugated iron awning which her son Abel had erected for her, watching the men at their work.

Everyone was afraid of her small, black eyes watching them, motionless but intent, while a young boy with a bunch of ostrich feathers waved the flies away from her face. She wanted to look up and tell them: I am glad to be here where the hands of men have a firm grip on things and Toorberg's affairs are properly transacted. But she had lost the power of speech.

When they wheeled her past the mirror in the passage, she saw her own reflection: a twisted, shrunken, bitter old woman, with a crookedly drooping mouth, expressionless jet-black eyes, her old hands shrivelled and distorted like the broken wings of a bird.

She'd grown more and more bitter until Abel sent for Katie Danster, then a young girl whom Andries Moolman, Floris' shame-child, already had his eye on, to push her wheelchair round the farm and to talk to her.

'Tell her whatever you like,' Abel told Katie Danster, 'but just see that you talk to her. And put this piece of locomotive grease into her hands every day and see that she kneads it with her fingers.'

Katie Danster pushed her all over the farm, with a strength and fierceness one would never have suspected in one with such a small frame. All along the access paths to the planted fields she wobbled early each morning, then up to the concertina gate, round the stock pens and outbuildings – once Katie Danster even wheeled her right down to the gateway to the farm, where they sat and watched the buses at the Halt. Katie Danster talked incessantly, about every subject under the Toorberg sun, including the stories about Floris Moolman, for – like everyone else except Granny Olivier's son Abel – Katie thought the old lady's brain was dead.

But she heard it all. She heard about the farm labourers' lives in the thatched cottages on the slope of the mountain. She heard about bitter, young Andries Moolman who used to come courting Katie each evening after Granny Olivier had been bathed and put to bed. She heard about the heroic deeds which Andries's great-grandfather, the missionary, did amongst the people and about how Andries had sworn to have a son who would imitate his grandfather – a son who would lead his people out of the misery of bondage into the free country which the Lord had prepared for them.

'Andries says you Moolmans are just Boer bastards,' Katie chattered on as she squatted in front of Granny Olivier's lifeless face. 'You're as grasping as hell itself, but what you don't know is that moth and rust corrupt.' At first Granny Olivier felt rage rising up inside her, but when she looked into the open, honest eyes of Katie Danster and Katie pressed the locomotive grease into her hands, saying: 'Knead it, little granny, knead yourself to life so that you can take control of your house again. Without you the servants are idling in the kitchen,' she softened towards her. If she could, she would have smiled at Katie. But she wouldn't even try to defend the Moolmans. What, after all, what did this young *meidjie* know of the hard road which FounderAbel's faith and daring had carved through the wilderness, away from the Dutch and British domination of the Cape? What did she know of the great task of converting the heathen in this black land, of exterminating vermin and of ploughing and sowing this soil?

208

Gradually, Granny Olivier's hands regained their skill. Life seeped back into the old joints. Every week Katie went searching along the railway line for a fresh chunk of locomotive grease, and each week Granny Olivier's kneading softened the stiff lump faster than the week before. Her face, however, remained numb, even though her insights were more penetrating: she developed a greater understanding of the actions of the Moolman brothers – even of that moody Soois's rebellion. She got to know De la Rey much better; De la Rey, her wanderer son, the one who turned his back on Toorberg, because he felt he didn't belong there. Or because Ella preferred Abel?

She understood everyone better, except poor Postmaster who had gone and married that papist Amy O'Leary. 'You'll never tame an Irishman,' OldAbel had said, 'particularly not if he is also a Catholic. They've got one idol only, and that's the Pope. What's worse is: they worship a woman – the mother of Jesus Christ!' Catholics were impure. No son born of such a union could ever be a Moolman.

But Postmaster had put his foot down. For once in his life he had refused to bow before the will of his fathers. It was the last time, too, for when the postmaster at the Halt was bitten by a mad meerkat and died of rabies, Postmaster Moolman – obsessed since childhood with postage stamps and envelopes, which he hid in an old trunk – was appointed in his stead.

They were difficult years for OldAbel, particularly when he had to cut De la Rey out of his will. It was at this time, too, that the Eye began to dry up. One evening Abel had come home dusty and worried. 'The Eye's seventh mouth has been muddy since yesterday,' he said.

'Perhaps there has been some movement under the earth,' she consoled him. She was afraid it might have been the comet which had passed over, but she didn't mention this to him: he was not a man for superstitions.

The next morning OldAbel went up the mountain before breakfast to check. He found the Eye's seventh mouth dry: it had stopped running during the night. OldAbel immediately sent a team of men up the Toorberg with picks and shovels. Granny

Olivier followed them up the mountain, despite the high blood-pressure that made her head throb. They dug open the seventh mouth, past thin reeds and rushes and long strings of half-dried duckweed. But as the day wore on and they were forced to use crowbars to break through the stone slab, OldAbel realized there was nothing blocking the spring. The empty black channel disappearing into the earth lay open, slimy, washed smooth by the years. But dry.

The other six mouths of the Eye bubbled forth strongly for another seven months, but by the end of the summer they, too, were losing some of their strength. The water no longer had the same pressure. Too much of it was filtering away into the river-bed and too little was reaching the fields. When OldAbel said: 'I shall have to dig a furrow and line it with concrete,' Granny Olivier read in his eyes a fear she had never known in him before. 'The farm is going to dry out under my feet,' he said, as though he was personally to blame for the subterranean water drying up.

When he started the digging of the furrow, from high up at the Eye right down to the dam in the Vlei, Granny Olivier's blood pressure was so high that on some days she could do no more than sit dizzily at the sitting-room window. She lost her enthusiasm for crochet and it was many years, when her hands were once more skilful from Katie Danster's patient care, before she again began to crochet. Then Abel, who regarded the recovery of her hands as the direct result of his own faith, stopped in front of her one day and said: 'Crochet a table-napkin for me, Ma, and embroider my initials on it. Come on, Ma, show me you can.'

At such times Abel could be like a second De la Rey. If he had been like that more often, life would have been a great deal easier for Ella Coetzer. The Coetzers of Altydsomer were wealthy people; an old family, but they never set the same standards for themselves that the Moolmans did. When their grandfather perished in foreign parts while searching for old President Kruger's state treasure, they learnt humility.

If only Abel and Ella had spent more time talking together,

as her daughter-in-law was doing in the sitting room with the magistrate at this moment! It was almost like old times: the young De la Rey and Ella, sitting on a low wall in the orchard on a bright spring morning, their heads close together, deep in conversation among the first peach blossoms. Until Abel, his sleeves rolled high up on his upper arms, his wet hair clinging to his forehead, came striding back from the fields. Without a word, Ella rose and followed him to the homestead.

Suddenly Granny Olivier had a vivid recollection of a peach tree, the sultry drone of bees among the boughs, Ella's fluttering pale blue frock, and De la Rey with his chin on his knees.

Only once, when Ella made her choice, was there a flash of the Moolman lightning in De la Rey's eyes. 'I'll come back, Ma,' he had said to Granny Olivier. 'For Ella.'

Chapter 37

Ella sent for the Malay to throw the bones for her.

The wizard had sent a message before she summoned him: a ragged boy came to the back door and stood there wide-eyed and nervous till the boer mastiffs had sniffed him up and down. Then he blurted out: 'The wizard can help, the wizard says, if you need him.'

Ella considered his offer while she sat listening: Tilly was singing quietly in her locked room. The magistrate was taking one book after another from the bookcase in the library, paging through and then replacing them. Silence, Granny Olivier always said, was Toorberg's meanest asset: you could always hear guests breathing in their rooms, an Abel knocking out his pipe in the library, servants scraping their knives as they peeled potatoes in the kitchen. It was the high ceilings, the deep cellar under the floors and the steep roof which amplified all sounds.

Let him come, she decided, and later that morning she took CrazyTilly by the hand and went out into the front garden to where the Malay had already cleared a bare patch of earth with his cunning hands. He had been a long while coming, he explained, as the magistrate stood to one side and watched him, because he had first had to go searching up among the cliffs of the Toorberg in the early morning mist to pick wet leaves – leaves with the night's dew still on them, leaves speckled with the shining, fat droplets of life.

He'd had to search for a long time, he said, as he undid the skin pouch at his hip, because the mist was dense and the plants had misled him: first he'd gone down a ravine, then he'd run into a blind cliff-face, then he'd taken fright at a sudden herd of antelope, and then he was lost, wet and cold, wrapped round in white mist. But, he explained as he blew across his collection of little bones, no matter how he listened, he could not hear Abel anywhere. He'd gone up to TameBushman's cave to listen there, too, but the wind had nothing to tell him either. All the wind would sing about, he said with a quick, cunning glance at the magistrate, was the sad death of Trickle, the child of the wild geese, the child who looked up and up at the geese and suddenly stepped into a borehole, the child who looked down and down and suddenly fell into the wet belly of the earth, the child who trod gingerly, tiptoeing through the reeds, as though a ghost had him by the hand, as though the wind was his father.

His words seemed to liberate a rhythm within her, and CrazyTilly gently started rocking as she held Ella's hand. Then the Malay cast his bones onto the open patch and crouched on his hands and knees to read them. He capered about once or twice, breathing heavily, snorted like an affrighted goat, and suddenly looked up the length of Ella's legs, slowly, right up to her face. Then he looked at CrazyTilly, and then at the magistrate who was trying to match the same malice, the same cunning knowledge, in outstaring those little yellow eyes.

The Malay's hands were fluttering like bats above the bones, like dancing shadows. Here, he pointed, there . . . and Tilly, her hand over her mouth and her eyes starting out of her head, slowly sank down onto her haunches.

Just as it seemed that the Malay was about to detect some significance in the lie of the bones, CrossAbel's motorcycle came growling round the corner of the ram shed, slithered in wild esses across the yard and raced up to them. Pulling the crash-helmet off his sweaty face, he exclaimed roughly: 'O Ma, you're not listening to this crook again, surely? Can't you see he's full of dagga? There we are, searching ourselves to a standstill up in the mountain, and you sit down here playing in the yard!'

Getting off the motorbike, he kicked out the stand and then strode over to them. 'Go on, Malay, clear off.' He stamped his boot down among the magic bones. The Malay looked past the boot, then hastily raked the little bones, copper rings and leaves of succulents together, and limped off across the farmyard till he disappeared behind the ram shed.

Ella looked at CrossAbel for a long while and sighed. Then she took CrazyTilly by the elbow, checked to see whether the magistrate was following her, and slowly walked back to the house. But the magistrate remained standing in the same position for a long time, even after CrossAbel had raced off again. He looked at the eye cleared in the gravel of the farmyard. At its centre, like an iris, was the print of CrossAbel's boot.

Chapter 38

'This farm cannot ever dry up,' FounderAbel told OldAbel. 'Not with an Eye that spouts the sweetest water north of the Hottentots-Holland mountains. Water as sweet as this comes straight from God Himself – we have a divine calling in this place.'

It was the burden of this heavy calling that had exhausted OldAbel Moolman so early in life. He was the one who from his youth had to tame this stubborn soil. He was the one who had to pray for rain. He was the one who had to witness the drying up and the death of the Eye. If only he was a latter-day Moses who could strike the rock so that it would crack open and spew forth life-giving water! He was the only one who had to obey Founder-Abel's words: Celebrate Life!

Who could blame him for waiting in the shade of the pepper tree in front of the Agricultural Co-op on the day the magistrate arrived at the town to lay bare the tragedy of Toorberg? Invisible, he stood, suffused in the scent of the pepper berries, dead still, with the moving shadows of the branches falling through him. And when the man with the missing arm came walking along the street, an immense fury raged in OldAbel. Who gave this armless creature the right to take up position wherever he liked on the Toorberg farmstead, like that drilling machine of young Abel's, and delve for the truth? Who gave him the right to guess the secrets of the family graves and to peer into the sins of the fathers? Who gave him the right to visit the Skaamfamilie's cottage and sit and have coffee out of their mugs, like someone with no sense of discrimination or propriety?

He would have forfeited fifty ewes to be able to stop the interfering stranger, for he knew, without any doubt, that nothing good could possibly come of it. It was odd that from under the pepper tree he could also see the Malay, seated in front of the small Cash Store across the road. With a knotted flour bag in his hand, the Malay was sitting under the shadow of the roof and

OldAbel had the impression that the scaryman – as they had called him as children – was looking straight at him.

As the magistrate came round the corner at the bottom of the street, the Malay shifted his position, and when the magistrate was right in front of OldAbel – so close that OldAbel could make out a brownish mole on his neck – the Malay bounced to his feet, sat down again, stood up again, just like a meerkat at the entrance to its burrow.

Fifty fat ewes would OldAbel have given, to stop this stranger poking his nose into Toorberg's affairs. A farm that is choking to death is not a pretty sight. When you're dying you don't want an audience. Crossing over to the other side is a humiliating experience, because you have to leave your dead body, no matter how much you love it. You don't want spectators watching you.

Sitting in the shade of one of his aqueduct's tumbledown pillars, OldAbel watched the magistrate standing behind an aloe observing the Malay's hut through binoculars. That was what he didn't like about magistrates: their never-ending suspicions. Anyone who has suspicions devotes his time to searching for proof that will confirm his suspicions. Fickle people, magistrates. Clever Lucius had been like that too, on his visits from the city: his head full of foolish notions about God and man, and everlastingly searching for confirmation of his theories.

He had built this aqueduct with his bare hands when the Eye began to dry up. First they'd had to build a concrete sluice to divert the water from the pool at the eye, and then he'd had to use the theodolite to line up and measure and decide where to excavate and where to build up to ensure that the water channel gradient was right all the way to the dam in the Vlei. OldAbel discovered an unsuspected talent in himself for making such calculations when he had to work out the run of the water, the fall of the ground, the speed of the stream and the ideal strength for the wall of the Vlei dam. To maintain an even flow they had to dig down to the height of a man in some places, and for over four hundred metres they had built pillars to support the great water channel.

216

'An aqueduct!' Judge Lucius had exclaimed in astonishment, in the course of one of his visits. 'The Romans were building them thousands of years ago, brother. Stunning constructions!' OldAbel would willingly have consigned Lucius to hell. Get back to your book-learning, brother, is what he wanted to say. Toorberg hasn't got time or room for your kind of knowledge. Nor for Andreas's artiness either. Rather give me Soois who at least stood his ground up here in the mountains against the British patrols. But for the sake of peace he kept silence. Also because Toorberg was drying up and this awareness lay like a lead weight on his chest. These were his worries during the building of the water channel, while Lucius, relaxed and on holiday, sat on a rock with sketch-pad and pencil, drawing the aqueduct to show his colleagues at the Bar.

'The sun drinks water, the sun drinks blood!' sang the labourers with the picks. For how many months had they dug and built to get the water from the Eye diverted into the Vlei dam at last! For OldAbel, time stopped; he rang the farmyard bell before dawn and then cursed and tongue-lashed the sleepy workers to wakefulness as they trudged to work. One morning, after they had spent a fortnight working away at a single huge boulder with their picks and the wind had carried the sulphurous smell of broken stone all the way to the farmyard itself, he'd had to take his whip to the muttering convicts. His own folk worked faithfully, but the hired convicts were becoming surly and defiant.

That was when he had decided to use dynamite. He had to plead with the magistrate in town for a licence first, though. They packed in such a large charge that afterwards they had to fill in half the hole they'd blasted: OldAbel had miscalculated the force of the explosive. One of the convicts was never seen again, but everyone said he'd deserted because he was an idler and hard labour with a pick was not to his liking.

The sun had required blood, but there was rejoicing on Toorberg when with Granny Olivier by his side OldAbel opened the sluice-gate at the Eye and the silver snake spouted down the concrete furrow: a rushing, shining streak of water flashing faster than the eye could follow it over the pillars of the aqueduct till it spread, foaming and bubbling, over the dry bed of the Vlei dam.

There was a crowd of workers standing down at the dam. When the shining tip of the water spouted from the channel, they cheered and cheered, and from the top OldAbel and Granny Olivier and the other team of workers could see the shining trail of water all down the slope of the mountain. Granny Olivier burst into tears. That afternoon OldAbel had two oxen roasted on the spit for his workers and the convicts, and until late that night the fires in front of the farm cottages burnt high.

Next morning there was blood on one of the pillars of the aqueduct. OldAbel had risen early to check the whole length of the channel for any possible cracks or leaks, and he'd noticed the blood. Another convict was missing. He'd also deserted, so the others said, at the eleventh hour.

The sun had taken its blood and the aqueduct straddled two dead men as it bore the water from the Eye to the Vlei dam. Other farmers from the district came to gape: only the Moolmans would ever have had the drive to attempt such an undertaking, they said. Only a Moolman could so shamelessly alter the course and fall of God's water.

It was marvellous standing on the wall of the bulging Vlei dam. The water stretched from edge to edge of the dam, and even though the pump was regularly turned on to release irrigation water, the supply from the Eye always kept the dam full. The wild geese returned and nested in the reeds beside the pump. At night OldAbel and Granny Olivier slept with their windows open so they could hear the frogs croaking. One night when the moon was full Granny Olivier, high blood-pressure and all, took OldAbel out onto the dam wall and right there, amid the lush smell of the water, with the pot-bellied moon hanging over them, they cavorted as wildly as any two panting newly-weds.

OldAbel shifted his position under the weathered pillar. Round him lay chunks of mortar and great blocks of fallen stone. A gecko on top of the pillar was looking at him. There were only fragments of masonry left where the channel had formerly run along the stone pillars which had been built with such care. One night, when the Eye had dried up, the channel had suddenly tumbled down.

OldAbel sighed. With the binoculars round his neck, the magistrate was slowly coming towards the remains of the aqueduct. He leant against one of the fallen stone supports, idly kicking against it. The gecko wriggled its tail nervously and slipped away. The magistrate came right up to OldAbel, picked up some of the stones, tested their weight and absent-mindedly dropped them again.

Suspicions, thought OldAbel bitterly, suspicions ever in search of proof.

Chapter 39

'My dear wife,' wrote the magistrate as he sat in front of an open window in De la Rey's room. It was midday, just after dinner. Ella was taking a nap, and CrossAbel was sulkily searching the drawers of his father's desk for possible clues.

'A strange thing has occurred,' he wrote. 'The owner of this farm, who happens also to be the prime suspect in my investigation, has disappeared without a trace. As you will conclude from the address above, I am still on Toorberg, partly to lend moral support to Mrs Moolman – who is already acting like a widow – but also to keep my finger on the pulse of events affecting the course of my investigation.

'As I have previously written to you, I have become involved here, against my will (or could it perhaps be voluntarily after all?), in a matter which I find extremely strange. The *ratio* of Criminal Law has always rested on three concepts: transgression, guilt and punishment. The second of these concepts raises the question: What conclusion should the investigator draw before finding that a person has committed a criminal offence? That is the question which I have to investigate. It is also the reason why I have seized this opportunity of staying in the Toorberg homestead myself.

'There are many questions in my mind, my love, many questions which you might regard as unnecessary, but in all those years on the Bench I have lost the capacity to think spontaneously. I number my questions and I need to have the answers in the correct sequence. When confronted with a situation such as this, however, I feel I am in danger of losing my trust in the Law.

'I realize of course that I have grown rusty. Years of ruling on housebreakings and stabbings are not conducive to honing the legal mind. The formulas which are appropriate in the criminal courts are simple and I have needed to do no more than compare each set of facts with those formulas. But here, in this

220

part of the country, there is something ominous which lies outside my experience. Could that be the reason why in his report my colleague asserted that there was no reason to suspect foul play? Would it not be better, safer – more convenient even – simply to close the book?

'I do not know, so it is with unresolved questions in my mind that I must now conclude. I hope to settle this matter soon: my integrity and Justice both expect it of me. Justice has been good to me over the years and I shall do my best to meet the Department's requirements.

'Ever your longing husband and friend,
Abraham van der Ligt.'

Chapter 40

Streams of living water, thought Abel as he breathed in the rich, cool smell of the stream spouting from the Eye. Light was breaking through the green branches of the thorn tree in full bloom beside the pool. The delicate yellow tassels shed by the tree tumbled down onto the water, floating with the motion of the water past the child's narrow white shoulders, damming up against the rock, breaking free again and trailing away through the rapids and down the mountain.

Abel watched the child tumbling in the water, splashing, shrieking with laughter, bouncing up and then diving down again. The ripples spread right to Abel's feet as he knocked out his pipe against his boots and slowly repacked and lit it. Earth, he thought, my most fertile earth, slopes covered with redgrass and sourgrass. Sit on a horse and the top of the grasses will reach your stirrup. Paradysberg was the other name which Founder-Abel was said to have considered for the farm, but when the evening mist rose out of the marshes and the wild geese started their crying and the Bushman paintings were flickering on the rocky faces of the cave in the firelight, he thought: Mysterious earth; enchantingly, magically beautiful: Toorberg.

Now the child was chasing a dragonfly across the water. He stalked the insect hanging over him in the air, leapt suddenly and made a grab for it, but the dragonfly flashed sideways and the child landed on his haunches in the shallows with a splash.

Only the previous day Abel had sat watching the Malay clambering about among the cliffs, constantly stooping to pick moss and herbs and stow them in his leather pouch. People believed he had an extra eye, so Abel took care to keep his head down under the branches of the thorn tree at the Eye. He motioned to the child, too, to keep still, crouched among the rushes, until the wizard had disappeared down the ravine on the opposite slope.

Only once did the Malay stop, look round and stare fixedly

at the Eye. Abel could see the whites of his eyes, the fine caste-scars on his cheeks, the brass ring in one ear. Then the Malay jerked round angrily and hurried away, disappearing down the ravine. Later they heard him chanting his strange songs.

It was the Malay who had made life bearable for him and Ella with CrazyTilly. There had never been any hope for her, but the Malay's dagga-tea was a godsend in her really unruly times. Eventually Ella planted a whole bed of dagga plants alongside the herb garden, and although the police were aware of the fact, they never took any action.

In his long nights alone in the library, calculating bushels of wheat, gallons of water, acres of farmland and bales of lucerne, Abel sometimes had a sip of the tea himself. The taste was rather acerbic and rough on this lips. Suddenly the Malay loomed up before him with his bracelet of magical bones and his laughing yellow teeth. Later Abel received repeated visitations from Old-Abel and FounderAbel, seated solemnly in the easy chairs on the other side of the writing desk.

'Abel,' FounderAbel's voice would rumble. 'Abel,' the echo resounded through his days and nights. 'Abel!' he heard, high up on the windmills in the lean months after the troubles round the boreholes. Abel, where are you taking your patrimony? Are you farming successfully, like your fathers – or are you failing? Have you found water for the acres you have inherited? How many bushels did the Ouland yield this year? How many bales of lucerne were there in the Hartseerland? How many gallons are you using to irrigate the Vlei?

The arrival of the drilling machine, red and shining and higher than the roof-ridge of the great house, brought Abel some temporary respite: the visitations of the ancestors decreased, as every day the hammer blows of hope resounded across the farmyard. It was the handsomest piece of machinery the district had ever seen: with its shining rods, its grim, tungsten steel drilling head, its tough iron elbows, it would not be denied.

But as the machine was moved from one spot to another, in obedience to the dictates of Dowser's divining rods, the noctur-

223

nal visitations started up again. All at once De la Rey's footprints appeared in the kitchen garden: the marks of his lameness were unmistakable, one print deeper than the other. Ella took to wandering feverishly round the house. She had the farmyard freshly raked every evening and went out first thing in the morning, before her coffee even, to look for footprints. The boer mastiffs would growl on the verandas at night, but the only sounds when one went to investigate were the hiss of the rams urinating on the floor of their shed, and the jackals howling up in the distance. Nothing but the night, the mountain looming black against the stars, sometimes a white-haloed moon.

People always said: If Ella had not been two or three inches taller than De la Rey, she would have married him. His hand was gentler than Abel's, his mind was as sharp as Lucius's, he was as artistic as Andreas – but he was a man with the city in his blood, a man with an urge to wander. Ella had chosen Abel instead. He was a man who decided early in life that there was only one way of taking and that was by grabbing. Have a good look and snatch what you want. Set your sights and shoot straight at your target.

The day De la Rey's footprints appeared Abel sent for the Malay – and had him come into the tractor shed, so that Ella would not know. 'There are footprints on my property,' he told the Malay. 'One is deep, the other is shallow.'

The Malay narrowed his eyes. 'The man whose tracks they are will return,' he said. 'He may not look the same as you remember him, but you will know who it is, because he will wander round and round you. He will speak round and round you, with everyone else but not with you. When he appears, you will know it is the man who leaves two sets of tracks, one deep, the other shallow.'

With a green banknote in his hand, the man in jackal skins limped back to his mountain hut and Abel returned to the library. Dully he looked round at the portraits, the hats, the books. Family tradition had it that under the floorboards there were four fire-blackened stones, unmoved since FounderAbel and Grandmother Magtilt had cooked their meals there in front of their wagons.

Now the magistrate was there, the quiet man who was questioning everybody on the farm: first Katie Danster, then Mailbag Moolman and Dowser du Pisani, Amy O'Leary Moolman, later Ella herself; Oneday Riet in goal, too, apparently. The man had the law and righteousness on his side, so he was now walking around the farm as though he owned it. 'No Moolman surrenders jurisdiction,' OldAbel once said when the government had decided at cabinet level that the Toor River should be dammed. The government wanted to build the wall of a state dam just above the homestead to supply water to the Upper Camdeboo – to the Kinghorns, the Van der Merwes, the Minnaars, the Van Heerdens and the Jordaans, all of them on the verge of bankruptcy as a result of plagues of locusts and the movement of water tables. But at the gate of the farm OldAbel had taken up station with his shotgun and stared coldly at the petty official who had been sent to survey the land. OldAbel stared him quite out of countenance, people said. When the letter from the government arrived, OldAbel noticed the official ink-stamp, gave it one look and went out to the pens to dip his sheep.

But now the magistrate was leaving his tracks all over the farm. The windmills of the district were beckoning to Abel: he longed for that glorious sensation of sitting beside the whirling head and talking and shouting as loud as he liked. The wind in the shining vanes was deafening as it tugged at his hair; the legs of his trousers flapped in the immensity of the power of nature. He could talk to the gods, call out to the mountains, curse the earth, as he sat with his legs spread wide above a hole tunnelling down into the nether waters deep under slabs of rock where only water insects and algae lived.

Only the widow had never made demands on him. She was only too glad to receive the attentions of the foremost farmer in the district. Eventually he used to park his Land Rover quite unashamedly right in front of her house. Let all the district see, let the entire town tie their tongues into a tangle, let the deacons and the elders on the church council knot their cocks on account of him – he couldn't care less. 'Celebrate Life, and keep it holy,' he told the widow in her simple cottage where the cuckoo hopped out of its little clock door every hour to chortle about the flight of time.

If only Ella had created such restfulness for him in his own home! If only she had honoured him as the widow honoured him, without demands or questions, simply with love. Late at night, as he drove back to Toorberg, there were the red eyes of spring-hares in the road. Once something limped across the road: a baboon, or the *tokoloshe*, or perhaps the Malay. One night there was a wild goose in the middle of the road, half-lamed, and dazzled by the headlights. When he went to town again the next day he noticed the goose dead at the side of the road.

When you pick up a spoor, OldAbel had taught him, never let it go – but what does one do when it is the spoor that keeps running round you? When you cannot trace it back to its origin because it runs in circles which you cannot penetrate?

Not even the minister, who was old enough to be his father, remonstrated with him, about the widow. And neither the captain of police nor the detectives nor the commissioner of oaths nor the town magistrate raised any objections when he announced his intention of erecting a marble slab over the borehole – why go digging out the poor child only to bury him again somewhere else? Toorberg was his jurisdiction, he celebrated life here in his own way, and no one dared gainsay him.

Marvellous, magical earth, this Toorberg. Earth like a block of stone. Earth which sometimes would suddenly resist him and announce implacably: Abel, stop!

What was the use of thinking round and round the borehole, round and round that morning with the wind stirring the silver leaves of the poplars? Because it was a morning on which everything that was Toorberg had come to a head: Soois's blood liquefying every twelve months on the garden wall; Tilly baring her swollen white belly under the pealing schoolhouse bell; CrossAbel telling how he had shot his first black in the location, disappearing in the Land Rover, returning late that night hopelessly drunk and crashing into the rose garden; Ella standing in front of him with her diary in her hand, announcing: De La Rey has returned.

Abel beckoned to the child. There comes a time when escape is no longer possible, when life becomes a dodder twining round you and in you at every point with its tendrils. Cut it off wherever you can, somewhere there will always be a thread of the creeper left to start entwining you once again with its relentless fecundity. As the child swam closer, Abel looked out over the valley. He noticed a bunch of people in the farmyard; Cross-Abel's bakkie drove up in a billowing cloud of dust, spun round with a swagger and lurched to a stop.

You are the Abel now, thought Abel, as he watched Cross-Abel getting out of the bakkie, arms akimbo. He felt neither heartache nor regret, however, nor sympathy nor even pity for the birthmark across CrossAbel's ear. It could as easily have been me, he thought, but now, mercifully, it is a different Abel: Abel the Fourth, perhaps the stubbornest of them all. Probably, given his barren loins, the last Abel, who would one day sit on the stoep looking out over the farm, an old, bitter man. What would he see? What would he hope for? What would he flee from?

As the cool body of the little boy leant against him, Abel touched the child's wet hair. They saw Ella walk out onto the veranda and CrossAbel gesticulating. Behind Ella, in the shadow of the veranda, stood the magistrate. From here one could not detect that he had only one arm.

The bunch of people split into two. One group climed up hurriedly onto the back of CrossAbel's bakkie, which drove off before the last man was properly over the railings. The second group ran down the footpath through the poplar grove, leaving Ella and the magistrate alone on the farmyard.

'Look,' said Abel to the boy. 'Look, Noah, they're searching for me. They're looking for me in all the places where they think I ought to be.'

227

Chapter 41

LittleKitty had seen Trickle playing round the borehole, but she was too scared to tell anyone, not even Mailbag, what she'd seen.

With his little face almost touching the blades of the grass, he stalked the hole and then suddenly rolled over on his back. At first she heard him rummaging among the dead leaves, but then he lay still as he listened to the wild geese flying over. She saw him chasing a dragonfly that was circling the mouth of the moist hole. The next moment, when she straightened up again after stooping to pull some dead wood free of its covering of leaves, Trickle had disappeared down the hole.

The dragonfly still hung over the hole for a moment, but when LittleKitty found her voice again, it shot off into the trees. As she ran screaming up to the great house, she met the wizard draped with skins and rings on a bend in the footpath. He simply stood there, looking like a jackal caught up against a fence. She later thought she'd seen him putting a dead dragonfly into the pouch at his hip, but how could she be sure? And how could she tell anyone – even Mailbag – if she wasn't sure?

She burst out of the grove and the nearest thing to her was the farmyard bell. She hung onto the rope with her whole weight and kicked herself up and down. The great clapper started swinging sluggishly, but then found its own rhythm and rang out louder and louder until Ella emerged on the back veranda in amazement. By that time, Abel Moolman was already on his way to the borehole. How had he known? Who had told him? Or did time stand still when one was in the presence of the wizard, as the backvelders all believed? What happened between her first scream at the borehole and the moment when someone pulled her away from the bellrope?

Later, when everybody was gathered round the borehole, her confusion had dissipated, but her fear of the wizard made her resolve to keep silent. She would say that she had heard Noah calling from the borehole and had rung the bell. More

228

than that, she decided, she would never say nor enquire into. What was the wizard, like a forest *tokoloshe*, doing near the borehole? Had the Malay cast a spell on Noah to get him to grab at the dragonfly and fall in? Was he after Noah's little balls?

He was the same wizard who had forced GranmaKitty to drink a concoction to make LittleKitty's father, Andries, come away. The Malay had always been there. Some folk said he'd even been there before FounderAbel, Jan Swaat and TameBushman trekked into the valley. Others maintained that FounderAbel had had him fetched from Mozambique. There were those who believed he'd come from the Malay Quarter in Cape Town, since he was half-Malay. Another group held that he'd come from Central Africa, because he threw the bones like the people who lived in the rain forests at the equator.

The wizard had always known when to appear. With every baby of Meisie Pool's, the Malay had been there at the moment when the birthpangs began. He would suddenly appear at the door of the Stiefveld cottage with a little bag of herbs in his hand, curious to know the sex of the child. When Andrew Riet was born with a stiff little prick, his greedy hand had grabbed at the child. Ma Katie had instantly knocked his paw away and, later, washed her hand in turpentine because she had touched the scaryman.

From early morning on the day GranmaKitty breathed her last, the Malay squatted in the shadow of the rabbit hutch, waiting for her spirit, and for the next seven days he could be heard up among the ravines of Toorberg keening her death. The scandalmongers said the wizard used to visit GranmaKitty in her lonely times after Floris Moolman had been driven off the farm. The wizard used to come drinking her blood, they said, and stealing breast-milk out of the mouth of the bastard child Andries Riet. That was what made Andries Riet, who had been born without a father and with the wrong surname, so bitter all his life.

It was the Malay, too, who by the power of his thought had killed Soois Moolman, because that cross-grained Moolman had once caught him among the motherless lambs, with one lamb sucking at each of the wizard's ten fingers. In obedience to his aggressive instincts, Soois climbed into him then and there and gave him a terrible thrashing. The wizard then put a curse on him and the very next year Soois died with a bullet in his throat.

Who was she to ask, thought LittleKitty, what the Malay was doing with Noah du Pisani among the trees? Had she seen what she saw? For how long had the wizard's eyes brought time to a stop in the grove?

Mailbag, quite unconcerned and as randy as Shala's leading ram, wouldn't listen to her, either. Not that she blamed him. He had never discovered that she was the one who rang the bell. In the turmoil no one ever thought of asking her straight out what had happened.

Perhaps, she thought, she ought to discuss it with Oneday. But Oneday refused to listen to anything about the Malay. 'The *tokoloshe*,' Oneday once told the congregation in the lucerne shed at Overwood, 'is not a monkey-devil sitting on the Malay's shoulder. There's no such thing as a *tokoloshe*. He's nothing but a spook in your heads. Forget that idea and stop calling the Malay every time an owl perches on the roof of your cottage, or whenever you slaughter an animal at full moon and there is only air in the bones instead of marrow. Stop running to the Malay every time a cow shoves a back foot into a pail in the milking shed: rather tie the cow's legs together. Stop crawling to the Malay whenever a child is born with a pearl on the eye: go to the clinic instead. And when you feel death coming over you, or sin stirring within you, then come to the Lord God who sent His Son Jesus Christ to the workers of the world to live among us and lead us forth to liberation.'

But Ma Katie could not forget the *tokoloshe*. Some nights she would scream and sit bolt upright in bed, trembling. Her chest heaving, she would pant: 'The *tokoloshe* was sitting there on the wardrobe. He spat at me.'

One night she panted: 'He's got blue balls like a male ape!' and they had to make her a poultice of hot eucalyptus leaves and keep it on her tight chest till the daystar shone brightly above the Toorberg. When Kitty opened the back door, she and Meisie

Pool both saw the wizard standing beside a huge fire in front of his house on the opposite slope of the mountain.

'What's he making a fire for at this time of the morning?' asked Meisie Pool. At the time Meisie had been on the point of running away again, back to the Camdeboo, because she wanted to live under the love of a man, not under Ma Katie, and Oneday had been away travelling for weeks, preaching about the liberation which Jesus Christ brings. 'Everybody's got to know!' Oneday cried. 'Especially in these days when people are being shot on their own doorsteps!'

During the weekends Shala would disappear over the mountain, apparently to Eerste Station, where he later became involved in helping with Oneday's work. He would return on foot, exhausted, all the way from the Camdeboo, on Monday mornings. Sometimes his body was black and blue where he'd been beaten, and his eyes would remain red and stinging until the middle of the week, but he wouldn't ever say anything. All he would say was that he would skin that Malay alive if he ever again sent the *tokoloshe* to perch on Ma Katie's wardrobe in the middle of the night and spit at her.

All these things made LittleKitty decide: it was by the wizard's sorcery that Noah had fallen down the borehole. Years before, the Malay had appeared in court in connection with the disappearance of a young boy from Voetpad. The police had discovered a dried little scrotum in the wizard's hut, but the court had not been able to prove anything. The Judge pronounced the Malay half-mad, but no one had been able to prove beyond doubt that the wizard had actually murdered the little boy.

Sometimes LittleKitty dreamt that all the boreholes on the farm were stuffed with little dead boys – and it was the wizard's hands had made all of them disappear.

But these were things she could never tell the magistrate. When he came slowly walking up the path to the Skaamfamilie's cottage a second time, LittleKitty knew: this time he was coming to talk to her. Perhaps on top of everything else the Law was going to arrest her because of her involvement with Mailbag? Or perhaps the wizard had gone around spreading a tale that he'd thought up about her and Noah at the borehole?

As the magistrate was struggling to open the concertina gate with his one arm, she opened the small iron door of the rabbit hutch and crept into the musty, sweet smell of the rabbit droppings and lettuce leaves. The white rabbits bounced around her and one stopped right in front of her, its red eyes staring intently into hers. It's the wizard himself, she thought in terror, right here beside me in the rabbit hutch, but she gritted her teeth and remained motionless till the magistrate's legs had passed the hutch on their way to the front door of the cottage.

She heard him knocking and wriggled her legs in under the damp, mouldy straw. Ma Katie came to the door, walked all round the cottage with the magistrate, but then shook her head and pointed up towards the mountain. The magistrate said goodbye and passed the hutch a second time. Through the wire mesh LittleKitty noticed that despite their thin layer of Stiefveld dust, the magistrate's shoes were very highly polished.

She remained sitting there for a while longer. Only when Ma Katie went back inside the cottage did she crawl out again and shake the straw out of her clothes. Inside the cottage Ma Katie turned round from where she was stooping at the hearth and looked straight at LittleKitty. 'There's straw in your hair, child,' she said. 'What were you crawling around in the rabbit hutch for?'

LittleKitty didn't ask Ma Katie whether the magistrate had been looking for her and Ma Katie didn't say anything either. But that evening Shala mentioned that he had seen the magistrate up at TameBushman's cave. The man with the one arm had crept right into the cave and spent a long time inside, said Shala.

'And all that,' said Ma Katie, shooting a jet of tobacco juice into the hearth, 'to try and explain the death of Noah du Pisani.'

232

Chapter 42

'My love,' wrote the magistrate, propped up against the pillows, beside the sash window which he had pushed up for the night so that he could see the outline of the mountain etched against the stars. 'Irony of ironies, the ruler of this small republic is still missing. He has disappeared, escaped me, probably gone into hiding somewhere or taken his own life in one of the inhospitable ravines of the mountain. It would therefore seem that I shall not have the opportunity to interview him after all.

'Perhaps, in the perfection of this silent night, I should take this opportunity to reveal to you what is on my mind. It concerns matters which have been brewing within me since I first arrived in this district and had my first encounter with the people and legends of this part of the country.

'Even if Abel Moolman, suspect number one, has disappeared, and even if I do not get the opportunity of a conversation with him, I already know him as well – or so at least I feel – as I should ever have got to know him in the course of any conversation. I know his idea of right and justice, the *lex aeterna* which he put into practice here like one of Machiavelli's princes. (You may recall that Machiavelli's were the only politics which I ever did read.) Like them, Abel Moolman arrogated to himself the right even to act indecently and dishonourably, if this best served the interests of maintaining and promoting the welfare of his state. Have I now, at this late stage of my life, become an adherent of natural law? You know, my dear . . .'

He looked out of the window, slightly shifting his position among the pillows. Abel, Abel, are you somewhere up in the mountain with your cold gun in your hands, looking down on the flickering torches of the search parties, on the swinging lanterns with their puddles of light, on the illuminated windows of your house? Are you sitting up there with the gun in your hands, weighing up against each other in one terrible moment of decision, your life, full and active and ill-tempered, and your

233

death, cold and as darkly silent as the ravines, with the cold mist of nothingness stealing over you and condemning you and obliterating you like nothing else ever could?

'. . . that my daily duties on the Bench precluded my participation in so many things. This is something you realize even better than I do, of course. You have had to live with it day after day for years: the never-ending horde of knifers, pickpockets, prostitutes, confidence tricksters and wife-beaters queueing through my mind, all with the same terrible demand: acquit us, be merciful to us, attach your labels to us but at the same time free us from them. I remember how irritated you were when, in my early years as a public prosecutor, I used to bring books to bed with me, thick tomes by Augustine and Voet, and now I struggled to follow the Latin texts with my finger, through the elegant rhythms of the conclusions, through the rise and fall of the syntax: the incantations of a classical manner of thinking which made my duties in the criminal court the next day seem quite absurd. Later, when I had been appointed to the Bench, my judgements, which I tried to compose with such particular care, seemed to me so many extracts from the yellow press.

'Everyone allows something to slip through his fingers in the course of his life. That is what life is: the slipping away, the unstoppable disappearance of things. You know this even better than I do. My standard concepts – *dolus*, *culpa*, *animus* and all the other labels which my subject connects with virtually every shade of human endeavour, lust, deviation or omission – have proved inadequate. Now, here, on this farm, in this isolated district, these concepts again prove inadequate. Even in the cell of Oneday Riet they are inadequate. I sit in my office in the court building, listening to the voices of the public prosecutors barking through the walls, to the shuffling feet of the accused, to the long mumbling pronouncements of the magistrate. I hear the cane strokes being administered in the courtyard under the supervision of a bored district surgeon, for the duration of which the sound of the convicts raking the courtyard gravel is silenced. Those concepts are inadequate even then.'

Again he shifted his position among the pillows. Had he

heard something outside? Yes, it was the dogs sniffing under the window. Ella was allowing them to sleep outside at night, in case they caught Abel's scent when the air was free of the smells of the daytime activities.

'And now, with this letter, which will be the last before my departure, since my visit has already lasted too long, the impossible has, finally, become possible for me. I am sorry, my love, that you are unable to experience it with me. If I may say so: I admire you. And if you will permit me: I love you. In spite of. Or because of. You will understand.

'Your husband,
Abraham van der Ligt.'

Chapter 43

When Shala saw the search party coming past TameBushman's cave and slowly moving down the mountain slope, he knew: Abel Moolman was dead. No one needed to tell him. It was enough that when he went up the mountain with his goats that morning he saw the Malay standing outside his hut. Shala caught the smell of the Malay's brew as they were still making their way up the dry course of the Toor River, and it was the unmistakable smell of the deathbrew. He could never forget that smell, for when his father Andries Riet died, the Malay smeared that same brew on the doorposts of the Skaamfamilie's cottage. It would afford the bitter Andries Riet a safe journey, said the Malay.

In the early afternoon Shala drove his goats home again and into their pen. Ma Katie was still asking whether he was going to help in the search for Abel Moolman, when he was already saying goodbye. He had his dassie-skin jacket and his hat on, and his knapsack was slung over his shoulder. 'I've got to go down to Eerste Station, Ma,' he said.

The track he took was known only to him and Oneday. It ran past the Eye, diagonally across the crown of the Toorberg, then all along the ridge to where the steep slopes fell away sheer to the plains of Camdeboo. There was a narrow ledge, a pathway known to their feet only, hidden under spiny trailing vines. If you knew where the footholds were, you could make it down to the bottom. There were klipspringer droppings everywhere, some of them still fresh and steaming slightly. To the right of him gaped the abyss and the blue plains. To his left, ever higher and higher, towered the cliffs.

Suddenly he heard the bark of a baboon and noticed the troop a little way ahead of him on the path. He waited till the leading male slowly turned round and, growling, clambered up the cliff face, with the others following. Shala waited until he could no longer hear them breaking through the bushes, then he climbed past the handful of bulbs which the baboons had dug up and left behind. Abruptly coming round a bend in the path, he found himself on level ground. He looked up. The early dusk lay cool on the cliffs and the Toorberg's late afternoon shadow stretched out ahead of him across the Camdeboo.

He realized he would have to run if he wanted to catch the train to Eerste Station. The firebreak running along the foot of the Toorberg cliffs had recently been cleared of undergrowth, so he loped off along it at an easy trot, the knapsack bouncing at his hip. At Sukkelkop he lay in wait for the train slowly trundling its way up the steep slope. Smoke billowing from the locomotive swirled round Shala as he lay on the ledge above the cutting waiting for the train to pass through below him. When the last wagon was directly below, he jumped and tumbled into a pile of tarpaulins in an open truck.

When he sat up, out of breath, the train was gathering speed again as it ran down the slope. Sukkelkop lay behind them as they steamed down onto the Camdeboo plain.

At Eerste Station he slipped over the edge of the truck, ran along through the shunting yard and eventually swung off to the left, out of the station gate and up the hillside to the location's cluster of hovels. It was deep dusk by this time, and there were fires burning in front of the small cottages. He noticed stooping women picking up lumps of coal between the railway tracks. When a police van drove past they ducked behind the signal box.

These are Oneday's people, thought Shala. This is where Oneday preached his great sermons at the huge funeral gatherings for the children who fell to the soldiers' bullets. From far across the plains of Camdeboo the people had come, clinging like weaver-birds to the outside of goods trains all the way to Eerste Station, and then jumping off and running away before the Railway Police could arrest them for illegal staffriding. Rickety donkey carts came struggling up out of the valleys of the Great Fish and Sundays Rivers. Dusty buses and trucks drove in from the Moordenaars Karoo.

On the rocky hillside above the railway tracks they congregated in front of the loudspeakers while one of Oneday's deacons led the hymn singing until everyone was seated: a dense mass of people swaying in time to the songs.

At first people had brought only their hymn books and Bibles. Later, there had been a few flags as well. But at the last funeral before Oneday was arrested by the police, there were large banners and placards, the people had worn caps and sung new songs. There were few Bibles or hymn books in evidence, but there was great rage. When the singing reached a climax, Oneday drove up from the direction of the station in the black car belonging to the man from the city. The crowds parted to allow the car to pass, touching the bodywork as it slowly moved up to the top of the hill.

There Oneday got out and took the microphone in his hand: Oneday, his own younger brother, who had been far away to learn how to lead the people from the suffering of life under the white farmers. That last funeral day Oneday first calmed the people with a prayer over the microphone. Then he led them in the singing of a song they had already learnt in small groups in the barns and on the farms – a song about the liberation which Jesus brings. As the last strains of the song died away, the coffins were carried in. Three police vans and a Casspir were parked on the hillside opposite, with a group of soldiers standing motionless beside them, watching through binoculars. There was also a man with camera fitted with a long lens taking photographs. When all the coffins had been lowered onto the outcrop of rock at his feet, Oneday began to speak, and Shala wished that their dead father, the bitter Andries Riet, could have been there to hear him.

'My earthly father,' Oneday began, wiping away the sweat from his forehead with a snowy white handkerchief, 'vowed at my birth that my name should be Oneday. Because my father, Andries Riet from the Stiefveld, said at my birth that one day the day would come. And I say to you, one day the day does come. And that one day is no longer still coming. One day is not tomorrow or the next day any more now. Jesus Christ is not coming to liberate us one day in the future. He's coming now. One day has arrived. One day is now. One day is today. Jesus Christ is with us, to liberate us, today!'

Oneday took out the handkerchief to mop his brow again. He freed the microphone from its stand and strode up and down in front of the crowd holding it. 'My father, Andries Riet, has not lived to see this day, but his son Oneday would like to tell him, before all the people and the dead gathered here today: one day is today! One day has broken! And woe to him who says to the Lord God: "Not today, Lord, tomorrow. Not this day, but some other day." One day is right now!' The crowd was on its feet, shaking its fists in the air, waving banners. Shala thought: Ma Katie, you should see your son now – you'd be afraid. There was no mistaking the power Oneday had in him. When the coffins had been lowered into the hard earth and the crowds had dispersed, there was nothing left on the hillside. The crowds had trampled to dust every anthill and shrub. Nothing but bare earth remained.

Walking across the ridge now in the deepening dusk, Shala could just make out the crosses on the graves of the group of children they had buried that day.

Why had he come here today? He didn't know. He only knew that Abel Moolman's death signified something, and that by some means Oneday had to be informed of it. Perhaps one of Oneday's people would be able to smuggle the message through to him in goal. When they were small, sitting at the mouth of TameBushman's cave, watching Abel driving around in the Vlei, he and Oneday had thought that their world would forever be dominated by an Abel.

An Abel is an Abel, people had said ruefully. When Founder-Abel was no longer there, OldAbel was there to take his place, and when he died Abel was there waiting, and after him came CrossAbel the soldier. Shala touched his ear. But this is the end, he thought, for me and for you, too, CrossAbel, for both of us with the blemish on our ears.

The only one left was Mailbag Moolman, and he wasn't even capable of managing his own small herd of cattle, not even when he got both the grazing and the cattle for nothing. He had bankrupted himself within a year.

So, it was all over. And that, Shala suddenly realized as he

239

neared the tin shanties, was the message he wanted to convey to Oneday.

He knocked at a door. Someone peered through the window, before the door opened. 'Is that you, John?' asked the man.

'Yes,' replied Shala.

Four men were sitting round a table in the dim light, playing cards. 'We hear Abel is dead,' said one.

Shala looked at them in amazement. 'I was just bringing you the news.'

'We've sent a message through to Oneday.'

Again he was surprised. He nodded, and sat down to watch them play. When a train passed, Shala remembered how at the first big gathering Oneday had constantly had to stop talking every time a train passed. The next time the man with the black car had brought the small generator and the loudspeakers.

'Oneday will be pleased to hear Abel Moolman is dead,' said one of the men.

Shala watched the hands nimbly picking up and putting down the cards. 'I don't know,' he said softly. 'I don't know whether he will be pleased or not.' He thought of Oneday's words in TameBushman's cave at noon one day when they had been watching CrossAbel racing round his track at the Vlei dam: 'God is the one who gives, and God is the one who takes away.'

Chapter 44

The magistrate struggled up the outside ladder to the door of the loft. Dowser held the low door open for him, but before he stooped to enter, he looked down just once more – at Ella standing in the bright sunlight on the raked gravel of the farmyard, surrounded by the pawmarks of the boer mastiffs all over the neat rake-strokes.

It was the refusal of the dogs to leave the outside ladder that aroused Ella's suspicions. The search parties had been combing the slopes of the Toorberg for days on end, advancing like firefighters, men, women and children all together. They had swept systematically across every acre of ground, but not a trace could they find of Abel, nor of his Land Rover once it had swerved off the road to the Halt.

Early that morning, when the magistrate was still in De la Rey's room having his morning coffee, Ella noticed that the dogs were continually hanging about the yard. Later, as the heat of the day increased, they lay down against the wall, right under the door to the loft.

'It's terrible, Your Worship,' said Dowser as the stooping magistrate edged past him into the loft. For a moment the magistrate caught the sweaty smell of Dowser and his pipe tobacco, but when Dowser stood back, the musty smell of dust hit the magistrate in the face. 'Over there, Your Worship.'

Seated in the dark corner of the loft, a good twenty metres beyond the pile of books, furniture, lanterns, old trunks and china dolls, was Abel Moolman, awkwardly slumped in a chair, with coir stuffing bulging out past his pale, lifeless hands. Diagonally across his knees gleamed the only new thing in the room: the shining metal and polished wood of his hunting rifle.

Slowly, guided by the beam of light from the torch in Dowser's hand, the magistrate made his way towards the corner. The light opened up a pathway for his feet across the covers of forgotten magazines, across an old theodolite probably used by one of the Abels to survey fields for cultivation or for the construction of the aqueduct, across a brass telescope and a beautifully preserved china doll with a fixed, childlike smile.

He lost his balance for a moment and shuddered when the hand he put out to save himself sank into an old mattress. There were rat droppings everywhere. In the corner beside Abel's left foot were the grinning jaws of a dead bat. Carefully, the magistrate bent over Abel. There was no sign of a bullet wound. No one had heard a shot either. The face lolled back crookedly. The eyes still had a slight gleam as the light of the torch moved over them.

The magistrate looked back at Dowser. 'He's dead,' he said. Carefully, so that Dowser would not see what he was doing, and deliberately shuffling his feet to drown the rustle of the paper, the magistrate tugged the sheet of paper out of Abel's dead hand. Folding it, he slipped it into the pocket of his shirt, then wiped his hand on his trouserleg: the corpse was sweating as he sat in his chair, stiff and grim in the attic of his own house, among the lumber of his ancestors.

Returning to the door, the magistrate looked down. Ella was standing as though in expectation of tidings. Slightly behind her, in his army uniform, stood CrossAbel.

The magistrate waited until he reached the ground before he would trust himself to speak, but even on the gravel, once he realized that Ella already knew, he still hesitated. 'Let's go inside,' he said, putting his arm round Ella's shoulders.

He turned round in confusion when CrossAbel shouted: 'Oh, fuck!' The heavy boots marched off rapidly across the gravel. Ella called to him, but from around the corner they heard the roar of the motorcycle engine. The bike shot round the corner, punched through a thick garden hedge and then headed straight through the vegetable patch, leaving a trail of broken and tumbling stalks in the plot of young maize, then cut a swathe through the yellow heads of a bed of sunflowers, wobbling crazily as they teetered and collapsed in CrossAbel's wake. At last, giving the garden gate a kick as he passed through, CrossAbel raced out into the open veld and they watched him charging up to the foothills of the Toorberg.

242

'Leave him be,' said Ella, and added, as though in an attempt to throw a bridge across her dead husband: 'He's his grandfather's child. He has his own way of doing things.'

The magistrate sat down in the sitting room opposite Ella. She was silent. The head of the lion on the floor stared glassily at them.

'I had the yard raked yesterday afternoon,' she said then. 'For footprints. I was sure there would be footprints.' He looked at her enquiringly, his head held to one side in a wordless question. 'The yard always shows footprints,' she explained, 'and I was certain that I'd heard footsteps the night before last and the night before that as well. I thought . . .' She left the sentence unfinished, but looked up at the portrait of De la Rey.

Uncertain about what to do next, the magistrate lit a cigar. Should he disturb the corpse and lower him (but in what?) in a humiliating final journey, without even the dignity of a coffin, wreaths and a decked grave? 'Do you mind?' he asked, pointing with the cigar to the blue smoke already hanging round him.

Later he stood at the telephone. The undertaker's tones were confidentially hushed. The sergeant on duty at the police station promised to despatch a patrol van immediately. 'What about the family?' the magistrate asked Ella, who was still sitting in the sitting room. She shook her head.

Dowser lowered the unwieldy sheet of canvas containing the corpse, whose limbs formed stubborn bulges at every point. Abel had stiffened in the sitting position and they had to tip him absurdly onto his back to get him onto the canvas which was spread out on the worn-out old mattress. Abel slid onto the canvas head first, his knees and elbows crooked, his feet at right angles to his legs, for all the world as though he was trying to crawl along upside down, perhaps on the ceiling at which his glazed eyes were so fixedly staring.

The canvas sank down onto the yard. The boer mastiffs, locked in the wagon house, leapt up against the doors, barking. Ella watched through a window, screened by a lace curtain and mosquito-gauze. The servants in the kitchen were unashamedly crying into the elegant table napkins. Abel Moolman's initials

243

had been embroidered on the damask by the steady hand of Granny Olivier all those years ago when, after her recovery, she wanted to prove that her eye was still as sharp as her needle.

After the departure of the undertakers, the magistrate stood on the back stoep. He heard the nagging sound of CrossAbel's motorcycle in the distance racing round the track at the Vlei. The sound would die away, then approach again, change pitch, sputter a bit, growl and bellow. For a long time the magistrate stood there. So it is over then, he thought. Or is it?

As he walked past the silent servants in the kitchen and down the long passage, his shadow fell across the gleaming floor. In fact it was more than a shadow: it was a true reflection, since he noticed his stump comically swinging as he walked. Ella, dressed in black, with a high collar of fine black silk reaching to just below her ears, was in the sun-porch, bent over her diary. Through the window, the magistrate noticed the farm workers under the trees beside the wagon house. To one side, as though waiting for a sign, sat Dowser.

Tilly came by, barefoot, swinging along in a bright white dress, an excited red blush on her beautiful face. She ran along the track left by the motorcycle, following the esses through the neatly raked gravel and through the broken maize stalks till at last she disappeared, bobbing and floating, among the broken yellow heads of the sunflowers.

The magistrate went up to Ella, taking from his shirt pocket the title-deeds to Toorberg, which he had tugged out of the dead grip of Abel Moolman.

'It was your husband,' he said, 'wasn't it?'

She looked at him for a long time, then bent over her diary again. When he had long since sat down in one of the deck chairs and absent-mindedly lit a cigar, she said: 'This is one of those days when I don't seem to have anything to write about.'

Chapter 45

CrossAbel kicked his motorbike into gear, accelerated sharply so that the back wheel spun in the gravel and jerked the front wheel up. In strength, in strength, in strength, he gritted his teeth. In strength, in strength. He rode away round the homestead, chasing the boer mastiffs out of his way, from where they were dozing in the sun after their restless night. He raced all along the edge of the grove, criss-crossing sheep paths, earth walls, clods. He charged through the lambing ewes, making the fat-uddered beasts trot off in alarm and leaving the scattered and terrified lambs bleating for their mothers.

All over the Hartseerland, so called because between dawn and sunset they could break the spirit of any man, bales of lucerne lay scattered, baled there before Abel's disappearance. CrossAbel made an exciting obstacle of them, zipping between the bales, kicking some of them out of his way as he passed, slithering and sliding, since the lucerne tussocks offered little grip to the grinding, bucking wheels. He lost his balance at one point and fell, sliding with his bike across the field. Complaining, its wheels spinning, the machine slewed gradually sideways. CrossAbel, cursing and swearing, dusted off his jacket, tucked his tie back into his buttoned shirt, mounted the bike again and tore off over the wall of the Vlei dam and up one of the sandy courses running down from the Eye, until the hot smell from the engine groaning between his thighs suggested it might be seizing up and he was forced to stop for a while.

He thought back. He was standing, no more than a little nipper, down on the ground at the foot of a windmill that reached up and up into the sky. Wet and slimy, the rod was thrusting in and out of the earth. Looking up, his eyes screwed tight against the flickering sun behind the vanes of the windmill, he saw his father sitting high up on the platform beside the whirling head, higher than the whistling flight of the pigeons, higher than the sky, beckoning to him. 'Come, little Abel, come on now, climb up. It's not so high.' The labourers laid down their tools and waited, grinning, as they watched him grasp the first rung of the ladder, look up the length of the windmill, haul himself up to the next rung . . . Their faces were turned up to him now, their feet absurdly small below their bodies. The boer mastiffs were only backs moving around restlessly on his father's tracks. He suddenly saw the plain from a new, dizzying perspective. Things were growing smaller, trees were shrinking, the wind was whirring in the vanes of the windmill and the iron was trembling against his body. 'Climb, little Abel, climb!'

Someone down below said: 'Shala climbed right up to the top the last time we had to fix the head. Shala went up the windmill like a monkey!'

And when he couldn't go on any more, when he couldn't understand this new world around him, the ground had come up to meet him, and when he hit it his breath had hiccuped out of his body, but he still had enough wind left to limp across to his bicycle and pedal away up the path to the farmyard.

'Abel! Abel!' came his father's voice half-above, half-behind him.

CrossAbel sat in the dry bed of the Toor River for a long time, but at last he grew restless again. It was getting hot and the collar of his church shirt was choking him. There were grease and lucerne stains on his trousers. He kicked the motorbike to start it. Stuttering a little at first, it then roared into full-blooded life. He mounted it and shot out of the watercourse up towards the ravine, through the dip and up the other side, roaring off to the Skaamfamilie's cottage.

Leaving the concertina gate lying open behind him, he rode up the stony track, cautiously over broken bottles and old tins, cursing the Riets: how could these people make such a mess! Katie Danster came to the door of the cottage, holding her hand up to her eyes to shield them from the sun. Kicking the machine into a lower gear, CrossAbel performed an S-bend in front of the goat pen, slithering in the dung at the gate, and then thundered past the rabbit hutch where the red-eyed rabbits were bouncing in terror behind the wire gauze.

With the engine now reacting exuberantly to his every whim, he raced round the cottage one more time, nearly killing a couple of fowls, and then stopped in front of Katie. She regarded him disapprovingly, with LittleKitty in the dark doorway of the cottage behind her and one of the children crying sleepily inside.

'CrossAbel!' said Katie. 'CrossAbel, what do you think you are doing? And in your church suit at that!'

He pulled the crash helmet off his head and glared at her furiously.

'Abel,' he said. 'You will now call me Abel.'

Then he charged off, bouncing over the rocky path, through the gate, until all they could see was the sun glinting on his helmet, as the droning of the engine echoed off the cliffs of the Toorberg.

Chapter 46

He bent down among the splinters of glass to pick up the small portrait. The photograph was cold to the touch as just for a moment his fingers touched Abel, touched Ella. Crouched on the highly polished floor, he looked up along Ella's legs, past her hips, past the string of silver pearls.

'Oh, please don't bother about that!' she exclaimed.

'I . . . I am so sorry,' he stammered, crouched on his haunches, pointing to the shattered glass on the floor all round him, even on the furry back of the lionskin. 'It simply slipped out of my hand . . .'

'A magistrate feeling guilty?' she teased. 'Come, let me give you a hand up. It's ridiculous for you to be picking up splinters of glass on the floor. Let the servants sweep them up.'

He took the cool, smooth hand she held out: the hand of a widow, he thought suddenly – the servitude of death.

'I really am extremely sorry,' he repeated when he was on his feet again. 'It must have been of great sentimental value to you. Why I should have . . . and now of all times . . .'

In the sitting room the grandfather clock chimed the hour. In the kitchen the oven door of the Aga stove banged. Outside the clerk hooted a second time. So it is all over then, he thought.

'Please forget about it,' she gestured. 'It's really nothing. We'll simply put it in another little frame. CrossAbel will do it in a twinkling.'

He had to take his leave. 'I must thank you,' he began, formally.

She smiled at him. 'Call me Ella.' She was wearing fresh make-up.

'I must also tell you,' he said, repeating the phrase he had formulated in De la Rey's bed as he listened to the jackals wailing up in the mountain in the wee, small hours, 'that . . .' He took her hand. It was a clumsy, contrived gesture. 'I must tell you that I . . .' He hesitated. The arm, he thought. Resolutely, he finished the sentence: 'that I admire you greatly.' He nodded, as though the interview was over. He stood before her, uncomfortably, stroking his stump, thinking: for me, that was something of a judgement. A kind of pronouncement on this woman, this house. But on nothing and no one else: not on the stubbornness, nor the avarice, nor the pioneering fury of that man in the shattered engagement portrait – that proud Abel with his hand resting proprietorially on Ella's shoulder; she with delicate lace at her throat, her eyes gentler then, still expectant – even joyful. He looked at her now, in front of him.

She made no reply. Then, a moment later: 'That sounds so like De la Rey, years ago, in the peach orchard. He also said that. "Admiration".' She considered the word. 'Admiration,' she repeated, waiting for his response. He shrugged his shoulders in uncomfortable silence. No more and no less, he thought. The limits of love elude us. We may talk round them, evasively. In a sense it was a crime, he wanted to tell her, in the way that the law regards an attempt as a crime, or in the sense that the Bible regards the intention as the deed. Here we are, there already, but never there. To be judged as though we were indeed there. And therefore all the more culpable.

The clock struck the quarter. A quarter of an hour! he thought. We have been standing here face to face in the silent dining-room for a quarter of an hour, with the lion's head staring at us in fury and Abel's bakkie growling round the sheds. Outside, under the window sills, there was the crunching sound of the restlessly patrolling boer mastiffs on the gravel of the yard.

Up and down they wandered, always on the shadow side of the house. As the day advanced, they would move along a different wall, as though searching in the shade for their dead master; waiting for the bark of his powerful voice, his command to them to leap up onto the back of the Land Rover, the impatient tip of his walking stick, the innumerable smells on his hand when he bent down for a moment to pat their heads. Perhaps his smell was still seeping out through the windows. Perhaps it was driving them mad with longing for the man whom they had followed like the sound of his own footsteps.

'I must go,' he said at last. 'The clerk out there has been waiting for a long time.'

'Goodbye,' she said, and suddenly came right up to him. Then her pale face was beside his own. For a moment her lips brushed his. They walked down the passage.

When she opened the front door they saw the clerk impatiently pacing beside the car, small puffs of dust rising in front of his toecaps. He looked reproachfully at the urine stains on the tyres: he'd again been too late to stop the mastiffs.

Once out on the veranda in the sunlight, the moment was past. Standing there in front of him, Ella seemed tired. There were rings under her eyes, worry lines at the edges of her mouth.

'And who, would you consider,' she said, assuming the formal tone which he had observed throughout, 'is the one who is to be singled out as the criminal in your report?'

He looked at her for a long time. Then his gaze swept across the farmyard to the road winding away through the dry trees, across the rise, onwards to the Halt and from there to the town and his cramped, temporary office in the court building. He thought of the cabinet with its files, each one labelled, with notes on Abel, CrossAbel, Ella, Dowser du Pisani . . . even OldAbel, Judge Lucius, De la Rey . . .

He waved his hand vaguely, looking out over the garden again. A sprinkler was rhythmically spraying crystal clear water across a flower bed.

My dear wife, he thought. Here you stand, reincarnated before my eyes. Forgive me that I allowed you to die in my hands, that it is all over, that I was not prepared to share the blame. And I, who in unaddressed letters kept returning like a dog to your scents and memories, as though with my everyday concerns I could entice you back to this world in which I have to categorise so many inexplicable matters using such basic concepts as guilt and blame, crime and punishment – I shall forgive you, if you will forgive me, now, through this woman in front of me. Perhaps it is forgiveness, and not the chill, focused jet of judgement and sentence, that is the clearest water of all.

Understanding, he thought, looking at Ella. 'I cannot give

250

you an answer,' he said, and went down the low steps of the veranda. From there he looked up at her, but said no more.

She nodded, then asked: 'What about your department? Justice?'

He looked at the clerk beside the car, then at her again. He shrugged. I simply cannot give you an answer, he thought.

Inside the house CrazyTilly was crooning her lullaby. 'Antjie Somers . . . Antjie Somers . . .'

He smiled at Ella. 'Perhaps Tilly knows more than all of us.'

She looked straight into his eyes for a moment. He could not fathom her now. Was she expecting more from this farewell: a formal apology? A judgement, correct and legal? Surely not. A commission report would not trouble Ella. Perhaps, he thought as a moment of electric excitement shot through him – just for one brief impossible moment – perhaps she is expecting me to . . .?

'I am sorry that I never met him,' he said after a while.

She shrugged. 'An Abel is an Abel is an Abel,' she said, matter-of-factly.

He nodded. 'I understand.'

He turned round and walked to the car past the sniffing muzzles of the mastiffs. He nodded to the clerk and they got in. For just a moment, driving away from the homestead, the car's tyres crunching over the gravel, they caught the scent of the shining water from the sprinkler, the scent of damp earth. The magistrate was aware of entering the shade of the avenue. Sunlight shifted across him, across his lap, his stump, his face. He did not look back in a parting greeting at the woman on the veranda. He imagined her standing there: silent, unfathomable, in silver pearls and black silk, too alone for the endless acres stretching out on all sides around her, too small for the dark mountain looming behind the homestead, too eccentric – after so many years lived in the shadow of the Moolman delusions – for the narrowness of life in the town house which she might conceivably choose.

He imagined her, with the feverish face of CrazyTilly behind her, in the sleeping wing of the great house, looking

251

through the mist of her own breath on the window pane at the car which was taking Antjie Somers away through the trees, taking away the man who was supposed to bring rain, the man who brought nothing.

He imagined Ella, hesitantly, tentatively, walking into the great house, touching the furniture with her fingertips, as though experiencing something of a farewell in her lonely return, this time as a widow, beyond possession. She was free now, she was the possessor; possessor also of dead Abel, since his memory was her will.

He imagined De la Rey's silent bedroom, at the moment when he stopped at the door, seeing De la Rey's portrait on the wall and feeling the heavy drag of the suitcase on his shoulder. Well, he thought, the room may now revert to being the other man's, the man whom she so desperately sought for in him, quietly bending over his hand with the nail-clipper; or at table, with her eyes passing from his averted face to the portrait of De la Rey on the mantelpiece; or standing waiting on the veranda with a hand shading her eyes against the sun, looking towards him with such feverish expectation as he and the clerk drove down the avenue and into the yard.

Would she be able to read his letters? And understand them? Or would she shy away from them, as he had that evening when she had wanted to show him her diary in the stillness of the night, and he had refused? 'It would not make any sense,' he had insisted, 'confessions of guilt made in your most private moments, journeys through your own mind – such things are no concern of mine.'

'But isn't guilt what you're searching for?' she asked.

'Not like this.'

'Well, how then?' He turned away. 'It is late,' he said. 'It is time we retired. Tomorrow will be a long day.'

Recalling the episode now, he smiled wryly. An episode, he thought as they swung out through the farmyard gate onto the dusty road. They drove past the Halt. Mailbag and Postmaster were standing in the shade of the veranda, a crumpled, half-filled postbag at Postmaster's feet. There was a bus waiting at the pump under the pepper trees. The magistrate tried not to catch their eyes so that he would not have to wave. 'An episode,' he whispered.

'Pardon, Your Worship?'

'Nothing,' he said. 'I was just thinking aloud.'

'Oh.' Sinking low in the driver's seat, the clerk drove skilfully, his arm extended. By now he knew the road well. He cleared his throat. 'Have you completed your report, Your Worship?' he asked. 'All the guys in the office have been wondering if it was that Abel Moolman who murdered his grandchild.'

The magistrate did not answer the clerk. He lit a cigar instead. What do you know, he thought angrily, you and the rest of the chattering apes behind the counters of the Magistrate's Office? He was surprised by the sudden vehemence of the rage which gripped his chest. What do you know, he was tempted to ask, about guilt and complicity?

He veiled himself in his own blue cigar smoke. The clerk coughed uncomfortably at the silence which greeted his question.

Later, as they neared town, the magistrate asked only: 'Please stop at the pharmacy. I need more ointment.'

So it is all over with Justice, he thought, as he waited at the counter in the pharmacy. To return to Head Office after so many months and confess: No report. It is a matter of profound regret that I cannot give you an answer.

Later, in his hotel room, after his fourth whisky, he thought: That is a sentence. He smiled wryly. What I have established, people of Head Office, is the unlimited nature, not of the impossible – that which we were never prepared to admit – but the unlimited nature of the possible.

And since I am no longer the one sitting in judgement but one of those pleading the law, this is for me the *litis contestatio*: the close of pleadings.

He smiled again. For a long while he looked out at the gravel pit in the hillside. Eventually the light began to fade and at last evening closed in, leaving him standing in front of the open window, wavering between melancholy and joy.

253

Chapter 47

The sadness of a great, full-grown man was the most touching of all, Katie Danster was to say afterwards, when the mist came down over the Toorberg and the geese up in the cliffs were crying as though deserted by God and man alike. At such times she would be thinking back to the powerful figure of Abel Moolman standing with his legs apart over the borehole, surrounded by nothing but the footprints of his own folk, with only the trunks of the trees silently watching him.

When she began to talk like this, Shala would lose patience with her, stride off to the goat pen, walk straight into the middle of the flock and slap some of the boer goats on the rump, or angrily grab a ram by the horn and wrestle with it until he had worked his impatience with his mother right out of his system. And then she would think back to her clever Oneday – now in gaol in the city somewhere – who would look up from the book he was reading, take her by the hand and say: 'Ma, the *tokoloshe* has got nothing to do with it. The *tokoloshe* has been dead and buried for a very long time now. Forget about the Moolmans and all their nonsense, Ma. We are the Riets – and in the power of God, we are looking ahead to the future.'

That was one of the last conversations she had had with Oneday. Shortly after Abel's death he had been released, but two months later he was picked up again in the location. This time they sent him to the city to await trial. The man with the black car, she heard, was also going to have to appear in court.

Her children never knew that she, too, had attended the great funerals at Eerste Station – including the one where Oneday had preached about Andries Riet. Unobtrusively, she had gone to watch her clever son behind the microphone and then she had anxiously taken the bus back to the Halt. Oneday was too big for the Stiefveld, she thought. He had too many thoughts. Now he was trying to drag everybody into his world with him.

And even if her children did lose patience with her, she would stand her ground on the sadness of a great man, for she – she, Katie Danster – had found Abel Moolman, high up in the windmill near the OuMurasie, when everything was over and Trickle had been buried in the borehole, and the marble slab had been laid across the grave by the hideous-faced undertakers in their mourning suits.

She had been on her way to the Halt to fetch her pension money, at the time. As she walked, keeping a careful eye on the ground for the devilthorns which those horrible children of Oneday's sometimes scattered on the path when they knew she was about to set off for the Halt, she heard something strange above the whirring vanes of the windmill. Looking up, she thought at first it was a great crow perched up there. But when she narrowed her eyes and the blur sharpened into an image, she saw Abel Moolman clambering about like a mad thing inside the framework of the windmill.

He was climbing higher and higher, not up the narrow ladder, but crosswise between the iron struts until his head was dangerously near the flashing vanes. Katie set off at a trot towards the windmill, the sharp stones hurting her bare feet. She had struggled to apply and then tighten the brake, but with a long groan the head of the windmill gradually stopped turning. The tail wagged north and south a couple more times, but then it too came to a complete stop.

By that time Abel was right on the platform, high above her. 'Release the brake!' he yelled at her. The wind was strong between them and she was having to cling to the wet shaft of the windmill. It was disgusting, she later recalled, that slimy shaft, wet from all its labours in Toorberg's belly.

'You get down there, Abel Moolman!' she had shouted back at him, holding on to her headscarf. 'You must put away your sins, Abel Moolman!'

But Abel had stayed up there, perched like a crow looking out over the plains below – at the whirlwind spinning far away on the open spaces, at the white flocks of sheep which belonged to him but which he could not see, at the Toorberg where his grandfather had once lain thinking that by the grace of God and the nose of his tame Bushman he'd ridden into Paradise itself.

'Get down from there, Abel, before the wind rips you down!' But Abel was rigid, like a dead man, stuck up there with only his own thoughts.

Eventually Katie left him there, after first making sure that the brake was properly locked. She pulled her headscarf tight and low over her eyes as a protection against the coming sand-storm and struggled back over the low bushes and stones to the footpath. Shortly before she reached the Halt the sudden pain in her feet made her curse her mischievous grandchildren, for a neat row of fresh devilthorns had been set right across her path. Tonight, she decided, she would beat the daylights out of them.

Often she would also think back to the man with only one arm, the magistrate on commission, who had arrived long after Abel's windmill climbing period was over, to dig everything up again. He was the one who had driven Abel to climb up into the loft of the Toorberg homestead, to die there, alone and lonely among all the old lumber. On the day of Abel's funeral, when the magistrate was due to leave, Katie Danster stood on top of the rabbit hutch, her hand over her eyes to ward off the sun, and saw the magistrate standing with Ella in front of the great house for a long time, talk-ing. Then she saw him walk slowly to the car and drive away up the avenue towards the Halt and the town. Ella stood on the yard for a long time without moving, watching the car disappear. When the last dust had settled, she walked solemnly back into the house and Katie could tell from her bearing that she, too, had the feeling which Katie herself had: that something had ended.

Perhaps Ella knew more about Abel than all the rest to-gether, the magistrate included. Perhaps, in their long dark nights in the great house, Abel told his wife what it was that the winds in the windmills told him. Or perhaps, when all the ser-vants had gone home and CrazyTilly was asleep after her dagga-brew and CrossAbel was racing around on the dirt roads of the district, perhaps then Abel told Ella about the feelings he'd had on that last day at the borehole.

She, Katie, would never, ever, forget that last day: the only

256

day in the long history of Toorberg when the entire family had been in agreement about something.

It was early morning, after a long night in which the hole the men were digging had reached shoulder-depth in the shiny black soil of the grove. But then the roots of the poplars obstructed them: white, curling roots, twisted and stubborn. The men had to saw through them and the white sap dripped from the sawblades. The hands wielding the saws were wet up to the elbows. The roots had a sourish smell: the same smell you got when you bent over the borehole and sniffed at the cold air rising out of the darkness, out of the place where the child, without either sound of voice or breathing any more, was stuck.

Abel had to stop the digging, because from all the interference with the soil whole chunks of earth were coming away from the walls of the borehole. When they tumbled down and splashed into the seepage at the bottom, the diggers would stop, while for a moment everybody listened: Ella with her hands across her eyes; CrossAbel covered in dust and mud, his hands angrily on his hips; Dowser, his face tear-stained and smeared with mud from peering down the hole and calling to Noah. 'No,' Abel said at last. 'It's no use. You'd better stop.' The diggers struggled exhaustedly out of the hole to the tin mugs of brandy brought from Toorberg's back stoep.

The pre-dawn light was just stealing across the grove in fleecy little white clouds. Everybody sitting there, the whole family – the stolid Shala had returned from the mountain, her clever Oneday, even CrazyTilly leaning stiff and half-asleep on Ella's shoulder – looked tired and dirty, their hair wet with morning dew.

Earlier, CrazyTilly had escaped from the feed store and come walking slowly through the trees with a hessian bag wrapped round her shoulders. Oh, it's a ghost, thought Katie, since this happened before the lanterns were extinguished. The morning star was shining brightly above the Toorberg beacon, like a sign from God Himself, and in the deepest silence of the day, in the pre-dawn hush, CrazyTilly appeared from among the poplar leaves and walked slowly round and round the hole.

She stared closely at the diggers, then intently at Abel who

257

was watching to see that she didn't do anything stupid, and then at all the people sitting there. One step at a time she moved, round and round the hole, as though she knew that there was something there. The only member of the family who was not there, as Tilly must surely have seen, was Noah. And perhaps, in her madness and in the intoxication brought on by the wizard's dagga, she had a premonition of her child's death. For right there she began to speak to the ancestors. First to the calloused white trunk of the tree behind Postmaster: 'Oh, Great-grand-father Abel,' she whispered softly, and her voice cut through everyone there like the lightest of morning breezes.

'And Great-grandmother Magtilt,' she murmured, reaching out to a dense tuft of leaves on another tree. Slowly she came closer, right up to Ella. 'And Great-uncle Lucius!' she exclaimed, putting out her hand.

Then suddenly she jerked away, whirled round and round, kicked over three lanterns and caught her hair and the hessian bag in the low branches of the trees on the edge of the clearing, as her feet crackled through the leaves.

When CrossAbel grabbed hold of her and brought her to Ella, everyone could see that she'd been crying. Her whole face was bright with tears. Not for this one death only, Katie thought later, but for all the deaths which she had recognized in that single moment – all the folk of this sad farm, Toorberg, who had lived and died here in the sweat of their countenance.

After that, Abel disappeared. He went back to the homestead, and when he returned, everyone could smell the brandy on his breath. He'd started drinking earlier, in fact. When the meathook had been lowered into the hole on his orders and then reeled in again, he'd taken the point of the hook in his hands and seen the blood and mud sticking to it, along with a piece of Noah's little red shirt and a scrap of flesh. Then he had disappeared to pour the diggers some brandy. And he had drunk with them, for he was the master of the farm and the agony of Toorberg was his own – more so than any other man or woman round the borehole in those days.

Now that there was no hope left, Abel was coming back

along the footpath from the great house. And like all the others, Katie Danster tried not to see what it was he had in his hand as he came walking through the silver morning. Dowser was crouching over the hole again, his dusty face screaming down into the depths. CrossAbel was stacking the picks, all the handles in the same direction. Weeping, Ella was searching through the footprints left by all the commotion round the hole.

That was the sadness of a grown man, Katie said afterwards, even if Shala did turn his back on her, and even if Oneday reproached her for saying so. Abel was the Moolman who had walked back to the great house, who had gone into the library and taken his descision alone, who had then come back to the hole where his entire family was gathered together in witness. He must have believed in what he was doing: only faith could drive a man as far as that.

Abel had walked up to his oldest living brother. 'You, Postmaster?' he asked. He had then turned, tiredly, to his wife: 'And you, Ella?' after she had risen to her feet. She looked at him, as a woman looks at her husband.

Then Abel had walked over to her, Katie Danster of the Stiefveld. From sitting among the fallen leaves, her old legs were almost too stiff to stand on, but she struggled up, while he waited until she stood erect before him. She had never before been so close to Abel Moolman, the nephew of her Andries's father. She would never forget his face, for in it she could see how hard many Abels had worked to tame Toorberg, and how Abel in the half-light of that morning at the borehole had taken upon himself the burden of generations of his family.

'And you, Katie Danster?' he asked.

After her, Amy O'Leary Moolman and CrossAbel, who was so angry about his own sadness that he couldn't look his father in the eye. Mailbag, too, self-consciously touching his ear. Then Oneday, and Shala, and LittleKitty – everyone in the family had their turn.

At last Abel stopped in front of CrazyTilly, seated on the fuel drums beside CrossAbel. He didn't ask her, but for a long time he looked at her, the most beautiful girl in the district, her hair full of poplar leaves and damp from the morning dew, her cheeks red from the struggle when CrossAbel had grabbed hold of her, her neck soft and white above the rough hessian bag round her shoulders. Without saying anything, they looked at each other. Perhaps she realized what was happening, perhaps not.

And finally, Dowser. 'You are the father,' Abel said to him. 'You must say.'

Abel went and stood with his legs apart over the hole. He did not look round him again, as a man of lesser strength would have done. When CrazyTilly jumped up and broke away through the trees, CrossAbel set off after her, and Mailbag too, with a hoarse sob – Ella knocked over the fuel drum by accident – Oneday turned his head away – the grove broke apart as bodies burst through the branches and feet trampled on footprints and disappeared, until at last there was nothing left but the silence.

She, too, wanted to run, to get away from the man who with everyone's consent was now standing with his legs apart over the borehole. But she was too old and stiff to move that quickly. So in the silence, beside the dead lanterns and the still picks, in among the confusion of footprints, only herself and Abel Moolman were left.

Supporting herself on her elbow, she struggled to her feet and limped over to Abel. Gradually the blood flowed back into her limbs. She walked right up to him and put out a hand, looking for a moment at the dirt under the nails on the hand she had laid on his arm. She knew just how hard it was for him.

Katie took the footpath up to the Stiefveld, to the cottage on the slope. Out in the open, the wind tugged at her. She imagined she could hear the wild geese crying and see Noah standing in the footpath ahead of her listening to the wind, but she could not be sure. She fancied Andries Riet was walking along beside her, his hand under her elbow, his strong tread accompanying her struggling old feet. Then, suddenly, as though they would never again be able to come to rest, the wild geese clattered up out of the poplars. Crying, they flew over her head, dived through the wind and swung away into the white mist that was tumbling down over the head of the Toorberg.

260

Glossary

Antjie Somers:	traditional bogeyman character, in folk lore often represented as a man wearing women's clothes; a child-taker, who moves rapidly through space and time
bakkies:	light utility vehicles with enclosed cab and open loading platforms with low sides and back
bokkoms:	dried fish, often bloaters (sometimes spelled 'bokkems')
Casspir:	armoured troop-carrying vehicle, standing high above the ground, used by police and army units in the townships
dagga:	cannabis, marijuana
dassie:	hyrax, also sometimes called 'rock rabbit'
dolosse:	small bones of sheep and goats used as primitive children's toys
donga:	ditch, gully, pejorative reference to 'the gutter'
Familie:	family, dynasty
impi:	a group of black warriors
kraals:	stock pens, often constructed with dry stone walls
koeksisters:	plaited pastry deep fried and drenched in syrup
meerkat:	mongoose
meidjie:	(derog.) little maid; referring to young 'coloured' girls, especially domestic servants. Diminutive of English *maid*.
Meisie:	a young girl; here used as a name
melktert:	a custard tart, dusted with cinnamon and nutmeg
Moordenaars Karoo:	(lit.) The Murderer's Karoo, Killer Karoo

morgen:	an area of land roughly equivalent to a hectare
OuMurasie:	Old Ruins
Paradysberg:	Mount Paradise; (lit.) Paradise Mountain
Skaamfamilie:	Family of Shame, Family of Guilt, The Tainted Family
staffriding:	passengers clinging to the outside of railway carriages
Stiefveld:	Step Land, Grudgelands
tokoloshe:	powerful, usually malevolent spirit being, often manifested in the form of a tiny, wizened old man
toor:	to cast (a) spell(s) (on), to enchant, to practise sorcery, to make magic, to bewitch. Used of both good and evil
velskoens:	shoes made of rawhide
zol:	a hand-rolled cigarette often containing dagga